POWER AND POSSESSION

Also by C. C. Gibbs

All He Wants
All He Needs
All He Desires

POWER AND POSSESSION

C. C. GIBBS

FOREVER

NEW YORK BOSTON

This book is a work of fiction. Names, characters, places, and incidents are the product of the author's imagination or are used fictitiously. Any resemblance to actual events, locales, or persons, living or dead, is coincidental.

Forever
Hachette Book Group
1290 Avenue of the Americas
New York, NY 10104

www.HachetteBookGroup.com

Printed in the United States of America

RRD-C

First Edition: September 2015
10 9 8 7 6 5 4 3 2 1

Forever is an imprint of Grand Central Publishing.

Library of Congress Cataloging-in-Publication Data

Gibbs, C. C.
Power and possession / C.C. Gibbs. — First edition.
pages ; cm. — (Reckless)
ISBN 978-1-4555-3259-9 (softcover) — ISBN 978-1-4789-0478-6 (audio download) — ISBN 978-1-4555-3258-2 (ebook) 1. Billionaires—Fiction. 2. Women graduate students—Fiction. 3. Sexual dominance and submission—Fiction. I. Title.
PS3607.I2254P69 2015
813'.6—dc23

2015021784

POWER AND POSSESSION

ONE

Monte Carlo, Monaco, August 1

Nicole Parrish squinted against the sun pouring in through the bedroom windows, her uncle's penthouse apartment curtainless for some ungodly reason. Or more practically because it was forty stories above the ground. "I'm up, I'm up, okay. I heard you." Her friend, Fiona, was standing at the end of the bed, looking fresh and bright, every golden hair in place. "Seriously, you're sure it's not a problem?"

"God, no. It's a mega yacht. I Googled it. Two hundred fifty feet, six decks, helipad, swimming pool, hot tub, gym, spa, crew of thirty-three, built two years ago of aluminum for speed and fuel economy—how's that for an oxymoron. And the guest list is always huge, the invitations allow for escorts, partners, friends—whatever. So it's not a problem."

"Still." Nicole pursed her lips. "It feels like party crashing."

"You're too sober. That's your problem. My cousin says this is a not-to-be-missed party." Fiona Kelly, dressed in a green shimmering bikini that matched her eyes, lifted her mimosa. "Want some of my breakfast? Your uncle has one kick-ass champagne selection."

Almost lost in the huge bed, Nicole lazily stretched. "It

was a late night—actually morning, by the time I got home. I need food."

"The buffet is set up in the dining room as usual thanks to the food fairies." Nicole liked her privacy so Dominic Knight, her uncle, had given his staff orders to be discreet.

"Any breakfast tortillas?"

"Of course. Your uncle runs a tight ship. Or maybe you're his favorite niece."

"He's good to all of us. Did Mom call?" While her uncle was laissez-faire in his oversight, her mother wasn't.

"Only three times." Fiona grinned. "She must get up at dawn."

"Yoga at sunrise," Nicole muttered. "I didn't inherit those genes."

"Don't I know it, Miss Night Owl. Anyway, I didn't tell your mom you rolled in at seven. I told her you were busy Skyping with your new grad counselor at Columbia. A mix-up with your fall class schedule."

"Which isn't entirely untrue."

A lift of perfectly sculpted brows thanks to the spa at the Hôtel de Paris. "Only because you haven't actually registered yet."

Nicole groaned. "We're not all programmed for a career path from birth," she grumbled. "Some of us—"

"Want to be a screenwriter with a chem degree. Or work with that gorgeous Yash on his happiness research in Singapore. Which has more to do with *your* happiness than research."

"Hey—I'm trying not to think about any of that this summer."

Undeterred, Fiona said, "The summer won't last forever and you're going to have to deal with it. Just saying."

A mocking glance. "Thanks, Mom. Now be nice," Nicole murmured, still not fully awake. "Or you'll go mega-yachting alone."

"You be nice or I won't tell you what that lovely boy you were with last night sent in the way of a thank-you for"—Fiona flashed a wide smile—"your charming company."

"I already know. I smell the roses. And he *was* lovely." A hint of pleasure echoed softly in her voice. "Andre right?"

"With a whole lot of other names after that—don't forget."

"You're the one who likes titles. I just like to have fun."

"I try to combine the two since we're in Europe. So how was darling Andre? Scale of one to ten." The proverbial female question the morning after.

Nicole thought for a moment. "An eight. He was a little too sweet. Not my favorite thing. We went clubbing, dancing, had a last drink at some little bistro on the beach. He wasn't trying to score right out of the blocks. I liked that."

"Sometimes you like that." Fiona and Nicole had been talking boys since grade school. Nothing was sacred. "And sometimes you don't—a few occasions, one in a bar bathroom—come to mind."

"So?" Another lazy stretch.

"So nothing." Fiona drained the flute, set the glass on the dresser, and strolled to the windows overlooking the Mediterranean. "Wow. This isn't Kansas, Dorothy. Even more yachts in port than yesterday." She spun around, her long blond hair swinging in a silken arc, and threw her arms open wide. "Come on—it's almost one. Get up or the party's going to start without us."

Nicole glanced at the bedside clock and made a grumbly noise.

"Look, we have only a month left of summer break. That's thirty more days to rub shoulders and other more interesting body parts with the rich and famous before we're back to the academic grind. Or at least, I'll go back to the grind. Slackers like you, who knows?" Fiona walked to the bed and pulled the covers back. "Go take a shower. *Vite. Vite.* I'll pick out a bikini for you."

"And a cover-up," Nicole said, swinging her legs out of bed. "As a sop to my mom's sense of decorum."

"None of which rubbed off on you. You're lucky your uncle always bails you out of trouble without telling your mom or dad."

"Dominic understands craziness. What can I say?" Nicole smiled as she came to her feet. "And you should talk. You were with me most of those times." She sniffed the air. "God, I love roses. I must have told him that last night."

TWO

Nicole was lost.

Even after two crew members had pointed her in this direction, every corridor looked the same on the huge yacht. She was facing miles of burled tulipwood and polished brass with every cabin door identical—none with identifying signs, which meant she was probably in the private quarters of her host.

Damn. She'd probably had one drink too many. But the well-trained waitstaff was always passing around another tray of yummy summer drinks, the Mediterranean sun was hotter than hell, and Fiona kept saying, "It's a party. What are you waiting for?"

So here she was in another posh corridor, looking for a bathroom and facing nothing but closed doors.

What now? Just start opening doors until she got lucky?

Oops.

She skidded to a stop on the threshold of a large stateroom, the couple on the sofa went still, and she met the hooded, amber-eyed gaze of her host.

"Oh—God, sorry... wrong room," she stammered, feeling like a deer in the headlights under that hard, assessing stare, as well as seriously underdressed, although every other woman at the party was in a bikini too. "I was... just... looking for the loo." She started backing up.

"Wait." Tossing a feathered sex toy behind the sofa, the gorgeous man on the couch quickly rolled off the woman beneath him and, coming to his feet, zipped up his khaki shorts. "Use this one." He motioned to a frosted glass door across the large stateroom.

Having come to a stop, Nicole recognized Rafe Contini and tried not to stare at his broad shoulders and ripped torso, not to mention the semi-nude blonde casually lounging on the sofa, as if it were the most obvious thing in the world for people to watch her. "Really, I couldn't," Nicole murmured, focusing instead on a striking Picasso painting over the sofa. "I'm intruding."

"Not at all." Responding to her unease, Rafe grabbed his polo shirt from the carpet. "Silvie has to leave soon anyway."

"I do *not*!" The tawny-haired blonde punched Rafe's leg.

His head and arms slid out of his white polo shirt and the fabric dropped over his hard abs. "I just meant Emilio will be looking for you. Aren't you dining with Shokov?" Rafe said smoothly, ignoring Silvie's pouty scowl. "But stay as long as you wish. I'll open a bottle of that wine from Georgia you like." Bending down, he pulled a black lace top over her large breasts, slid the straps over her shoulders, and stood upright. "Please"—he glanced at Nicole—"go on in." He jabbed a finger toward the door, then raked his fingers through his long hair and flipped it behind his ears with a pivot of his wrists. "I'll get us drinks. Any preferences?"

A flicker of a smile drifted over her mouth. "I've probably had enough if I want to find my way back up to the main deck."

"Don't worry about it." His voice dropped slightly, his golden gaze turned warm. "I know the way."

His low, husky voice vibrated softly through her senses. Gently, without urgency, almost weightless—and she found herself saying, "Okay. Any drink is fine. Surprise me." Stepping into the room, she shut the door and moved toward the bathroom. Surprise me. Now there's a plan. And he watched her walk across the broad expanse of pale carpet with a breath-held wonder even he recognized as bizarre.

He didn't remember her, Nicole thought. Two years ago, Rafail Contini, head of R&D for his father's Swiss firm, Contini Pharmaceuticals, had been presenting a paper on the future of targeted chemotherapy at a conference in San Francisco. She, along with a group of chemistry undergrads, had been introduced to him by their professor. He was as gorgeous then as now: tall, superbuff, and starkly handsome, with long, dark hair and intense amber eyes. Magnetic, jungle-cat eyes.

The kind of man who brought a hush to a room when he walked in.

Serious centerfold eye candy.

Jesus, enough! Get a grip. He was probably just being gracious by offering her a drink.

And it was clear that Silvia Fermetti—trophy wife of the Italian ambassador to France, darling of all the gossip rags for her wild ways—had no intention of leaving.

In fact, when Nicole exited the bathroom a short time later, the same voluptuous blonde seated beside Rafe at a small table gave her a if-looks-could-kill glare as though to emphasize that point. Caught in the crosshairs of the murderous look, Nicole had a moment of doubt. Did she really want to be in the middle of a possible battle royal? Should she refuse the drink and get the hell out? But before she'd taken more than a few steps, Rafe was walking toward her, holding a martini glass.

"See if you like this Novatini," he said a moment later, handing her the drink. "Hendrick's Gin, white cranberry juice, half a lime, squeezed. Come, sit. You're an American aren't you?"

"Yes. San Francisco." Nicole took the offered glass.

"I know the city," he said as they moved to the table. "I spent a couple years at Stanford." He pulled out a chair for her.

Nicole glanced up as she sat. "Small world. I just graduated from Stanford."

He grinned. "It must be karma."

Conscious of Silvie's glowering expression, Nicole murmured noncommittally, "If you say so."

"No doubt in my mind," he said very softly, even though he'd never actually believed in karma. Nor in the word *mesmerized*, which described his reaction to this lithe lush beauty. Sitting down, he nodded. "You've been swimming." Nicole's long dark hair fell in damp ringlets.

"The swimming platform was inviting."

He smiled. "No one ever actually swims around here."

"I do."

"Often?"

"Every day."

He leaned forward. "Where are you staying?"

"Goddamn it, you shit! I'm right here!" Silvie spat, making a scene as natural as breathing to her.

"Relax, Silvie," Rafe said. "I'm just making conversation."

"I want her to leave!"

"Really, I probably should go," Nicole said, setting her glass down.

"Nonsense." Turning to Silvie, he said, very softly, "Behave."

Grabbing her wineglass, she was about to fling its contents at Rafe, as if she were once again playing the Italian soap opera role that had brought her to prominence, when the stateroom door abruptly opened.

Emilio Fermetti paused in the doorway. "Ah, there you are, Silvie." Well dressed in a custom-tailored fawn linen suit, the tall, white-haired patrician was fully capable of artifice after thirty years in the diplomatic service. "I thought I might find you here," he said with a bland smile.

His wife dropped her glass on the table. "The sun was too hot on deck," she said with a defiant little shrug.

"Of course. And you with such fair skin," he said gently. "But we do have to leave now, darling. Dinner with Shokov." He dipped his head to Rafe. "Thank you for your hospitality, Rafail. If you'll excuse us."

"Certainly. A pleasure to see you again, Emilio. Make sure you let me know what you need for your Sudan aid mission. I'll see that the drugs get there."

"I'll send over an inventory list. To you or to the Contini Foundation?" The ambassador smiled faintly. "Is Isabelle still in charge of your charities?"

"She is. Would you like her to call you for the list?" Isabelle was young, beautiful, and unmarried, not that marital status mattered to a lecher like Emilio. But Isabelle could take care of herself.

"I would, thank you. And thank you too for your continuing philanthropy. I can always count on the generosity of Contini Pharmaceuticals."

"Our pleasure. We like to help. Do you need any more of those three-D printers we sent you?" A new, inexpensive robotic hand was one of Rafe's personal projects.

"Absolutely. We were able to fit forty people, mostly children, with artificial hands last quarter."

"Must you always talk business, Emilio?" Silvie said, with a pettish little sniff, preferring to be the center of attention. "You know I dislike it."

Her husband didn't respond other than to cock one eyebrow. "But a necessary annoyance when it comes to charity, my dear." He turned to Rafe. "If I wouldn't be imposing, Rafail, another twenty printers would be useful."

"I'll see that Isabelle's notified. And if there's anything else we can help with, don't hesitate to—"

"I'm leaving if you aren't!" Rising from her chair in a petulant huff, her boobs thrust out in an unsubtle ploy for attention, Silvie spun away, marched to the door, and slammed it behind her.

Emilio dipped his head, giving Rafe a rare smile of sincerity. "You're not your father's son, Rafail. Your benevolence is commendable."

Rafe recognized the double entendre and grinned. "Thanks. I've tried very hard not to be my father."

The ambassador sighed. "At times I envy you your youth. Not often though." His diplomatic smile appeared. "I find the drama enervating."

"Come now. I've heard all the stories." Emilio always reminded Rafe of an eighteenth-century courtier. Worldly, rational to a fault, morally ambivalent.

Emilio shrugged. "Shokov will put her in a better mood. He's young and aggressive."

"And is thinking of running an oil pipeline under the Adriatic to Italy."

"Exactly. It's the only reason I eat his very bad food. Did you know his chef was a chemist first?"

Rafe groaned.

"You see my dilemma." Emilio raised his hand slightly in adieu, and a moment later followed his third wife from the room.

As the door closed on the ambassador, Nicole raised her brows slightly. "He seems to like you, and you like him. I'm confused. Is she your girlfriend?"

"You can't be serious," Rafe said.

"Ah."

He didn't respond to her insinuation, nor to her arched look. Instead, he slid down in his chair, lifted his gin and tonic to his mouth, and surveyed her over the rim of his glass for a moment before he drained the drink. Fishing an ice cube out of the glass, he held it up. "See this?" When she didn't answer he said, "The length of time it takes for this to melt is about the extent of my interest in a woman."

She grinned. "Your numerous charities aside, you really *can be* an unmitigated shit."

"Somehow, I'm finding you the exception to my rule," he drawled, dropping the ice cube back in the glass. "If I believed in the idea that a mysterious stranger could enter my life and change it in a split second I'd say it was when you walked in the door." His mouth twitched slightly in amusement. "Since I don't, I'm going with instant lust."

"Fine with me." A novel concept in her life, unique to this man; although she liked the equally mysterious notion of second chances. "I've met you before, you know."

He quickly sat up. "Fuck if you did." He set his glass down. "I would have remembered."

"You were with a woman."

He didn't want to say that was too common to jog his memory. "Tell me where?"

"San Francisco. Two years ago. You spoke on the targeted chemotherapy Contini Pharmaceuticals was developing."

"And I met you?" He smiled. "Were you in disguise?"

"I was with my chem class; our professor introduced us as a group." She didn't say that the beautiful blond doctor on his arm had been whispering in his ear at the time, which may have distracted him. Nor that, afterward, she and a classmate had discussed the probable size of his dick, his scorching good looks, and the fact that if he'd even crooked a finger in their direction, they would have jumped into bed with him, alone or together.

"Forgive me for not remembering you." He suddenly grinned. "But there, you see, it's an example of awesome fate and opportunistic probability that we met again."

"Somehow I don't see you as a spiritual guru."

He shrugged. "Whatever. But I'm glad I met you again."

He didn't care if it was the work of pixies or the hand of God; he wanted her. "Where *are* you staying?"

"At my uncle's apartment."

"Come to my place." He folded his hands on the table, leaned forward a little, his gaze focused, her appeal powerful as a riptide, ignoring the fact that what he was about to say was messing with his head. "I'll kick out everyone else."

"Everyone else? Meaning?" She didn't lack confidence, and he was notorious for his casual sexual encounters.

For some reason he didn't mind her impertinence. "Only male friends. I never allow women to stay with me." He smiled. "Until now. So how about it?"

"Sure, I'd like that." *And suddenly the summer takes an interesting turn.* So far the boys of summer had been only mildly interesting. "But not for long." She wrinkled her nose. "I have to go back to school in a couple of weeks."

Rafe suddenly went still; her little nose twitch reminded him of a child. "Just for the record," he murmured, "how old are you?" People graduated college at any age; he had at nineteen.

"Worried?" Nicole flashed him a grin. "How much does it matter?"

He scowled. "It matters."

"Or?"

"Or you're gone."

"Now neither of us wants that," she said, amusement in the blue of her eyes. "Do we?"

He didn't move a muscle, even his breathing quieted. "Don't," he said, very softly. "No games."

Nicole's voice was lush with provocation. "Really? I've heard you like games."

"You heard wrong." He held her gaze for a moment, then sighed. "Tell me your age or get the fuck out." Hand of fate or not, he didn't do stupid.

"Twenty-two." Her brows rose in perfect arcs. "So, are we seeing blue skies and rainbows once again?" Honeyed sarcasm dripped from each word. "Or do I find someone else at this party to entertain me?"

Rafe's smile slowly unfurled and his eyes took on a predatory glow. "You could try, I suppose. But you wouldn't get out the door."

"Oh dear, oh my, I do declare," she lamented in playful parody. "Am I your captive?"

"You are." Smoothly rising from his chair, he strode toward the door. "Now I'm going to lock the door, then fuck you till morning."

"And then what?"

Whoa. The unmistakable note of demand in her voice brought him to a stop. He turned. "I'm sorry, did you say something?"

She met his insolent gaze and smiled. "I said—and then what?...As in afterward."

Audacious or foolhardy? Fascinating certainly. He winked. "Afterward, you can tell me your name. How's that?"

She winked back. "I'll think about it."

He went very still. "Is this a contest?"

"I hope not," she murmured, gazing at him from under her long, dark lashes. "I hope I get what I want."

"Which is?"

"Do you need a list?"

"Do you know what you're doing?" Unsure whether it was anger or lust igniting his senses, his voice took on a raspy edge and his golden gaze turned cold.

"I can't answer that definitively, but right now it looks like your dick knows what it's doing," she noted, with a languid lift of her hand.

He looked at her for a moment. A woman had never taunted him before and he wanted to pick her up and shove his dick so far up her pussy he'd need a road map to get out.

"Don't," she said, very, very softly. "This could be really good... mind-blowing in fact. You have to know that."

"Fuck you," he whispered, shifting his stance enough to ease the pressure on his erection.

"Anytime... Just not that way, okay?"

He dragged in a ragged breath. "Don't tell me what to do."

She held his gaze, unflinching. "Nor you me."

A smile slowly overcame his discontent as he held her contentious stare. "Why don't we see?" he said very gently. "You might like it after all." Then he reached back, turned the key in the lock, slid it into his pocket, and moved toward her.

THREE

Only two people in the world were feeling what they were feeling, the sensations like a lightning flash illuminating the universe.

That they were both young, wild, and willful was deeply consequential. Perhaps even the sweet scent of summer played a role. Or maybe it was nothing more than the combustible combination of alcohol and easygoing hospitality on the yacht that day.

But whether fate or chance, lust or circumstance drove events, their dawning recognition that not only was this unprecedented, but might be real was stark.

The word real brought Rafe to an abrupt stop just short of the table where Nicole sat. A frown deepened on his brow as he slowly contemplated the stunning, barely dressed woman looking at him with an increasingly puzzled look as the silence lengthened. "I'm freaking out," he finally said. "Because this situation falls into the category of unnecessary complications and, as a rule, I generally avoid attachments." He smiled wryly. "Always, as a matter of fact. So"—he took a quick breath—"no disrespect, but I'm going to pass on this."

She didn't doubt him. He'd spoken plainly enough. "How much?" she asked.

He looked at her sharply. "I beg your pardon."

"How much do you want to pass on this? Give me a percentage." She sat up straighter as if she knew she dealt from a position of strength. And when he looked at her expressionless and silent, she said, "Do you want me to tell you why you're spooked?"

Sitting there quietly, her self-possession struck him as strangely seductive. He wanted to be angry with her, but she was so assured, he couldn't help but admire her. And, of course, he wanted to fuck her too. "Really?" he muttered, frustrated by his contradictory emotions, by his riveting interest in this woman. "You have all the fucking answers?"

"Maybe just a few." She raised her brows slightly, immune to his male phobia on relationships. "Or would you prefer I leave?"

He dragged in a breath, stared at her, and knew he was going to regret it even before he said, "No."

"Then be nice. I don't need you to make my life interesting. I can do that on my own." She smiled just a little because he was looking at her with such blunt curiosity it was clear she didn't conform to his type of sex partners. "With all the single men on your guest list today, finding someone to entertain me won't be a problem."

She was a cheeky little thing—actually not so little everywhere, he corrected himself, letting his gaze settle briefly on her lush tits. Suddenly, his misgivings were irrelevant, evaporating like rain in the desert after a hundred-year drought. Slipping his hand into his shorts' pocket, he pulled out the door key and held it up. "One slight drawback to your finding other entertainment."

Her eyes widened slightly. "You're serious?"

"As death and taxes," he said softly.

"Hmmmm." She measured the distance from the table to the key.

He followed her glance and suddenly smiled. "In over your head?"

She smiled back. "Never."

It was his turn to say, "Hmmm." She was relaxed, her breathing steady, not even a hint of unease in her lounging posture, despite the fact she was locked in a stranger's stateroom and wearing very little. "Don't tell me you have a black belt in karate or something?" Pocketing the key, he dropped into a chair opposite her.

"Not a black belt, but I do have *something*." Her blue gaze sparkled with amusement. "Something you want."

"I could just take it."

She gave him a look of mild forbearance. "Now where's the fun in that?"

He placed his hands on the marquetry table, slid them forward, and, leaning over, held her brilliant blue gaze. "Tell me about this fun."

"First," she said gently, "let's clear away the obstacles. We're both feeling this incredible attraction, excitement—whatever it is. Don't panic—I'm just stating a fact, I'm not looking for permanence. I have a life. You have a life. And that's not going to change. You don't have to explain anything to me about what you've done in the past or why you've done it." She leaned back a little in the shagreen and aluminum sculpted chair and smiled at him. "And if it makes you more comfortable, I don't have boyfriends probably for the same reasons you don't have—what—attachments? Are we good now? Can we just enjoy ourselves? I'm sure you know how and if you don't"—she laughed a little—"I have some suggestions."

Her soft laughter was without artifice and damned charming. Sliding back in his chair, he smiled warmly. "Are you a bloody therapist?"

"No—just realistic, fickle, superbusy—like you I'm guessing. By the way"—her voice was amused—"do you give that all-worked-up speech about no attachments often?"

He rolled his eyes. "Not until I met you."

"So I'm special," she said, her eyes alight.

"Yes. In every impractical, improbable, disturbing way." Then he exhaled, releasing his lingering doubts. He'd spent a good many years chasing new sensations and no one had ever provoked this sort of reaction in him. No one but this beautiful, smiling woman. "So the complexities aside"—he said, sketching a small circle in the air with his index finger—"this thing we've got going—you and me—us… karma—whatever the fuck it is, I'd like to take it slow and easy if you don't mind."

"You mean stamp the date and time on our psyches, tattoo it on our hearts, send word balloons out into the ether?"

His sudden smile was dazzling. "I'm obviously more sober than you, but yeah—something like that."

She grinned. "Personally, I'm going with the liquor rather than magic."

He sighed. "I'm not so sure. But I do know I don't want to rush this. That okay with you?"

"Maybe."

His brows spiked upward.

"You can't plan everything, that's all I mean. Sometimes shit just happens."

"I know."

"Like this."

"Yes." He held out his hand. "Like this."

His long, slender fingers closed over hers, and rising from his chair, he pulled her to her feet and drew her near. "Christ," he murmured, squeezing her hand lightly. "Did you feel that?"

Her breath caught, but she said hesitantly, "I'm not sure."

"Fuck if you're not. Tell me you don't feel anything." Enveloping her other hand in his large grip, he dipped his head until their eyes were level—deep, vivid blue and a warm, unshadowed gold. "Tell me you're not touched by the mythical electricity."

She slowly exhaled. "I'd prefer not going there."

"Don't tell me the lady who advised me not to be spooked is afraid of a little romance?" Pulling her closer so their bodies lightly met, he smiled. "Come on, take the leap. It could be an incredible rush."

It helped that she felt the hard, solid strength of his body, so she was reminded who he was and what he was; how she'd seen him casually rising from the sofa not long ago with another woman. "You and romance? Seriously? You'd have to have a personality change from what I hear."

"Don't believe everything you hear," he said, brusquely dismissive. "And this is different. We both know that. Maybe we should Google *romance* and set up a game plan for novices," he suggested, only half in jest.

"Speaking of game plans within the realm of possibility," Nicole said drily, "I do have to let my friend Fiona know I'm staying over. *And*—in the event even *some* of the gossip about you is true—just a quick FYI. I don't take orders."

"You never know," he said, smoothly.

She jerked her hands free and frowned. "No, I know."

"I can change your mind," he contradicted. She didn't so much as blink. He liked that she wasn't intimidated.

"I'm not here alone." She lifted her chin in willful challenge. "Fiona's with me."

"It doesn't matter." His lashes dropped infinitesimally. "At all."

"Because this yacht is yours, the crew is yours—"

"And I can buy anything and anyone," he finished softly.

Her skin prickled. But a second later she reminded herself that her uncle Dominic had given her a glimpse into both the joy and misery of great wealth and power. "Look," she said, briskly, "I don't care if you can paper the world in money, but Fiona needs a heads-up."

"Then I'll have someone tell her." A brief, perfunctory statement.

"No." Her voice was curt. "I'll tell her. She has my phone too by the way. I need it."

Rafe was in no rush to exert his authority. Hell, it might be interesting to show this blue-eyed beauty the finite details apropos who did what to whom. "Suit yourself." His voice was urbane, his smile well-mannered. "Would you like me to find someone to entertain your friend?"

She grinned. "You know when to stop pushing."

He inclined his head slightly in acknowledgment. "I do." He laughed. "But don't get reckless."

"I hope that's not part of the orders."

Her smile dazzled and for a split second it bothered him that she handled herself so well. But a split second later he reminded himself that he wasn't looking for innocence; he never had. "Of course not," he said, polite as hell. "Now does your friend need my help?"

"No thanks," Nicole answered because she could be polite too when she wanted something. "Fiona likes to make her own selections from the titled ranks. It's her thing this summer."

"Then she's in the right place. There's a full range of titles on board. If she needs any introductions, I'd be more than happy to oblige. Tell her you'll be gone for a while though." He smiled. "I have plans for us—with your approval, of course," he added smoothly.

Nicole grinned. "Women don't talk back to you much, do they?"

"Not often, no."

"And if they do?"

A small pause before he said, "It depends."

"On?"

She was fearless. He smiled. "What I want."

"I may want things too," she warned. "So you still have time to change your mind."

But you don't. "I think I can deal with it." A quick flash of white teeth. "I'm a problem solver."

"Speaking of problems," Nicole said, suddenly groaning. "I have five brothers and sisters and a mom and dad who like to be *involved* in my life. So I'll have to coordinate stories with Fiona. My mother calls at least once a day, usually more often."

"Don't worry about it. I'm an only child—sort of," he added. "My mother remarried after my father died and I now have a stepbrother. But Mother's also part of the business—always has been—and we stay in touch. But I'll be quiet when you're on the phone and vice versa."

"Christ, why do I feel like I'm fifteen and out past curfew?"

"I can't speak for you, but with the brevity of my ah… friendships with women, phone calls have never been an issue before."

"Jesus, maybe it really is karma. I've never had to plan past a few hours either."

"So everything's brand-new with us," he said, husky and low.

"Fresh as spring." She gave her head a little shake. "I don't actually believe it."

He smiled, imminently comfortable now with the wisdom of his choice. "Maybe I can show you—make you a believer."

"Or I'll show you," she said with a grin.

He laughed. "Be my guest. I'm easy." If she was talking about sex though, he guessed his skill set was more varied and sophisticated than hers. Not that he was questioning her expertise, but few people were introduced to the flesh markets of the world at fifteen as he'd been by a father whose taste for vice was notorious.

"What?"

"I was trying to decide to what degree sex enters this new emotional world of ours."

"You better be kidding."

"Ah."

"Damn right—ah." Nicole slid her hands down his chest, brought her palms to rest on his fly. "Because I have plans and apparently you do too," she said, smiling up at him as his erection swelled under her fingers.

"But not right this second," he murmured, lifting her hands away and taking a step back. "I'm going to take a quick shower first. It won't take me long. In the meantime," he added, moving toward an intercom on the wall, "if you tell me what Fiona looks like, I'll have someone bring her here and you two can coordinate your schedules." He paused before striking the call button. "Although say the word and I'll see that she has a companion with any title she wants."

"Really? You can do that?"

"Absolutely. A lot of these aristocratic families are short of cash. I'm not. So she can put in her order." When Nicole hesitated, he added, "Or if you prefer, she could come with us. We could sail somewhere—the Adriatic, the Greek islands. The weather's nice this time of year and most businesses, ours included, are on semi-holiday." Whatever she wanted she could have; whatever made her happy made him happy. The imaginary word, *happy*, come to life with her. Not that he was going to begin to parse the strange earnestness of his feelings; he preferred uncomplicated sex.

"Is that what you want to do?"

"I want to do whatever you want to do," he replied politely, though he had an explicit personal agenda; he'd not developed into a paragon of beneficence regardless of the novel circumstances. "Our time is limited if you're going back to school." His gaze suddenly narrowed, a compelling urgency glittering in the golden depths of his eyes. "Tell me your name."

"Nicole Parrish."

He didn't move for a fraction of a second, his brow furrowed. Then he took a breath and smiled the most beautiful smile. "A pleasure to meet you, Nicole Parrish. We're going to have fun."

"I know," she said with a lavish grin. "I find you very attractive."

He laughed. "And I find you," he said, his voice taking on a husky resonance, "my reward for ignoring every cautionary precept in my life." His gaze shuttered slightly as he contemplated her. "I'm both disturbed and obsessed, but," he added more softly, feeling an improbable pleasure, "I'm looking forward to my obsession."

"Is this where I say I'll be gentle and not take advantage of you?"

"God no." His smile was sunny. "By all means take advantage of me."

"Don't say I didn't warn you," she teased.

She was too tempting, he thought, as she stood before

him, barely clothed, confident and assured, aware of her extravagant beauty, and for a moment, his gaze cooled.

She could see that he was uncomfortable; too many compliant women had left him unequipped to deal with her directness. “Forgive me. I only meant it in fun. If you like, I promise not to be demanding.”

Her astonishing offer made him smile. “You couldn’t do it.”

The light of mischief shone in her eyes. “For you, I’d really try.”

“You’ll have to show me then,” he said circumspect and polite, as if she’d offered him some superficial kindness.

“My pleasure.”

Rafe smiled. “I know,” he said cryptically. “Now—give me a description and we’ll get Fiona up here.”

FOUR

Shortly after Rafe left to shower, there was a discreet knock on the door and a crew member ushered Fiona into the stateroom, then quietly withdrew.

"Holy shit! Is that a real Picasso?" Fiona moved toward the painting over the lime green sofa.

Nicole smiled. "I guess. It's signed."

Fiona surveyed the enormous painting of Picasso's young family on the beach at Juan-les-Pins. "I recognize this from Art One." She swung around. "And that and that," she added, pointing at several more works of art. "Fuck this is *real* money." She waved her arms. "Everything here is like antique or designer. Did you really score the god himself?" She grinned. "Or am I in a museum?"

"No museum. And he's just a man, so relax."

"Yeah, right. Like Brad Pitt is just the boy next door and Justin Timberlake is just a kid who dances well."

"Okay," Nicole said drily, "I get the picture. He's got something else going for him."

"About a gazillion somethings. Where is he?" Her face fell. "Oh, God, sorry. Did he hit and run? Am I here to take you away?"

"Have a little faith, babe." Nicole grinned. "He likes me. I like him. We like each other." She gestured over her shoulder. "He's in the shower washing off the scent of Silvie

Fermetti. It looked like they were about to have sex when I accidently barged in."

"You're kidding!"

"I couldn't see for sure, but he was zipping up when he came to his feet."

"Oh my God!" Fiona dropped into the nearest chair as though knocked off her feet by the shock. Then her smile appeared, widened, and crinkled the corners of her eyes. "Tell me every little sordid, titillating detail." She shoved herself upright. "Mostly how he got rid of the firebrand Silvie Fermetti. You know how wild she looked in those pictures in *Paris Match* last week. And that guy she was punching—"

"I'll tell you later." Nicole glanced over her shoulder. "Privately. What I wanted to tell you was that I'm going to stay with him for a while."

"Awhile!"

"Calm down. Seriously, it's not that big a deal." Nicole took the chair beside her friend. "And Rafe said if you want to come sailing with us, you're welcome. Also, if you want introductions to anyone, or if you want him to set you up with some titled dude, he's willing."

"Wow. So I can put in my order and he'll do the pimping?"

Nicole smiled. "It sounded like it. See anyone you want today?"

"Lordy, lordy, if I have that big a menu," Fiona murmured. "Lemme think..."

While Fiona was trying to decide, Rafe had already made a few decisions. First, he'd prefer being alone with Nicole.

Second, the title of prince seemed to have a certain cachet with women. And last, his cousin Giacomino, owed him a favor.

Picking up the phone in the shower, he gave instructions for someone to find Prince Giacomino Santori and a few minutes later, the phone rang.

"How busy are you?" Rafe's Italian was rapid-fire. "I'm in the shower. I don't have much time."

Giacomino knew that tone of voice and with a smile for the lady he was flirting with, he moved away from her. "Not that busy, Rafe. What do you need?"

"I'm calling in my marker. Do this for me and we're even."

Since Giacomino owed Rafe three hundred K, his answer was predictable. "Name it."

"There's a lady in my stateroom I need you to take off my hands. I haven't seen her, but I'm assuming she won't hurt your eyes. Her name's Fiona, she's blond, and since I want her friend for myself, I need you to entertain Fiona somewhere else for a few days."

"Presumably this Fiona has a choice. What if she's not interested?"

"We both know you can make her interested. So just do it. Take her shopping, to the casino, wine and dine her. Spend what you need to make her happy—although I'm not paying for your lack of skill so don't run up any charges at the roulette table. Carlos will give you a credit card. Use it, no questions asked. Okay?"

"Fuck yes."

"Oh, and be sure you see that Fiona is happy sexually

too—or she'll move on. Apparently she's adding up her conquests this summer."

"*Cristo Dios*—you don't want much."

"Actually, I do. I want three hundred K and expenses worth of fucking. We both know you can do it. Hell, you might even like her. See you in five."

Rafe was walking out of the bathroom, dressed in fresh clothes, his T-shirt faintly damp against his skin, rubbing his hair with a towel when the corridor door opened and a tall, blond, very handsome man stood on the threshold.

Rafe smiled. "Jack, come on in. I looked for you earlier. Did you just get on board?"

"A few minutes ago," Giacomino said, picking up his cue. "Am I interrupting anything?"

"No, have a drink with us." Rafe dropped the towel on a chair, quickly finger-combed his heavy hair and waved his cousin in. "I'll introduce you to the ladies."

Fiona and Nicole were seated beside each other on matching chairs upholstered in white duck hand-painted in a colorful Japanese dragon design.

Arriving from opposite directions, the men met at the chairs. Rafe lifted his hand briefly in his cousin's direction. "Jack, may I present Nicole Parrish and Fiona"—he hesitated, and Nicole interjected, "Kelly"—"Fiona Kelly. Jack's my cousin and his entire name is Prince Giacomino Franceschini-Santori, but he prefers Jack. Nicole, Fiona, Jack. There, that's done." Rafe smiled. "Now what does everyone want to drink?" He winked at Nicole and lowered his voice. "Another surprise for you?"

"Sure." She held his gaze and spoke as softly. "I like surprises."

A small hush fell, a faint frisson of anticipation ruffling the air, the ripe sense of opportunity palpable.

Fiona and Jack exchanged glances. "Would you like us to leave?" Jack asked. "We can find a drink on deck." He moved to Fiona's chair, held out his hand, and smiled with incredible charm. "Or if you're tired of the crowd here, we could go somewhere else. Anywhere you like."

As he pulled her to her feet, Fiona grinned. "Paris, Rome, Madrid?"

He looked down at her, his gray gaze amused. "Which one first?"

"God no, I was just kidding. But I couldn't resist a line like that." She did a little flutter of her fingers. "This—yachts and such—is rarified air for a girl from the suburbs."

"Why don't you two fly to Ibiza?" Rafe said, his gaze still on Nicole, wondering how one woman could make him so goddamn needy, thinking he'd never seen such flawless skin, a mouth as soft and pink. Feeling his erection begin to rise at the thought, he quickly said, "The nightlife and beaches there are prime. Take my Gulfstream. You've two more weeks of vacation, right?"

"Uh-uh—a month," Fiona corrected.

Rafe shot her a sharp look over his shoulder then turned back to Nicole, the warmth in his eyes extinguished. "A couple of weeks?" There was a sudden hostile edge to his voice.

She stared right back. "You'd just explained your ice cube policy to me." She shrugged. "I was giving myself options."

His riveting eyes narrowed. "What makes you think you have options?"

"Fuck you," she said through her teeth, starting to rise.

Moving with surprising speed, he shoved her back down with a stunningly soft push and, planting his palms on the chair arms, leaned in close. "Don't be childish," he said under his breath.

She glared at him. "I decide when I leave, okay?"

"Come on, kids, no fighting on a nice summer day," Jack drawled.

Rafe silenced him with a raised palm.

"Really, I don't need a protector, but thank you," Nicole said into the electric silence, not a trace of anxiety in her expression. She smiled at Jack over Rafe's shoulder. "Why don't you get our drinks while Rafe and I talk?"

Jack had recovered his equilibrium. "Only if you two promise to make up," he said with a cheerful breeziness.

Rafe glanced at his cousin. "I'll have a whiskey. Neat."

That clipped tone didn't suggest further conversation, nor did the prince's large debt inspire him to persist. And when Nicole said, "The same for me, thanks," Jack readily surrendered his conciliatory role.

As Fiona and Jack walked away, Rafe pulled up a matching hassock so close to Nicole's chair her feet were in imminent danger. But before her alarm fully registered, Rafe slid his hand under her legs, lifted them, dropped the hassock, sat, and placed her feet in his lap.

Then, quietly infuriated, half hoping she'd resist, he leaned forward, slid his palms up her legs, her inner thighs, and when his thumbs came to rest on the flowered silk covering her crotch, he looked up and met her angry gaze. "I told you this isn't a game," he said, his voice taut with challenge, pressing his thumbs deeper. "Did you not get the message?"

It took her a half second to reply with the lustful jolt shimmering through her senses in a totally outrageous give-it-to-me *now* response. But the blue of her eyes sparked flame hot when she snapped, "Our messages must have crossed then, because I distinctly remember telling you I don't take orders. That includes me telling you everything I'm thinking in advance."

"So is it two weeks or a month?" he growled.

"If you don't change your damned tone, it'll be two minutes."

Rafe slid his thumbs under the bikini bottom and gently stroked her silky wetness. "Two minutes?" His smile was knowing. "I'm guessing a pussy this wet is going to want longer than that."

"Stop it," she snapped, attempting to draw away.

Hooking his thumbs in her slick heat, he dragged her back. "Liar," he whispered, the single word uttered in a low, husky, obscenely sexy tone, the soft assertion rich with authority, making her squirm and turn liquid around his fingers. "You like that?" he said, amused. "Or are you just glad to see me?" His thumbs stroked up and down, gently, deftly, divinely, while she melted inside, grew slippery with longing, and tried not to openly pant.

Rafe shot a quick look toward the bar. "Give us some privacy," he said in Italian. "Go."

Jack smiled at Fiona. "Want to fly somewhere?"

Fiona didn't understand Italian, but Rafe's sharp, staccato delivery had been clear. "One stupid question first, and it really doesn't matter, but are you really a prince?"

Jack grinned. "I'd better be or I'm going to have to send back all the monogrammed towels."

"Perfect," Fiona said cheerfully. Turning to Nicole, Fiona raised her voice enough to be heard across the large salon. "Hey, babe, are you going to be okay if I leave for a few days?"

"She'll be fine," Rafe answered crisply.

Fiona touched Jack's hand. "Be right back."

As Fiona walked toward them, Rafe turned back to Nicole. "Don't fucking move," he murmured and pressed both thumbs down on her swollen clit with flawless dexterity.

Stifling a gasp, reality momentarily eclipsed by a wild, scorching delirium, Nicole suddenly wondered if the awesome pleasure Rafe offered was worth forfeiting her independence. Quintessentially willful, however, the answer was only briefly in doubt, and drawing in a small breath, she said, "Maybe I'll leave with Fiona."

His expression held a hint of triumph. "No you won't, because you want me to put my big, stiff dick in your wet pussy and get you off." Swiftly rolling his wrist, he slid his index and middle finger palm-deep into her sleek, pulsing warmth and at her shocked surprise, whispered, "Just. Like. That." Then smoothly withdrawing his fingers, he sat back and casually wiped them on his shorts.

With Fiona drawing near, Nicole suppressed her shudder and tried not to think about how desperately she wanted to screw the egotistical prick. That Rafe was watching her, clear-eyed and brilliantly relaxed, made her unspeakably pissed and shamelessly horny. Damn, his quiet arrogance was hot.

Fiona stopped at Nicole's chair and not entirely sure she wasn't in the midst of a war zone, asked cautiously, "Are you going to stay or come with us?"

"I haven't decided," Nicole said, when, of course, she had, with her libido full speed ahead in its not-to-be-missed rendezvous with destiny.

Rafe couldn't recall a woman ever challenging him—acquiescence the rule when it came to the females in his life—and he briefly wondered if he'd be picking up the tab for a holiday that didn't include him. *Probably not—actually no way in hell*—because he wasn't going to let her leave without him. Nicole Parrish intrigued him, made him curious to discover what made her different. Although it might just be her prickly defiance that made him hard.

Whatever the reason, a swift adjustment to the personal dynamic was required. Lowering his voice, Rafe said softly, "I'm really sorry." Reaching out, he touched Nicole's fingers where they lay on the chair arm. "I'll apologize any way you wish. I had no right to take offense. Forgive me?" His golden gaze was warm, his smile innocent as a child's. "Two weeks is perfect."

Nicole stared at him for a second, then a small smile twitched at the corners of her mouth, broadened a moment later to light up her eyes. "Goddamn, you're smooth, Contini. Even better than my younger brother when he wants to drive my car."

Rafe returned her appealing smile. "You can drive my car—cars, yachts, planes, choppers. Anytime. Anywhere."

Then he left the silence undisturbed.

He was entirely too good-looking. Too familiar with a revolving door of women making asses over themselves to please him. She could choose not to join that vast legion. But then her rendezvous with destiny was beckoning like a mirage in the desert. And like mirages everywhere, the lure was irresistible. Perhaps not completely irresistible, because a little voice inside her head reprimanded, sharply: *I'm disowning you if you cave completely. I need a quid pro quo.* "Just so everything's clear," Nicole said, hardwired not to cave with or without a niggling voice. "We're agreed on two weeks?"

He recognized her challenge, said as much with a look.

She laughed. "They always just say yes, don't they?"

"Of course not," he lied.

Nicole looked up at Fiona, who was failing to follow the subtext of the conversation. "I'm going to stay," she explained. "You and Jack have a good time."

"You're sure now?" There was a note of uncertainty in Fiona's voice.

"Rafe said he was sorry." Nicole gave him a smug smile. "So everything's good. What about you? Are you fine with"—she wiggled her fingers—"wherever you're going?"

"Are you kidding?" Fiona let out a throaty giggle. "I feel like I won the lottery!"

Nicole laughed. "Have fun then. Oh, hell," she said. "Do you know where my phone is?"

"With mine. I'll go get it."

"I'll go with you." Jack set down the two whiskeys he held, intent on giving Rafe the privacy he wanted.

Rafe glanced up. "Carlos is in the wheelhouse. I told him you'd be up."

Nicole waited until they were alone before offering her own apology. "I'm sorry too. I have a short fuse." Whether her mother's admonitions about common courtesy were prompting her or she was trying to semi-manage the uncharted craziness, she wanted to clear the air. "Can you deal with the fireworks? We'll probably fight like a couple of cats."

He offered her a lazy grin. "Cats?"

"Not you I suppose—unless it's some huge jungle animal." Her gaze flicked up, a playful glitter in the blue depths. "Points to you on weight class."

"Why don't I promise not to use my size to my advantage?" His smile could have melted the last of the Arctic ice. "Deal?"

She nibbled her bottom lip. "Deal, but still...last warning—I can be difficult. You might be better off with someone else."

"In what way?"

"Less angst. More compliance." She smiled. "All those yeses you like."

His brows rose. "Tut, tut. You want compliments? You want me to tell you how special you are? How I can't live without you?"

"Screw you," she muttered, taking offense at his silky sarcasm, chafing at her flagrant attraction to a man who only knew adoring women.

"Oh you will," he said softly, "a hundred different ways. And," he added with a smile, "if I'd wanted someone else, I wouldn't have sent Silvie away."

His deep voice was like a caress, his smile sensual, the subliminal message so overt, she felt the pleasure ripple through her body, particularly where his fingers had so recently rested. But he was watching her, so ignoring his lazy smile and her fevered senses, she spoke with deliberate coolness. "You forget, her husband came for her."

"I could have dealt with it. Silvie likes to fuck me. She would have stayed."

Nicole gave him a sharp look. "You really are an arrogant bastard."

"But that's what you like. You don't want someone too nice, do you?" When she didn't answer, he said very softly, "I'll tell you what you want. You want raw, sweaty, rock-your-world sex. You want to be pushed and pushed and pushed some more until you're dripping wet and desperate, until you'll do anything to be taken over the fucking orgasmic edge. Because under all that sass and audacity of yours you don't really want a man who takes orders, do you?" Her heart was pounding, her ears buzzing, her breath caught in her throat, and as if knowing what he'd done to her, he held her heated gaze, gave her a mocking smile and repeated in a whisper, "Do you, Nicole?"

She didn't have to answer. The insolent smile on his face said it all. She should tell him to find someone else to fucking push over the edge. But she didn't because all she felt was an insistent, impossible craving that she was powerless to contain and she wasn't entirely sure she wasn't going to simply melt in a puddle of lust right before his eyes. So with a noticeable wince because she'd never before said anything so abjectly submissive, she answered, "No."

"That's what I thought," he said, amused.

She gave him the finger and he only said, "You're going to be a great fuck."

"Maybe I don't need you," she muttered, sullen and testy.

"Need and want are two different things." His smile was warm. "I can show you."

Annoyed by that lovely smile—a reflex for a man used to getting what he wanted—she held up her hands and wiggled her fingers. "FYI—these work just fine."

"I'm going to teach you a whole new meaning of the word *penetration*," he said gently, as if she'd not spoken. "Nothing extraordinary or shocking," he added at her nervous start. "Just a different kind of compliance." His brows lifted faintly as he watched the color rise in her cheeks. "Don't tell me you're afraid. Or does it turn you on—the thought of what I'll do to you?" Looking at her directly, he lowered his voice to a sultry whisper. "It's about me setting the rules and you obeying them. Willingly. Totally. Without complaint," he whispered as she uttered a soft breathy moan. "You'll be sore in the morning, but you'll come so many times you'll be grateful and"—he grinned—"knowing you, probably resentful. But I guarantee you'll enjoy it."

Even as lust in all its torrid, earth-shaking intensity roared through her senses, she bristled at his assurance. "You can't guarantee that."

"Fuck if I can't. You're getting wetter just thinking about what I might do to you, aren't you?" His voice was exaggeratedly soft. "Wondering how it feels to submit for the first time in your spoiled life." He took an exasperated breath. "Don't pretend you don't know you're beautiful."

They looked at each other for a taut, simmering moment, both defensive and defenseless. Both stunned by a rare feeling of freedom lost.

Then with zero interest in shutting down this freaking flame-hot drama, Rafe reached out and gently slid a damp curl behind her ear. "I'll make sure you're happy with the arrangement," he whispered. "I promise."

The door abruptly opened and Fiona and Jack walked in.

Instantly, Rafe's face was wiped clean of expression. "So no more arguments?" His voice was bland. "Only sunshine in paradise for us?"

Less practiced in casual prevarication, it took Nicole a second to regain her composure. And a further second to answer as blandly. "I'll give it a try." Her smile was carefully rationed. "That's all I can promise."

"Trying's good," he said, smooth as silk, glancing up as Fiona reached them. "You found the phone. Perfect." He held out his hand, took Nicole's purse, and set it beside him on the hassock.

"We should check in every day," Fiona said. "In case our mothers need some explanation."

"Or we do," Nicole noted, unsure of the length of her stay.

"Agreed. When?"

Nicole shrugged. "I don't care. I talked to my mother earlier, so I'm off the hook today."

"One-ish then, tomorrow. Anything else we should agree on?" Fiona's voice plainly conveyed her reservations.

Rafe smiled. "You two have your code words in case Jack or I misbehave?" Lifting Nicole's feet from his lap he lightly kissed her toes. "And just for the record," Rafe said, glancing up and smiling at her, "I've never done that before."

"I do so like to be special," Nicole purred.

"And you are, pussycat." He winked. "No doubt in my mind."

Conscious of his cousin's unprecedented show of affection, Jack immediately made their adieus with a promise that he and Fiona would stay in touch.

With the door closing on their friends, Rafe glanced at the clock, as if fixing this extraordinary event in his memory. He'd always been a practical man, but his feelings for Nicole offered him no reference points in his past. This holiday was about play, but not just play; it was something more. Something honest and joyful, something that made him happy when he'd always been critical of it before.

And for the first time in his life, he was planning on spending more than a few hours with a woman.

Weeks in fact.

Perhaps...the less infatuated portion of his brain reflected, as did the deep-seated pragmatic centers of his subconscious.

This was, after all, a completely unorthodox situation.

No sense in jumping to conclusions.

"Hey."

He looked up.

Nicole gazed at him from under lowered lashes, her smile playful. "What if I said you're the sunshine of my life, and you're probably a little bit right about everything you said?"

He laughed. "I'd say give me whatever you're smokin'." Then his voice softened and he said quietly, "You make the sun shine for me as well…the moon and stars too, I'm guessing." His mouth twitched. "We'll find out tonight."

FIVE

Suddenly wary of having said too much, Rafe quickly sat up, reached out, swept Nicole up in his arms, and swung her onto his lap. Bending his head, he kissed her cheek. "Now, what do you want to do? Or," he added, amusement in his voice, "more to the point, where do you want to do it?"

Her smile was teasing. "Maybe, I should...like, pass on this."

He laughed. "You won't any more than I did."

"Hey." Her mood abruptly altered. "Don't do me any favors."

For the space of a second he hesitated, then a smile slowly formed on his beautiful mouth. "Maybe just a few to begin with. See what you like."

"Oh, Jesus," she said on a soft breath. "I'm sorry. I should say thank you."

"You should. You will, we both will. So where do you want these various favors to take place?"

She hesitated at the broad scope of his query, wondering next how long it took to master such a bland expression when offering carte blanche sex. But she dismissed her quibbles a second later. The idea of carte blanche sex intrigued her more than she was willing to admit. "There's way too many people here."

"Definitely soul mates, babe. I was thinking the same thing. Noisy as hell." It wasn't, of course, in the quiet of the insulated suite, but the party wasn't going to end until morning and he wanted complete privacy. "Here are our choices. My house up in the hills, a small cruiser that's over in the next marina, or we can fly somewhere else quiet. I have a villa at Split. It wouldn't take long to get there."

"My apartment first so I can pick up a few things, then your house."

He was tempted to say "soul mates" and mean it this time; he wouldn't have to wait and he could fuck her in comfort. "Got it. You have your phone, what about shoes?"

"My shoes are—shit. I don't know where I left them."

"It doesn't matter. Someone can find them later." Rafe suddenly went quiet, then slowly exhaled. "Christ—I feel like a goddamn adolescent on his first date."

"No you don't."

He laughed, quickly stood, and set her on her feet. "Well, like I imagine one would feel."

"And I'm feeling like I imagine all your women friends feel. Eager, impatient, horny." She smiled. "I told you I think it's the liquor, not the magic."

"Spoilsport, when I'm feeling the magic."

She snorted. "As if."

"Well, you're freaking rockin' my world." He winked. "How about that?"

The *Discovery II* was anchored offshore so they made their way to where the custom-built Dariel limo tenders that shuttled guests were moored. As they approached the stairway to the lower deck, a female voice rose above the sound of music drifting down from the main deck. "Rafe darling! Come give me a kiss!"

"Ignore her." Gauging the distance to the stairway, Rafe exerted slightly more pressure on Nicole's arm to speed up their departure. But then a waitperson blocked their way for a moment and a second later, Rafe put the brakes on and softly swore. A tall, dark-haired, minimally dressed woman with her eyes flashing *do me,* had stepped squarely in his path.

"*Mia caro,* don't run off." The cover-model smile was sultry, her voice a sex kitten purr. "I haven't seen you since that night in Rome and you definitely weren't in a hurry then. In fact—"

"I'm in a hurry now, Bianca." Rafe lifted his brows and stared at her. "So if you'd move, I'd appreciate it."

Nicole had to tilt her head to look up at the supertall, flawlessly beautiful woman in a string bikini so inconsequential she might as well have been naked, while the words *night in Rome* pissed her off for no earthly reason with a man like Rafe. If all the stories were true, he was a man without limits, out of reach for women looking for more than just sex. Skilled at evasion. For anyone to expect more was idiotic.

Bianca didn't move. "I just wanted to say thank you, darling." Her voice was soft as silk. "I didn't have a chance to do that properly in Rome. I fell asleep. You wore me out." She ran her fingertip down Rafe's cheek. "You were so wild that night, all brute force and out-of-control—"

"You weren't invited to this party," Rafe said, stepping

out of reach. "So why don't you be a good girl and move. I have things to do."

"Anatole was invited." There was a faint irony to her smile, as if she were helpless against his demands. "And I'm his guest."

Rafe sighed. "Then go talk to him, not me. Or have a drink, fuck the DJ—you remember him. Last year, Capri? Just stop breaking my balls. I'm not in the mood." He was trying to avoid a scene. Bianca loved scenes. But then she was seriously messed up, like so many people he knew. Himself included.

Understanding what Rafe *was* in the mood for, Bianca looked at Nicole for the first time, lips pursed, head slightly askew, as if she were unacquainted with what she saw. "You're not his type." She looked at Rafe, brows arched in derision. "Since when did you fancy wholesome?"

"Jesus, Bianca, how would you know what the hell I fancy?"

"Actually, I'm not sure Rafe has a type," Nicole interjected, her smile sweet as pie. "I know I don't. So I was thinking Rafe and I would just use each other for mind-blowing sex. No mercy, no remorse, until we run out of breath or collapse or both." She glanced up at Rafe. "You're good with that, right?"

He smiled down at her. "Sounds lovely."

"Apparently hard core runs in the family," Bianca sneered, her glittering gaze on Nicole. "I saw you with your uncle in Cannes this spring." Her mouth twitched into a malicious smile. "Dominic prefers subversive kink too. Or maybe your uncle's already shown you the kind of kink Rafe likes."

Waylaid and impatient, Rafe hadn't been listening. Instead he was scanning the crowd for one of his security men, but at the words *subversive kink,* his gaze returned to the women and he heard the last sentence. "Jesus, Bianca, shut the fuck up!"

"Really, Rafe, you of all people, suddenly virtuous. Aren't you on video in every private sex club in the world?"

"We're done here." Glancing up, Rafe finally caught the eye of one of his security staff. "Apologize to Miss Parrish." He spoke with such aggression, Bianca started.

Then her eyes narrowed. "Fuck you, Rafe." Flipping him off, Bianca turned to Nicole. "I was married to Dominic you know— Oh...you didn't know? He always did live by his own set of rules, didn't he?" she added, sly and artful. "We were married in Fiesole. Ask him."

Nicole shot a shocked look at Rafe. "Who is this?"

"Nobody." Rafe grabbed Bianca's arms and began dragging her aside.

Struggling to free herself from Rafe's grip, Bianca hissed at Nicole, "Ask Dominic about his marriage to Bianca! He can't deny it! We had a *child*!"

Nicole gasped at the word *child,* cringing at the thought of Dominic married to this woman. Told herself a bitch was a bitch and this bitch was *lying.*

A large man who looked as though he could bench-press a truck suddenly appeared and Rafe shoved Bianca at him. "Lock her up until we're gone. Then escort her ashore. And tell Anatole Regnier if he brings her onboard again, I'll personally beat the shit out of him."

"You goddam son of a bitch!" Bianca raged as she was

being hauled away. "I'll make you sorry for this! I swear I will!"

"Too late," Rafe muttered, leading Nicole to the stairway. He gently squeezed her hand. "Sorry about that. Bianca's a total head case."

"It sounds as though she really liked *you* in Rome."

"Trust me, she likes any man with a beating heart and money."

"What did she mean about my uncle? She's lying, right?"

"That's all she does is fucking lie. Believe me, she was just trying to get a rise out of you." He'd never heard that Bianca had had a child. He also knew a lot of people named Dominic, although, with Bianca, that was probably another fabrication too.

"Jeez, I hope so. She's a major skank." Nicole angled a pointed look at Rafe. "I could ask why *you* were with her, but I think I know the answer."

"Won't happen again, believe me. It was a onetime deal, short and sweet. I'm guessing I was drunk. Now watch your step," he said, handing Nicole into the sleek tender, hoping like hell the conversation about Bianca was over. "Hey, Jules. We're going to the car."

"I'm done with this," Nicole said, watching Rafe jump down.

"Good." He was fucking grateful. "Come stand with me up front." He held out his hand. "You don't see much when you're sitting."

Reaching the shore in record time, Rafe helped Nicole onto the dock and nodded at a black sedan idling in the marina parking lot. "There's our ride." Sliding his fingers through hers, he drew her along with him. "We'll pick up your stuff and head up the hill."

"Jules is rockin'. I *love* speed. When I was young, my car had a governor on it." She grinned. "No more."

"We'll have to go driving. See how good you are behind the wheel."

She shook her head. "Later. I have plans."

"Good to hear," he said in an entirely different tone, thoughts of fast cars and driving eclipsed by the velvety resonance in her voice that seemed to reach out and touch him. "That way I won't inconvenience you." He beat back the worst of his wildness, took a small breath, and said, in a raspy whisper, "With some of *my* plans."

At the flash of heat in his hooded eyes, the hair on the back of Nicole's neck stood up, but every sex-deprived nerve in her body was immune to fear. "Lucky me," she murmured.

Pulling her to a stop, Rafe spoke with an honesty unheard of for him in situations like this. "Lucky us, you mean," he said softly, holding her gaze until she stopped breathing. And when she mutely nodded, he experienced a frighteningly wild happiness that would have brought a dead man back to life.

But a second later, his expression mirrored his shock, and understanding that they were both operating in the same clueless haze of mind-altering desire, Nicole suddenly dragged in a breath and grinned. "New territory, right? No maps. No GPS. Nada."

"Fucking A." He frowned, momentarily baffled before he sorted through the crazy mind fuck that had blown in with Nicole Parrish. "Look, if it's all the same to you," he said with empty politesse, "I'd prefer to file this *us thing* under lust." He smiled. "That way it's safe, familiar, nothing that'll wreck the comfortable pattern of my life."

"You're preaching to the choir, dude."

He did a double take. The women in his life were notoriously calculating, all after the same thing—marriage to a billionaire. He had no illusions.

"Don't look so surprised. I'm on summer break. Lust is the reason I'm here." Nicole lifted her chin as they reached the black Mercedes sedan and spoke in a deliberately disinterested tone. "Nice car. Armored." She smiled up at him. "Looks like you bring all kinds of excitement with you."

"Just a practicality," he lied, grateful for her well-mannered change of subject. "I have too many attorneys. They hate problems." Opening the back door, he waved her in. "Give Simon directions."

Since Dominic's apartment was practically on the water, it was only a few minutes before the car pulled up to the building entrance. Rafe held up his phone. "If you want company, I'll come up with you. Otherwise I'm going to take care of some business." He smiled. "Seeing how you and I are going to be busy for the foreseeable future." His smile widened. "No mercy, no remorse. Should be fun."

"Here's hoping." Grinning, Nicole held up crossed fingers. "Make your calls. I don't need company."

"Simon could come with you and carry—whatever."

"Nah, I'm good. I travel light."

Opening the car door, Rafe swung his legs aside and

gave her ass a little pat as she eased past him and stepped out onto the pavement. "Don't be gone long."

There was something in his tone—a casual, boundless authority. Nicole turned back. "Or?"

He smiled and his voice shifted downward. "Or I'll have to come up and get you."

He was way the hell too good-looking and so totally sexy, she didn't even need that soft, killer tone of voice to make her turn into a damp, aching mess. Shutting her eyes, she let the sweet pleasure melt through her body for a fraction of a second before she hauled herself back to reality.

He didn't think he'd ever seen anything hotter. "You gonna make it?" His voice was whisper soft. "Maybe I should come with you." *Fuck you while you're packing.*

She sucked in a breath. "Tempting," she murmured, as if she could read his mind, as if they were both on the same supercharged, X-rated wavelength. "But better not. Sometimes staff is around."

"So?" Gently suggestive, a flash of heat in his amber eyes.

"So I'm not looking for an audience right now." But she shuddered a little as a quivering warmth coiled deep inside her.

He grinned. "Come on back in. Simon won't look."

"No." His casualness helped. Made her less likely to fall into his arms like every other woman.

"No?" he said very low, a small constraint in the word. "Are you offended?"

A muscle briefly twitched in his lean cheek, then he

grinned and said with teasing irony, “Fuck no. It’s just sex. I’ll catch you later.” His grin widened. “I’ll show you a good time whenever. Your call.”

She laughed, back in control, not entirely sure he hadn’t helped her get there. “You make me so crazy hot, I’m in the mood for just about anything.”

His smile lit up his eyes. “Now there’s incentive to up my game.”

“Hold that thought, Contini.” She offered up a sexy wink, then swung around and moved, all fancy-assed grace and awesomeness, toward the front door.

The doorman’s eyes looked like one of those cartoon character’s stunned by a gigantic hammer; he was opening the door in a slow-mo daze. Not that Rafe blamed the guy. Just watching Nicole’s sweet ass in her teeny, tiny flowered bikini sent all the blood in his brain south to his dick and he was seriously thinking: *Screw the staff. Her bedroom door must have a lock.*

Just as he was about to push the intercom button and tell Simon he was going to be gone awhile, his phone rang. Shit. He briefly considered the possibility of divine intervention or random bad luck or both. But he’d been waiting for this ringtone, so he took a breath of restraint and tapped the Answer bar.

“Anatole and Bianca have been set ashore.” Carlos’s voice was professionally cool and composed. “I gave orders they weren’t to be allowed onboard again.”

“Thanks. Appreciate it.” Carlos Sanz filled a variety of roles: personal attendant, lecturer, fixer. Ex–Basque separatist, ex–French Foreign Legion, ex-mercenary in lawless regions of the world, he'd been with Rafe a long time.

"Not a problem. Jack and Miss Kelly also left for the airport in Nice. Jack said you might be gone a few weeks. I know you told me that, but just double-checking."

Rafe smiled. "Worried?"

Carlos grunted. "Skeptical."

"I don't blame you. I am too. But it is what it is."

"Your stepfather will want to know your plans. He called me when you didn't answer. I told him you've gone ashore with one of your guests and might have turned off your phone for a few hours."

"Thanks. Whatever he needs can wait until tomorrow." Anton had brought joy into his mother's life, but if the term *overprotective* could be attributed to anyone it was his new stepfather. "If he calls you back, tell him as little as possible. Honestly, I'm not sure myself what my plans are."

"I'll do my best. But—"

"Do what you can." Not that Rafe and his stepfather didn't get along. In fact, Anton was a real asset to the company; his management skills were outstanding.

"Keep me in the loop. I'll text you if any emergencies come up. But make sure you answer your mother's calls."

"I will. I might fly to Split for a few days. So far that's all I know."

"Do you want me to vet this girl?"

"Fuck no. No," Rafe added more firmly. "Don't even think it. She's my new learning curve."

"If you say so."

That was too vague a reply. "I do, so chill." Rafe exhaled. "At least for now. And if anyone asks, you don't know her name. Although I expect you do."

"Of course."

Rafe chuckled. "The Mossad could only hope to have an intelligence service like yours."

"Your mother worries," Carlos said simply.

Rafe sighed. "I know." He'd always been a target. For his wealth. For the Contini business that attracted industrial piracy. Because his father had introduced him into a vice-ridden, dangerous world. He didn't blame his mother. But security had its down side on occasion.

"Miss Parrish *is* a refreshing change," Carlos acknowledged. "Enjoy yourself. Just don't forget your obligations."

"Do I ever?"

"Not to date, no."

"I'm not sure I like the insinuation I might. I won't," Rafe said brusquely. "But a word of warning: even if you find out Miss Parrish is a bigamist with six children and an empty bank account, don't tell me. I don't want to know yet. Clear?"

"Affirmative."

Rafe slowly inhaled, held his breath for a tenuous second, exhaled, and said very softly, "It may not be a game this time, so I just want to play it out. Privately. In my own time."

"Got it. If you need anything though, don't hesitate to ask."

Rafe dropped his head back on the padded leather seat, stared at the ceiling, and spoke softly. "I know what

I'm doing, Carlos. There's no need for alarm. Two weeks, a month at the most, and life goes back to normal. I can almost guarantee it."

"I'm simply offering my help. I'm not questioning you. You're not a capricious man."

"With a father like mine, I couldn't be. Someone had to have their head screwed on straight."

"Right. One last business matter before you start fucking. Ganz tried to call you. I intercepted and called him back. He's coming in next week. He said another attack from the same state-sponsored hacker is looming."

"Jesus, what's that—the tenth, eleventh?"

"Ganz said the twelfth."

Rafe sighed. "Okay, start bringing in the teams to my place here. Provided Ganz approves."

"Already on it."

"How about the police chief in Zurich? Is he doing his job?"

"So far. Ganz and his mother are safe. No activity at your farm. The chief has set up round-the-clock surveillance shifts and not a ripple of activity anywhere. But your property is off the grid. It makes it harder to find."

"Thanks. You know how to get hold of me. Ah, here comes Miss Parrish," Rafe said, pleased their business was more or less concluded, pleased as well that she'd put on a shirt that covered some of her nakedness. For some reason, he didn't feel like sharing—the thought so shocking, he quickly dismissed it. It smacked of permanence, of something beyond the simple pleasures of this holiday, of feelings too intense, too inappropriate, for his life. "Has the house been cleared out?" he asked, returning to more ordinary considerations, watching Simon walk around the front of the car.

"As of ten minutes ago. Roddrick had to be carried out," Carlos said drily. "No surprise. But everyone's been transferred to a hotel of their choice."

"Excellent. Ciao." Rafe looked up as the door opened and smiled. "That was fast."

"I was in a hurry." Nicole handed him her backpack.

Taking it from her, he set it down and helped her into the car.

Dropping down beside Rafe, she waited for Simon to shut the door, then leaned over and ran her hand over his fly. "No pressure," she said, glancing up with a saucy grin, "but I needed to come—like an hour ago."

He laughed. "That's the kind of pressure I like." He touched her bottom lip with the pad of his finger. "Want one for the road? There's time."

She hesitated.

His erection surged higher.

Then she shook her head. "You said you wanted to take your time. I do too." She gently stroked his hard, rigid length with a brush of her hand. "I want to feel you in me and over me, slowly, deeply, your naked skin on mine, your heat and strength, everything you've got making me crazy for a *very, very* long time." She looked up at him from under the soft curl of her lashes, cupped the head of his dick, and softly squeezed. "I'm selfish. So I want that first"—she smiled a big-eyed, dead-ten, fuck-me smile—"before you push me over the edge."

SIX

Rafe's *house up in the hills* was a gross misrepresentation of the Renaissance-style peach-colored palace that came into view as the car topped the steep gated drive. An enormous four-story facade lay squarely before them at the very end of a lengthy row of boxwood-framed parterres ablaze with colorful flowers.

"Seriously?" Nicole muttered, rolling her eyes at Rafe. "Your house?"

"At the moment. It's been in the family a long time. Actually, I prefer the carriage house. Does it matter to you?" Women were invited to parties at the main house; he understood its cachet.

"So your friends hang out there?" She flicked a little wave in the direction of the palace.

"Did. They're gone now. So." He smiled. "Where would you like to stay? Take your pick."

"Does the carriage house have a sea view?"

"Both places do."

"Staff?"

"At the main house."

"Do you cook?"

"Not much. Scrambled eggs if I'm desperate."

"Can we get takeout?"

Since there was an industrial-size kitchen at the main

house with a chef and his team, the answer was simple. "Sure."

"Then I'm opting for the carriage house." Nicole wrinkled her nose. "I don't like people around."

Rafe grinned. "When you're fucking."

"Particularly when I'm fucking. I hope that's not a deal-breaker." She sat up a little straighter as though instinctively adding emphasis to her comment. "Especially since I've been wanting to check you out," she said, her voice a hushed purr, a warm twinkle in her blue gaze. "In terms of my personal fulfillment."

He lifted an eyebrow. "So I'm to perform?" A small friction lay beneath the pleasantness of his tone.

"Of course. Otherwise, what's the point? I have a vibrator at home." She smiled then, an irresistible, blatantly seductive smile. "I'd really prefer to see what you can do for me before I go home."

"Don't worry, you won't be going anywhere." There was quiet rebuke in his voice, finality. "You've heard the saying—as long as I have breath in my body? I'm operating on that principle."

"Am I supposed to be alarmed?" She cocked her head slightly and looked straight at him. "I'm not."

Did she realize what she was saying to someone who flirted with the dark side of human nature? It took an act of will for him to not take advantage of her. "I'll try not to alarm you," he said. "Ah, here we are."

The car came to a stop before a rusticated limestone building fronted with several large pots of topiary and draped in a tumble of climbing white roses and bougainvillea.

Nicole shot Rafe a look. "Simon can't hear us in here, can he? So did I even really have a choice?"

He looked amused, her mutinous personality strangely attractive. "Don't be so prickly. Simon just knows I usually stay here. But speak up if you'd rather go somewhere else. The South Pole for all I care, so long as I can fuck you." He had his finger on the intercom button. "You want to give Simon directions? The airport's not far. The Gulfstream's gone but the 757's there."

"Oh God." She blew out a breath. "Sorry. I told you I could be difficult."

"Bossy, you mean," he said, smiling.

Instinctively responding to his male interpretation, she met his gaze with a faint frown. "I mean assertive. You know, like men are assertive, but women are bossy or stubborn or obstinate. *That* way. No offense, of course," she added with a sudden grin.

He held up his hands. "None taken. I can deal with any kind of assertive you've got, or, more precisely, I'm willing to deal with it because you're making me crazy in a supernice way. Although, just out of curiosity—do you give orders in bed?" When she hesitated, he chuckled. "That'll be a change. I'm guessing we'll be flying blind."

A tip of her head. "Meaning?"

"I like to give orders too."

His deep, husky voice triggered every needy, X-rated nerve in her body, the essence of his words settling with a shimmering jolt deep inside her, and with a soft gasp, she felt herself open in welcome as if he'd touched her where she most wanted to be touched.

"Want to give it a try?" he said softly, watching her. "My orders first?" And without waiting, he lifted her into his lap and tapped the intercom. "Get the door, Simon. We're staying here." Then he slipped a finger under her bikini bottom, stroked her throbbing pussy, and whispered, "I guarantee happy endings. How soon do you want to come?"

"Yesterday," she said on a caught breath, damp and aching. "Last week, last year."

"So I should let you come quickly. Is that what you want now?"

At the sudden edge to his voice, she looked up, accusation in the brilliant blue of her eyes. "Don't you fucking dare."

His driver was almost back to the car door. "Do you want Simon to watch? Or are you going to wait?" He shrugged. "Your call."

She shoved his hand away. "Asshole. Maybe I'll make *you* wait," she hissed as the car door opened and then added under her breath, "Put me down."

"Just leave Miss Parrish's backpack in the foyer, Simon." Swinging his legs out of the car, Rafe rose to his feet smoothly, despite having Nicole in his arms. "And tell the kitchen we're not sure when we'll have dinner." As his driver reached into the car, Rafe wondered if Nicole would make a scene, not sure what he'd do if she did. But she only stuck out her tongue.

Seriously, soul mates; he disliked public drama too.

Simon swiveled back up with Nicole's pack in hand. "I'll let the chef know the dinner hour is uncertain." Tall and trim, with military-cut hair, a gold earring in one ear, and a bespoke linen jacket tailored to conceal his shoulder holster, the driver smiled. "Since you're Henny's go-to guy when he loses at the tables, he'll overlook your nonschedule."

"I figure." Rafe turned and moved toward the entrance. "You'll be around?"

Simon kept pace. "Where else."

"We might go to Split."

Simon's smile flashed. "Excellent." He had a girlfriend there.

"No set itinerary yet. So it's not for public consumption."

"Understood." Simon lengthened his stride, reached the door first, and opened it.

As Rafe walked through, he glanced back over his shoulder. "I'll check in with you tomorrow."

Simon gave him a quick finger gun salute, mouthed the word *enjoy,* dropped the backpack on the marble floor, and softly shut the door.

"Goddamn bloody tyrant," Nicole grumbled the second they were alone. "I don't suppose it would do any good to say, 'Put me down' now."

Rafe dropped a light kiss on her forehead and strode toward a curved stone staircase carpeted in a faded red-and-blue flame pattern. "Nope."

"So you're calling all the shots?"

He gave her a quick grin. "Only until you're not having fun."

"Maybe I'm not having fun."

"Give me a couple seconds. We just have to get upstairs." And he took the remaining stairs two at a time with lithe, athletic ease.

Nicole bashed him on the shoulder as they reached the top of the stairs. "Goddamn, Contini, all that flash and dazzle muscle and strength is a major turn-on." She grinned. "I might have just come. Wanna do it again?"

He gave her an impatient glance. "Fuck no." He didn't alter his swift stride down the wide hallway. "And FYI, baby, just watching you breathe is a turn-on for me. In fact, I'm not equipped to deal with this crazy, out-of-control need. I'm not sure how to play it."

"Just so long as I come in the next few minutes, play it any way you want. I won't complain."

"But then you're not giving the orders, are you?" he murmured, nudging a door open with his foot, entering a large bedroom with an incredible view of the sparkling Mediterranean, and heeling the door shut.

"Ohmygod! I have to go see that! Put me down this second or—"

His grip tightened. "Or?" A soft hint of warning in the word.

She patted his cheek. "Save the Neanderthal shit, okay? I just want to stand on your balcony and drink in that fantastic scene. Come on, Mr. You're-in-Charge. I'll be ever so good. Just put me down."

He grinned. "You good? That I gotta see." Setting her on her feet, he gently prodded her ass. "Go. I've seen it before."

Quickly discarding her shirt and dropping it as she ran, a moment later she stood on the wide balcony, her arms raised to the sky, like some acolyte to an ancient sun god.

Motionless, Rafe took in the beauty of her celebratory

pose, the supple grace of her body, the beguiling vision of exultation. He couldn't help but smile. She was the human equivalent of delight, completely open and natural, frank about what she wanted. And she wanted him—not a rarity in his world—but rare in the pleasure it afforded him.

He actually wanted to make her happy, like she did him. It was the most exhilarating feeling he'd ever had, quickly followed by more predictable alarm bells reminding him not to be gullible, delusional, or both. Furiously warning him that this might be an immense error.

He almost turned and walked out.

But Nicole suddenly swung around and held out her hand. "Come." She wiggled her fingers. "I think I can see Algiers from here. Tell me if it's true."

He hesitated. She'd messed with his head from the first. And here in his bedroom—where he always slept alone—he was suddenly feeling unmoored.

"Did I do something wrong?" Her brow furrowed and her voice turned soft with concern. "Of course I did," she said with a small sigh. "I tend to bowl people over with my"—a sweet smile lit up her face—"assertiveness." Another little sigh. "And you're only familiar with women who say yes, yes, yes, and *yes*. I could probably do that—for a little while anyway. Is that what you want?"

"I'm not sure what I want." The fact that he answered honestly only unnerved him further. Sex and honesty were mutually exclusive in his world.

"Please don't tell me to leave. I really don't want to." She blew out a breath and began walking toward him. "I probably don't know much more than you do about whatever is between us, but I do know that I'd like to stay—at least for a time."

Her smile was so artlessly seductive, he said brusquely, "Don't smile," and took a step back.

She abruptly halted. "Sorry."

The silence was thick with indecision and bafflement.

Rafe's nostrils flared, then he said slowly, "I don't like feeling this way."

She could have said, what you don't like is actually feeling something, anything. But she understood his dilemma. The difference was she didn't mind feeling something new and different. "Would it help if I left in the morning? That way we could take advantage of this crazy attraction between us—enjoy it, have some fun." She looked up into his shuttered gaze. "Then go our separate ways tomorrow. Would that work for you? No strings attached, no untoward feelings, just us getting off a few times."

As the silence lengthened, she said, "Maybe some other time then," and turned to get her shirt. She'd never begged for sex; she wasn't about to start. Call it pride, female power, fucking hot-tempered crankiness. And whatever his problem was, she suspected it was beyond the simple remedy of a night of sex with her. Too bad. He was insanely hot.

He watched her walk the few feet to where she'd dropped her shirt, pick it up, put it on, and then move toward the bedroom door.

Nicole's hand was on the latch when Rafe said, "Wait."

But she didn't wait. She opened the door and walked out into the hall.

"Do you want me to say I'm sorry?" he called out.

In reply he heard her footsteps receding down the corridor.

Fuck, fuck, fuck. Now what?

By the time he made up his mind, she was already out of sight. Racing down the corridor, he saw her as he reached the top of the staircase. Swiftly descending the wide, carpeted steps in great leaps, he scooped her up in his arms just as she reached the bottom of the flight. "You can't leave," he said, turning swiftly and moving back up the stairs. "I don't know why, but you can't."

"Want me to tell you why?" Although seriously, she'd need a degree in psychotherapy.

"No."

Typical male introspection. "Do I get a fuck at least? Hey"—she gave his chin a sharp snap with her thumb and middle finger—"look at me."

His amber eyes glowed like flame. "The fucking's guaranteed, babe."

"I'm not your babe," she said tartly. "I'm not anyone's babe."

"You are right now," he growled, beginning to travel down the long hallway. "For as long as I say you are. And the way I'm feeling, it's gonna last awhile."

"Well, if that's the case, wiseass," she said, pissy and hot-tempered, not in the mood to fold without considerable compensation, "I'm going to need that apology."

"Or?" A narrow-eyed glare.

"Or you won't enjoy the fucking."

"Don't be stupid."

"Jesus, is that supposed to frighten me?" Her voice was all sass and insolence; she was intrinsically unafraid. A character trait like that of her uncle Dominic, whom she'd challenged since childhood. "You might want to think about saving your unprotected dick from my retribution instead of threatening me."

He suddenly smiled. "Retribution? That's cute." Entering the bedroom, he pushed the door shut with his shoulder.

"Whether it's cute is for me to know and you to find out."

He came to a stop in the middle of the room and looked at her with a small frown. "Christ, you're mouthy."

"Yeah. So?"

"So I should kick you the hell out."

"Go for it. You could go fuck that bitch from Rome." At his sudden grin, she said, "What?" when she already knew the answer.

"I don't want to fuck her." The warmth in his eyes had nothing to do with temper. "We both know what I want to do. So if it helps, I apologize."

"Accepted."

He lifted one brow.

She wrinkled her nose, then smiled. "I apologize too. I'm guessing you're going to be worth an apology or two."

"It depends on how you feel about continuous sex," he said pleasantly.

Her smile was mischievous. "Wow, you're that good?"

"You can let me know in the morning."

"So all the stories are true."

Unabashed by the insinuation, he said, "Fuck the stories. This is different; we're different." He grinned. "Mostly you're different. I've never stopped anyone from walking away before. I usually would have been out the door first. But with you, I can't even visualize the end game."

"That decision's not just up to you." That voice of female power was persistent, or perhaps just on call twenty-four/seven.

Of course it is. "I know," he said instead, not about to start another argument about something so ludicrous. "You decide when it ends." Walking to the bed, he sat down with her on his lap, feeling strangely content with no expiration date on their amusements, gently kissed her cheek, and said softly, "Your schedule, okay?"

"At the moment I don't have long-term goals." She ran her finger over his bottom lip, feeling all warm and fuzzy in the aftermath of their dispute or her temper tantrum or whatever it was, liking the way he felt holding her close. "Only super short-term goals having to do with an orgasm or two for me."

Capturing her finger, he kissed it, then folded her hand in his. "I can do that." His whispered words touched her cheek, warm and seductive. "One or two orgasms first?" A neat and pragmatic solution, a cure for the ache inside her. "Any preferences on methodology?"

"You inside me, first, second, then ask me again." The desperation in her voice exposed her need. "Just so you know, I don't like to be desperate," she said on a suffocated breath. "So if you don't mind one small order. Fucking hurry."

He laughed. "Got it." He reached for the tie on her bikini top.

She brushed his hands aside. "I'm just slightly past seduction. About a hundred miles. Put me down and get undressed."

He chuckled. "More orders, pussycat. Will they ever stop?"

"Yeah." She ran her hand over the bulge in his shorts. "Guess when."

SEVEN

Standing up, Rafe set Nicole on her feet beside the large four-poster bed covered in a Le Manach zebra-print fabric and nodded. "Sure you don't need help?"

She pointed at her itsy-bitsy, flower-print bikini. "I'll be in bed before you." She grinned. "Waiting."

Already kicking off his blue leather sneakers, he laughed. "There's a living wet dream." He jerked his white short-sleeved Henley over his head and was reaching for the zipper on his striped shorts when Nicole pulled the bow at the back of her neck loose with one hand, unsnapped the hook on her bikini top with the other, and let the small scrap of flowered fabric drop to the floor.

Rafe's breath caught in his throat. "Nice tits," he said softly. "You must hear that a lot." He was looking at the Venus de Milo of breasts—flawless, sex-bomb plump, the deep rose nipples mouth-wateringly kissable.

"Not really," she lied. "I expect you hear a compliment or two about"—she flicked her hand toward his chest—"your ripped torso. Only a little moral restraint kept me from jumping you when I first saw you in your stateroom." She grinned. "And your dangerous girlfriend too."

No way he was touching the topic of Sylvie again. "Right now, the only danger is *my* lack of restraint," he said, unzipping his shorts. "This might be the fastest fuck of my life."

"Music to my ears, dude." Sliding her thumbs under her bikini bottom, she wiggled once.

"Jesus." Rafe went still as the silky material slid down her legs. It wasn't as though the small bit of fabric had hidden much, but what it had was seriously fuckable—the perfect little minimalist V of soft dark curls, glistening and dewy wet, was kicking his libido into the red zone, adding inches to his dick.

Intensely susceptible to her own fierce need, Rafe's full stop was unnerving; he'd already tried to back out twice. "In case it matters, I'm asking real politely for you to hurry, okay?" She kept her voice supercalm, like one would coaxing a lion into a cage. But with her current level of horniness, she wasn't above resorting to plan B. "Or I might have to go it alone."

"No fucking way," Rafe growled. "And I mean it real politely," he murmured, each word thick with sarcasm. Although with her creamy ass and the tantalizing glimpse of slick pussy she gave him as she briefly kneeled on the bed before dropping onto her back, he was going to be hard-pressed to stay within the boundaries of acceptable behavior, let alone politesse. Sucking in a breath, he told himself to fucking *chill,* and tamping down the worst of his brute impulses, he shoved down his shorts and boxers and stepped out of them.

She gasped—a soft, explosive sound.

Not an unfamiliar sound. He looked up.

"So it's not an urban legend after all," she whispered, coming up on one elbow and holding out her hand as little tremors raced up her spine and she turned liquid inside.

"That... is... *wow*—big." She took a quick breath, blinked. "And gorgeous." All her nerve endings began to sizzle and *please, please, please* lit up her brain. Rafe Contini was the poster boy for *hung*. Her wide-eyed gaze levered up, met his, and her voice went velvet soft. "Come closer."

"I'm way past even minimal control." His voice was a low rasp. "So don't touch or I might go off. I'm assuming you don't want that." For the first time in his life, he didn't trust his dick to comply, and motionless, he waited for her answer.

She smiled. "No touching—promise. I wouldn't want to deprive myself of— Oh, Christ." Her hand began to quiver and, abruptly dropping it on the bed, she drew in a slow, even breath. "This never happens," she whispered, her eyes locked with his. "Never."

"No shit," he said on a suffocated breath. "I'm hearing bloody violins like some goddamn silly girl."

The sudden silence was fraught with chafing discontent.

Then Rafe restlessly raked his fingers through his hair. "Fuck it. We'll deal with it." He didn't say that his libido was calling the shots, that he had no intention of letting her go.

"Right." She wasn't about to voice her purely selfish thoughts about instant orgasms either. He wasn't looking real reasonable right now, with a kind of suppressed fury in his eyes. And she had plans.

"So you still want to look?" He spoke with such admirable control, he could have been asking her if she wanted one card or two in high-stakes vingt-et-un.

Even his breathing had quieted and she forced herself

to speak as dispassionately as he. "Yes, please. I'm locked down tight again." She gave herself points for matching his cool, detached gaze. "Observe." She held up her hand. "Steady. Now let's see that art up close and personal."

"Just for a minute." Moving the few steps to the bed, Rafe lay down beside her and, turning his head, held her gaze. "You'll have plenty of time to see my tattoo up close and personal in the weeks ahead." At the quick lift of her brows, he added, "Open to discussion of course." *When it wasn't.* "Right now, though, just look or I'm going to come all over your hand." His voice was curt. "There are physical limits."

"Don't worry. I have no intention of missing out on your impressive hard-on." Her gaze flicked downward to his dick at full stretch. "I can see why women adore you," she added coolly. "I expect you don't have much competition."

"And I expect you can pick and choose your bed partners," he countered, experiencing a shocking twinge of jealousy, when he'd always had zero possessive instincts. "Forget it," he muttered. "It's none of my business."

"Same here." *Christ, what was she thinking?* Coming up on her knees, she pointed at the magnificent length of his erection arched navel high against his stomach—a masterpiece of both virility and artistic talent that was making her melt inside, that spurred a small breathlessness in her voice when she spoke. "Hokusai, right?"

With his gaze on her pussy only inches away, it took him a fraction of a second to reply. "Right."

An exquisitely detailed image of Hokusai's iconic *Great Wave* was inked on the underside of Rafe's rampant, upthrust dick: foam-topped waves, small figures of men in boats, a wide, beautiful, pastel sky. Then her gaze came up in fleeting surprise. "The water's moving!"

"Traditional tattoo work respects kinetics and muscle movement." He flexed his lower body and his erection swelled—animating the billowing waves, pitching and tossing the boats.

"That's amazing." Her overwrought whisper encompassed both the moving image and the ostentatious size of his arousal. "Did it take long?"

His gaze widened, the discrepancy between her tremulous tone and the bland question confusing. "Is this conversation going to be lengthy?" His voice, in contrast, was edgy, because his dick was aching something fierce and politesse had never been his strong suit.

She stiffened at his tone. "What if it is?"

He dragged in a breath, asked himself if this cheeky bitch was worth all the trouble, and, even before the thought was fully formed, knew the answer. "It took a week to finish." He smiled. "Is there more?"

She liked when he smiled like that, indulging her. "When? If you don't mind?"

Yes, he did mind—a whole freaking lot. "I had it done when I was sixteen. You know, kid stuff, a spur-of-the-moment impulse that ended up taking longer than I thought." A severely edited version of his youthful rebellion against his father's oppressive monitoring of his sex life.

"The colors are splendid: the luminous gold sky, the complex blues in the waves, the creamy foam flecked with bubbles. Subtle coloring like that has to be rare." She smiled and tilted her head slightly. "Not to mention the rarity of a dick your size that allows scope for the entire scene." She looked up. "That's me asking to see it all."

"Just don't touch. Seriously, I'm on a fucking hair trigger." Prying his rock-hard erection off his stomach, he forced it upright. "The rest of the scene continues around to the front. You can see a small image of Mt. Fuji there"—he pointed—"and another boat cresting a wave." When she leaned in to look, he grabbed her shoulders, rolled her under him, and smoothly settled between her legs. "End of art lecture, pussycat. Let's see if we fit."

The head of his dick slipped past her slick folds.

"Hey, hey, hey!" Jamming her hands hard against his chest, she vehemently shook her head. "You need a condom. Those are the rules."

Feverish desire glowed flame hot in her eyes. *He could change her mind.* And largely immune to reason with the head of his dick engulfed in her soft warmth, when all he had to do was push and he'd be where he'd wanted to be since he'd first laid eyes on her, he was indefensibly reckless. "I have a doctor on staff, I'm superclean, and I'm *this* close to losing it. So I'm willing to take a chance with you."

"Are you fucking crazy?" she screamed in a voice that would shatter glass.

His body went rigid. "Probably, yeah. Ever since I met you." Then he rolled off her because his ears were ringing, he was seriously pissed, and losing control wasn't an option if he ever wanted to fuck her—like, nonviolently. "You're totally screwing up my life, you know," he growled, turning his head and glowering at her. "Make up your fucking mind. Do you want it or don't you?"

"Well, for sure I don't want you screwing up *my* life because you can't use a condom!" Coming up on one elbow, she slammed her fist into his arm. "What the hell were you thinking!"

"Fucking tone it down," he muttered. "My hearing's just fine. They can hear you in the main house for Christ's sake."

"Ask me if I give a shit," she snapped, rising to her knees in a surge of fury, her eyes butane blue. "Now where the hell are your condoms? I'll get them, I'll put one on you, we'll both get off, then we'll repeat the fun and games until you want to stop. No one has to take a chance with anyone. That's how it's done in the real world, asshole."

"Screw you. Maybe I don't want to now. Maybe my libido took a hike." He laced his hands behind his head, stretched out his large, muscled frame like the king of the jungle settling in for a nap, and insolently smiled. "Now what are you going to do?"

She gave a little nod. "It doesn't look like your dick got the memo." In a flash, she ran her fingertips up his erection from base to swollen crest.

Slapping her hand away, he sucked in a breath as his dick pulsed and twitched. "Christ," he breathed, "I hope you know what you're doing." A smoldering heat darkened the gold of his eyes. "I don't have very good manners, sometimes none at all."

She shrugged off his threat. "I'm not looking for manners. Just a condom. I'll even do all the work." She jabbed a finger at his engorged cock. "As long as you bring that to the party. So where are your condoms?"

He groaned. "I wish I could kick you out. Seriously, I would if I could. This is all so fucked up."

"But it's awesome too, don't forget. And so rare"—another little lift of her shoulder—"we'd be stupid to walk away."

"Or smart."

She looked at him with a trace of a smile. "Don't you ever take a chance, go for broke, just wing it?"

"I was going to and you wouldn't let me," he pointed out, his eyes locked on hers.

"That's because my brain is still working. And that's not what I meant. I meant go for broke like"—she gave him a wicked wink—"with your feelings."

"I don't do feelings. I prefer zero emotion, no drama."

"How do you ever have fun?"

He laughed. "I thought I *was* having fun until you walked in the door."

"Seriously, with someone like Sylvie Fermetti?"

He lifted an eyebrow. "Orgasms register as fun in my world."

"But ours will be better."

"Maybe they won't be. I'm just saying."

"Okay, I'm done talking. You're not cooperating." She jumped off the bed. "Now, come on, where are your condoms?"

"I don't have any here. I sleep alone."

She spun around, her smile pure sunshine. "See. What

did I say? It's gonna be a whole lot better—guaranteed. So can we call a drugstore and get a delivery?"

Rafe exhaled a deep sigh, rolled up into a sitting position, and swung out of bed. "There might be some at the main house. I'll go look."

"Why didn't you say so before?"

"Because I'm not sure there are any."

"Someone could look, couldn't they, and bring them over?"

He smiled. "Thanks for the advice. But I'd better do it." He didn't say the party last night had probably decimated the supply of condoms, and if there were any they'd be somewhere obscure enough not to have been found when Roddrick was tearing the house apart screaming, *You gotta be kidding? We're out?* "I'll send Simon into town but he won't be back for a while. Are you desperate?"

"No more than you," she said pleasantly.

"Yeah." He grunted, reached for his shorts, and said a little prayer his search wouldn't be in vain. Because desperate didn't begin to define his ache for her.

"I'll come with you. Let me get my backpack and put on some clothes."

"Grab one of my robes." He pointed to the dressing room. "Just for the record, I'm fucking desperate, so hustle."

She walked back into the bedroom a few minutes later wearing one of his shirts. "Your robes all dragged on the floor. And you have ten of these blue oxford cloth shirts. I figured you wouldn't miss one." She'd rolled up the sleeves and the shirttails covered her legs to her knees.

He didn't want to think about her nakedness under his shirt, so he moved toward the door. "Come on." He reached out his hand. "I called Simon. He's on his way into town. In the meantime, let's see if we get lucky."

"At least I'm thinking semi-clearly again," she said, taking his hand.

"I'm trying. No guarantees though." Although the small break had mitigated the worst of his loot-and-pillage mentality, his remaining horniness was only mildly problematic.

But once they were outside and the world intruded, Rafe was better able to restrain his libido. The flagstone path to the main house was smooth and warm on their bare feet, the gardens scenting the air, and when Nicole gently squeezed his hand, they both felt the same warm enchantment.

"Nice," she said softly, smiling up at him.

He nodded.

"I'm glad I went to your party."

"Me too."

She grinned. "Are we having a moment?"

"If it's not going to piss you off, I'd rather not talk about shit like this."

"Gotcha. I have another question. No romance, strictly business."

He finally smiled. "That I can handle."

"Are you really superclean? I mean, even with all the women? And don't look at me like that. You know you and your dick are notorious."

He sighed. "Everyone's a goddamn voyeur. As for the women, I use condoms." He frowned. "You happen to be the exception condom-wise, like you are in every other way, okay? And don't ask me why because I already told you I haven't a clue."

She glanced at him sideways. "That's really kinda sweet."

"No, it's a mind fuck," he grumbled.

She had no intention of arguing with him, especially since she was feeling all warm and fuzzy about him when no other guy had ever made her feel that way. She knew better than to belabor the point, since it had to do with feelings—a universal male phobia. "You said you had a doctor on staff? Is he here?"

"Actually, I have two and, yes, they're in town. With the size of my crew and various households, having private doctors is convenient. You can't always find a local one you like."

"Maybe they could show me your clean bill of health and one of them could check me out. Not that I'm worried because I *always* use condoms, but to ease your mind. I mean, if you'd like."

He dragged her to a sudden stop, slid his hand around the curve of her hip, and pulled her close. "Fuck yes." He laughed. "You're just so contrary, I didn't dare mention it."

She grinned. "So I scare you?"

He dipped his head and held her gaze. "Uh-uh, I'm just being selfish. I want you in my bed. That means not pissing you off." Then he raised his head, smiled, and pulled his phone out of his shorts' pocket. "I'll call one of the doctors. Simon can bring him up." He paused. "You sure now? I don't want to force you into anything."

"I'm sure. I'm selfish too."

He went silent for a moment, struck again with that strange happiness he'd prefer not to be feeling. Dropping a quick kiss on Nicole's nose, he murmured, "Selfish. Good word. We'll check it out." Then he punched in a number on his cell.

She stood and watched him as he made his call. He wore only shorts, so his big, powerful body was on display—tall, tanned, and virile—his dark beauty so absolute, she felt as though she'd won every roll of the dice in the universe. There was no mistake, in terms of the world's gene pool, Rafe Contini had walked off with the prize. Not to mention, he could be really sweet, like considerate and charming. She almost said, *Pinch me,* because where he preferred emotionless objectivity, she was a sucker for the mystical hand of fate.

But then she was from northern California. If it wasn't yoga and crystals, it was surfing and powerpunk music, the psychic mysteries of the mind or the transcendent wonder of fine weed. The word *emotionless* wasn't in her vocabulary.

"Done," Rafe said. "Simon's picking up one of the doctors." Shoving his phone back in his pocket, he smiled and twined his fingers through hers. "It might be an hour or so before they get here. Let's see what we can find at the house."

EIGHT

They walked past an infinity pool overlooking the Mediterranean, entered the house through a terrace door, and stepped into an enormous sunlit room with an Olympic-size indoor pool.

"You swim a lot?" Nicole asked, admiring the colorful Moorish mosaic lining the pool as they passed by.

"A fair amount, but the pools were here long before me. Actually, I prefer the sea. You said you swim every day. Where?"

"A small private beach down the coast. My uncle's."

"An American, I assume." A statement rather than a question apparently, because he opened one of two glass doors on the opposite wall and waved her through into a light-filled, arcaded hallway. "Up those stairs. We'll check the bedrooms first."

All the interior walls and floors were faced with marble—a golden hue on the ground floor, pale green on the main floor, the wide marble stairway a neutral white and richly carpeted. As they ascended the stairs and continued past the dramatic entrance hall illuminated by a fifty-foot-high, stained-glass cupola and filled with enough art nouveau marble nymph sculptures for a museum, she murmured, "Very impressive, Contini. I think I'm underdressed."

He shot her a glance and grinned. "With any luck you'll soon be overdressed. But you can see why I prefer the carriage house."

"This is definitely nice if you like palaces. Or a sense of history."

"Actually, Eiffel built this place in the 1870s shortly before his major achievement in Paris. There's a certain amount of interest in the house, so we open it for tours one weekend a month."

"Which means no parties for you and your friends then."

"Or just small ones. My private quarters are closed to tours. Here we are," he said as they reached the third floor, the hallway on this level a muted pink marble.

"Why is no one around?" She smiled at Rafe as he began to move down the corridor. "Ashamed of me?"

He turned to her, his gaze amused. "You want a compliment?"

"I was just asking why we're alone, but I'll take a compliment too," she finished with a grin. "Something over the top."

"How about we take turns being on top? Is that what you meant?" He feigned surprise when she gave him a jaundiced look. "Would you prefer: Thou art more lovely and temperate than a summer's day? And may I add *way, way* more tantalizing than Shakespeare," he murmured, a sudden heat invading his eyes. "So watch out."

She smiled. "Maybe you should watch out too. I'm not the passive type."

One eyebrow lifted. "You don't fucking say. But be a

good girl and tone it down for now. We need a condom or no one is going to do anything to anyone. Don't say it," he muttered, as she opened her mouth to speak. "I'm not in the mood for alternatives. Not after waiting this long." Rafe glanced at his watch. "And to answer your question, everyone's in the kitchen. It's dinnertime."

"How many everyones?"

"Fifteen, twenty, maybe more. The chef is temperamental. He's always hiring and firing people on his team. Here, let's look in this room first," he said as they reached the end of the corridor. "It's smaller so it's not used as much." Opening the door, he waved her into an opulent room decorated in the Belle Epoque style, with floor-to-ceiling windows, a bed large enough for a crowd, gilded furniture, and plush carpets soft as silk. "Find somewhere to sit. I'll do the search."

She didn't say, *Wow,* although she was thinking it. "I can help if you like," she said instead, scanning the sumptuous room. "Although you'd hardly expect to find condoms in a room like this."

"I use the house mainly for parties," he said. "So."

"I see."

"What?"

"Nothing."

But her eyes were cool and he briefly debated his answer. "Look," he said quietly, "I just met you. I'm not apologizing for my lifestyle, if that's what you want."

"Did you have a party last night?" *Some lunatic was speaking for her.*

"Yeah, the usual warm-up for my annual bash offshore.

If I'd known you then, you would have been here with me. Okay?"

"Did you get any sleep?" *Clearly, her psyche was demented.*

"Not much. Do you have a lot more questions?" His gaze had chilled. "Just asking, because yesterday is fucking irrelevant."

"I have no right. I understand." *Finally, the voice of reason.*

"Good."

She suddenly grinned. "Maybe I'll make you pay."

"You already have. Believe me, this is not the kind of foreplay I had in mind."

"But I'm worth it."

She was smiling at him, like some beautiful, barely dressed enchantress with the keys to the kingdom. He sighed. "So it seems."

"I'm not apologizing for shaking up your world," she said brightly, paraphrasing his earlier comment. "And extended foreplay isn't my idea of a good time either. So can I help?"

He liked her quixotic moods, although there wasn't much he didn't like about her. "Why don't you check out the drawers in here," he said quickly, wishing to avoid thoughts about liking any woman so indiscriminately. "I'll see what I can find in the bathroom and dressing room." Not that he was overly optimistic after Roddy's frantic search last night.

Hundreds of drawers and ten bedroom suites later, Rafe walked out of the last dressing room, stopped in the doorway, and looked at Nicole sprawled in a chair near the fireplace. "I'm about out of ideas."

"Think." Nicole made a face. "Because I'm seriously frustrated."

"You're not the only one. I've never worked so hard for a piece of ass in my life." He smiled. "When I said I wanted to take it slow, I didn't mean this slow." Bracing his outstretched hands against the doorjambs, he stared at her. "I don't suppose you feel like being rash. Or semi-rash. Really, I don't foresee a problem."

She met his gaze. "I'm twenty-two years old."

Suddenly the hair on the back of his neck rose as an issue so rare as to be almost obsolete jostled his consciousness. Did her concern about condoms have something to do with birth control? She was offbeat enough to have her own weird reservations about taking pharmaceuticals. "You're on the pill, right?"

"What if I said no?"

His adrenaline spiked. "Then I'd say it might be a good idea if you were."

She smiled. "You didn't ask."

"I assumed."

"Really, with your track record? That's a dangerous assumption."

His voice had a brittle edge to it. "Spare me the editorial. A simple yes or no will do."

"Yes."

His eyes snapped shut for a second, then he dropped his hands. "Glad that's cleared up," he said smoothly, picturing spanking her creamy ass for his near heart attack.

"Then we'll just wait until Simon gets back. Would you like dinner?"

She gave him a raking glance as he stood in the doorway, all hard-muscled, male splendor with an endless supply of sex appeal and enviable urbanity. "Not unless you're on the menu." She could do smoothly unruffled too.

He sighed. Then he suddenly grinned as a switch flicked on in his brain. "How easily are you embarrassed?"

"The word has no meaning."

"Come on then. You can meet my staff."

Ten minutes later, because the house was gigantic and it took them that long to traverse the numerous hallways and stairways, they walked into the ground-floor kitchen.

"Don't get up," Rafe said as several men and women began to rise from their dinners. "I have a request. But first, may I introduce Miss Nicole Parrish. Nicole, meet everyone."

A round of *bonjour*s were exchanged as if she weren't barefoot and nude under one of Rafe's shirts. Then a young, slim, dark-haired man with Slavic eyes came to his feet. "What do you need? I'm sure we can find it."

"I'm not so sure, Basil. I've already gone through every drawer upstairs. Which brings me to a personal question. Does anyone here have condoms?"

As numerous smiles appeared and titters erupted, Basil snapped his fingers and instant quiet ensued. "You heard Mr. Contini. Those who can help, please do so immediately."

Most of the staff came to their feet.

Basil tapped his very expensive watch, which went with his bespoke ivory shirt and dark slacks. "Five minutes everyone. *Vite, vite.*"

As the room quieted after the mass exodus, a large, heavyset man in a stained yellow T-shirt and canvas shorts, his ginger hair close cropped, his eyes at half mast, leaned forward, folded his hands on the tabletop, and smiled at Rafe. "Simon said your dinner plans were uncertain."

"I'm afraid so. I'll call later."

"Am I going to be up all night?"

Rafe glanced at Nicole. "Is Henny going to be up all night?"

Regardless that she'd told Rafe that she was beyond embarrassment, and had been until now, Nicole felt her cheeks flush at the russet haired man's blunt query. She shook her head.

"There. Relax, Henny. You'll get your beauty sleep."

"Do you like dessert, Miss Parrish?" The chef was smiling faintly. He'd never seen one of Rafe's women blush. And they were staying at the carriage house. Interesting.

"Yes, very much."

Even more interesting. All the svelte models, actresses, and privileged young women hardly ever ate anything. Especially desserts. "Chocolate? Please say yes, because I have a penchant for chocolate desserts."

Nicole smiled. "So do I."

Henny clapped his meaty hands. "Capital. Keep this one, Rafe. I'd like to cook for her."

"I intend to." Rafe shot a quick grin at Nicole. "Miss Parrish, however, is unsure of her holiday plans."

The chef leaned back in his chair, exposing a glimpse of a green-and-black dragon tattooed on his neck. "Should I send over some menus, Miss Parrish? See if I might tempt you to stay longer? Rafe's taste in women has been deplorable until now."

"Watch it, Henny," Rafe said, only half in jest, knowing his chef's unfettered views on civility. "You're in hock to me for some major gambling debts."

"Fortunately, my quarterly funds will arrive soon. Not to mention my wife makes a fortune keeping people out of jail."

"Then be polite for *me,*" Rafe said gently. "I'm trying not to scare off Miss Parrish."

Henny grinned. "So I shouldn't tell the truth. I could tell her about the puppy you had when you were ten. Or about the time you helped—oh shit, maybe it wasn't an old lady across the street. Come to think about it, she wasn't that old. How about I just lie."

Rafe grinned back. "Good plan."

Nicole was intrigued with the rapport between employer and chef. Although they were close in age. Had they known each other long before?

"Henny and I went to school together," Rafe said, deciphering her speculative gaze. "Or rather, we were kicked out of the same boarding schools. Henny likes to mouth off, as you may have noticed."

"And Rafe despises rules," the chef drawled.

Rafe shrugged. "So do you." He waved his hand in the direction of the table. "Basil completes our nonconformist trio. He preceded us at a truly gruesome school in Lucerne."

The slim man with the face of an ascetic saint—a very handsome saint—grimaced. "I still have the scars to prove it. Rafe and Henny arrived just in time. I was about to be dropped from a fourth-floor window."

At Nicole's quick intake of breath, Rafe gave her a charitable smile. "You must have avoided boarding school. Those institutions offer an incomparable apprenticeship in survival of the fittest—picture *Lord of the Flies* for eurotrash." Rafe glanced at Henny. "Do you think it taught us ruthlessness or were we born that way?"

"Speak for yourself. Turn the other cheek, that's me."

Rafe snorted. Henny was as tall as he was and heavier. Neither one of them had ever turned the other cheek or avoided a fight.

Just then a young man entered the kitchen, smiling. And before long, the rest of the staff returned with the necessary items. Basil collected the condoms without comment, placed them in a drawstring muslin bag he pulled from a drawer, and handed the bag to Rafe. "A pleasure to meet you, Miss Parrish," he said, a genuine warmth in his eyes. "Enjoy your holiday."

"We'll call for dinner later." Taking Nicole's hand, Rafe lifted the bag to the room at large and smiled. "Thank you, everyone."

As they left the kitchen, Rafe wrapped his arm around Nicole's shoulder, drew her close, and, dipping his head, kissed her cheek. "Everyone liked you. Henny, in particular; he rarely talks to strangers. He prefers to cordon off his world. You dazzled him."

"I don't know about that, but he seemed very nice. Friendly."

Rafe chuckled. "I don't think I've ever heard anyone

say that about Henny. Other than his wife, who looks after him like a mother hen. His family background was traumatic, although none of us grew up in ideal conditions. Money aside, of course."

"So I should be kind to him."

He flicked her a startled glance, the word *kind* a rarity in his world. But he replied in a casual tone. "I'm sure Henny would appreciate it."

"Not a problem. As the oldest of six kids, I've done my share of mothering."

He was caught off guard again, the concept of mothering with regard to the hot, sexy woman at his side surprising. "I see."

Recognizing the faint bewilderment in his tone, Nicole glanced up. "Sorry. I didn't mean to introduce so outré a subject as motherhood. Relax."

He laughed. "Gladly. My image of you is quite different."

"That works out then. Because I can't see you as a father under any circumstances."

He frowned. "What the hell does that mean?"

This time *she* laughed. "Seriously—you don't really want to go there, do you?"

He had the grace to look rueful. "No."

"So to change the subject, what's first on the agenda? Although I warn you, my G-spot requires a whole lot of loving."

He grinned. "G-spot? What's that?"

"I'm leaving." She playfully pulled away.

He pulled her back. "No worries, pussycat. I'll make sure your precious little G-spot is petted all night long."

"Ohmygod," she whispered, his softly uttered words spiraling downward between her legs in a wild seething tremor. "I felt that. Say it again."

He came to a stop, turned her slightly, dipped his head so their eyes met, and said, very softly, "By morning your G-spot will begin to throb just at the sound of my voice. Because I'm going to give it some real special attention, make an unforgettable impression, see that that little bundle of nerves is so hair-trigger jazzed you'll come the instant I touch you there. Clear?"

She'd shut her eyes halfway through his graphic description.

"You have to open your eyes, Nicole, or I might decide to neglect your G-spot. There's a good girl. And you really shouldn't scowl. I *could* be sensitive. Now that's better. You look much nicer when you're not scowling."

"Fuck you," she said with a smile.

"Soon," he said with an answering smile. "Very soon." Then he swept her up in his arms and started to run.

NINE

At the same time Rafe and Nicole were swiftly covering the distance to the carriage house, Rafe's mother and stepfather were having dinner on the terrace of a villa overlooking the Adriatic at Trieste.

"Carlos told me that Rafe went into town. He neglected to say that he'd turned off his phone." Rafe's stepfather raised one brow. "Unusual."

Rafe's mother smiled at the man she'd loved since she was fifteen. "Surely whatever you have to say can wait until morning? I could call Rafail then if you like."

Anton smiled wryly. "Because he always answers *your* calls."

"It was only us for all those years," she said gently. "You know that."

"I do." He'd watched over them as best he could from a distance, but the measure of his influence had been limited when she was married to someone else. Mother and son had faced the trials of life with Maso Contini largely alone. "I'm glad it's finally over."

Camelia glanced at Anton's young son sitting back in his chair intent on his video game, then smiled at her new husband and switched from French to their native language. "There were times when I regretted the decision you made for us."

"I wanted a better life for you. You deserved it."

She gave a little shrug. "I'm not so sure it was better." She smiled. "You always came to me when I needed you though."

"You were my heart. I would have come from the ends of the earth for you," he said softly, reaching out to touch her hand. "But in my line of work, you would have been at risk. You know that. I couldn't allow it."

Anton and Camelia had both come from a poverty-stricken village in Romania controlled by the Mafia. Anton had joined the organization in order to survive and when Camelia had finished school, he'd persuaded her to go to London and enter the Miss World contest. It would be their ticket out, he told her.

She'd won. He'd never doubted it. She was the most beautiful woman in the world. He'd sent ten dozen white roses in congratulations, along with a note telling her that he'd married the daughter of the Mafia chief.

When Camelia married a wealthy man, Anton knew his sacrifice hadn't been in vain. He didn't know until later that the marriage was deeply troubled, nor had he discovered until recently that Rafe was his son.

He'd been told two years ago after Maso Contini was found dead in a Bangkok hotel room, a plastic bag over his head in a last act of autoeroticism. Six months later, Anton's wife was discovered lifeless in one of the Istanbul Four Seasons' garden suites. An overdose it was said. The young man lying dead beside her in bed wasn't mentioned in the police report.

Separated from his wife's family business by gratuitous

circumstance, Anton retired soon after and proposed to the only woman he'd ever loved.

"Let's talk about something else." Camelia ran her fingers through her thick, dark hair in a quick, restless gesture. "Forget the past. We're happy now."

"Good things come to those who wait." Anton's smile was tender. "And you don't look a day over seventeen, sweet Mila."

She blew him a kiss. "Flatterer." But she was still stunning at fifty-two, tall, slender, with exquisite bone structure and glorious golden eyes.

Anton shook his head and smiled. "It's the truth, *ma chou*." A few years older than his wife, he hadn't aged as gracefully. Almost too thin, like a marathon runner who'd run one too many races, his hair was gray, his face deeply lined by the stress of a long criminal career. "I'm pleased Rafe has your looks, not mine."

"He's determined like you though." Camelia smiled. "I recognized that same unshakable will when he was still very young. Remember how you kept all the bullies away from me when we were growing up?"

He smiled. "You were too beautiful. Some people resent that."

"And too poor, don't forget."

He frowned. "That always amazed me—the poverty in our village. A pecking order was pointless."

She shrugged. "Nevertheless, it existed and you were my protector. Later, Rafail took over that role. Regardless of how he liked to bluster and threaten, Maso was always a little afraid of Rafail. It was a blessing that as he became more disturbed, he was rarely home." A small sigh. "If he hadn't threatened to disown Rafail if I left him, I would have walked away a thousand times. But even as a young child, Rafail was always in the labs when he was home. Maso knew how much he loved the company." Her eyes closed for a second, then opened again. "Tell me I wasn't foolish to stay."

"Of course not. You wanted the best for Rafe."

"And you were married to—"

"An organization equally ruthless, survival a constantly moving target." He lifted his shoulder in a small dismissive shrug. "We both did what we had to." Although Anton wished there was a way to kill someone over again; Maso deserved it. But he only said, "Rafe turned out well. You deserve all the credit."

Camelia laughed softly. "I'm not so sure. He was a law unto himself from the cradle. But he had all my love. And I had him. We survived."

"Perhaps there really is justice in the world," Anton murmured, though he knew better, he knew you made your own justice. Reminded of that law of the jungle, he said, abruptly, "Do we have to worry about Rafe not answering his phone? Or his going ashore? I wouldn't have thought he'd walk away from his annual party."

Camelia smiled. "You worry too much. He's very competent."

"Humor me. I have many years of fatherly worry to make up for." Anton's lashes lowered faintly. "You really should have told me about Rafe, you know that."

"And you know why I didn't. You might have interfered

and been hurt. Or Rafail or I could have been hurt. Maso was unpredictable."

Anton sighed. "You're right, of course."

The young boy seated beside them at the table suddenly sat up, waved his smartphone, and screamed, "I won! I won! I won!" He beamed at his father. "I told you I wasn't too young to beat this game, Papa! I told you!"

Anton smiled and answered his son in French, the young boy's first language. "Congratulations, Titus. Now finish eating."

"Can't. I'm doing the next level." His thumbs were already flying over the icons, his attention fixed on the screen. "I'm going to win that too." He glanced up and grinned.

Memories of their afflicted pasts were abruptly set aside to attend to a six-year-old boy who didn't have a care in the world other than losing an occasional video game. He'd been cosseted since birth by his father, his new stepmother was very kind, and his older stepbrother could play video games like a wizard. "Can I stay up late?" Titus asked without looking up. "Can I? Can I? Please! This next level is awesome!"

TEN

When they reached the bedroom, Rafe set Nicole on the bed, tossed the bag of condoms beside her, slipped his cell phone from his pocket, punched an icon, and raised his finger to curtail her comment.

A second later, he spoke briskly. "Wait downstairs. I'll call you." Dropping his phone on the nightstand and picking up an elastic band, he smiled. "I didn't want any interruptions. That okay with you?" Pulling his long hair back in a rough queue, he wound the elastic around it with a few deft flicks.

Sitting cross-legged on the bed, Nicole gave him a thumbs-up, then slid Rafe's shirt over her shoulders and down her arms at the same time he discarded his shorts.

"Be still my beating heart," she breathed, only half teasing, her gaze on the sizable splendor of his tattooed dick arching upward against his stomach, the pulsing veins outlined in high relief. "That is *so* fine."

In the process of kicking his shorts aside, he glanced up, his gaze blazing a scorching trail of approval down her lush nudity. "You have the most perfect tits," he said with a small smile, grabbing a condom from the bag. "To go with your smoking-hot body. And that." He indicated her pussy with the foil pack. "Definitely awesome."

She took a quick breath as his erection surged higher.

"Jeez—rein that in or it's not going to fit," she whispered, even as her reckless libido was busy ramping up all her erogenous zones into do-me-quick mode.

Intent on rolling the condom over his tattoo, Rafe just shook his head. "Don't worry. I know what I'm doing." The task completed, he looked up and smiled. "Ready?"

His question was way too nonchalant, like he'd done this a thousand times before, like maybe she was a nameless means to an end. And while the rational portion of her brain was telling her not to self-destruct, her quick temper jumped the gun. "What if I said no?"

He went still. "You're kidding."

"Well, maybe we could just wait a minute."

His amber eyes drilled into hers. "Because?"

She ignored the tick suddenly flickering over his high cheekbone. "Why did you say *don't worry* and *ready* like that?"

"Like what?" There was a brittle edge to his voice.

"Like supercasual, like it could be me or anyone, like it didn't matter where you put your dick. Like maybe I'm the ten thousandth woman you've fucked."

By the time she finished, he was trying to figure out why he was still standing here, why he hadn't walked out the door. What the *fuck* was the vast mystery that made him want her enough to keep arguing? "It's not like that," he heard himself say—or maybe it was just his dick being practical. "You've got it all wrong."

"It didn't sound like it to me," she said with her own kind of edginess. "I'm thinking maybe this is just wham bam and I'm out—"

He had her pinned to the bed in a flash, his biceps bulging as he held his powerful body lightly above hers, his dick nudging her pussy, his hot, glittering gaze signaling he'd hit his limit. "Normally, I'd be happy to argue with you," he growled. "But right now I'm not interested in conversation, so let me make myself—you and me, this whole bloody mind fuck—crystal clear."

He took a deep breath because he felt like hitting something and that wouldn't be real useful right now. "To begin with, I've never walked out of my party before. I've never brought a woman here before. I've never even thought about bringing a woman into... this... bed," he ground out. "And in case it slipped your goddamn mind, I was willing to risk my fucking life to have sex with you without a condom. How the hell casual does that sound?"

"Sorry," she said on a suffocated breath, shocked by his startling confession, beyond flattered by his concessions, fully conscious as well of his dick poised to enter her entirely unconflicted, hot, and bothered pussy. "I was completely wrong."

"Goddamn right you were." Shutting his eyes, he dragged in a breath through his nose. *You know how close you are, right?* his libido warned. *Get a grip.* Then he opened his eyes and softly exhaled. "Look, I'm operating way the hell outside my comfort zone with you. In a good way, so don't get all tense again. You're suspicious. I get it. Personally, I'm so far out on a limb I don't know what the hell I'm doing most of the time." Then he offered up a tentative smile because the warmth had returned to her eyes. "So how about I try not to piss you off, you maybe could step out of the ring for a little while, and once we deal with the worst of our bat-shit crazy lust, we can think about acting normal again."

She smiled. "Is that your version of romantic sentiment?"

"If it gets me over the goal line it is," he said, with a cheeky smile, nimbly rolling onto his right side in order to catch her swinging fist. "What am I going to do with you, tiger?" he whispered, holding her hand loosely in his, one brow arched upward, his rigid dick pulsing against her thigh.

"Am I supposed to tell you?" A playful glance.

His smile was wicked. "Why don't you show me?"

"Let go of my hand."

His lashes drifted downward. "You hurt my dick, no guarantees."

"Now why would I do that?"

He held her gaze for a moment more before releasing her hand.

Neither moved.

A thin-skinned, edgy tension strummed through the air, spiked through their nerve endings, lit up their brains for a cool, clear-eyed pulse-beat.

Then he watched her move her hand with the unshakable vigilance of a man interested in protecting his dick. He watched her place her fingertips lightly on her silky pubic hair and felt his tension melt away. He smiled as two of her fingers disappeared inside her slick cleft and when she looked up, glanced at his responsibly clad erection, and said, "If I ask nicely, do you think he might like to come and play?" his smile was a thing of beauty.

"He accepts your kind invitation," he said with exaggerated courtesy.

"Finally," she whispered and tugged on his broad shoulder.

Lifting her hand aside, he rolled back between her legs and dropped his head so his mouth brushed her lips. "I guess some people are worth the wait," he said with the faintest twitch of his lips. Then he flexed his hips delicately, exerted a slight pressure, slowly slipped inside her heated warmth, and abruptly stopped at the jaw-dropping, adrenaline-pumping pleasure.

"Jesus." His voice was rough, breathless.

Clinging to him, Nicole raised her hips, so he glided in deeper and, beginning to tremble faintly at the extraordinary, unbearably beautiful pressure, she lifted her wide, blue-eyed gaze. "It's not the same is it?"

The glow in her eyes almost stopped his heart. "Not even close," he said with a mild unease, feeling as though some tide was building, getting stronger. His eyes drifted shut for a moment before he gently sighed. "If I had half a brain, I'd get the fuck out."

She held his gaze for a tremulous moment, then slid her heels upward so her knees were bent, and her thighs opened wider. "I want you. It's as simple as that," she whispered, filled with an unspeakable hunger, less terrified of cautionary judgments and things not easily undone. Touching the black silk of his hair framing his face, she said hushed and low, "Sometimes that Taser just zaps you and there's nothing you can do."

He knew what she meant.

He wouldn't have understood a few hours ago.

"So fuck it, right?" His sudden smile was improbably tender. "Screw danger and the mysteries of the universe."

Her smile was sweetly seductive. "I'd like that if you could see your way clear to indulging me despite your reservations."

"Not a problem." He grinned. "My dick is single-minded." Cautiously pushing forward into her soft flesh, he moved deeper in a fluid stirring of muscled constraint, forcing her sleek tissue to yield to his deliberate progress. "Stop me if I hurt you."

"Don't stop." Her eyes half shut, her breathing unsteady, her nails leaving marks in the corded muscles of his shoulders, she wallowed in the glorious feel of his hard, rigid length filling her by slow degrees, the pressure so agonizingly lurid she whimpered.

His body tensed. "Too much?"

She shook her head against the pillow, her eyes half closed. "No, no, please—more," she gasped, overcome by a dizzying rapture, impatience echoing in her hot demand, tiny preorgasmic shudders beginning to vibrate up her spine.

She was wetter than wet, eager and willing, but his concern wasn't without precedent. "Sure now?"

"Yes, yes—yes," she panted, hovering on the veritable brink. "Don't—fuck this up."

For a nanosecond he didn't move. He couldn't remember the last time anyone had given him an order. But his imminently practical libido immediately overruled any momentary displeasure. "Yes, ma'am," he murmured, softly caustic and silky smooth. Then, with astonishing speed, he flexed his strong legs, swung forward, and plowed into the tightest pussy he'd ever had the good fortune to fuck, slamming home with such a jarring jolt of pleasure a deep groan swallowed up his breath.

Thoroughly impaled by his rock-hard erection, feverishly aroused, her body hot and slick, her climax hovering—damn it—just . . . out of . . . reach. She punched his shoulder hard. "Hey! Remember me?"

Dragging himself back from a stunning glimpse of nirvana, he almost laughed. You had to give her credit. Nothing daunted her. Gazing down into the blue heat of her eyes, he smiled. "You should think about being more polite."

"And you should think about moving," she hissed, slamming her palm into his immovable chest.

"Like this?" He pressed forward an infinitesimal, carefully calculated distance more.

Her small hungry scream vibrated in the stillness.

"Feel good?" he whispered. "Want more? All you have to do is ask."

"I'm thinking," she muttered, when they both knew she wasn't; when she was slick with desire, quivering and needy, her heartbeat so strong they could both feel it.

"Why don't I help you decide." Placing his hands on her hips, he splayed his fingers wide, held her firmly in place and slowly withdrew until the crest of his erection was nuzzling her clit. "Now, be a good girl and apologize."

Her eyes flared wide, then narrowed into a glare while she momentarily weighed various unsatisfactory options.

Intent on making her decision easier, Rafe delicately massaged her throbbing clit with the head of his dick, sliding his swollen crest barely in, then out, around and around, incredibly gently, with the most refined pressure.

Oh my God, that felt good! She might just come with that lovely, glorious friction alone. No apology required. *Oh, oh, oh, yesss!* Shutting her eyes, she suppressed a blissful sigh.

"Uh, uh, tiger. Not gonna happen." He slid back on his heels.

Her eyes snapped open at his sudden withdrawal. "Jesus, are you always a prick like this?"

"Do you always give orders in bed?"

She suddenly grinned. "Oh, shit, I'm just supposed to say yes."

He snorted. "That'll be the day. You argue about every goddamn thing."

"Maybe you like to argue."

He gave her a contemplative look from under his long lashes. "I never argue. Or at least I didn't until you entered my life."

"That's because no one dares argue with you."

He shrugged.

"There, see—I'm right. Maybe I bring some excitement into your life. Have you thought about that?"

"Jesus, baby, I have all the excitement I want, whenever I want it. Now, could we just please"—he sighed—"do this?" He grimaced. "Before I fucking explode."

She gave a quick glance at his really explosive-looking dick, beautiful and colorful even through the stretched condom and really huge. “Okay.” She wrinkled her nose in a little bunny twitch. “Do I have to apologize?”

“Right now, I’ll fucking apologize if we can get this show on the road.”

“No need,” she said cheerfully, and, sitting up, she took his erection in her hands and falling back on the bed, brought him with her. “I’m guessing you can take it from here,” she murmured, placing the head of his dick against her throbbing pussy.

His smile was very close. “Good guess.”

She began climaxing the moment he entered her, her wild cry shattering the silence.

“Wait, wait,” he whispered, although he wasn’t sure she could hear him with the sheer volume of her scream. So he drove back into her lush body with feverish haste, intent on sharing the seething ecstasy. And as her clamorous pleasure cry filled his ears, the room, and the gardens beyond the open balcony doors, his orgasm surged through him like a tidal wave and, catching up with her, he climaxed in a ferocious ejaculatory rush so violent it ripped the air from his lungs.

She was shuddering afterward, hot, breathless, a luscious ache spiraling through her body, bathing her senses.

He gently rocked inside her, not quite willing to relinquish the rare, extravagant pleasure, wanting to prolong the tremulous bliss.

For hushed, roseate moments, the world disappeared, there was no past or future, only this inarticulate, primal aftermath of passion and the harsh rhythm of their breathing.

Rousing first, Nicole's voice was a wisp of sound. "So did the earth move?"

Rafe's eyes were shut, his breathing rough. "It—didn't just—move." His lashes lifted marginally, revealing a sliver of his golden gaze. "It fucking—blew up." A smile slowly lifted the corners of his mouth. "So I'll be... keeping you."

Still in the grip of the blissful aftershocks, the world all warm and magical, she wasn't inclined to be overly contentious. "Sure you can do that, big boy?"

"Oh yeah." His grin was blatantly sexual, his lethargy replaced by a new resolve. "No doubt in my mind. And with that pleasant thought"—he began withdrawing—"we should talk to Aleix."

"No offense to whoever that is, but not now." She sighed, her eyes half-closed. "I'm still floating somewhere in space."

"Soon, then. Aleix's one of my doctors." A man on a mission, Rafe quickly stripped off the condom, leaned over the edge of the bed, and discarded it in a wastebasket. Rolling back, he propped himself up on one elbow and gazed at the woman who'd shattered all his preconceived notions of priceless. "The sooner we see Aleix, the sooner we can dispense with condoms," he said. "Your call, of course."

Softly exhaling, she forced herself to think. "No condoms is risky," she finally said, her blue gaze wide open now and direct. "Like seriously."

"You got that right." His shoulder lifted in a small shrug. "But fuck it. It's not every day"—he winked—"the earth moves."

Conscious of his eyes on her, she stared at the coffered ceiling and went through a swift list of pros and cons again before she met his gaze. “This really is irrational.”

“Agreed.”

“Have you ever done this before?”

“Never.” He ripped off the elastic holding his hair back and tossed it on the nightstand.

“Really? No bullshit?”

“Really. No bullshit.”

“You can guarantee your health screen is genuine?”

“Jesus. Why wouldn’t it be?”

“Okay, then. What do I have to do?”

“Aleix will take a blood sample, do a quick exam if that’s all right with you. And in a couple of hours, we’ll both have the stamp of approval. No need for Russian roulette.”

“Hmmm.”

“Is that a yes?”

She hesitated a second more, then nodded.

Not about to prolong the conversation when he had what he wanted, he asked, “Do you want me to hold your hand with Aleix?”

She shook her head.

“Embarrassed? Don’t be.”

Nicole smiled. “I’m not embarrassed. I just prefer doing it myself.”

Leaning over, he kissed her gently. “Whatever you want. And thanks.” Then he sat up and reached for his phone. “Not that I’m anxious,” he said with a grin, punching in a number. “But let me tell Aleix I’m coming down to get him.” He paused, blew her a kiss, and when someone answered, said, "I'll be down in a minute." Dropping the phone back on the nightstand, he turned back to Nicole. "Need anything?"

"You back in bed."

He sucked in a breath. "No shit." He grinned. "Seriously. You're going to have to be the one who says enough." He leaned over and kissed her again, and this kiss wasn't gentle at all. It was all pent up lust and feverish desire and they were both panting when he finally rolled away. "Fuck, I gotta go," he muttered, leaping from the bed. "We need Aleix ASAP."

"You *could* call and say you'll be a little late." Gazing at his splendid erection, she looked up and smiled. "It wouldn't take long."

He blew out a breath. "I'm going to be the adult here, get the hell dressed, fetch Aleix, and see that this screening gets done. How's that for sane and rational?"

She touched her pulsing clit. "Knock before you come back in."

"Don't you fucking dare," he warned, stepping into his shorts. "I own that clit for the next month."

She stared at him. "I beg your pardon?"

"You heard me. Keep your hands to yourself," he growled, zipping up his shorts. "I'll be back in two minutes." He frowned. "And I'm not going to knock."

ELEVEN

Nicole briefly debated whether two minutes was enough to get herself off, or whether she minded if she had an audience. Probably not and probably, she decided with a grumbly sigh. Still—she disliked orders. From Rafe or anyone. Although maybe having him tell her what to do turned her on just a smidge. Or maybe more than a smidge. She shivered, remembering the hard, solid feel of him, the fluid strength, the explicit challenge she found so enticing. Damn, everything about the beautiful, golden-eyed Rafe Contini was incredibly hot.

Sliding off the bed, she quickly crossed the room and walked out on the balcony, needing to cool her fevered senses, control her lust. Talk herself into a more rational frame of mind. She prided herself on being sensible; she'd never been the flighty type.

So craving Rafe like some teen rock star fan was a huge freaking change. Probably slightly demented as well, considering he viewed women as disposable. Then she suddenly grinned. But in terms of gratification, he was dynamite, so screw it—literally.

While Nicole was coming to terms with loss of control versus impetuous desire, Rafe was giving instructions to Aleix.

"Miss Parrish has agreed to see you, but she's skittish,

so be scrupulously polite. And she prefers seeing you alone. You know I've never done anything like this before, so whatever you do in terms of an exam"—he took a quick breath—"keep it as brief as possible." He held the young fair-haired doctor's gaze. "Can you do that?"

Aleix's eyes were amused behind his gold wire-framed glasses. "I'll try not to look. Is that what you mean?"

Rafe exhaled a long slow breath. "I don't know what I mean. Just be nice, okay?"

"I'll treat her like a nun."

"Good."

Aleix concealed his shock. He'd been kidding; Rafe wasn't.

"You've brought the health reports?"

"Right here." Aleix took some stapled pages out of a small leather bag and handed them to Rafe. "Should I explain to her that you're conscientious about condoms?"

"I already did, but sure why not?" Rafe nodded to Simon. "Aleix won't be long." Then he waved his doctor forward and as they reached the stairs, asked, "How soon will you have the results?"

"By morning."

Rafe's gaze flicked sideways. "That long?"

Running to keep up with Rafe's swift, long-legged ascent, Aleix glanced up at the man he'd only known as the most casual sexual partner to a great many women. "When do you want the results?"

"An hour ago."

Another startling response. "I'll see what I can do. I can't promise anything. It depends what I find."

"I don't want you to find anything," Rafe said a little impatiently.

"But then I'm not certifiable like you right now."

Rafe sighed. "Sorry. Do what you have to do. But quickly. That's all I ask."

"She must be something special."

"You'll see for yourself." Rafe shot him a grin. "And I should know."

"No argument there," Aleix agreed, having witnessed an unending succession of beautiful women passing through Rafe's life.

Rafe paused at the bedroom door. "Now just the minimum of tests. I don't want her upset."

Aleix smiled. "I got the message. You're crazy and I have to accommodate you."

"Good," Rafe said, no smile. "We're in sync then."

A moment later, they walked into the bedroom and after a quick scan of the empty bed and room, Rafe saw Nicole standing on the balcony. Stark naked. "Give me a minute." Quickly easing Aleix back into the hall, he quietly closed the door.

Dropping his health report on a chair, he walked into his dressing room, randomly selected a robe from one of the closets, returned to the bedroom, and moved soundlessly on bare feet to the balcony. "We have company."

Nicole turned and glanced past him.

"He's waiting in the hall." Rafe held out the white seersucker robe. "I don't know about you, but I find I have a prudish streak after all," he said, forcing his dick to behave at the sight of her world-class tits, curvaceous hips, and legs that went on forever. “Put this on before I let Aleix in.”

A trace of a smile fluttered across her mouth. “He’s going to see me anyway.”

“Not all of you. Humor me. I don’t like to share.” This from a man well known for group sexual amusements. Taking her hand, he slid it through one sleeve, pulled the robe over her shoulders, and, turning her slightly, slipped the other sleeve up her arm. “It’s a little long. Just as well,” he said under his breath, and a second later looked up from the fabric puddled at her feet. “Lift it out of your way when you walk.” A definitive statement, brisk with authority.

For a fleeting moment, Nicole almost said no, just for the hell of it. But she’d enjoyed his barely audible comment. Was there a woman in the world who didn’t like a little male jealousy? And watching him carefully overlap the robe to cover her breasts, knot the tie at her waist, then tug the neckline tighter made her smile. “Relax. The doctor isn’t interested in me other than as an exam subject.”

“I’m sure,” he said drily. “Just don’t take off the fucking robe.”

“Yes, sir, whatever you say, sir.” She cocked her head and looked up at him with a playful lift of her brows. “So long as I get rewarded.”

He laughed. “You can count on it. And I apologize for my new prudish streak. Aleix called me certifiable just now. I probably am. You make me crazy.” His smile was one of ineffable charm. “I mean that in the nicest way.”

“Hey, I’m losing it too. I spent the interval while you

were gone telling myself it didn't matter if I was flipping out because the sexual payoff was awesome. And I'm not interested in walking away from awesomeness any time soon. So give me a kiss, let's get this over with, and then"—she reached up and lightly ran her warm palm down his hard, muscled chest—"you can reward me."

Dropping his head, he kissed her gently for a slow, lingering moment, sliding his tongue into her mouth just before raising his head—as if marking his territory. As if to say *There's more when this is over.* Then he touched her cheek with his fingertip. "I can hardly wait to push you over the edge." His smile was easy, his golden gaze fixed on her. "It's going to be fun."

Aleix was brought in, Rafe made introductions—"Dr. Aleix Rovira may I present Miss Nicole Parrish"—adding a brief description of the doctor's impressive credentials from Europe's top medical school before he left the room.

The doctor looked young, dressed in chinos and a white shirt. That he was slight of build with refined features and pale disheveled hair enhanced the image of youth. And as he began to detail the procedures, Nicole was certain that Rafe had intimidated him because his explanation was not only scrupulously respectful, but cautious in the extreme.

"Please, call me Nicole," she interrupted, wanting to put him at ease. "I think I understand the fundamentals." She smiled. "And ignore whatever Rafe said to you. This isn't a problem for me."

The doctor softly exhaled. "Please then, Aleix," he said,

brushing a wave of ash-blond hair off his forehead. "If you'd like to sit on the bed and roll up your sleeve, I'll take a blood sample first."

Moving to the bed, she sat, slid the loose sleeve up to her shoulder, and held it in place. "Have you been with Rafe long?"

"Quite a while." He began wrapping a tourniquet around her upper arm.

The doctor wasn't chatty. Not that she was deterred when she wanted to know if this was the ten thousandth time Aleix had run these tests for Rafe. In her experience horny men and the truth weren't even in the same zip code. "Does Rafe have you do this often?"

"You'd have to ask him." The doctor tore open a sterile pack that held a syringe.

Okaaay. Maybe signing a nondisclosure statement was required for employees of a major stud like Rafe Contini. But then she wasn't an employee, so she could keep asking—in this case a more pointed question. "Would Rafe take it out on you if I shut this down?"

A startled, wide-eyed look behind his wire-framed glasses.

"It's okay. I won't." She smiled. "But just in general terms, is Rafe fairly truthful?"

"In most things, yes," Aleix said in lieu of a legitimate answer, bending over her arm to test the vein.

"You're not going to tell me anything are you?"

He didn't look up. "This might hurt a little."

She pulled her arm from his grasp, tamped down her rising temper, and addressed Rafe's gatekeeper with the tone she'd use to coax a toddler from its twentieth teacup ride at Disney World. "Rafe told me he'd never done this before. I just want to know if that's true. You can just nod or shake your head if you don't want to perjure yourself."

A slow smile formed on Aleix's mouth. "You're going to give him trouble aren't you?"

"Not particularly. But all this"—she did a little twirl of her fingers—"the house, the staff, the women, the parties. Let's just say, I'm not inclined to add to his arrogance."

"You're the voice of moderation?" His voice was sardonic.

"God no. But, unlike all the others, I need a reason to say yes."

Aleix lifted the syringe. "Like this?"

She grinned. "Rafe and I agree on the merits of self-indulgence."

"So long as you set the rules?"

"Maybe." She shrugged. "I don't know."

Rafe had spoken with the same uncertainty—and he wasn't an uncertain man. Nor was Miss Parrish, unless he missed his guess. "Rafe's never had me do this before." Aleix glanced at the clock. "He's also in a hurry. So if I've answered you satisfactorily, you might like to look away while I draw some blood."

Never before? Was that lovely or what? "I'm not afraid of needles," she said, supercool, like she wasn't smiling inside.

"Excellent." Aleix eased the needle into her vein. She didn't so much as flinch. Miss Parrish was not only breathtakingly beautiful, but undaunted and self-possessed. There was no mystery as to why Rafe was attracted to her.

"There, done," Aleix said a moment later, withdrawing the needle and capping it. Unwrapping the tourniquet with one hand, he placed it along with the syringe in the bag he'd carried in. "Now, if you don't mind," he said with exquisite courtesy. "I'll take two fluid samples, if you'll lie down on the edge of the bed. Right here, please." He patted the bed and smiled. "No need to disrobe."

As she moved into position, he slipped an elastic cuff supporting a small flexible light around his left wrist and snapped on latex gloves. Then without meeting her gaze, he drew her legs up, placed her feet flat on the bed, and eased her hips forward. "This will feel a little cool." Having taken a disposable speculum from its sterile packaging, he deftly slid the instrument inside Nicole.

She did more than flinch that time, she gasped.

"I'm sorry. Are you all right?"

"No."

Alarmed, his gaze flew up.

She grinned. "I'm fine. I just never had a chance to say that before."

It took a moment to calm his racing heart. Rafe's instructions had been explicit; don't upset her. "Be sure to tell me if anything else hurts."

Ignoring the familiar platitude, she nodded and took a breath.

Forewarned, Aleix proceeded with caution and very gently took the two swabs he needed, placed them in a container, carefully eased the speculum out, pulled off the latex gloves, and held out his hand to help Nicole sit up.

"Thank you very much, Miss—er...Nicole." Pulling the light from his wrist, he placed it in the bag with the rest of the equipment. "I apologize for any pain or inconvenience."

"It was relatively painless." Nicole smiled. "And I expect you're going to be more inconvenienced. Rafe wants this yesterday doesn't he?"

The doctor's lashes drifted downward fractionally. "Rafe's in a capricious mood. I'm just glad he didn't neglect this altogether."

"Oh, he tried. I said no. One of us had to be rational."

Shaken by her disclosure, Aleix kept his voice steady with effort. "Then please accept my appreciation. I'm afraid Rafe never hears the word no."

"That's why we get along," Nicole said with a grin. "I dislike the word as well."

A brisk knock suddenly echoed in the room, the door opened, and Rafe walked in and stopped just inside the threshold. "You must be done by now." He really meant, *You are done now.*

Nicole grinned. "You have no patience."

"I don't. Thank you, Aleix. We'll hear from you soon?" It was an order and dismissal, no matter the soft diffidence in his voice.

"Yes, of course." The doctor shut his bag and picked it up. "A pleasure to meet you, Miss Parrish." With a smile for Nicole, he walked toward the door.

Rafe stepped aside, quietly said, "With all due speed,

please," as Aleix moved past him, then shut the door on the doctor, turned, and leaned back against the painted wood. "Count down, baby." He glanced at his watch, then smiled. "If I start shaking, smack me."

"Don't tempt me." She grinned. "You of all people *need* a smackdown."

"Ha! Miss Mouthy giving me shit." He slowly inhaled, then exhaled even more slowly before he spoke. "Seriously though, we're going to have to find something to do while we're waiting for Aleix to call. Otherwise I might just say, 'The hell with it' and jump you." He held up his thumb and forefinger, only a sliver of space dividing them. "I'm this fucking close."

"We could play cards," she said with a smile.

He gave her a look from under his lashes that signaled his disdain.

"Watch TV?"

"If only I was twelve," he drawled. "We need people around. I'm undependable right now. Correction, my dick is undependable. Let's go have supper. Do you mind eating in the kitchen? That's not really a question. I can't be alone with you."

"Got it. Do I have to dress?"

Another of those are-you-kidding looks.

As she jumped off the bed, he took his phone from his pocket like a gunslinger checking his six-gun to see that it was working, slid it back in his pocket, and held out his hand. "I'll give Aleix an hour. After that, there are no guarantees."

Coming up to Rafe, Nicole slid her fingers through his,

rose on tiptoe, and waited for him to dip his head so she could kiss him. A few moments later, when she dropped back on her heels, they were both breathing hard.

"No more kissing," he muttered, gently pushing her away and opening the door. He flashed her a hard, heated look. "I mean it. Or we're going to be defying the odds. And I don't think you want that."

TWELVE

The kitchen was quiet when they walked in, only Henny and Basil still at the table, a dusty bottle of cognac between them.

"We're killing an hour," Rafe said, moving into the large room. "Feel like feeding us?"

Henny met his gaze. "Here?"

"Here would be good." Rafe lifted his chin in the direction of the table. "Is that the '75?"

"None other. Want a taste?"

"Of course they do." Basil was already reaching behind him for two more glasses from a massive cabinet painted in Provencal colors. "Eighteen seventy-five was a very good year." He slid the glasses across the table. "Please, sit. Do you want company?"

"That's why we're here." His friends were safety and comfort and if he wasn't exactly thinking clearly, they'd grab him by the shoulders and pull him back from the edge.

"I figured. You lit a fire under Aleix, I hear." When something was dodgy, Basil always felt it first, like splinters in the air. A survival technique learned early. "We'll lock you in for an hour."

Rafe grinned. "Is nothing private? I suggest you ignore them as much as possible," he added, smiling at Nicole as he pulled out a yellow wooden chair for her. "We've known one another too long."

"Not a problem. Fiona and I share everything too. That's what comes from being friends since grade school."

Henny came to his feet and ran his palm over his close-cropped head as though triggering his action mode. "Any special requests? American food, French, Italian, snacks?"

Rafe looked at Nicole; she shook her head. "Whatever you have that won't take much time," he said, sitting next to Nicole. "I'm serious about the hour time limit."

"Ah, impetuous young love," Henny mocked, walking to a wall of refrigerators. "It warms the heart and gives new meaning to the word *appetite*."

Rafe rolled his eyes, and, pouring them cognac, said under his breath, "I can't shut him up. I hope you don't mind." He flicked his gaze to the cognac level, then across the table to Basil. "This obviously isn't your first bottle."

Basil shrugged. "I haven't been counting."

"I'm guessing Henny drank more than his share. Is he in any shape to make supper?"

"He can always cook, drunk, high, or sober. You know that. Simon said you're thinking about Split," Basil said, Henny's state of inebriation so common as to be incidental. "A large party or small?"

"I haven't decided."

"Mireille is in London for a week if you want Henny's food in Split."

"You okay with going to Split, Henny?" Rafe called out. Mireille liked her husband home as much as possible, so Henny arranged his schedule around his wife's.

"I'm free for a week." Henny's voice came from the depths of the refrigerator. "Take me anywhere."

Rafe glanced at Basil. "You?"

"Sure. I never have plans." Basil gave new meaning to the word *introvert;* even his poetry and documentary films were supremely esoteric.

"We'll figure out something then." Rafe dipped his head and smiled at Nicole. "Henny's wife's in London, so we can have company. Unless you have reservations."

"None." She smiled. "You decide."

Rafe leaned in close and kissed her, a quick, cognac-tasting kiss. "Where have you been all my life?" he whispered, his comment innocent of reason, his smile disarming.

"Waiting to be found by you," she whispered back, aware of how charming and practiced he was and not caring.

Basil didn't know where to look for a moment. Henny stopped dead in the middle of the kitchen, his arms laden with food, his mouth agape. The Rafe they knew was legendarily unromantic.

Immune to his friends' shock, Rafe slid his chair back, picked Nicole up off her chair, and set her on his lap. "There, that's better," he said with a smile. "Want me to feed you?"

"Do fish swim?"

Rafe laughed. "Goddamn. I'm not even going to try to figure this out."

"Me either. Not for thirty days."

He lifted his brows. "So no two weeks?"

She shook her head rather than try to put her contradictory feelings into words.

He saw the uncertainty in her eyes, but no way was he going to prolong this discussion with thirty days of red-hot sex on the horizon. "Ready to see what Henny found for us to eat?" Looking up, he smiled at his friend, who quickly shut his mouth. "What? I can't be affectionate?"

"It's never too late, I guess." Henny grinned. "Although I would have appreciated some warning. This is going to cost me."

"You bet on this?"

"Of course." He shrugged. "Mireille's a romantic."

"Serves you right then to have so little faith in miracles. Yours included. You're lucky your wife puts up with you." Rafe smiled. "Are you going to need a loan?"

"Uh-uh."

Rafe chuckled. "You bet something other than money, didn't you? Tell Mireille she may thank me—actually, Nicole—for my new tender sensibilities."

Henny snorted.

"Watch and learn." Rafe gave him a mocking smile, then turned to Nicole. "Tell him, tiger. We're both burning bright."

Nicole reached up and lightly traced the curve of one dark brow with her finger. "You've definitely become a matter of riveting curiosity for me." Her gaze was warm, faintly teasing. "That much I know. When all else is chaos."

"But a good chaos," he said very gently.

He was staring at her, no teasing in the depths of his golden eyes, no smile, waiting. "Yes," she said, feeling such pleasure at the sight of him that it took an act of will not to embarrass herself in front of his friends and tell him she was fly-me-to-the-moon happy and off-the-charts sexy. "There's a new kind of real pressing in around me, like the world is wonderful and terrifying at the same time." She gave him a lopsided grin. "Leaving me breathless and giddy." A sudden catch of her breath. "Ridiculous, right?"

He gave her a full-on grin. "Nope. It's grand, full of a million different possibilities, all good." He had his hand on her back, just lightly, felt her soft warmth on his thighs, against his chest, smelled the perfume in her hair, saw the unprotected need in her eyes, and almost said, *I can't wait an hour. Neither of us has to wait.*

Henny closed the distance to the table in two long strides and dropped the plates he was carrying on the table with a clatter. "Crostini with fresh cheese and honey for the first course," he announced in a tone capable of reaching the last row in the gallery. "We had some for supper so it's still warm."

Rafe glanced up, blinking.

"You're waiting for Aleix to call," Henny said, taking care of Rafe as he would for him, as they both did for Basil, their protective bond forged in their troubled childhoods. "I have two nice steaks I'll cook with thyme. Your favorite."

"Ah." Rafe took a breath, then nodded, his equilibrium restored, the strange layers of feeling safely unstacking. Reaching for the plate of hors d'oeuvres Henny pushed his way, he picked up a crostino layered with fresh cheese drizzled with honey and held it to Nicole's mouth. "You have to try this. Henny learned to make this local cheese from an old lady in Nice." Rafe looked up. "What was her name?"

"Madame Bardet. May she rest in peace." Henny made the sign of the cross over his stained T-shirt. "I was fifteen, she was ninety-five and the best cook I ever met."

"We hardly saw Henny that summer. She took him under her wing, told him he couldn't swear in her kitchen, and set him on his path to culinary glory. She was the grandmother you never had—right?"

Henny glanced up from arranging half shells of chilled mussels on two plates. "The family I never had. Rafe likes lots of mayonnaise." Dipping his head toward Nicole, he closed the door on any discussion of his family. "Do you have a preference?"

She swallowed. "Lots is good."

Rafe grinned, then offered her another bite of crostini. "Really, I'd say separated at birth if it wasn't illegal for us."

"Mmmpf," Nicole said through a mouthful of delicate honey and cheese.

He understood her mumbled reply was another one of agreement and for the first time in his life believed in good fortune over and above the casino table.

As Henny put a dollop of mayonnaise on each mussel, Rafe picked up a toast, popped it in his mouth, chewed, swallowed, and sighed. "Jesus, that's good. I think I forgot to eat today." And later, after Nicole had eaten her fill, he finished the remaining appetizers.

The mussels were a rustic specialty consumed tête-à-tête to the continuing astonishment of Rafe's friends. Although Henny's and Basil's raised eyebrows went undetected by Rafe and Nicole as they devoured the tasty morsels between kisses and soft murmurs.

With perfect timing acquired in the best restaurants in Europe, Henny whisked away the plate of empty mussel shells and served a salad of baked fresh figs with crumbled goat cheese and hazelnuts. But after setting down the plates, he pulled out Nicole's chair and gave Rafe a pointed look. "Play Romeo and Juliet later. My food deserves your undivided attention."

Rafe smiled at Nicole. "Henny's a demanding artist. Do you mind?" It was a rhetorical question, and without waiting, he placed her on the adjacent chair.

The figs were at their peak in August, compellingly sweet and flavorful. Nicole didn't mind in the least giving her full attention to Henny's delicious masterpiece arranged on a bed of dressed arugula. Between bites of syrupy figs and blissful sighs, she showered him with compliments until Rafe muttered, "Careful, babe, he's already conceited enough."

Henny turned from the stove, where he was searing rib eyes and smiled. "Don't knock it, Rafe. A woman who likes to eat? When's the last time you saw that?"

"Okay, you're great. We agree," Rafe said in lieu of answering questions about the women he'd known. "How much longer on the steaks?"

Well aware of the reason for Rafe's topic shift, Henny held up the skillet. "Observe. It's going in the oven. Relax. Have another drink." And he slid the pan of steaks along with a bundle of thyme, flamed, blown out, and added to the skillet for flavor into the oven.

Under Henny's watchful scrutiny, the meat was roasted to a perfect juicy pink. Placing the steaks on toast brushed with olive oil, Henny set a small bowl of fleur de sel, a pepper grinder, and a pot of Dijon mustard between Rafe and Nicole and said with a flourish of his hand, "Enjoy."

A tame word for the gustatory pleasure of thick, tender, superbly prepared meat. Nicole stopped eating well before Rafe, full from all the previous courses. When Rafe flicked his fork at her steak and lifted his brows, she said, "It's all yours. I couldn't eat another bite."

"*Non, non,* just a taste of chocolate sorbet and one mocha meringue," Henny murmured, sliding a plate before her.

Nicole looked up, a twinkle in her eyes. "How can I resist?"

"Indeed," he said with a grin. "A little chocolate always makes the world more livable, *ma chou*."

Nicole blushed at the endearment.

And Henny now understood another facet of Nicole's appeal. She could be sweetly naïve, not to mention devastatingly beautiful and a woman of appetites. All of which had inspired Rafe to jettison his preference for personal privacy.

While Rafe ate his steak and hers, Nicole finished her dessert, just as Henny set a crème brûlée in front of Rafe. "This is Rafe's favorite—lavender scented." He smiled at Nicole. "Would you like to try one?"

When she hesitated, Rafe muttered, "Leave her alone, Henny." Then shooting his friend a don't-fuck-with-me look, he picked Nicole up and set her back on his lap.

Understanding Rafe's weighted look, Henny immediately raised his arms. "I'm not interested in pistols at dawn. Look, I'm sitting down," he said, his gaze amused. Reclaiming his chair, he lounged back and watched, fascinated, as Rafe alternately fed crème brûlée to Nicole, then himself, in what only could be characterized as explicit sexual foreplay. Turning to Basil, Henny murmured drolly, "What do you think? A spring wedding for our lovebirds?"

Basil smiled. "Sure Rafe can wait that long? I'm thinking next week."

"Shut the fuck up, you two." Rafe flashed them a mocking grin. "I've never felt so good. Tell them, baby. We're living the dream."

"It's madness," Nicole said, equally blithe. "But irresistible. Like chocolate and catching a prime wave."

Henny exploded in a booming laugh, Basil raised his cognac in salute, and Rafe pushed the empty bowl aside and said without a qualm, "Am I lucky or what?"

Both men understood that they were in the presence of a bona fide miracle. Since their precocious youths, Rafe's interest in women had always been brief and supremely casual—as in names were not a requirement.

Rising from his chair, Henny spread his arms wide. "This momentous occasion calls for vintage champagne."

Rafe didn't need an interpreter. "I agree. The '92."

"Coming up," Henny said, moving toward the wine cooler. But he'd no more than opened the nineteenth-century champagne from the Contini family vineyard when Rafe's phone rang.

Taking his phone from his pocket, Rafe glanced at the caller ID and hit the Answer bar.

"Enjoy your holiday."

"Thanks, Aleix." Sliding his phone back in his pocket,

he looked at Nicole. "Did you get enough to eat?" His voice was ultra soft, his smile, easy, relaxed.

She nodded.

"Ready to go?"

How could he speak so quietly when lust was lighting up her brain and her speech synapses had jammed to a stop like a LA freeway at rush hour?

Maybe he was a mind reader because he didn't wait for an answer; he stood with her in his arms and nodded at Henny. "Thanks for supper."

Powering through her LA traffic jam, Nicole said in an explosive rush, "Everything was wonderful, the company too."

"Anytime." Henny grinned. "Sweet dreams, children."

"See you in the morning," Basil added with a shy smile.

Once they were alone, Henny poured Basil and himself champagne, then raised his glass. "Mark your calendar," he drawled. "Rafe's gone over the fucking edge."

"I'm not so sure." Basil studied the bubbles in his glass for a second, then looked up. "She's a novelty. By definition novelties are fleeting."

Henny shrugged one massive shoulder. "You never know. Hell, I never thought I'd marry. And then Mireille walked into my kitchen in Paris with—what's her name... the woman you were fucking?"

"Claudine."

"What happened to her?"

"She went back to her husband and family."

Henny made a face. "Sorry. Are you heartbroken?"

Basil smiled faintly. “She called last week.”

“And?”

“And I told her I’d think about it. I don’t give a shit about her husband, but she has two young children. And you and I both know how unsettling divorce can be.”

Henny laughed. “Especially the second and third.”

“Keep it up,” Basil muttered. “And I’ll never call Claudine back.”

Recognizing his friend’s grim, self-absorbed stare, Henny quickly veered back to their original conversation. “Want to give me odds on when Rafe gets tired of Miss Novelty? My call is he’ll last the entire thirty days. According to Carlos that’s when she leaves.”

Basil looked up with a small flicker of surprise, as though reentering the world. “Thirty days is a lifetime for Rafe,” he finally said, having rallied his senses. “I’d say, ten—at the most. Actually, five is more realistic.”

“How much?” Both men were wealthy in their own right. Friendship rather than necessity brought them all to Monaco each summer.

“Five K. And I’m going to modify five days to an even more realistic three. Once Monday comes, Rafe’s going to check in with Geneva and get back to business.”

“I’m not so sure. He’s in deep. Make it ten K and we’re on.”

“Fine. But the odds are against you.” Basil’s form of crazy was personal; in all else, he was eminently rational.

“I like a long shot. And you have to admit,” Henny said with a big grin, “just seeing Rafe play Romeo is worth the goddamn price of admission.”

THIRTEEN

Kicking the carriage house door shut behind him, Rafe set Nicole on her feet. "I'm a couple hours past taking it slow," he said, his fingers quickly undoing the tie on her robe. "I apologize if it matters."

"And if it does?"

His gaze came up but he didn't stop pushing her robe off her shoulders. "Then add some jewelry of your choosing to this apology."

She laughed. "Really? Has that worked for you?"

Always. "Could we have this conversation later?" He arched one brow. "Seeing how you're naked"—he tossed her robe aside—"and my dick isn't in the mood for chitchat."

Her libido zeroed in on the overtaxed fabric of his shorts stretched taut over a truly impressive erection that was about to be hers in all its au naturel glory. "Fine," she said, giving him a brilliant smile and reaching for his zipper. "We'll talk later."

He lifted her hands aside. "Let me. I'm faster."

Fuck—like the speed of sound. A second later, Nicole watched him step over his shorts on the floor. "Great skill set." She frowned.

Catching her chin with his forefinger and thumb, he forced her head up. "Don't pout. You're everything beautiful and surprising in my life." He hid an involuntary wince at his earnestness. "It would be easier if you weren't."

"You and I both know the reason I'm here is because it *isn't* easy." Arching her throat, she pulled away from his hand. "It's volatile. You like that."

He suddenly laughed, leaned in, and smiled, a wide, fabulous flash of white teeth and golden-eyed warmth. "What I *like* is fucking you. And you talk too much," he added, grinning into her audacious blue gaze, shoving her gently backward until she was pinned against the cool stone wall.

Bracing his hands on either side of her shoulders, he smoothly eased forward until his powerful body was lightly resting against hers. As if he were politely offering himself and his considerable physical assets. As if he awaited her approval.

When he knew damn well that there wasn't a woman alive who'd refuse him, she understood, particularly with the hot, hard arc of his massive erection advancing the offer. Pressing gently into her belly, reminding all her fomenting carnal impulses of the wild orgasmic payoff he so easily delivered.

"Am I supposed to say yes?"

He kissed the tip of her nose. "Are you?"

"I thought you were in a hurry," she said, a noticeable restiveness in her words.

He almost smiled at her willful evasion; not that a little friendly tutelage wasn't going to make her more agreeable. But in the meantime, he had no complaints. She was hotter than hot. "You sound breathless," he whispered, bending his head and kissing the fluttering pulse in her throat. "Does it turn you on—the novelty of uncharted territory—no protection, all the barriers down?" He smoothly slid his middle finger down her pulsing cleft, drew it back over her slippery softness, then lifted his head and lightly touched the pad of his finger to her lips.

She shivered, her body jolted by his touch.

"I'd say that's a yes."

He lifted one brow at her dazed look, raised his finger to his mouth, and licked. "One more time just to make sure?"

When he gently pressed her clit, she stifled a cry as a hot, flaring warmth raced through her senses and melted into a fiery pool of burning desire between her legs.

He watched the color rise in her cheeks, his thumb resting lightly on her pulsing nub of engorged flesh. "Your jazzed little clit is talking to me even if you won't," he whispered, rubbing the pad of his thumb up and down the sensitive bundle of nerves before he gently flattened it.

She groaned, a soft, frantic greedy sound.

He raised his head. "Feel good?"

He was smiling at her, there were creases at the corners of his eyes, a small lift to his midnight-dark brows, an amiable openness in his gaze. He nuzzled the small bridge of her nose, then took her face in his hands. "Talk to me."

She shook her head, her breathing shallow. "Rafe…"

There was both hesitancy and panic in her voice, a rare glimpse of unsureness in her eyes. He was just about to respond to the plea in her voice when she shoved her hands between them, swept them downward at warp speed, curled her fists around the swollen head of his dick, and in a sex-deprived frenzy squeezed—*hard*.

His breath hissed through his teeth.

"Oh, God." She dropped her hands, looking almost as pained as he felt. "Did I— You know...are you..." Her voice trailed off.

He took a step back, glanced down, saw that his equipment was still in working order despite the crushing abuse, looked up, and smiled faintly. "We're good. I think I still can have children." His smile widened. "Obviously, you're ready."

"Just a little."

Her sweet, downcast gaze was obscenely hot—as if she might be asking forgiveness, as if an act of submission wasn't out of the question. His dick took notice in an indelicate and sizable display of lechery.

"Oh. My. God."

It was the merest sound, tremulous and breathy—but it shot to the top of his list of best compliments ever. That his house guest was flushed, trembling, ravenously impatient, was a factor. That she radiated a rare compliance spoke to his own brute idiosyncrasies.

Catching her around the waist, he swung her off the floor. "Instant gratification, baby. Legs up." Pressing her against the wall, he helped her circle his waist with her legs, quickly guided his dick to her throbbing sex, and smoothly entered her.

"Me first," Nicole gasped.

Rafe tensed, then said smoothly, "No problem."

His casual assurance shouldn't set her teeth on edge,

especially now when her body was laying out the welcome mat. *Ignore it.* "Just like that? Cool as ice?"

"Relax, tiger. Everything's not a personal challenge. I can do it if I have to, that's all."

Like your dick is programmed after the millionth fuck?

As she opened her mouth to reply, Rafe cut off the discussion by giving her something else to think about—like penetrating a fraction more into her supertight, totally awesome, made-for-optimum-sensation body.

After waiting so long to feel the unprecedented skin-on-skin sensation, the degree of pleasure flooding her senses was epic and truly awesome. Rafe's enormous erection, thick, hot, turgid, imprinted itself on every sleek surface and tremulous nerve ending, touched every feverish cord in her high-flying sensual spirit. She felt blissfully ravished, gloatingly indulged, and so spectacularly horny she wanted to say, *You can own me if you want, lock, stock, and barrel.* She didn't, of course, because she was never so lost to reason; instead she whispered, "You feel really nice..."

"And you feel perfect. Velvety—tight... um—*that's* tight." His concentration momentarily slipped as the extraordinary pressure on his dick electrified his senses, and without thinking he drove in more forcefully than intended. Under normal circumstances, a perfectly ordinary stroke; in this instance, the sensitive head of his dick suddenly banged into a non-resilient surface.

Rafe grunted on impact.

Nicole flinched.

Jerking back marginally, wondering if she was swollen

from their earlier sex, Rafe murmured, "Sorry—need a break? Or would you rather we stop completely?" An offer he was hoping she'd refuse.

"No, no, no, no, no, no! Don't stop!"

Her wild litany of negatives, not to mention the nail marks on his shoulders, had his dick doing the happy dance. But his brain was still functioning, and though he was pretty much with his dick on the full-steam-ahead plan, he politely gave her a last chance to refuse. "Sure?"

The heat in her eyes could have fueled a rocket to the moon. "I said *don't stop,*" she hissed.

For a reckless moment he considered giving her what she wanted. But saner counsel quickly prevailed. This wasn't his first fuck or even his thousandth; he knew better than to hurt her and blow his chances for the rest of the night. And when it came to getting what he wanted, he was a pro. "You're first on the agenda, tiger, don't worry. But we need to slow down. Deep breath now, okay? Then relax and let me make you feel good." He waited for what he recognized now as her normal reaction to instructions or commands. "Come on," he whispered, contemplating the tiny flicker of resistance in her gaze. "Guaranteed satisfaction if you do what you're told."

"Christ—sorry." She let out an explosive breath. "I'm struggling here. In fact"—she paused—"it's just that— Oh hell, forget it."

"No, tell me." He was halfway home in terms of sexual satisfaction, his dick midpoint in a provocatively snug pussy. He could wait a few minutes more.

She shut her eyes and grimaced.

"I'm not going anywhere," he said mildly. "So you might as well tell me."

She frowned. "This is so stupid."

"You know I can see you even with your eyes shut." His smile echoed in his voice.

"Okay, okay."

The brilliant blue of her eyes contemplated him through the lush canopy of her lashes, a faint irony visible in their depths, and he suddenly wondered if he'd be sorry he asked.

"If you must know…" She hesitated, feeling as though her brain had been taken over by aliens. Since when did she talk feelings during sex?

"Oh, what the hell," she muttered. "I want you way too much…like an idiotic fourteen-year-old with a crush and it's freaking me out."

Her rush of words set his world back on track. He grinned. "Christ, I thought I was going to have to talk you out of something weird. But if you must know," he said, mimicking her preface, "I've got you beat—idiot-wise… because my dick's never been this horny. So I'm freaking out too." He grinned. "Ready to come a few times?"

Her mouth pursed. "Are you always this cool?"

"If I was cool about you, I would have fucked you on the yacht and sent you back up on deck." He smiled. "I didn't."

She smiled back. "That works out then because I'm not sure I would have gone."

This wasn't the time to apprise her of the broad powers his wealth allowed him. "Lucky me," he said instead.

"And now *I* want to get lucky," she said with her usual frankness. "Give me those orgasms."

He suppressed a smile; she never asked. She told. On the other hand, he was already on board with her plan and his ego was flexible when it came to imminent orgasms. He adjusted his grip on her bottom.

She lifted her brows. "Tired of holding me? We could go upstairs."

"I'll let you know when I get tired. Right now, it feels pretty fucking good."

"Yeah, no shit," she said with a small sigh, wiggling her hips a little around his partially submerged erection. "Supergood. Tell your dick not to forget my G-spot, okay?"

He laughed so long she finally grumbled, "I just thought I'd remind you."

He grinned. "Has anyone ever told you that you're the fuck from hell?"

"Gimme a break," she said sweetly, like the totally hot fairy-tale princess of every man's fantasy. "Do you get complaints?"

"So we're irresistible?"

"Tempting, I guess. I've never asked. So?"

He lowered his head, his voice. "Your G-spot's on my list, pussycat. Now shut the fuck up and let us do our job."

She opened her mouth.

One dark eyebrow lifted. "I said I'd take care of it."

She shut her mouth.

He knew better than to smile, although her first small capitulation made him want to at least say *Thanks.* Instead, he showed his appreciation by demonstrating the sexual artistry he'd mastered since his disreputable youth. In the interests of mutual consummation though, he progressed with extreme caution, waiting between each progressive advance for Nicole's body to open, part, slowly yield to his invasion. Watching her from under his lashes and monitoring the flush rising on her throat, the rhythm of her breathing, the increasing pressure of her fingers on his neck.

Until, finally, his dick filled her completely.

She whimpered.

He dragged in a shuddering breath.

Paradise found.

Splaying his fingers wider, he held himself motionless inside her for a moment, supporting her weight, his hands cupping her bottom, her thighs resting on his forearms, pleasure washing over him in fierce, hot waves.

Every nerve and heated bit of flesh, every functioning brain cell, was stimulated, then overstimulated, her arousal at fever pitch, prodigal surfeit surging through her body so wildly she began to shake.

Quickly adjusting the angle of penetration, Rafe brushed her cheek with a kiss. "Better?"

Eyes shut, her fingers tangled in his dark hair, she nodded.

"Ready to go over the edge?" His voice was a low rasp.

She twisted her fingers more tightly in his hair.

A slightly painful, but recognizable answer. He zeroed his dick in on her sensitive little G-spot nerves, focusing on a gentle, consistent pressure, on the smooth, silken friction, withdrawing marginally against her frantic resistance, slowly plunging back in to her grateful sighs. Until soon, she was shuddering on the frenzied brink, and he was contemplating clear sailing to the orgasmic shore when he was brought up short by a brutal jerk on his hair.

"Now, now, now!" she cried.

Christ, he'd probably lost some hair. But that wasn't all he'd lost. He'd been on his best behavior for too long or maybe he didn't know what good behavior was. Or maybe she'd simply given him one too many orders. "You want something?" he said sharply. "Open your eyes. Tell me and I'll think about it."

Suddenly he was looking into an angry blue gaze. "Don't fucking scream," he growled. "Ask me nicely."

She glared at him and shoved at his shoulders. "Why don't I find someone who doesn't make me work for a fuck?"

"That wasn't nice." Spinning around, her weight incidental to a man his size, he strode toward the stairs.

"Ask me if I care," she muttered, fighting to break his grip. "There're plenty of parties in town besides yours and I've met a lot of— Oh shit." Her struggles had only deepened his penetration, ignited potent little shimmers of arousal, provoked an unwelcome deluge of slick need.

He smiled. "My party looking more interesting?"

She stared at him sullenly. "Screw you."

"You'll be screwing me all right," he drawled, not even breathing hard as he took the stairs in a run. "You've been in the driver's seat too long, tiger. Time for a change."

"I thought everything wasn't a personal challenge," she snapped.

"You haven't learned when to stop pushing. I'll teach you."

"Like hell you will."

Rafe laughed, his extraordinary eyes fixed on her. "Let me explain a few things to you," he said gently. "You know—clear the static." Ignoring her eye roll, he continued in the same extrasoft tone that those who knew him well recognized as dangerous. "First, I outweigh you by at least a hundred pounds. A Neanderthal standard, I know, but reality. Second, I'm guessing I can change your mind." He smiled faintly. "What with your interest in my dick and a talent I've acquired over the years that recognizes when *no* means *yes*. And, finally, you won't find anyone else handy tonight, so I suggest you humor me if you want sex."

"Maybe I don't want sex." Even to her ears, her response lacked the slightest evidence of sincerity. But then his enormous erection was rocking against her highly stimulated nerve endings with each racing step and it took real effort not to openly pant.

"Sure you do," he said, walking swiftly down the hall. "Do you think I can't feel how wet you are?"

Annoyed by his insolence, not to mention his long-legged stride that was obliterating the last of her self-control, she punched his arm hard. "Put me down, damn it! You think every woman wants you! I don't!"

Rafe came to a screeching halt, dropped her on her feet, dipped his head until their eyes were level, and said very, very softly, "Fucking grow up. I'm not interested in your juvenile prick teasing. Who the hell are you kidding? You want to get off. We both know it." He took a small sustaining breath because his dick was aching like a son of a bitch and he had to fight the urge to throw her down on the nearest flat surface and fuck her until he dropped.

"I brought my trusty vibrator, so getting off's not a problem," she said, pissy as hell. "And FYI, I decide who I want to fuck and when, not the other way around. I suppose you point and choose." She smiled tightly, then lifted her chin and held his gaze. "Maybe I do too. Maybe that's our problem—command and control, no begging." She paused, wondering if she was letting her temper get out of hand and missing out on some fine ass, but decided a second later that, bottom line, she didn't do submission. "So." She stood, eyes blazing, beautiful and casually nude before him. "Regardless that you have a prize dick—and you do—it's not the only dick in the world. I'll live without it."

"Are you done?" She was really magnificent, confident and forceful, hotter than hell; he began thinking, *Indefinite stay.*

"You find this amusing?"

"A little." But he stifled his smile in the interest of future orgasms. "You're naked. In my house. It's a long walk into town, although you probably wouldn't have any trouble getting a ride." Since she looked like she was getting ready to strangle him, he quickly curtailed his litany of obstacles to her leaving. "Forgive me, that was rude."

She snorted. "You think? And I *have* clothes."

He bit back his first ten comments that had to do with his personal power and authority.

"What?"

"Nothing."

"I *brought* clothes with me."

"Yes, I know."

"And I could call a cab. I have my phone."

"You're very resourceful," he said, in lieu of mentioning that none of that mattered.

"Fucking A, you arrogant prick."

His eyes went flat and for a second he didn't move for fear he'd do something uncivil. "Have you ever thought about bottling that in-your-face shit you specialize in? I'm sure there's a market for it."

"You don't like women to talk, I suppose."

"Usually not when I have a raging hard-on."

"Why don't I leave you to deal with it?" She turned away.

He grabbed her wrist and jerked her back. "Just a minute," he said as politely as he could when the urge to explode was almost overwhelming.

She looked down at his fingers circling her wrist, then up at his face, one brow arched in derision. "Do I have a choice?"

Faced with salvaging a situation that would be personally satisfying in terms of sexual gratification, he didn't question his venal self-interest; his belief system was rudimentary. Ignoring her sarcasm, he smiled. "I apologize if I offended you. I didn't mean to. And since you're the oldest of your siblings, you're more familiar with giving orders." He looked at her directly, bowed his head a little. "I should remember that."

Her eyes widened a fraction, like one would on seeing

a unicorn decked out in gold sequins. "Seriously? You're apologizing?"

"I am." He smiled warmly. "Tell me you forgive me."

She bit her bottom lip. "I don't know if I believe you. But fuck—it's tempting."

"How tempting?" He grinned. "Make sure you consider my prize dick before answering. He's waiting to make you happy."

She sighed. "You're just too goddamn beautiful, if you must know. How's that for stupid?"

He understood what was left unsaid—about the women, the *unending* women. And for the first time in his life he recognized the discomfort of need, of desire, of truly *wanting* someone. "You should talk. I'm ready to punch out any man who comes near you. And that's *really* stupid."

"Jesus, I don't like to be this confused. I like to be able to say thanks and walk away."

"You're preaching to the choir, pussycat. But I suggest we put our past behavior aside for the next month, not let it get in the way, and enjoy our crazy new feelings. What do you say?"

She pursed her lips; the silence lengthened.

"I'll let you come whenever you want."

She laughed. "Christ, are you laying down your last card?"

He shrugged and made a wry face. "Let's just say it's a unique offer."

"I don't want to know." She paused. "You understand?"

"Then you better tell me you've never been with a man," he said defensively.

Her smile was pure innocence. "How did you know?"

His shoulders relaxed. "Because you have the tightest little pussy I've ever seen." Suddenly feeling a surge of relief wash over him, he pulled her down the hall, swept her up in his arms when they reached his bedroom, and carried her to the bed.

He was inside her before she'd fully made contact with the mattress, filling her slowly and gently until her eyes shut and her small moan warmed his throat. "Do you like me better now?" he teased.

Looking up into his affectionate smile and tender gaze, she languidly smiled. "I like you as much as a girl can like a guy. Add a couple truck loads more likes and we're in the ballpark."

He winked. "Then my work is done."

"It better not be." But her voice was very mellow.

"Not for at least a month, pussycat. So enjoy the ride." If someone had asked him what he was feeling, he couldn't have explained. A woman had never mattered before, heartfelt sensation was a foreign concept, and the thought of a month with one female would have sent him into therapy. But he did know how to please a woman; sex was his forte. "Let me know when you've climaxed enough. If you don't want to talk, hit me, okay? This is for you."

She came the first time so quickly even he was surprised, and when she whispered, "I'm sorry," he knew what she meant.

"Let's make sure you feel this one." Dipping his head, he lightly kissed her cheek. "We'll make it last longer than five seconds."

Her eyes fluttered open. "I'll pay you back," she promised softly, then her lashes fell as she absorbed the thick, rigid length of him with a low, sensual groan.

"You are already." But she didn't hear his throaty reply; he might not have wanted her to. He might have preferred not saying it at all, his sense of personal upheaval disturbing. But she made him feel a fierce, breathless pleasure he'd never felt before—like now...oh Jesus—like that. Then he slowly glided in and out in a prolonged rhythm of leisurely arousal, and after she began to pant in an exquisite little feverish cadence, when her frenzied, passionate cries reached fever pitch, he finally buried himself deep, deep inside her and went utterly still. A nanosecond later, her orgasm detonated, her scream filled the room, and he met her climax with his own explosive torrent, pouring into her in a wild, ferocious turbulence that left finger marks on her ass, a raw, deep-felt pleasure vibrating through his senses, and insufficient air in his lungs.

Braced on his forearms, gasping for breath, he dropped his forehead on the bed. Her body was exquisitely soft beneath him, her lush, gently pulsing warmth enveloping his dick, echoing the soul-stirring beat of his heart.

After long, hushed moments, he felt the warm flick of her tongue on his throat, and he lifted his head, shoved his hair out of his face, and looked at her with a smile of expanding delight.

"You're incredible." Rosy-cheeked and beautiful, she

smiled up at him. "Not that you don't know it, but add me to your fan list."

"And you're mind-blowing." He grinned. "I never before knew what the word meant."

"Don't panic and run for the door, but I really like you," she said simply.

"No panic. I like you too." His voice was velvety soft. "It's an amazing feeling, isn't it?" His dark lashes veiled a portion of his eyes. "When so much in life is uncertain."

"But not this—here, now...for us." She smiled. "Too equivocal?"

"That's life," he said gruffly. "No guarantees."

He suddenly looked so comfortless, she quickly redirected, like she always had when her younger siblings had been unhappy. "So what do you think comes first—the sex or the feelings?"

"Fuck if I know. Shit happens. You deal with it." Scowling, he pushed up on his elbows, rolled away, and lay sprawled on his back, eyes shut.

That was grim. "I hate to bring this up," she said, not sure of his response with his morose expression. "But I'm dripping all over your bed."

His smile broke first, then his eyes opened and a second later he was propped on one elbow, grinning down at her. "Jesus, baby, you have no fucking filter, do you? But the drips are my fault, not yours. Don't worry about it." He bunched the sheet between her legs. "How's that? We'll take a shower later." Another flashing grin. "Right now I have other plans—if you don't mind, of course."

She laughed; the contradictory, beguiling, playful man

who charmed so easily was back. "As if it matters what I mind."

"It does," he said quietly. "It matters a lot."

She gazed up at his strong jaw and fine straight nose, at the stark beauty of this man she found irresistible. Her chest constricted briefly and she knew how foolish it was to fall under his spell. Like being infatuated with a cinema star. "You don't have to say that. I have no expectations."

As though streaming the same strange, emotional vibe, he looked at her in mild disbelief, then sighed. "You're the only woman I've ever wanted badly. It offends me. It pleases me. It fucks me up." He smiled. "In a good way. In a don't-wake-me-up-if-I'm-dreaming way."

She gave him a little bunny twitch of her nose in wordless agreement. "Sometimes I think this is the dumbest thing I've ever done. Just because I'm way the hell outside my comfort zone," she quickly added at his sudden scowl. "Not because of you. In fact, I may not leave quietly when you tire of me. Just a warning." She looked at him calmly, neither helpless nor insecure. She never had been.

His dark brows came together in a brief pensive moment—turning her comment and it's repercussions over in his mind. "Then we understand each other," he said, his expression clearing, his gaze direct. "Because you won't be leaving."

Her mouth quirked. "This from a man with an ice cube policy?"

"I'm accountable to no one." For a second, coolness darkened his eyes, then he blinked and smiled. "That's my warning to you."

Cocooned in a warm, sumptuous euphoria, she dismissed that momentary chill in his eyes and lazily stretched. "Have I mentioned how pleased I am to be here?"

"Not as pleased as I, tiger." She was all female softness and willingness lying on his bed, tempting as Eve. He imagined winning the lottery felt like this. "Rest five minutes if you need to, otherwise"—he swept a hand toward his rampant erection and gave her a killer smile—"we're ready."

FOURTEEN

Actually, give me a minute," he said, and rolled off the bed. "I'll get some towels."

As he walked away, she watched him just like a teenager with a crush. Funny, because she'd never experienced a wild fascination like that in school. Better late than never, she cheerfully decided, feeling the bewilderment and obsession, the wonder and thrill—taking pleasure in the sight of Rafe's tall, athletic form, his powerful muscle and stark virility, his dark, sleek hair lightly brushing his shoulders as he moved with an easy grace.

Crossing the threshold of his dressing room, he spoke without turning. "Don't move. I'll be right back."

Then he disappeared from sight.

"And no touching your pussy."

Jerking back her hand, she looked up, expecting to see him since she had heard his voice so clearly. No; she was alone. But his curt command had sent another lustful shudder rippling through her senses, ratcheted up the throbbing between her legs, and made her question the human powers of speech when Rafe's words alone could turn her into a desperate, sexified mess.

"Are you being good?"

His voice rang out over the sound of running water and she briefly debated the necessity of compliance. "Depends what you mean by good," she shouted back, taking a personal stand for female power. The bathroom lay beyond his dressing room. How would he know? What could he do if he did know? Fuck him.

Or not.

She hesitated, weighing her current cravings against the merits of waiting for Rafe to more substantively assuage her. Meanwhile, her warming passions were morphing into a frantic ache, the echo of his provocative orders reverberating through every erogenous zone in her body. Fretful and restless, in an uneasy limbo with personal independence and pleasure at odds, she tersely swore, then rolled over on her stomach, cupped her pussy in her palms, and flexed her hips into the mattress.

Her low moan was whisper soft.

Yet of conspicuous significance to the man walking into the bedroom.

"I'm back just in time I see," Rafe said with a grin, tossing the towels on the bed. "Hands where I can see them. *Now.*"

The soft hint of a reprimand in his voice shouldn't make her cream her pussy, nor incite an almost unbearable horniness. Or conversely—mess with her head, when acquiescing would set precedents she didn't want to set.

"I can help you." His voice was silken, assured, as if he were witness to her internal debate. "All you have to do is move your hands where I can see them. There you go... that's the way."

As she slowly drew her hands out and placed them at her sides, he felt a staggering pleasure out of all proportion to the simple event. Perhaps the California-girl wholesomeness pouring off Nicole stoked something untapped inside him or maybe her cheeky defiance offered an even rarer challenge. Or maybe he just needed to get laid. Regardless of the reasons, at the moment she was compliant and his for the taking. "Roll over and spread your legs."

After a small, defensive pause that didn't surprise him, she did what he asked. "Thank you." His chin rose. "You look delicious."

"You do too. The waves are moving." Her smile was warm and alive. "A lot."

"He's definitely on board." His amber gaze glittered for a moment, wicked and edgy, then he slowly inhaled, reminding himself that this didn't have to be complicated. So she pushed all his buttons. Chill. A rush is a rush. "We're going to have to make room for my ink." And he arranged her legs to his satisfaction—knees drawn up and apart. "You're being very dutiful." He ran his palms up her smooth inner thighs, slid his thumbs up her slick, swollen cleft, and smiled as she shivered. "You must want something."

At the soft mockery in his voice, her gaze came up and met his. "I want the same thing you want." He was standing beside the bed, his prize dick at full stretch, twitching gently against his flat stomach. "Come closer."

"Not yet." He picked up a wet washcloth he'd carried in. "Open yourself for me," he instructed. "We'll start with your clit."

She smiled, feeling less defenseless with the evidence of his arousal pulsing in time to his heartbeat. "I need a more polite tone of voice."

"I know what you need, and it's not that." He lifted his brows. "So—anytime."

She wrinkled her nose. "Don't be rude."

He laughed softly. "Jesus, are we having fucking tea?"

"What if I resist? I could. Until you're nicer."

He closed his eyes for a second. "That's not going to happen—me getting nicer. If your other bed partners let you get away with this bullshit that's their problem. I'm not the altruistic type. So—I repeat...anytime."

She breathed out her displeasure. "Give me the damned washcloth. I'll do it myself."

"If I wanted you to do it yourself, I would have said so. Now show me your sticky clit. *That's* a fucking order."

She felt the blood in her face rise. "This is preposterous," she muttered, dropping her legs and rolling away.

With blurring speed his fingers closed on her shoulder and, flipping her over, he shoved her back on the bed and swept his hand downward over her breasts and rib cage until his palm came to rest firmly on her stomach. "What's preposterous is your constant defiance," he said, meeting the fury in her gaze with mild annoyance. "What the hell? You want to come, I want to come. I don't see the problem."

"Let me go!"

He splayed his fingers wider, exerted more pressure, and angled his head as if trying to decide if this was just a game. "You like this don't you? It's turning you on."

She looked up to his face, her brows drawn in anger, but her skin felt hot, her heart was pumping madly in her chest and it took her a few seconds to reply. "No."

"You don't mean that," he said. "Even if you think you do," he added softly. "So here's me playing God. And you playing the game my way. Show me your clit or I'll tie you up, clean you up, then see that you don't come for thirty days. I'll have sex with you but I'll be the only one who climaxes. Clear?"

She was speechless for a moment, confused, rebellious—oh fuck—stunned by tiny, tingling spasms pulsing through her body in embarrassing arousal.

"You don't have a choice," he murmured, helping her out, giving her leave to accept the inevitable, not mentioning the telltale carnal flush rising up her throat.

Aware of her limited options, his smile promising he'd make even submission worthwhile, she shut her eyes and silently complied, reaching down to touch her pink folds, sliding her index and middle fingers in slightly deeper, opening her slick flesh enough to expose her clit, mortified to feel it so engorged that there was no question she was interested in whatever he considered worthwhile. *At what price?*—her mutinous voice of reason snorted. Suddenly overcome by panic, not sure she could deal with Rafe's total autonomy, she forced aside the impetuous, gimme, gimme fever gripping her senses, opened her eyes, and stared at him stonily. "Don't."

He smiled. "You're way past don't, tiger." Her guilty need was graphically evident in the insistent little pulse swelling her clit. "You like me, I can tell." He carefully touched her slick, swollen nub, and the tiny rocket of sensation that kicked against his fingertip pleased him. "So don't pretend. Come on, it's not the end of the world"—he paused, gave her a tender smile. "Not even close. It's only sex... a little wider now so we can get you cleaned up... there, perfect, good girl—don't move."

She shivered at the first touch of the wet washcloth, flushes of warmth ran through her, flowed into all her slippery, greedy places, making her squirm, and she rose into his hand with a low, muffled sound, forcing the pace.

"Hey, hey, not so fast."

She made a face at him and he grinned. "It doesn't have to be wild every time. Relax." Then he delicately swabbed her clit, taking his time, thorough in his cleansing. "Everything good so far?" he murmured as she lay, fists clenched, dragging in shaky breaths, glaring at him. "Need a little more speed?"

But by the time he'd finished sponging, she was panting raggedly, frantically writhing her hips, so near orgasm he was tempted to humor her. If he didn't prefer less argument with his sex, he would have. If he didn't want to screw her obsessively, he could have overlooked a fight or two. But he didn't care to deal with perpetual drama for the next month; she needed to recognize there was a downside to her confrontational style. This was lesson one. Tossing the washcloth on the floor, he bent down and dropped a kiss on her nose. "I'm going to climax first."

Nicole's eyes flared wide. "You're kidding!" she gasped, her orgasm terrifyingly close, blissful relief beginning to swell inside her.

"I'm not," he corrected. "I washed him for you. You'll have to come closer." He pointed to the edge of the bed where he was standing.

Overcome with fury, she hissed, "I'll do—myself," and quickly slid her hands down her stomach.

With frightening speed he pinioned her hands to the bed and leaned in close so his narrowed gaze was only inches away. "You can do yourself later." His eyes burned into her. "Right now, I want your mouth on me. Understand?"

"Screw you!" She fought against his grip—big mistake: a frantic-for-sex female without clothes writhing in his grasp seriously affected the size of Rafe's erection; it also triggered a stunning, fuck-me tremor that flashed through every functioning nerve in her body.

He was watching her with a ghost of a smile. "The sooner I come, the sooner you get off, tiger. It's pretty simple."

Never before faced with sexual extortion, she dragged air in through her nose and eyed him hotly. "I'm damned near there already. Do you really think you can stop me from climaxing?"

"Fuck yeah. For thirty days if necessary." He shrugged and smiled. "We can fight it out if you like. Your decision, of course."

"Why would you do that?" She wasn't stupid enough to ask, *Would you do that?*

"Because, my little hothead," he said very softly, his dark, silken hair brushing her face, his golden gaze so close she could feel the glow, "you can't always have your way."

His quiet certainty gave her pause; she had to swallow before she found enough breath to speak. "Does that mean you're going to make all the rules?"

Recognizing her wavering tone, he slowly released her

wrists and stood. "Not all of them—but more than you." He sighed, as if he were helpless against irksome reality. "You've been running wild too long."

Surprised at his choice of words—that it actually mattered to him—she let a small silence fall before she said, "Maybe I like it that way."

He gave her a teasing smile. "You'll like my way more." Then he circled his erection with his fingers, slid his hand downward, and added inches to his dick, the flaring head swelling sizably in a flamboyant display of virility. "So stop resisting, pussycat. It'll only get you in trouble."

"With you." Her mouth was in a tight line.

He lifted an eyebrow. "Yes. But trust me. I know what I'm doing."

"Do you know how offensive that sounds?" she complained.

He shrugged. "Do you know how good I can make you feel?"

"Don't be so sure." But her voice was scarcely a whisper and her slight frown signaled doubt. She took a small, emphatic breath. "If you must know, I don't like feeling defenseless…desperate." She gestured at his showy dick. "For him, you. It's unsettling. It alarms me."

"I understand the desperation," he said quietly. "But it's not so alarming"—he smiled—"to at least take turns. What do you say? I'm not interested in making you unhappy."

She sighed. "That's not actually possible." A flicker of a smile appeared. "Really. Even when I'm pissed. You're so extraordinarily handsome, it obscures objectivity. How's that for pure folly?"

He dipped his head. "None of this has anything to do with reason. When you walked into my stateroom, I felt the world shift. And I begrudge that feeling as much as you begrudge your defenselessness."

She grinned. "So we're motivated by an underlying umbrage."

He shook his head and grinned back. "Lust first, baby. Fuck the rest. So bottom line"—his grin widened—"you have to make up your mind how we're going to play this."

She nibbled on her lower lip, then sighed. "Okay, we'll *try* it your way."

"Fair enough," he said very calmly. "So, are you going to come closer or what?"

"If you ask me nicely."

"I thought I did. I know I did. Don't be a dick." And into the small silence that ensued, he added, "Thirty days without an orgasm." One dark brow inched up slightly. "That's a long time."

A little shiver ran up her spine, whether from the thought of such an unsettling eventuality or the more challenging sight of his blatant erection visibly expanding to a spectacular height as he spoke, she wasn't sure.

"Give in," he whispered.

She frowned, took a breath. "It's really hard, and I didn't mean that so stop grinning. I'm just not sure I can do it—*give in* the way you want me to."

"You mean even faced with no orgasms for thirty days." He couldn't imagine it.

She nodded.

"Seriously?"

"Could you? Beg?" Her voice was constrained. "Because that's what this is."

He didn't immediately reply, then said, "No."

"You see? You're asking too much. It's a double standard and you know it."

He looked amused. "Is this about equality?"

"It should be."

He rubbed a hand over his face in a nonverbal curb on his temper. "I'm not sure that's what I want with sex. I'm not sure you do either. Could we talk about this later?"

"After I go down on you, you mean."

"Yeah."

There was a quiet finality in his voice, an undiluted bluntness. "When later?"

He didn't quibble; he was tired of arguing. "We'll talk tomorrow. And you can come as many times as you want tonight."

Her brilliant smile could have been seen from outer space. "Why didn't you say that before?"

"Because I didn't feel like it before. Now stop talking before you piss me off again."

"Yes, sir." She licked her lips and grinned. "So, what exactly can I do for you?"

"I need your mouth here." He pointed.

"You want a kiss?"

He smiled. "It's a start, smart-ass."

He watched with pleasure as she slowly rose to her knees: the enticing sway of her spectacular tits as she turned; the slender span of her waist that made his fingers twitch; the sweetness between her legs that was currently his magnetic north, his consuming passion, his addiction.

When she was resting on her knees at the edge of the bed, she put her hand flat on his hard chest. "Mine," she said, feeling his power and strength, his potent maleness, the sexual heat escaping from him in waves.

He sucked in a breath at her touch, at the aberrant word no woman had ever dared say to him, at his heart-tripping reaction that rapped on every door he'd always kept closed. He frowned. "Dangerous territory, tiger."

She looked up to see his golden eyes darken, and caught in the wicked burn she suddenly felt cornered, captive to the too handsome, too rich, too improbably charismatic man. But a second later, she stopped freaking out because it usually took zero effort to make it happen if she wanted a man. Not that Rafe was a role model for conformity, but—what the hell...life was good, the sex was fantastic. "I'm not easily scared," she said with a nervy grin.

"I've noticed. That's part of the fun. You think you can handle me."

Their eyes locked for a moment.

"I always win, tiger."

She smiled. "Funny thing. Me too. In fact"—she was cut off; her comment, her breath, her ability to think, because Rafe was sliding his fingertips down her stomach and it didn't take a rocket scientist to know where he was heading. *Oh yess*...his fingers came to rest on her newly washed cleft and she involuntarily moaned as he slipped one finger inside and ever so gently touched her sweet spot.

Reality was instantly transformed into a lush, misty,

flower-strewn landscape with the prince of her dreams smiling at her. "I'm so on board with your style of winning," she whispered, her eyes half shut. "You have magic fingers, no question."

"Glad you like them," he said. "More?"

Awash in pleasure, feeling breathless and adored, humbled by Rafe's benevolence, she wanted him to feel the same incomparable wonder. Caught up in a sumptuous euphoria fueled by pheromones and lust, she jettisoned her conditioned resistance and lifted her lashes. "It's supposed to be your turn first."

"Don't worry about it. I'll catch you later." Untouched by tender sentiment, he thought: *Thirty days; plenty of time.*

"What if I want to?" She lightly touched the taut head of his erection, glancing up through her lashes. "I don't need your consent, do I?"

He laughed. "You got it, babe."

"I figured. You're pretty fucking worked up."

"Yeah," he said with a lopsided grin. "You too." He moved his finger an infinitesimal distance over the solid flesh of her pulsing clit.

"Jeez, cool your—jets," she gasped. "I can't do—two things at once."

"Sure?" His voice was soft as silk. "You might like it."

She made a growly noise. "How would you know, since you've never done anything like this before?"

"Right. But I've a great imagination. I dream about this shit."

His look of innocence was truly impressive. "Hmmpf!"

"Is that a yes?"

She was still glaring.

He grinned. "Don't bite, okay. That's all I ask."

"Maybe I'm not giving any guarantees."

"Even if I guarantee you one of the better orgasms of your life?"

"Hmmm."

"Now that's definitely a yes." Making an executive decision to move the party along, he quickly added a second finger to her superwarm pussy, which was already telling him yes in a hundred different ways.

She was softly moaning when she dipped her head and swirled her tongue around the flaring ridge of his erection and ran it down the throbbing vein underneath—definitely an added bonus to degrees of sensation, he decided, and stroked her G-spot in a friendly hello.

Really, why she even debated feeling this good was seriously overthinking sex. Rafe had the right idea. Just do it. Not that he might have operated on that premise a few thousand times more than her. But that didn't mean it didn't feel good all the same.

"What the fuck are you doing?"

It wasn't rude or harsh; the question was only whispered in bewilderment. Returning to the world, she realized she'd apparently zoned out. "Sorry," she said, her mouth full so it came out muffled; but he must have gotten the message because when she glanced up, he was smiling.

"You're supercute, tiger. But if you need instructions, just ask."

In answer, she grabbed his balls—not too hard, not

too soft; she wasn't expecting a coherent answer. There—a nice, guttural moan, like he really meant it.

Settling into her groove, she sucked and licked the velvety skin beautifully inked by some hotshot artist in Tokyo so each up and down lift of her head was like a trip to the museum. Lightly pumping his rigid length with one hand so the ocean waves totally rocked and rolled, she gently massaged the pliant flesh of his balls with her other hand, slid her head downward, taking as much as possible of the smooth, solid length of him into her mouth, then with added suction and some tongue slowly worked her way back up again. Rafe's low throaty growl played backup music to her performance.

His hoarse, raspy voice echoed her own volatile need as he touched and tortured her throbbing sex, caressed her nipples and breasts, made her all fluttery and needy, warm and tingly, like the pro he was.

Even his choice of soap was beneficent; he tasted of cinnamon. Cinnamon and Hokusai—nice combination, along with his huge dick in her mouth, which was stoking all her freaking hot and heavy, loaded-for-sex desires. In fact, in a total turnaround, she was thinking she'd be happy to take seconds with—like seriously—gratitude. So in terms of pure luck, barging into Rafe's stateroom was—

Rafe pressed down on her clit with his thumb, gently flattened it out and instantly drove any coherent thought out of her mind. With a high-pitched squeal, she jerked upright as raw, scorching bliss burned through her body at warp speed.

His fingers cupped her neck and he slowly forced her

head back down. "Give it a second." And a moment later, when her cry dropped to a restive little mew and the strumming aftershock subsided, he whispered, "Like this?" and rubbed his thumb so softly over her clit she purred.

"Better?"

His voice was husky, low.

Still trembling slightly, her mouth crammed full, she raised her lashes. "Amazing."

Damn near as wired as she, he grunted softly as her reply drifted over the swollen crest of his dick. "Do that again. Talk."

She took a deep breath. "Actinium, symbol Ac, atomic number 89, aluminum, symbol"—she felt his laugh, then his dick slid farther into her mouth as he flexed his hips. A second later, the pad of his finger ran over her G-spot with such finesse she almost begrudged him the experience required to gain that level of skill. But currently mesmerized by the shimmering enchantment lighting up her brain, jealousy issues faded into the ether.

Instead, the gloating pleasure flooding her body revived her earlier feelings of self-discovery and affection. He's mine, she thought: his inked dick; his charming, difficult, exasperating character; his beautiful face; his tall, lean form; his mind and spirit.

Granted, her fulsome ardor may have been stirred by Rafe's deft hands skillfully massaging her nipples and making her clit and G-spot smile. Or perhaps by his beautiful, enormous, cinnamon-flavored dick, which clearly demonstrated that size did matter.

Oh God, oh God, oh God. Her tightly wound-up G-spot

bundle of nerves wildly quivered as Rafe dragged his finger over the sensitive flesh. Overprimed, about to combust, she didn't hear Rafe's low, tattered snarl.

He pushed deep into her mouth.

She started to gag.

"Fuck, sorry." Jerking back, he stroked her cheek, nuzzling the solid feel of his dick with his fingertips. "Jesus—though, baby, that was—fucking extreme." Shaking his head, he blinked himself back into the world, gently ran his finger over her top lip, which was stretched around his dick. "You okay?"

He felt her nod way more than he would have liked considering he should probably make amends if he ever wanted her to blow him again. "Why don't I get you off first? How'd that be?"

She gave him a nice little suck he took as a yes.

A second later, her clit and G-spot were being treated to the world's most talented digits: two on her G-spot, his thumb on her clit, and as her orgasm started to swell through her sex, down her legs, up her spine, and then was turning her brain to mush, Rafe Contini, virtuoso lover of women who knew what he was doing and had for a decade or more, cupped Nicole's chin in his free hand, held her head firmly, and, guarding against overzealous momentum, timed his climax to meet hers—exactly. He also saw to it that the glory lasted for them both till the absolute, mind-blowing, ride-off-into-the-sunset limit.

Quickly withdrawing, Rafe breathed a litany of, "Fuck, fuck, fuck," in a tight, brittle riff as he grabbed a towel, wiped Nicole's mouth, and lowered her down on the bed.

Half-dazed, his chest heaving, he raked his fingers through his hair, rested his hands on the top of his head, and waited for the debris from the violent explosion to clear from his brain. "Christ," he said in a soft rush of air. Then he took a deep breath, dropped his hands, gazed at Nicole all flushed and fragile lying sprawled on his bed, and smiled so widely two rarely seen dimples were etched in his cheeks. "Want me to buy you Cartier? Just say the word, tiger, I'll sic my lawyers on them."

Eyes shut, she shook her head. "I'd buy it for you if I could. I almost died," Nicole purred. "You are *so-o-o* fucking good." Her eyes opened slowly, the pleasure glowing in the blue depths sunshine bright. "Thanks for giving me my turn first. I know why you're in such demand. You're chivalrous."

He was wiping himself off; he looked up and gave her an eye roll.

"No?"

"Just you, tiger. You're deconstructing my life"—he winked—"and I mean it in the nicest way." He dropped a clean towel on her stomach. "Now move the fuck over. I have to rest a minute." His smile was killer sweet. "But don't go to sleep. I'm not done with you."

"Oh goody."

He was on top of her a second later, kissing the grin off her face. "Winning with you is going to be survival of the fittest, no shit," he whispered, brushing a kiss along her cheek. "I feel like a fucking gladiator."

"Does that mean I'm Wonder Woman? She kicks butt, you know."

"You're a wonder all right, but it'll be a cold day in

hell when you kick my butt. Just saying." He rolled away, shoved a pillow behind his head, then turned and smiled. "You know somewhere down the line, it's going to be my turn first."

"Do I know that?"

"You will." He leaned over and kissed her. "You won't mind."

"Such confidence." She gave herself a swipe between the legs and tossed the washcloth.

"I'm getting to know your sweet spots and your tricky ones." His smile broadened. "Those take a little more concentration."

"For which I'm grateful."

He winked. "You should be."

"Is your minute up yet?"

He was still laughing when he entered her creamy warmth; she liked the feeling, almost as much as she liked his slow, deliberate penetration so every sensation was magnified by anticipation, every sensory tingle was indelibly etched in her brain, her need for him bordering on insatiable. "You're really good to me," she whispered, brushing his hair back from his face, resting her palms on his cheeks.

He smiled. "Only you."

"Just so you know—you can always win. I don't care."

He chuckled. "You'll change your mind after you come."

"When will that be?"

His smile was all sweet, cocky heat. "You need a time or just a promise?"

"I need you," she whispered. "That's all I need."

If any other woman had said that to him, he would have shown her the door. "You've got me, babe. Everything good now?" he added, unruffled by her demand, making her happy a business plan he was more than willing to sign off on. "And fast is fine with me if that's your schedule. Ready?"

As she nodded, she wondered if one could become a nymphomaniac in a matter of hours. Because all she wanted was Rafe Contini inside her, making her feel hot and wild and scary good.

Rafe was thinking maybe there *was* a God because Nicole Parrish had appeared out of nowhere and was introducing him to heaven on earth—in terms of maybe the best, most intense sex of his life. The shocking concept instantly generated a wave of panic, until his self-preservation instincts kicked in to remind him he'd said *maybe.*

"I don't want to wait," Nicole whispered.

But his moment of panic had sent a burst of adrenaline through his blood, fueling his fight-or-flight reflex. Or, in his case, attack mode—an indictment of boarding schools where survival came down to winning or losing; there was no middle ground. Struggling to rein in the pressure to hit something, Rafe muttered, "If I get out of hand, maybe you should have a safe word."

She gave him a curious look. "Out of hand—like how?"

"I've been known to lose it on occasion."

"With sex, you mean."

"Yeah, I guess." Since he didn't want her to walk out, he left it at that.

"Don't worry about it. I'm good." She slid her legs around his waist and smiled.

"What the hell does that mean?" He gave her a flat look.

"Jeez, relax. It just means I don't need a safe word."

Dead silence for a moment, then he lifted an eyebrow. "Are you saying you're into rough sex?"

She sighed. "No, I'm a virgin. Does that make you feel better?"

"How rough do you like it?" he asked, an edge to his voice.

"Could we drop this conversation?"

"Answer my question."

She unwound her legs and shoved against his chest. "Don't snarl at me. It's none of your damn business."

He lowered his weight on her just enough to get her attention. "I'm making it my business." He gave her a chilly look, forcing her legs wider. "Now, one more time," he snarled, just to get his point across. "How rough? And don't fuck with me. I'm not in the mood."

"I know what you're in the mood for," she snapped, glaring at him as his erection swelled inside her. "Your dick likes this stupid macho shit, doesn't it? You gonna pound the fucking answer out of me?"

She was all sulky and pissed, flushed and huffy. And so totally hot and sexy she was probably right about his dick. But he'd spent a lifetime dealing with frustration, schooling himself to control his emotions and his world. And after all the fucking debate his adrenaline had almost flatlined. Screw the stupid argument. He offered her a warm smile, raised his weight off her. "Sorry. I was out of line. So what would you like first? Slow, fast, simple, not so simple?"

"Christ, are you schizoid?" But she was smiling.

He smiled back. "Yeah, seriously demented. But that doesn't mean my dick can't make you all hot and bothered."

"No shit. And since it seems to matter, I've never done rough sex." She shrugged. "I'm not saying I'm against it. No one ever appealed enough to give it a go."

"You probably shouldn't say that."

"I just did."

A soft smile curved his lips. "Good to know. But I'm guessing I'm on the clock right now."

"If you don't mind."

He laughed. "So polite, tiger. You must really want it."

"You're fucking addictive. What can I say?" She slid her arms around his neck and wrapped her legs around his hips again. "Show me," she whispered. "I'll let you know if I like it."

Not an invitation any man with a heartbeat could refuse.

Quickly sliding his hands under her soft bottom, he tightened his grip and rammed home in one hard downstroke.

She sucked in her breath.

"Okay?"

She held his gaze and nodded.

"Let me know if you want to come up for air." His fingers pressed into her soft bottom, his hips swung forward, and, firmly securing his hold on her ass, he began to move in a wild, unrestrained rhythm, ignoring all the posted speed limits, driving through the stop signs, pounding into

Nicole's tight, creamy sex with his full and undivided attention. Each thrust ended in his grunt, her gasp, as he rode her faster and faster, her heels digging into his butt, straining to pull him in, while he shoved in so far his dick damn near bent on impact. But most of the blood in his body was making sure his dick stayed in the game, so there was no way he was going to stop over a few jarring jolts.

He was relentless.

She was quivering, and shuddering under his hands, desperate, spiraling out of control.

Seriously enthusiastic, he impudently thought, just before her teeth sank into his shoulder. He swore, hauled her hard into his dick, said through his teeth, "Don't say I didn't warn you," and put every hard ass muscle in his big body into his next powerful thrust.

She didn't seem to notice, or she noticed and liked it. Not that he gave a shit when he was getting close to blazing out. They were both wound up, switched on, pumping and grinding until their skin was slippery with sweat, their breathing labored, a mindless lust burning away reason.

"Now, now, now," she screamed, eyes closed, throwing her head from side to side, clawing at his shoulders.

He went still; his mouth went tight. "Tell me my name, goddamn it."

"Rafe, Rafe, Rafe!" A high, frantic cry, her nails scoring his skin.

His smile was instant. "I'm here, baby—lemme take you home." Plunging back in, he felt her climax begin to flutter up his dick, and holding himself deep inside her, swelled bigger as her tight pussy clasped and quivered around him in her frenzied rush to the finish. He waited a second, two, a polite third while the first hot orgasmic wave crashed through her body, then he joined her, coming hard, pouring into her, staking his claim in a way he would have found incomprehensible just hours ago. Softly whimpering, she arched up into his thick, rigid length, taking him into the very depth of her sweet, lush body. And he repaid the breathtaking rush of pleasure by prolonging the rapture for long, endless, heart-thudding moments.

The silent aftermath stretched out in a haze of sexual intoxication, a warm, powerful satisfaction curling through their bodies, the activity of the world briefly suspended. Only their breathing breaking the silence.

Nicole came up for air first. "I know who you are," she whispered, dropping her legs on the bed.

Rafe pried his eyes open and relaxed his grip on her bottom. "Sorry about that."

"I like that it matters."

He grunted.

She grinned. "Postorgasmic sanity?"

"Dunno." He dropped his head, kissed her lightly, and rolled away. "You feel good, that's all I know."

"So I won't be getting an engagement ring?"

He looked at her, unsmiling. "Fucking cute."

"Like your question," she said with a lift of her brows.

A muscle jumped in his jaw. "I'm not talking about this." Rolling up into a sitting position, he grabbed two towels, tossed one at Nicole, and began wiping up.

"I have a novice question."

His hands went still; his whole body tensed.

"Jeez, you're jumpy. I guess you don't get asked about engagement rings every day."

He gave his dick a last wipe. "No," he said, dropping the towel on the floor.

"I didn't think so." She smiled. "Stop scowling. My question is about something else. Was that what you call rough sex?"

He chuckled. "Not if you have to ask." He'd walked a fine line; no point scaring her off the first night.

"Sorry I bit you."

"I'll live. Feel like a shower?"

"Are we done talking about this?"

"Pretty much."

"Sorry, I always forget. Men never want to talk after sex."

He smiled. "Does that ever stop you?"

"Depends if there's something better to do."

"A shower good enough?"

"And?"

He did a quick double take. "Jesus, babe, you're driving me hard."

"Sorry." She tried to look contrite.

He grinned. "You're a shitty actress. And I'm just screwing with you anyway. Drive me as hard as you fucking want. I can't get enough. Ready to check out my shower?"

"You have some special plumbing?"

His smile was contagious. "Something like that." He held out his hand. "Come see."

He'd just taken her hand to help her off the bed when his phone rang. "Let it go," he said, as she glanced toward the bedside table.

"I thought you turned it off."

"I did for a while."

"But you can't for long." She'd seen Dominic on call twenty-four/seven; she understood.

"Not really. But whoever's calling can live without me for a few hours."

But they'd not taken more than a few steps toward the dressing room when the phone on the desk rang.

She nodded toward the desk. "Whoever it is knows you're here."

He grimaced, came to a stop, then dropped her hand. "Give me a second."

Walking over to the desk, Rafe checked the caller ID, then picked up the receiver. "I haven't forgotten," he said gruffly. "I'll be there later." Pausing to listen, he glanced at a small clock on the desktop. "I thought he wasn't coming until next week." A small frown creased his brow at the answer. "Okay, give me a half hour." His frown deepened; he shook his head. "I don't care if he's antsy. Give him some Cristal to relax. Shit—well, try to keep the blow to a minimum. The best I can do is a half hour. Yeah, yeah, I know, I know. Do what you can. *Ciao.*" He slammed the receiver down.

"Are you going somewhere?"

"*We're* going somewhere. I'll explain on the way. Let me call Simon and have the car brought up. Then we just have time to shower. We'll have to save our playdate for some other time."

"It sounded like trouble."

"Hopefully not." He reached back and lifted her in his

arms. "But my friend Ganz shows up when hackers are in the wings," he said, moving toward his dressing room. "So perhaps minor trouble."

"Don't let me get in the way."

He grinned. "Sometimes you can be so fucking polite. Mom taught you well?"

"You wouldn't believe. But I heard you on the phone, so any time just say the word, I can sit and wait until the storm rolls past."

"You can sit and wait with me. Just a nod, tiger. No argument. I have enough shit going on."

She grinned. "Yes, sir. Be happy to, sir."

"Fucking A." He dropped a quick kiss on her nose. "You're finally learning."

FIFTEEN

I'm going to shower in the other bathroom," Rafe said as they walked into his dressing room. "Otherwise, we'll be here all night. And this guy is unpredictable." Setting her on her feet, he dipped his head. "You need one of the staff to help you dress or anything?"

She smiled. "I don't live in a palace. I know how to dress myself."

"A half hour's a real pain"—he sighed—"but if you don't mind."

"No problem. Want me to meet you downstairs?"

"Fuck yes. Christ, you *are* perfect." He didn't say that most women he'd been with took a half hour to put on their lipstick.

"Yes, yes, I am," she said with a playful grin. "Five bucks says I'm first downstairs too."

"Let's make it worthwhile. First one downstairs gets to name their pleasure when we come home."

She spun around, waved over her shoulder and walked into Rafe's huge white marble bathroom that had, on first sight, made her question his avowal that he'd never had women at the carriage house. The room was palace-style luxurious and large enough for an orgy. French doors opened onto a balcony that overlooked the sea, a long countertop with three hand-painted sinks—zebras again—

ran along one mirrored wall, a separate room held a toilet and bidet, and the mosaic tub was large enough to swim in, while the shower would accommodate at least ten people with rows of showerheads lining the ceiling and walls and several mounted shower wands.

No time for speculation, though, when she was up against the clock. Fortunately, she'd had lots of practice dressing quickly for a night on the town; a piece of cake for a California girl familiar with putting herself together in a hurry after a day of surfing. Shower in five minutes, dry her hair in five more, dress in less time depending on her outfit. Makeup—another five. Hell, she even had time to check her e-mail tonight.

Some people, as it turned out, were more competitive than others.

Or perhaps the reward for arriving first was more compelling.

Showered, dressed in black linen slacks, a gray T-shirt, and sandals, and looking sleek and powerful, Rafe was downstairs checking *his* e-mail when Nicole appeared at the top of the staircase. Sliding his phone back in his pocket, he greeted her with an admiring whistle. "Smoking hot dress. What's underneath it is even hotter. Every guy in the club is going to want to nail you, myself included."

"Subtle, Contini." But Nicole was smiling as she moved down the stairs on silver strappy spike heels. "Your idea of flattery?"

"I'll flatter you later any way you want." He took a breath. "Right now, I'm sucking it up 'cause I have to."

His smile was supersweet. “You do look hotter than hell though, tiger.”

She wore a clingy silk metallic dress in silver and azure, with a deep V-neck, little ruffly sleeves, and a gathered bodice that cupped her breasts. “This is my traveling dress. It doesn’t wrinkle in a backpack.”

He frowned slightly. “Do you think you should wear a bra?”

“Can’t with this neckline.”

“Then you’d better stay by my side. Your tits are really out there.” He grunted. “Sure you don’t have something else to wear?”

“Let me check.” She tilted her head sideways for a second. “Nope.”

“I’ll take care of that tomorrow.” His voice was equally succinct. “Right now,” he said, holding out his hand as she reached the bottom of the stairs, “just stay close and I won’t have to punch out anyone.” He nodded toward the door. “The car’s outside.”

“Speaking of taking care of things”—she glanced at him as they moved toward the door—“and I mean it ironically—what’s that box of rope with a Japanese address doing in your dressing room?”

“Someone must have brought it over.” She might have asked him if he thought it might rain from the casualness of his tone. “Where was it? I didn’t see it.”

“In one of the wardrobes.”

He smiled and opened the front door. “Snooping?”

“I was looking for a pair of scissors to trim my bangs.”

His look was mildly inquisitive. “Find any? Thanks,

Simon." He nodded at the driver, who was holding the car door open.

"Yup." She flipped a finger through her long, jagged bangs. "All fixed." She waved at Simon as Rafe handed her into the car.

Rafe slid in next to her and the door shut behind him. "Sounds like you're low maintenance." He grinned. "Except for your sex addiction."

"I'm only addicted to you. Not that your vanity needs bolstering, but"—she shrugged—"it's the truth. So tell me about the rope."

He checked that the privacy glass was up as Simon pulled away from the house; with Nicole a conversation could turn volatile in seconds. "You didn't notice I wasn't answering that question?"

"Of course I did. That's why I asked again."

"It's for sex," he said simply.

"Duh. And?"

"And some guy in Japan makes the best bondage rope in the world."

"Really, the world," she said drily. "You've tried them all?"

Wondering for the hundredth time since he'd met her why he found this woman who demanded equality so fascinating, he sighed. "No, I haven't tried them all. My partner at this club we're going to has a Japanese father. Tomi lives part of the year in Tokyo and knows this Japanese artisan who makes traditional bondage rope. It's specially treated hemp that's soft, doesn't burn the skin, and holds knots." He gave her a scrupulously neutral glance. "Is that what you wanted to know?"

She narrowed her eyes. "I mostly wanted to know that you've never used it before."

"Then this is where I say that was my first ever shipment of rope," he said, without missing a beat because no way he was going down memory lane when it came to his sex practices.

"Goddamn," she muttered, dropping her head back against the cool leather and shutting her eyes. "Not giving a shit is way easier."

"But not so intense." He ran his finger down her warm cleavage, slid it under the silky fabric, and touched her nipple. "Right?"

She'd gasped, so there was no point in trying to pretend. "You probably shouldn't do that if you have to see someone in a few minutes."

He smiled and his voice dropped a husky octave. "We could have him come out to the car. How do you feel about exhibitionist sex?"

"The same way you feel about engagement rings."

He laughed, a teasing light in his eyes. "Then you'll have to wait. Practice a little patience." He brushed her jaw with a light sweep of his thumb. "I've heard it builds character."

"Or I could find someone at the club to help me out," she purred, because he was looking way too smug.

"Somehow I'm thinking no on that," he said with a quick lift of his brows. "Any guy so much as looks at you, no guarantees."

"Jeez, now your baddest-dude-in-town jealousy is turning me on."

"Everything turns you on, pussycat." He smiled faintly. "It's one of your many charms."

"Just everything about *you,*" she said, fighting the impulse to say more because he'd heard it all a thousand times before. She gave him a lavish grin instead. "Should I apologize?"

"No, I'm flattered." It wasn't as though women hadn't flattered him his entire adult life. But that Nicole did mattered; she gave him joy. Curious word that. Not that he was going to overanalyze his feelings. Therein lay danger.

"At least tell me we don't have to stay long."

He pulled her into his arms. "We don't. I just need to find out why Ganz came in a week early." He kissed the top of her head. "And you're not allowed to leave my side. I *will* require an affirmative on that," he said gruffly.

She lifted her face to him and whispered, "Yes, sir, whatever you say, sir."

He groaned. "We're going to have to make this a super-short visit."

But his partner, Tomi Nureki, was waiting outside when the car pulled up to the entrance of the private club.

"What the fuck," Rafe muttered.

"Trouble?"

"I hope not, but Ganz is a total cokehead. We'll know in a minute." He was out of the car before Simon came to a complete stop and motioning Tomi over before he turned to help Nicole out.

A moment later, Rafe said, "Tomi, Nicole Parrish, Nicole, Tomi Nureki. Is he crashing?"

"Getting there. Hi, pleased to meet you." The tall, handsome Eurasian man, dressed in jeans and a blue button-down shirt, smiled at Nicole. "Come on in. Ganz is in one of the banquettes in the back room." His brows flickered. "Entertaining everyone with his favorite topic. The corruption of civilization."

Rafe sighed. "Great."

"Yeah, no shit." Tomi waved them toward twin bronze doors. "If this wasn't a private club I'd worry one of his numerous enemies would take him out."

"We all have enemies," Rafe murmured.

"Some more than others. Ganz has a way of pissing off people."

The men were walking side by side and speaking softly.

"Our security is—"

"Ramped up," Tomi murmured. "At least while he's in town."

Rafe turned back to Nicole and smiled. "Sorry, business."

"I understand. That's why you're here." But she'd heard the word *enemies,* so understood it wasn't about something benign. With an uncle like Dominic, who traveled with a security detail and who had additional security teams for his family, she was aware of the dangers in great wealth.

Two huge doormen/bouncers in black T-shirts and slacks guarded the entrance, although other less visible protection was on duty as well.

"Evening, Rafe," they said in unison and swept the doors open.

"Hi, guys. Busy night?"

"Every night, boss. The rich and famous like to party."

Which was the reason Rafe and Tomi had opened the private club. No tourists, no wannabes, no oligarchs who traveled with muscle, no strangers. Mostly no strangers.

The three made their way past a welcoming committee of five female concierges seated behind desks in the large entrance hall—a virtual UN array of stunning beauty dressed in matching Chanel Pop Art summer dresses.

Rafe greeted the ladies with a smile as they passed through the large rosewood-paneled chamber, drawing Nicole by the hand past five gazes that turned icy when they focused on her.

"Have you slept with all of them?" she whispered, once they cleared the gauntlet of unhappy women and moved toward an imposing set of trompe l'oeil doors offering a view of the sea. "I'm getting frostbite from their looks."

"You're imagining it, pussycat," he said, like every man immune to the repercussions of fucking and running.

"Did you?"

"To be honest, I didn't notice who was even here tonight," he said, following Tomi through one of the painted doors held open by another buff, young man in a black T-shirt and slacks. "Want me to go back and look?"

Feeling a blissful glow from his casual answer, she shook her head.

"Until you came along, I never looked or asked names," he explained, candid and blasé. "So don't sweat them or anyone else. But I'm a little uptight over Ganz showing up early, so if I'm inattentive, please forgive me."

"Really, no worries. Pretend I'm not here." How sweet

he was to say what he did, even if it wasn't true about the women; Nicole was smiling as they walked into a large room vibrating with music and the din of shouted conversation. Two walls held long, neon-lit bars manned by a couple dozen bartenders and packed with people trying to get a drink, tables crowded with guests were arranged against another wall, and the fourth was floor-to-ceiling glass fronting an artistically lit atrium with lush plants and more crowded tables. The band was rocking hard, the dance floor was a writhing mass of bodies, and the crush of beautiful people in the club was testament to the personal trainers, hairdressers, plastic surgeons, couturiers, and rich parents and/or self-made wealth that made it all possible.

Rafe leaned over enough to put his mouth near her ear so he could be heard above the music and noise. "It's not possible to pretend you're not here. Just holding your hand has my dick going crazy." Then he quickly held his free hand palm out in a warding off sign to a man who pushed out of the crowd to greet them. A gesture he repeated several more times as they wove through the standing-room-only partiers.

They finally made their way to a plain black door, flanked by two of the biggest bouncers Nicole had ever seen.

While Tomi waited, Rafe greeted both the men by name, asked one of them about his recent wedding, and listened politely to the man's enthusiastic appraisal of matrimony.

"Sounds like you found the perfect woman," Rafe said with a smile. "Nice to hear." Then his voice took on a measured intensity. "I'm going to try to get Ganz out of here.

Bring up a few more men just in case we need them." He turned to the door, Tomi pulled it open, and Rafe escorted Nicole through to the inner sanctum.

As the door closed behind them, an immediate hush descended. The small room was subtly lit with low-wattage track lighting bordering decorative cornices as well as some spectacular Venetian chandeliers dimmed to a soft golden luminescence. A plush reproduction of the Pazyryk carpet in russet and gold covered the floor, the walls were dark teak; there were no windows, just the single door. A short row of russet leather banquettes lined the back wall, and a half dozen tables scattered about the room were occupied. Most of the people in the room were having dinner.

"Why is he quiet?" Rafe murmured.

Tomi nodded to a banquette in the far corner. "He's doing a line. Everyone at the table is waiting for his next harangue."

Rafe groaned. "Too bad he's so fucking brilliant. His path to self-destruction wouldn't be so bloody sad."

"But he *is* fucking brilliant."

"Yeah." Rafe took a deep breath. "Let's go see about saving his ass." He turned to Nicole. "Ignore anything Ganz says. He's pretty out of it. If possible, I'm going to hand him over to Henny and Basil tonight. They can keep him company while he comes down. Don't worry, someone else will drive him up to the house."

"I'm not worried."

Rafe nodded at Tomi. "After you."

As they reached the banquette, the man sweeping a short crystal straw over a line of cocaine on the table came to the end of the white powder, jerked his head up, and inhaled sharply through his nose. Only then did he open his eyes and look up at his visitors through a curtain of black hair. Flicking his hair out of his eyes with a sweep of his arm, he smiled in a wide flash of white teeth, shot a glance at Nicole, thrust his hand up to Rafe in greeting, and said in a low rumble, "Looks like I got you out of the sack."

"And it looks like I got to you a couple hours too late. Can you still walk?"

"Fuck, yeah." Heaving himself to his feet, he immediately fell backward and sat down hard.

"If we could have a little privacy." Rafe silently surveyed the ranks of druggies keeping Ganz company with cool deliberation. "Now."

Although Rafe's tone was extremely soft, the well-dressed entourage all lurched to their feet as if they'd been struck, and mumbling apologies they quickly cleared the table.

Nicole figured this wasn't the time to make some smart-ass remark, but she was tempted. That was authority in action, no question. And for the first time since she'd stumbled into Rafe's stateroom, she made the connection between two of her favorite people. She was watching a younger Dominic in action; a don't-fuck-with-me attitude was a common trait.

"Sit here," Rafe said, in an altogether different tone of voice—gentle, affectionate—and, pulling over a chair from a nearby table, he seated Nicole in front of the banquette. He slid in beside Ganz, and Tomi did the same from the opposite side, effectively blocking in their friend.

The large Asian man stared at Nicole for a moment, then turned to Rafe. "Introduce me to your"—he started to say something and changed it to—"lady."

Rafe gave a him a hard look. "Good choice. Your fucking brain's still working."

Ganz dipped his head and smiled. "Lucky for you it is."

Rafe took a breath and nodded. "Point taken. Nicole, Ganz, entire name, Ganzorig, one name, he's Mongolian. Ganz, Nicole Parrish, and make sure you treat her with respect."

"Absolutely. Excuse my disarray, Miss Parrish," he said, polished and urbane, his English colored with a faint French accent.

Nicole smiled at his good manners. "No problem. It's a pleasure to meet you."

"Known Rafe long? I haven't seen you before."

"Not long, no. I'm here on vacation."

"From?"

"San Francisco."

"Could we exchange pleasantries later?" Rafe muttered, feeling strangely possessive when he never was, when Ganz knew better than to poach anyway. "I have better things to do. Come up to my place and we'll talk in the morning when your head is clear."

Ganz's gaze swung lazily to Rafe. "You do have a sense of humor."

"Well, let's say clearer. You can party with Henny and Basil. They have roxy to let you down easy when you're ready."

"Why didn't you say so before?" He started to rise,

wobbled a little, brushed Rafe's helping hand aside, placed his palms on the table, and pushed himself upright.

"Just a minute," Rafe said. "We'll move the table out of your way."

The man who looked even larger standing smiled at Rafe. "You do love me."

"Damn right. You're my fucking savior."

"This time for sure," he said, swaying on his feet. "You have major problems. Government espionage, *mon ami,* from *my* special friends."

"Oh, fuck," Rafe muttered, lifting one end of the table while Tomi grabbed the other side and Nicole pulled her chair out of the way.

"Exactly. An epic fuck of epic proportions." He chuckled. "Lucky I'm an overachiever."

"Can it wait till morning?" Ganz had come in so early, Rafe wasn't sure.

Ganz nodded. "I slowed them down—balled up their systems so they've all been sacrificing their sleep to try to get back online. I'll save your ass in the morning."

"I'll have everything set up for you. Geneva is waiting too, I'm assuming. Hey." Rafe took Ganz by the upper arm and gave him a shake. "Pay attention, eyes open. Tomi and I are going to walk you out of here and into a car." Rafe turned to Nicole. "Give me a minute. I'll be right back."

By the time the trio had moved a dozen feet, four men had come up to help take Ganz off their hands. Nicole watched as Rafe gave instructions, the security team nodding, one asking a question, Rafe answering briefly. Most of the occupants of the room were indifferent to the transaction. But then security was a way of life for the haut monde and glitterati. As for drugs, they viewed that as a personal issue.

"Normally, Ganz controls his intake better," Rafe explained when he came back to Nicole, giving her an edited version of Ganz's drug habit. "But occasionally when the stakes are high or he's working nonstop, things get out of hand. Tomi'll see that he gets in a car. You okay? Not freaked out?"

She smiled. "Everything's good."

"I figured. Just checking. Let's get out of here."

The crisis contained, Rafe was more relaxed and on their way out, he stopped once or twice when friends came up. He offered a few, mostly yes or no, answers and fended off several invitations with a smile and a shake of his head before moving on, shielding Nicole with an arm around her shoulder as he wended their way through the crowd.

They exited the noisy bar, the doors shutting behind them, sealing off the pounding music and roar.

"Calamity averted, although tomorrow's going to be hell." Rafe squeezed Nicole's shoulder and dropped a kiss on her cheek. "You're welcome to join me in the war room, but you might rather read or watch some movies, or someone can take you shopping if you like. I have accounts in all the shops." *He'd not met a woman who didn't like to shop, particularly when someone else was paying.*

"First, fuck you on the shopping," she said, gimlet-eyed and direct. "And second—what kind of espionage?"

No way he was responding to her shopping statement,

but damn, that was a first. "Bad actors are always trying to upload our research. When it's a government player, they have beaucoup resources." He smiled. "Ganz will get it done though. He used to work for this particular group."

"Rafe! Rafe! *Darling!!*"

He glanced up just in time to brace himself against the twin blondes in skimpy, pastel dresses who launched themselves at him. Absorbing the impact of their bodies with a grunt, Rafe swiftly disentangled himself from their embraces, stepped back, whispered, "Sorry," to Nicole and reclaimed her in a one-armed hug. "We're just leaving." He nodded at the two models who were offering him their best camera-ready smiles. "But have yourself a good time. The band is rocking tonight."

"Screw the band," one of the women said, with a toss of her blond curls.

And she probably had, Rafe thought.

She'd certainly screwed Rafe, Nicole decided, although her little-girl lisp was really out of place with those humongous man-made boobs and six feet of blond goddess.

"We'll come with you," the other half of the matched pair said in a husky contralto that better matched her Nordic height and accent. "The more the merrier... isn't that what you always say, Rafe?"

"Sorry, ladies, I'm with Nicole."

"So? Our bed is big enough for everyone." The blond beauty glanced at Nicole. "You don't mind, do you? Rafe's always up to it"—she gave him a lewd wink—"aren't you, darling?"

"We're going to pass," Rafe said smoothly. "My girlfriend's jealous."

"Girlfriend!!" Their unbridled shrieks turned heads at the concierge tables as well as from guests passing by; the young doorman stifled his grin.

Nicole lifted her hand, gave a tiny wave. "That would be me. Rafe insisted, didn't you?" She gazed up at Rafe with adoration. "He's *sooo* romantic."

Ignoring the twins' gape-mouthed astonishment, Rafe played his part with equal aplomb. "Only for you, kitten." And leaning down, he gave her a lingering kiss.

A blast of music flowed outward briefly as the door to the bar opened and closed.

"Hey, *Nicole*! I thought I saw you inside!"

Rafe lifted his head, stared, then frowned. "You know him?"

Before Nicole could answer, Andre de Barre was standing before them, his gaze resting on Nicole's cleavage for a moment too long before he looked up and greeted everyone. "Hey, Mia and Tig, how's it going?" Taking note of Rafe's arm around Nicole's shoulders, he gave his rival the briefest of nods, then turned a beaming smile on Nicole. "I had a *great* time last night! Or morning, by the time we got home," he added with a wink. "Did you get my roses?"

"Morning?" Rafe's murmur was deceptively soft.

"I did. Thank you, they were lovely," Nicole replied, aware of Rafe's tone, and not intimidated but still wishing she were anywhere but here. The Valkyrie twins were giving her the evil eye, wanting her *gone*, wanting the Rafe they knew and lusted after back in their large bed. While sweet Andre, looking even more youthful next to Rafe's powerful masculinity, appeared oblivious to Rafe's icy glare. Shit.

"Looks like you're the lucky one tonight, Contini," Andre said in grudging complaint. But a moment later, he reminded himself that Rafe had a short attention span when it came to female company, so his smile was in place again as he turned to Nicole. "Maybe we could do something tomorrow. I'll call you in the morning."

"She's busy," Rafe said brusquely.

"The next day then."

"She's busy then too."

Andre's gaze swiveled from Nicole to Rafe, puzzlement writ large on his face. "Are you relatives or something? Is the family all here on holiday?"

"Fortunately we're *not* relatives," Rafe drawled, the cadence carrying a residual warning. "Now fuck off."

"Rafe, for heaven's sake," Nicole muttered testily, drawing away from Rafe's encircling arm. "Don't be rude. I'm sorry, Andre. Perhaps—"

"Get the fuck out of my club," Rafe growled, dragging Nicole back against his hard body. "Or I'll kick you out." And he waited a pulse beat, a muscle twitching over his stark cheekbone, hoping de Barre would make a move so he could beat the shit out of him.

The door to the bar abruptly opened and music poured out, along with two couples who were singing a popular song at the top of their lungs.

Reality intervened.

Everyone froze for a nanosecond, although the twins might have been wallpaper for all the notice they were given.

Rafe abruptly dropped his arm from Nicole's shoulders and grabbed her hand. "If you'll excuse us," he said, with suave discourtesy, rancor in every syllable as he stared at Andre. And he stood there a fraction of a second more, willing de Barre to take him on, every muscle coiled, ready to strike.

"That's enough, Rafe."

Rafe turned to Nicole, his nostrils flaring gently. "You don't want the problem, babe. Clear?"

"Just a minute, here," Andre protested. "Show a little respect or—"

"Or what?" Rafe snarled.

"Really, Andre, I'm fine. None of this is necessary." She squeezed Rafe's hand. "Let's go."

"Protecting your little boyfriend?" Rafe said under his breath.

"Could we talk about this somewhere else?"

"Of course," he said, softly ruthless. Wheeling to his left, he hauled Nicole away without a glance at the trio left behind, oblivious as well to the astonished glances and raised eyebrows of everyone in the entrance hall who watched him stride past them so swiftly that Nicole had to run to keep up.

"Jesus Christ, did you have to be such a major ass?" she lashed out, raging at his force majeure arrogance and also pissed at the two blondes and their ménage à trois history with Rafe.

"Don't bitch." He flung a hot-tempered glance over his shoulder, the image of Nicole fucking de Barre till morning burning a hole in his brain. "De Barre's still standing and his pretty face isn't smashed to hell."

"So I should be grateful...that you were...only rude?" she panted, her spike heels not meant for racing.

"Like I should be grateful that de Barre doesn't know how to fuck?" Rafe shot back, turning down a dim corridor. "I've seen him in action. Seriously, what were you thinking?"

"Not that it's any of your business, but I didn't screw him, okay? So cool your fucking jets."

"Yeah, right, like I believe that," he growled. "Miss I-Can't-Ever-Get-Enough." Coming to a sudden stop, he punched in a code, shoved a door open, pulled Nicole into a shadowed office, and kicked the door shut. "This won't take long. Lift up your fucking skirt."

"Fuck you," she snapped, fighting to break his harsh grip.

He smiled thinly. "That's why we're here." Jerking her forward, he spun her around in front of a desk. "Bend over."

"Who the *hell* do you—"

"*Bend* the *fuck* over." Planting the weight of his palm on her back, he guided her facedown on the desk, barely avoiding her kicking feet by nimbly stepping between her legs and forcing her thighs open. "Calm down, pussycat," he drawled softly, nudging her legs even wider with his muscled thighs. "This won't take long."

She could hear the smile in his voice. "Goddamn you!"

Slapping her hands on the desktop, she stiffened her spine and pushed hard against the confining weight of his hand.

Holding her in place with an effortless strength, he flipped her dress up with a casual flick of his finger. "You shouldn't have fucked de Barre, baby. Big mistake."

"I didn't! Everyone's not into indiscriminate sex like you, asshole!"

"You coulda fooled me. I got the impression indiscriminate was your style." Unlike the fiery scorn in her voice, his was tempered, cool. Although, bunching the sheer lace of her panties in his fingers, ripping the fabric, and dropping the shreds on the floor indicated a certain degree of discontent. "Nice ass—up high in those spike heels. Perfect." He ran his palm over her smooth, silky bottom in a casually possessive gesture. "Should I tattoo my name here?" He patted one of her ass cheeks. "As a memorial to some fine fucking?"

"No. No. And *fuck* no!" she screamed, furious at being subject to his facile strength and arrogance and treated like one of his bimbos. "Goddamn you, you're going to pay for this—damn indignity!"

He laughed. "Indignity? That's cute. Is Victoria still queen?" He ran his hand over the curve of her ass, spread his fingers wide over the soft fullness, and gently squeezed. "That is one perfect ass," he whispered. "Maybe we should give it a try."

She sucked in a breath as a streak of pure lust spiked through her senses. But her no-nonsense voice of reason quickly leaped in and barked, "Are you fucking kidding me?" Once again back in control of her traitorous libido, remembering where she was and the bloody injustice of it all, she snapped, "Don't you dare even think about it!"

He went still; nothing moved. "Probably not a good idea to use the word *dare* right now." His voice was velvety soft. "The mood I'm in." Then he lightened the pressure of his fingers and gently ran his palm over her ass. "Let's keep the beast in the cage, okay?"

A shiver ran up her spine, but she forced herself to speak calmly. "Look, why don't you let me up." But even as she spoke, she felt a finely drawn pleasure course through her body from the point of skin-on-skin contact, the warmth of his palm stroking her bottom disastrously undermining issues of personal autonomy. "Seriously, let me up." But her voice caught at the last as his hand slipped between her legs.

He heard that small suffocated sound, sullenly wondered whether de Barre had heard it too, or how often he'd heard it. And it took enormous self-control to ask in a tone of relative mildness, "Are you sure?" He slid two fingers up her sleek cleft, slipped them inside briefly in a quick vetting, and ignored her quick shuddering gasp. "You have a real friendly pussy, babe. Hot and slippery, nice and wet—see." He slid his damp fingertips down the bridge of her nose. "So I'm thinking maybe you want to be fucked after all."

"No."

But her voice was barely audible, and a tiny sheen of fresh moisture gleamed on her pouty sex. "Liar," he whispered. And suddenly, the image of de Barre tapping that sweetness relooped through his brain, obliterating all but a need for revenge. "Did you bend over for de Barre last night?" he drawled, a nasty edge to his voice as he reached for his zipper. "Am I getting seconds?"

"Jesus, let it go." Her temper instantly reignited at his bloody double standard, jealous too of the Nordic twins when stupid didn't even begin to explain the folly of that feeling, she fought against his casual control and the unwanted frisson of hot desire making her even wetter, and damn it, aching now. "Go fuck your twin bimbos," she muttered, pissed for reasons of her own, for stupid jealous reasons that didn't bear close scrutiny. "I'm not interested."

Splaying his fingers wider, he exerted more pressure on her back. "Calm down, babe. You're always interested, we both know that." Then, pulling out his throbbing dick past the well-designed zipper placket that kept his tender skin safe, without preliminaries, without so much as a hint of foreplay, he plunged into her sex and buried himself to the hilt in a single, hard, powerful thrust. "See, smooth as silk. You like to fuck, pussycat. I could tell the first time I saw you. There's one hot chick, I thought. Ready for anything. Like this." He drove in deeper, in a hard, deliberate stroke. "Feel that?" he unnecessarily murmured at her quivering moan. "And this?" he grunted, cursing her seductive allure and his insatiable hunger, wanting her to pay for what the gift of roses meant, for her goddamned availability, for her lush, welcoming warmth that Andre probably slid into all night long just like *that*. "Fuuuck."

She groaned, the stunning jolt registering as pleasure when it shouldn't, her body liquefying with longing when it shouldn't, the feel of him dragging back in a slow, lingering withdrawal making her whimper when it shouldn't. And desperate to keep him close, she squirmed, contracted her muscles, and tried to shift backward to maintain the acute, rapturous sensation.

He spanked her ass. "Don't move! This isn't for you. It's for me. And don't you dare come," he growled.

"Like you can stop me," she sneered.

"Damn right I can. And you will not be fucking de Barre again." He drove in with all his strength, as if he could dominate her with sheer physical force, make her submit to him alone. Another irrepressible thrust of his hips touched her deep in her core and left her whimpering, panting, pulsing up and down his entire hard length. "I need an answer!"

"Yes, yes," she whispered, defenseless against her need, a slave to her passions, to him, to the extravagant soul-stirring pleasure he dispensed with such ease.

"Yes?" He went still inside her, jealousy licking a fiery path of destruction through his brain.

She heard the thin-skinned resentment, the wild intemperance in the single word. "No, no," she cried, instantly aware of her mistake. "I mean, no I didn't, I won't!" she quickly added at his low, savage growl.

"Good. We understand each other." Having been given the required answer, there was satisfaction now in the undercurrent of his voice, the savagery restrained. "And if you like roses," he murmured, gently moving inside her so he touched all her sweet spots, "*I'll* get you roses. Okay?" Recognizing acquiescence in her soft little breathy sigh, he slowly slid his strong fingers over her hips, held her firmly in place, flexed his quads, and swung his lower body forward with a practiced, delicate, indulgent precision.

"Oh God, oh God, oh God..." She exhaled a soft, languorous moan, shifted faintly against his gentle grip, the world momentarily eclipsed by the most exquisite, inexpressible bliss.

The familiar sound of her pleasure thrilled him, made him wildly jealous of any man who'd ever heard it, made him grateful as well for his unaccountable luck in having her walk into his life. She was spectacularly sensual, easily aroused, quick to climax, and, in a purely selfish, carpe diem way, he wanted to keep her for himself alone. He didn't question his need for control, nor his capacity for managing his anachronistic feelings. He only said, this man without limits, "From now on, babe, consider me your personal cock-block. No one gets into your pussy but me. Clear?"

Shuddering with peaking desire, his huge erection filling her entirely, a dizzying, taut friction obliterating all but blinding need, she only half heard the rough query in his voice. "Yes, yes, whatever you say," she stammered, not sure what he'd said, but understanding an answer was required. "Rafe, please... hurry," she whispered, wiggling her hips in frenzied need, softly panting, impatient, seething. "Please... I'm so close... please, please. Oh God..."

She had no right, he thought, to be so provocative.

And so faithless. Did she even know who was cramming her full, making her tremble? Would any dick do when she was this wild?

He struggled for a moment with his aberrant feelings, with her bewitching sensuality, with a degree of outrage he'd never felt before. He was no different from all the other men who wanted her, he resentfully thought; not disengaged as was his custom, or, at best, marginally involved, but like a dog after a bitch in heat.

And for a man who'd known only female adulation, who viewed women as interchangeable amusements, who'd always been the object of pursuit, never the pursuer, it was a radical change.

A hugely objectionable change.

Suddenly, he had zero interest in anything but climaxing hard and fast. He had no interest in making it last or making it good for her. Ripping away her skirt, which was in his way, and tightening his grip on her hips, the heat of her body under his hands taunting him with its lush opulence, he started fucking her like there was no tomorrow, like the finish line was in sight, like coming without her would somehow right the inequities of the world. Or at least the world of de Barre, his bloody roses, and all the other men she'd known.

He felt her muscles quiver up and down his dick, heard her scream begin, and, swearing under his breath, powered up a straight path to nirvana, like he hadn't had a fuck in a decade. Like he might never get another. Like he owned her body and soul.

With his pulse thundering in his ears, with his dick rock hard, with only a tenuous thread of reason reining him in, he didn't stop his hard-driving, wildly explosive rhythm through one, two, three of her orgasms. By then, he was no longer sure if he was pleasing her or himself, whether her past even mattered, whether he'd ever understand the clusterfuck in his brain.

Whether he even fucking cared.

Just as he decided *no,* Nicole started whimpering. He recognized that familiar, mewling sound, knew what it meant, and with an impromptu combination of cynicism and awesomeness, he thought, *Bottom line, good times,* and whispered, "Ready to cap it off, tiger?" Then he smiled because there was no way she heard him and, with a sigh, realistic about the price he would pay in precedent for the pleasure she gave him, he deftly took her over the orgasmic edge.

But a moment later, as he was about to give her a small encore while he climaxed, she cried, "No, no—no more! I can't!"

His hesitation was brief; there was a certain principle of fairness. "Feel free to wait this one out then," he murmured, and like a well-oiled piston, he kept pumping and pounding, flat-out racing for the checkered flag.

At first when she started climaxing again he discounted the small tremors. But the tiny flutters were real and escalating; his dick took serious notice and, half angry, half pleased, he tightened his grip on her hips. "Hang on, tiger. Pedal to the metal." Tapping her hard, totally ready to blow after waiting this long, feeling as though he'd been superpolite through a helluva lot of her orgasms, he waited only for her scream to begin before he climaxed in an explosive white-hot rush, pouring into her, filling her with wave after wave of come in such brute hammering thrusts the torque on his spine bordered on painful. Forgetting all the rules of casual sex, of sex as inconsequential entertainment, of the messy risks in nonrandom chicks, he marked Nicole as his in the most elemental, unconstrained, barbaric way.

When the madness was over, he kissed her, his mouth resting gently on her nape.

In voiceless apology.

Then he gently lifted her in his arms, walked to a sofa only faintly visible in the light from the shaded windows, sat, set her on his lap, and held her close.

Only the sound of harsh breathing filled the silence.

Coherent thought still in abeyance.

Normalcy waiting in the wings.

The sudden tension in her spine should have warned him, but he was still coming down from one of the better orgasms of his life. So when Nicole swiveled around and slammed her palms against his chest, he automatically eased back.

Then she wound up and slapped him hard. "You fucking asshole!"

He winced but otherwise didn't respond; he deserved it.

"And if you're going to get pissy about who I was with last night," Nicole muttered, defiant and glaring, pelting him with a flurry of two-handed sharp, stinging slaps, "you better tell me who you were with."

Fuck, that hurt. She'd come enough times to be a little more grateful, he thought, bearing her assault with restraint. "Whoever it was," he said, a small irritation entering his voice at the thought of who she'd been with, "I didn't send them any fucking roses."

"Whoever?"

"Hey, watch it," he growled, jerking his head back. "I like my eyes. And if you need a fucking name—*names... but no way he was going to be that honest*—I'll ask Simon. He drove her home."

"God, you're a massive shit!" Nicole slammed his shoulder with a hard chop.

"Maybe if she'd entertained me as well as you did de Barre," Rafe drawled, cranky after that painful chop to his muscle, even more cranky about de Barre, "I'd remember her name."

"Fuck you!"

Grunting as her fist damn near broke his nose, he grabbed both her hands and put an end to the one-sided militancy. "You want to fuck, babe?" he murmured, his insolent gaze up close and personal, his fingers viselike on her wrists. "Why didn't you just say so?"

"Maybe if you learn some goddamned manners," she snapped, trying to shake him loose, "I might think about it." The brilliant blue of her eyes literally glowed with a palpable anger. "Do you ever fucking ask first?"

He softly exhaled, the answer not likely to please her. "What do you want me to say?"

"Oh, I don't know," she said with withering contempt. "Maybe something like the truth?"

He drew in a small breath before he spoke, reminding himself to keep the stricture out of his voice. "Okay, you want the truth? You're a hypocrite." His lashes drifted a fraction lower, the gold of his eyes only faintly visible. "You came five fucking times. You're welcome."

She went completely still.

"You've been indulged, pussycat." His voice was ultrasoft. "You're very beautiful. You're used to getting your way."

"And you're not?" He was expecting concessions from her—damn him—when he didn't know the meaning of the word. "You practically banged me to kingdom come, you prick! I hope you had fun!"

There was a small pause while he softly inhaled, debated various tactful and nontactful answers, wondered when the game had changed, why he didn't feel like walking out when she was—granted, in his selfish opinion—a bitch. "Look, I'm sorry," he said quietly, indifferent to all the myriad problems and subtleties of their volatile stances, wanting her anyway, every way. "Truly." He brought her hands to his mouth and kissed her knuckles. "You're right. I was a prick. There's no excuse. None." He dropped her hands, leaned back, spread his arms along the top of the sofa, shut his eyes briefly, then dipped his head. "Let me make it up to you."

She looked at him, penitent and contrite and so damned beautiful she didn't wonder that he had the world at his feet. Rich or poor. It wouldn't matter. And she understood too that they were both struggling with their new, challenging, occasionally righteous feelings. "I guess I could have been less bitchy," she said quietly. "But from now on, just ask first. Okay?"

His small startle reflex quickly contained, he gazed at her from under his lowered lashes. "Like how?"

"Lord, Rafe." Nicole sighed. "I don't know. Figure it out."

He ran his palm over his face and blew out a restive breath. "I don't do this... exclusivity shit. I share, for Christ's sake. It's part of the game. And now"—he bared his teeth in a rictus of displeasure—"I want to lock up your pussy and hang the key around my neck." He snorted. "How's that for a mind fuck?"

"If it's any consolation, I'm not sure I'd care if you did that. And believe me, that's so far out of my comfort zone, we're talking beyond this galaxy into the black hole of the universe." She grimaced. "You're not the only one obsessed."

He suddenly grinned. "So the sex is that good?"

"Fuck you." But she was smiling.

"You say that so often, I'm beginning to think you mean it," he said, hushed and low.

His deep voice resonated through every sexually addicted nerve in her body with predictable effect. She winked in open invitation. "So—wanna see if you can keep up?"

"You say the sweetest things, Miss Parrish." Straightening, he leaned forward and kissed her gently, a young boy's kiss, the kind he hadn't given even when he was a young boy. But she made the world seem fresh and new, brought with her an incomprehensible joy, made him believe in the word *relationship* as a meritorious concept. "Keeping up shouldn't be a problem, pussycat," he whispered, with another brushing, butterfly kiss. He ran his hands down her arms and smiled. “But let’s get out of here first. I’ll find you something to wear.”

Nicole’s eyes flashed wide. “If you say you have a closet full of women’s clothes, I’m going home.”

“You can wear one of my robes. And I’m not letting you go home,” he said, tapping her bottom lip with his index finger. “So take that option off the table.”

“You can’t make me stay.”

“Don’t start,” he said pleasantly. “I don’t want to fight anymore.”

“You can’t, that’s all.”

“You’re absolutely right. Forgive me.” This wasn’t an argument she was going to win, nor one he wished to have; she’d leave when he let her leave. “Now let’s wash up in some rudimentary fashion and have Simon drive us home. You good with that? Please?”

His smile was freaking beautiful, and cautious, like he was a little worried about her answer. She nodded. “Yup. I’m good.”

He exhaled. “Thanks.” Then he grinned. “First time walking on eggshells for me.” He quickly put up his hand at her lifted brow. “All good, seriously. You’re teaching me a lot.”

Nicole smiled. “I know what you mean. Obsession’s a bitch, right?”

“Hey, as long as you’re in the picture frame, I’ll deal with it willingly. Now I’m calling Simon.”

He told Simon to park out back, then picked Nicole up, rose from the sofa, and carried her into the bathroom. His office held a minimum wardrobe, and once they'd cleaned up, he changed into jeans and a T-shirt, offered her a choice of sweats or a robe, helped her into a light blue cambric robe, and carried her through the back corridors to an exterior door.

Manned by beaucoup security.

Nicole lifted her brows as the door was opened for them and they walked out into the summer night. "You must be important. Or is the crowd down here so rowdy?"

"Neither. The casino's close, a security issue; so is Ganz." *Not to mention Rafe's usual list of enemies.* "That's why I like the house. It's private. Hi, Simon." He handed him Nicole's shoes. "Mission accomplished. We're going home."

Nicole liked the sound of the word *home.* It was a total fantasy, of course, but screw it, she intended to enjoy every second, every breath, every lush sensation while she was here. Call it Zen, call it magic, call it bewitchment or the perfect alignment of the planets. It was pleasure, pure and simple.

And all because of a superbeautiful, badass, charming, incredibly talented sex god currently holding her in his arms in the backseat of his armored car.

She sighed softly.

He dipped his head and held her gaze, a faint frown visible under a fall of dark hair. "Everything okay? Need something? Just name it, you got it."

She smiled. "That was a happy sigh."

He exhaled. "Good. I'll see that it stays that way."

And for the first time in his life, he wanted to make a

woman happy, keep her happy. Keep her close. It was a strange, unapologetically glorious feeling that didn't bear close scrutiny. "Want some music?" He reached for the control; no point in getting maudlin. This was about sex. Good sex, crazy, obsessive sex, but that was all. "Who do you like? The car playlist has pretty much everything."

SIXTEEN

Nicole fell asleep in the car.

Looks like keeping up isn't going to be a problem, Rafe decided with a good-natured smile. Apparently hours of mind-blowing sex exhaust some people; he'd have to think about practicing a little discipline. She was more fragile than hard-core party girls, like a feisty kitten—all sharp claws and hiss—but surprisingly innocent underneath. Not as worldly as she supposed.

Not worldly at all in terms of his crazy-ass lifestyle.

When Simon opened the car door at the house, he took one look and spoke in a whisper. "Henny called wanting to know your plans."

"If Nicole doesn't wake up, I'll come up to the house," Rafe murmured, sliding out of the car carefully. "Let them know."

Simon nodded and quickly moved to open the front door.

Rafe stood for a moment in the entrance hall, waited for the door to be shut behind him, then took the stairs at a leisurely pace in order not to jar his sleeping beauty. The bedroom had been put to rights in their absence and, pulling back the duvet on the freshly made bed, he lay Nicole down gently, tucked her in, and watched her sleep with a slight air of wonder.

Having a woman in his bed was extraordinary. He couldn't have imagined the likelihood for a decade at least. Yet he felt no trepidation or disquiet; he felt instead a strange content. More: a feeling of peace. And he carefully stored the feeling away against the cold reality that would reclaim him soon enough.

He knew better than to believe in miracles.

A last look, then he walked to the balcony doors, quietly opened one, walked outside, and closed the door behind him. The night sky was brilliant with stars as he walked well away from the door, sat on one of the chaises, took out his phone, and called his cousin Jack.

Jack and Fiona had gone to his villa in Ibiza. He'd received a text after they arrived. This time of year it was nonstop partying on Ibiza; no one slept until morning.

When Jack picked up, Rafe said as loudly as he dared, "I need to talk to Fiona. Go somewhere quiet so I can hear her." The DJ music in the background was ear-splitting. "I'll wait." He thought about saying, "Call me back," but didn't know whether Jack was in any shape to remember a message.

He was getting worried by the time Fiona finally got on the phone. It was quiet, though; no club noise. They must have walked out on the beach.

"I thought I'd check in," Rafe said politely. "See how things are going. Are you enjoying yourself?"

"How could I not? Everything's sooo perfect. Your villa, Jack, the crowds of celebrities, even the weather is unbelievable—"

"Glad to hear it," Rafe interrupted when she stopped to

take a breath. Drunken women liked to talk and he still had calls to make. "I was wondering if you could help me with a couple of questions about Nicole?"

"Is she okay?" Fiona's panic-stricken voice catapulted upward.

"No worries. She's fine. She's sleeping now," Rafe replied, calm and soothing.

"Thank God." Fiona's relief vibrated through the phone. "I could just picture myself calling her mother with bad news. Nicole likes to take chances. Sometimes they backfire—nothing big ever, but well…occasionally things have gotten dicey." Her voice trailed off for a moment. "Anyway, thank goodness she's okay. And no wonder she's tired. She was out last night till morning."

He really didn't need that reminder. Tamping down his surge of anger, he returned to the business at hand. "I was wondering if you knew where Nicole bought her silver dress? We had an accident at the club. I'm going to have to replace it."

"If you spilled a drink on it, don't worry. It's cleans up easily. That's why she likes it. It's perfect for someone who can travel anywhere with only a backpack. I think her mother set that standard. Nicole learned about minimum wardrobes from her, although they definitely never bonded on yoga. Did she mention her mother does yoga at sunrise? Oh shit, you asked me something, didn't you?"

"I need the name of the store where Nicole bought the dress." He spoke very slowly so he wouldn't overwhelm her alcohol-soaked brain. "There's a tear in the skirt. It can't be fixed."

"Oh hell, it was a gift too. As for the shop's—"

"A gift from whom?" Rafe's voice was suddenly tight with fury. "If you happen to know," he quickly amended in a normal tone.

Fiona was several drinks beyond deciphering emotional nuances; Rafe's displeasure went unnoticed. "Her uncle gave her the dress. I think he owns the store or part of it. I know he owns a hotel in Rome because we stayed there. Anyway, we came to Monaco after a few days of sightseeing in Rome."

"The name of the shop?" Rafe gave himself points for polite forbearance.

"Lemme think. It had an Italian name, of course. Which is a problem when you don't speak Italian. Hey, hey, good news, I remember the location because I handed over the address to the taxi driver. It was on the Piazza Capranica. Wait, some of the name is coming back to me too. It starts with a D. Do you ever do that—run through the alphabet when—"

"The location should be enough." Rafe's patience was stretched thin; listening to inebriated women fell into his don't-give-a-fuck category.

"Degli! That's the first part. Or was it—"

"That's a start," he interrupted as politely as possible. "One last question. Any idea on size? I could check on the dress"—*if the cleaning crew hadn't tossed it by now*—"but in case the label is gone. I'm hoping to surprise Nicole."

"Then mum's the word," Fiona said with a giggle. "She wears a size four—that's American, so whatever it is over here—you'd have to ask. But she'll love anything you buy at that shop."

"Thanks. I appreciate your help. Wait—shoe size?" And he listened through a long description of possible sizes depending on shoe style until he finally *did* lose patience. "I think I got it. Sandals, heels, sneakers"—he listed off the sizes.

"Man, you're on top of things"—Fiona giggled—"like, in a good way."

"Now to see if I can find that dress," he said, deliberately changing the subject. "Thanks again. Could you put Jack back on the phone?"

"What's up?" Jack's lazy drawl indicated he was well on his way to getting wasted.

"Are you sober enough to remember what I'm saying?" Rafe spoke in Italian, in the event Fiona was close enough to hear.

"Probably," Jack replied in English, not wishing to be rude. "Text me if it's important."

"I'll text you the details, but a couple questions right now. Can you keep Fiona interested for a month?"

"Jesus."

"Watch what you're saying in front of her."

"No shit."

"I'll pay, of course. Whatever."

"Hey, hey, Fiona, don't go far. Okay, one more for me too. Make it two. There. She went to get us drinks at a bar on the beach. We're in a party mood like everyone else here," Jack said, switching to Italian. "Doing shots. She likes the pretty colored ones."

"Good for her," Rafe said drily. "Just don't lose her in the damned crowd. I'd be seriously pissed."

"Chill. I'm watching her, yeah, yeah, she's not going far. By the way, she rocks; I like her. When you asked me about a month, you just caught me by surprise. I'm not averse to the action. But a month for you, dude. Is the world coming to an end?"

"Sometimes it fucking feels like it. But in a good way. So go anywhere you want, do anything you want, so long as you keep Fiona satisfied and out of my hair. That's about it."

"Christ, don't hang up when you've just told me you're staying with one woman for a month. I need details for that kinda crazy."

"Too fucking bad."

"Okay, one question. What's different about this woman?"

Rafe laughed. "Everything. That's all you're getting. Make sure Fiona calls Nicole in the morning. I want everyone happy."

"You most of all."

"Naturally."

"Seriously, thanks Rafe. I'm having a good time too."

"Buy Fiona some nice stuff, take her shopping. Women like that."

"How would you know? You don't shop with your one-night stands."

"Some of them shop afterward, okay? I get thank-you notes."

"I didn't know people still sent thank-you notes."

"Depends how much they spend," Rafe said casually.

"Or if they're hoping for a second hookup."

"As if that's going to happen."

"But Nicole's different—right?" Jack's voice was mellow with liquor and friendship.

"Right. Which reminds me—you're on the clock for the full month regardless of whether I last that long or not. Your call. And for Christ's sake don't discuss any of this with Fiona."

"Your secrets are safe with me; we're family, dude. But, no shit, I'm consumed with burning curiosity about your upcoming holiday."

Rafe laughed. "Not as much as me. *Ciao.*"

After a glance at the time on his phone—midnight—Rafe's next call was to a personal shopper he used to buy gifts for his mother. "Sorry to wake you," he said with cultivated politesse. Although Alessandra was extremely well paid, so he wasn't unduly concerned about the late hour.

"You didn't wake me. I'm just back from dinner. What can I do for you?"

"I have a commission right there in Rome, although you're going to have to wake up some people. I need these things in Monaco by morning."

"When in the morning?" Alessandra Puglisi was never flustered. She'd been an assistant to Fellini in her youth. She understood improvisation and chaos.

"Early. I'll have a plane standing by tonight. You just have to messenger the items to the airport."

"Item one?" she asked, imperturbable and cool.

When Rafe gave the location of the shop, she immediately knew the name. "That's Degli Effetti. They stock several designers, all wonderful. What do you need?"

Rafe described the silver dress. "If it's available in other colors, send those as well. Then add whatever else you like in dresses—American size four. Shoes too, size six. I'd say more, but this lady finds it difficult to accept gifts."

Her trill of laughter was bright with merriment. "Where did you find this paragon of womanhood? I've never heard of a woman who won't take gifts."

"I'm not sure she's a paragon so much as difficult and troublesome." Alessandra was like an elderly aunt, charming, chatty, and blind to rules of conduct. He'd known her for years.

"Ah, that's why she intrigues you. She doesn't say yes. Good for her."

"We'll see."

"My dear boy, mastering one's feelings is much overrated. I understand you're dealing with some demons—with a father like yours, who wouldn't. But this young lady sounds fascinating. Put your reservations aside. Enjoy yourself. Need I remind you—there are no redoes in life. If you have a chance to touch the stars, however briefly, you'll never regret it. Now, enough unwanted advice," she said crisply. "Why don't I send along a few more things your little girlfriend might like—for your pleasure and hers?"

"I never said girlfriend." His blunt protest was manifest male phobia.

"Rafe, darling, have you ever once asked me to buy something for your—what do you call them—fuckees? No. So resist or not, and most men like you think they can go around sticking their dick into random women for the rest of their lives—until suddenly, *presto, like a shot*—the girlfriend checks in and knocks you on your ass. Now, I'll have the gifts nicely wrapped with pretty name tags that will make her happy, which will make you happy, et cetera, et cetera. So stop being obstinate and listen to your clever aunty."

He had a pretty good idea debating the point would be useless. "I should get a discount for a verbal flaying," he grumbled.

She laughed. "My pet, it's the best advice you'll ever get."

"I'm not saying I believe you completely," he said in a slow, considering tone, "but maybe the door's open an inch or two when it comes to a bona fide girlfriend. She *has* knocked me on my ass. It feels good though, so thanks—as always."

"You're such a sweet boy with such lovely manners," Alessandra cooed.

Rafe laughed. "No point in pissing you off when you're doing me a huge favor."

"Not just good manners but smart too. Your father died opportunely. I hear the company is doing exceedingly well since you took the helm."

"I'll never be as smart as you," Rafe said, a smile in his voice, enjoying Alessandra's delight in life, her directness. "Spend whatever you want. I don't care."

"I know that, darling. And I'd love you even if you were a pauper. Tell your Nicole she's very lucky."

"I'll think about it." He wouldn't, of course, but he might *show* her how he felt.

Next, Rafe chartered a plane in Rome rather than ask his pilots to make a round trip in the middle of the night. Then a last call. Monte Carlo was open late or all night in some cases, so finding a flower shop that would deliver wasn't an issue.

When all was arranged, he walked back into the bedroom and stood bedside for a few moments, feeling an unalloyed happiness. Alessandra was right. Why question every sensation, decision, possibility? Simply enjoy.

Nicole suddenly cried out and he smiled, recognizing the sound. She was dreaming—of him he hoped—but certainly she was enjoying herself. And he waited in the event she woke. But she didn't, and when she was sleeping deeply again, Rafe left the bedroom, softly shutting the door behind him. Walking downstairs, he stood outside, called the main house, and five minutes later, Madame Laplace, who'd been at the house as long as he could remember, arrived.

"Sorry, to keep you up, Josephine," Rafe said, speaking French, "but I need someone I can trust. Sleep in late tomorrow. Right now, I'd like you to sit outside my bedroom with the door ajar so you can hear Miss Parrish if she wakes. If she does, call me and I'll come right back. Don't frighten her, just call me. You have a phone with you?"

The plump, elderly woman nodded. "She's a lovely girl, Rafe." She'd met Nicole in the kitchen. "She has my endorsement."

Rafe smiled. "I'll let her know you approve."

"Be nice to her."

"That sounds like an order."

Her eyes twinkled with amusement. "Then we understand each other."

"I could fire you, you know," Rafe grumbled.

"No, you couldn't. The household would fall apart within a day."

Rafe grinned. "True." Josephine was the titular head of the property. "And Nicole is very nice, I agree." He dipped his head. "I won't be long. I'm just going up to check on Ganz."

Madame Laplace sniffed and brushed her palms down her serviceable skirt in a little restive gesture. "He's very disruptive as usual."

"But a damned genius. And I need him."

"I know. The computer room is being readied as we speak. Everything should be in place by morning. Seven, you said?"

"It'll probably be more like eight before I wake Ganz. But we can't wait too long."

She clicked her tongue. "Such nasty people in the world. They never give up, do they?" This wasn't the first time Rafe had assembled a defense against this particular government. She was familiar with the drill.

"They have a twelve-story building filled with people who aren't allowed to give up. Their job is to steal secrets, plans, and formulas from people who actually do the work. So no," he said with a sigh, "they won't be giving up."

"Make sure you get some rest at least," she said gently.

He smiled. “I will. As soon as I see Ganz to bed.”

“Good luck with that,” she said, her eyebrows sliding upward.

“Yeah, no shit.” Then with a lift of his hand, he turned and walked away.

SEVENTEEN

Ganz had decided he needed a swim, so Rafe found everyone in the pool room when he walked in from the garden. With a glance at the swimmer apparently trying to set new world records, Rafe moved toward his friends seated in the corner conveniently near the bar.

"He's on lap fifty," Henny murmured, tipping his brandy glass toward the pool.

"Did he take the roxy?" Rafe dropped into a cushioned chair, stretched out his legs, and sighed. "I hope so. I want him to sleep. I'm fucking beat."

"He took it, but not knowingly," Basil said, looking up from the martini he was stirring in a pitcher. "I put it in one of those iced coffees he likes. Coffee aside, he should be slowing down soon, maybe sleeping in a half hour or so, twenty-nine, thirty, and...a half." Basil made martinis like a scientist. "When does Ganz have to be up?"

"I'm getting him up at eight. Josephine said everything will be ready by seven."

Henny gave Rafe a jaundiced glance. "The usual suspects?"

"Fuck, yeah. I wish they'd get a new business model that doesn't involve ripping off everyone."

"That'll happen right after world peace becomes more than a roseate hope for the naïve," Henny drawled. "And none of us is fucking naïve. So can you do more than stop them this time? Can you ream them a new one?"

"I'm definitely in the mood. Since they took down Ganz's father in Paris two months ago, he's more than ready to do scorched earth."

"His mom's in hiding?"

Rafe nodded. "Remember that cop in Zurich whose daughter needed help on her drug charges? He's paying me back and keeping an eye on that little farm of mine outside town. Ganz and his mother have been holed up there. She's safe. He came in on a semi-legal chartered plane to avoid flight records." Rafe shot a glance at the swimmer powering down the Olympic-size pool. "Fuck, he's going to have a heart attack with all the pharmaceuticals in him. I better go and see if I can coax him out." Placing his hands on the chair arms, he paused a second, tired as hell, then heaved himself to his feet and smiled. "Wish me luck." He turned back after two steps and nodded at Henny. "Do me a favor. Fucking change your clothes tomorrow. You're ruining my appetite."

"Didn't look like it at supper. You ate like a horse."

"Come on. What'll Nicole think?"

Henny grinned. "Why didn't you say so. I'll even shave for her. How about that? I wouldn't want to piss off your latest dewy-eyed piece of ass."

"Watch your fucking mouth."

"Because?" Henny held his gaze, looking amused.

"Because he likes her, Henny," Basil softly reproached before smiling at Rafe. "More than most, right?"

"Abso-fucking-lutely."

Basil gave Henny a censorious look as Rafe walked away. "Don't tease him. He's goddamn happy after sleep-walking through tons of naked women who wanted to have sex with him—without ever once breaking a smile. Nicole's different; he's clueless why but he's willing to risk finding out. You fell in love, so you know what it is. I'm finally willing to give it a shot. Yeah, look surprised. I called Claudine. I'm going up to Paris in a few days, see if we can work things out. Look, all of us are fucked up in our own way, but Contini père's twisted view of women and child-rearing did a real number on Rafe."

"And you're saying this chick will open his eyes to love?"

"I'm saying she might. She's lasted more than a few hours and she's in his bed." Basil's brows lifted slightly. "Two recent miracles. So give him a break."

"God, you're sweet, like it's your God-given mission to spread happiness." Henny's smirk creased the rust-colored scruff on his cheeks. "I see why all the poetry-loving groupies jump into your bed."

Basil smiled. "There's something wrong with poetry?"

"Hell no, not if it gets you some fine ass," Henny drawled. "Hey, look." He jabbed his finger toward the pool. "Success. The man is fucking smooth. No wonder the ladies love him. He even has Ganz smiling and he was in a fierce, crazy mood."

"The roxy's taking him down."

"Whatever. Our boy, Rafie, could sell ice to the Eskimos. Not that I'm complaining. I wouldn't mind a few hours of sleep."

Henny and Basil were on their feet waiting when Rafe and Ganz walked up.

Henny grinned. "Anyone want a nice hot chocolate in bed?"

"You gonna tuck me in too?" Ganz was dripping all over the floor, seemingly immune to the coolness of the air.

"Of course, baby," Henny said sweetly. "I'll give you a kiss too if it will fucking put you to sleep. Morning comes early and I'm guessing everyone's going to want breakfast. Which means I have to get up and cook."

"Waffles. The ones you make with strawberries and whipped cream." Ganz's lashes drifted lower for a moment, then he jerked, his eyes flew open, and he was back in the world. "Café au lait with that hazelnut liquor of yours too."

"You got it." Henny surveyed the small group. "Any other requests?"

Rafe caught Henny's gaze, dipped his head toward Basil. "Nothing special for me. Can you all take it from here?"

"No problem," Basil murmured.

"Call me if you need anything," Rafe said cryptically. "Anytime."

"Will do. Sleep tight." Basil winked. "If she lets you."

"I still have a few things to do. So fingers crossed she's still sleeping."

"Whoa." Henny's eyes widened. "You're turning down sex?"

"What? As if I can't?"

"You can't."

"Can too."

"Cannot."

"Jesus, are you two in primary school? Get the fuck out of here, Rafe," Basil ordered.

Rafe didn't have to be asked twice. He was burned out. He hadn't slept last night, nor much the night before. And he had to be up at the crack of dawn. Even the warm night air conspired to add to his fatigue and by the time he reached his bedroom he was practically asleep on his feet.

Josephine clucked in sympathy when she saw him. "For pity's sake," she murmured, patting his back as she had when he was young and she'd put him to bed, "you're exhausted. Go right to sleep." She shook her finger at him as he started to speak. "Don't argue. The world won't come to a stop if you sleep for a few hours."

"Nicole didn't wake?" he said instead, because arguing with Josephine never got him anywhere.

"Not a peep. The darling girl is sleeping like a baby. See that you don't wake her—you hear?"

Rafe smiled. "Yes, ma'am. Am I dismissed now?"

She snorted. "Don't get smart with me, young man. Someone will call you at half past seven." She gave him a shove. "Now get to bed."

He wasn't planning on sleeping because he still had hours of e-mails that had come in while he'd been playing with Nicole. But when he sat down at the desk to log on to his laptop, he woke up a second later and found himself staring at his screen saver. Crap. A couple of hours of sleep might not be a bad idea.

Quickly undressing, he slipped under the covers and

gently eased Nicole into his arms in order not to wake her. But he needed her softness and warmth, her sweet scent and sweeter body right next to his. Ummm...he felt a quick shot of happiness, like he must have done something right and been given a present. A small, perfectly formed, beautiful gift that brought a strange sense of peace with her in the middle of the night. Perhaps it was just not being alone or the feeling of not being alone when his entire life had been intensely private. Or maybe just the feel of her in his arms made his world richer.

An almost invisible thought drifted into his consciousness, filling him with gladness: *Take good care of her.*

A first for him.

He fell asleep with a smile.

Nicole came awake to a low mutter of obscenities, half opened her eyes, and found the source of the sound seated at his desk, marginally dressed in shorts, his bronzed, muscled body a killer sight to wake up to. "Did you sleep?" she murmured drowsily, thinking once she woke up she was going to throw herself at him and beg for sex.

Rafe swiveled around, his smile bathing her in sunshine. "I did. It's still early though. Go back to sleep."

"What time is it?"

"Five thirty."

"What are you doing?"

He tapped his laptop with his finger. "E-mails." He grinned. "Some people actually want an answer."

She slowly stretched, then sniffed as a familiar sweet scent drifted into her nostrils. "Why do I smell roses?"

"There're a few roses here."

She came up on her elbows, scanned the room, gasped, and sat bolt upright. "A few?" she whispered. Every square inch of surface, floor and furniture, was filled with bouquets and baskets of roses.

"I told them to send what they had. I should have been more specific. I guess the guy figured this was his chance to pay for his kid's university education. There're more in the hall. And downstairs...everywhere downstairs." He took a small breath and held her gaze. "This is me trying to apologize for last night. I messed up and I'm sorry. You deserve better than some wild-ass animal going crazy." He smiled, a small private smile. "I don't actually know what's going on with us, but it's good. So maybe you should pull the covers up"—he exhaled, made a little motion with one hand—"because you're tempting as hell, I'm trying to behave, and I haven't had much practice." His mouth twitched. "I'm giving my hard-on a serious pep talk about right and wrong."

A playful light warmed her eyes. "So if I said I wanted to lick you all over, it might be a problem?"

"Just a little." He dragged in a breath, his gaze sliding over the round, luscious swell of her breasts, downward to the bit of sheet still covering her sex, then flicking back up to meet her eyes. "Toy with me," he said softly, "and I can't guarantee I'll behave." A small half smile slowly lifted one corner of his mouth. "Or are you looking for some serious action?"

"I was thinking more like wake-up sex," she murmured.

"There's not just one kind, pussycat," he said, hushed

and low, shutting down his laptop. "Put in your order. I'll see what I can do."

"You're going to piss me off is what you're going to do unless you reword that comment," she said, her eyes alight with resentment. "As far as I know, there's only one kind of wake-up sex."

He scowled. "Speaking of pissed off, I don't care to hear about that one kind, okay?"

Since she suddenly wanted to lick that pulse beating wildly at his throat, then move downward to taste his entire hard, drool-worthy body, she wasn't above reversing course. "My fault. Let's start over. How about we have our own version of wake-up sex?"

He blinked, got his temper under control stat, and came to his feet. "I can do that." He reached for the zipper on his shorts. "You start, I'll follow, that way we're both singin' the same song." But he'd no more than half unzipped when his phone rang. "Ordinarily, I'd ignore it"—he gave Nicole a quick smile as he pulled his phone from his pocket—"but there's so much shit going down this morning— Oh hell, I gotta take this." He dragged his zipper back up in some Freudian act of diffidence, hit the Answer bar, and said, "Hi, Mum. What's going on?"

Reaching the bed, he held up his hand, fingers splayed to indicate five minutes, then sat down and listened, nodding once, twice, before speaking. "I went to the club last night so I turned my phone off for a while. It's so loud there you can't hear it anyway. Nothing to worry about. Everything's good." He grunted. "No, really. Tell Anton to chill. If I'm ever in trouble, believe me, he'll be the first person I call. I know, I know. I should have answered last night. My phone's on now, so call whenever. How's Titus?" He knew that was always a topic of conversation during which he only had to listen. Which he did, his eyes on the clock and after a respectable interval, he made an excuse. "Henny's at the door. I'll talk to you tomorrow."

He set his phone on the bedside table. "Sorry." He smiled. "Where were we?"

"I was trying to decide what to lick first."

He laughed. "Christ, there must be a heaven after all." His shorts were on the floor a second later and a second after that he was sprawled on his back beside her. "Do your best, your worst, whatever turns you on." He flicked his glance downward, his erection rock hard. "We're already on our way, so it's not gonna take much."

She grinned. "It must be karma. I'm superwired. So let me see this awesome artwork." She'd just taken his dick in her hands and was lowering her head when her phone rang.

"What the fuck! Sorry." He sucked in a breath and smiled as pleasantly as he could under the circumstances. "You probably have to take that."

Nicole hesitated a millisecond more but that ringtone was her mother. She groaned. "It's *my* mother this time." She flexed her fingers around his dick in unconscious demur. "Do I have to be a grown-up?"

Squelching a throaty growl, Rafe steeled himself against the intensity of his desire, twisted his arm upward to reach for her phone next to his, and handed it over. "Be nice. You don't want problems." Then he shoved himself up into a seated position against the headboard.

"Hi, Mom. How's everyone?" Nicole grimaced. "Sorry, Fiona and I were at a party last night. Some people her cousin knows. On a yacht, so the reception was probably no good or I would have picked up your call. I'll try, yeah, I know, I'll really try, okay? Word of God. What's everyone been doing?" For the next ten minutes, she answered politely at first, later in monosyllables, hoping to shorten the conversation—to no avail, her mother didn't notice. "Okay, great!" she finally said, way too cheerfully. "I mean, that's too bad, but call me anytime. Of course I mean it. Anytime, Mom. Absolutely. Bye." Pressing End, she dropped her head and groaned. "Now I *have* to answer when she calls. My dad just walked in so she had to go, but I heard him in the background yelling, *Answer your mother's calls!*" Nicole frowned. "You don't fuck with my dad. If I worry my mom, next thing I know, he'll be hauling my ass back to San Francisco."

Rafe sighed. "How old are we?"

"Not old enough, apparently," Nicole grumbled.

He grinned. "I was an only child for years, so I have an excuse. What's yours?"

"I have a helicopter mom. I love her to death, but..."

He held out his hand. "Phone." Taking it from her, he set it down, then leaned forward, picked her up, and placed her on his lap. Dipping his head, he brushed her cheek with a kiss. "Should we try this again? We've dealt with the two people we have to talk to." His smile warmed his eyes. "Clear sailing now, tiger."

Wrapping her arms around his neck, she lifted her mouth to his. "Kiss me. I'm feeling deprived."

"Then I'd better take care of that."

His kiss was gentle at first, just the slightest pressure, but when she tugged on his hair, he got the message, forced her mouth open, slid his tongue over hers and offered her a hard, wet, toe-curling kiss that brought her to a groaning, hot and heavy breathless need with such ease she might have taken issue if she hadn't been in such desperate straits. "Now, now, now," she panted. "I'll lick you later, okay?"

He understood that it wasn't really a question. "Gotcha." And he'd just eased her up enough to guide his erection into her slick, hot folds when his phone started screaming in a ringtone that would wake the dead. "Jesus fucking Christ," he hissed, hesitating for a heartbeat before he lowered her to the bed. "I'm *so* fucking sorry," he whispered. "But that's big-time trouble."

Rolling over, he grabbed the phone, shut down the insane din, and said, clipped and curt, "I'll be right there." Turning back to Nicole, he sighed. "I feel like we're in the middle of some screwball comedy, only it's not fucking funny. Look, why don't I get you off before I go. Fingers. Mouth. Dick. You decide and I apologize up front, but I gotta make it quick. The bad guys are closing in, Ganz is cranked up to the max, and I have to be there in case one of those which-way-do-we-go decisions is needed."

Hearing the crackling tension in his voice and taking note of the small worry line between his eyes, she put a smile on her face. "Go. That's a thousand times more important. I'll catch you later."

He dipped his head. "Sure?"

"Yeah." She nodded. "Go. Ganz is waiting; the bad guys need to be smashed."

"Fucking A. You're a total sweetheart. Thanks." He rolled off the bed and reached for his shorts. "Take a look in the dressing room. I think I might have found a replacement for the dress I ripped all to hell last night. Let me know if I'm close."

"How did you manage all this while I slept?" She swept her arm to take in the room full of roses.

He was already zipping up his shorts. "Everyone took off their shoes and they got a bonus if you didn't wake up." He grinned. "Money talks, babe. Now," he said, his voice taking on a briskness she'd not heard before, "I'm on the main floor of the house, halfway down the hall, on the side facing the sea. Come see me when you feel like it. And Henny has breakfast in the kitchen. Just tell him what you want. Or call in an order if you'd rather eat here." He held her gaze. "We good?"

"Super. I'll see you later."

"Don't forget the stuff in the dressing room, tiger." His smile was flat-out beautiful. "Hope you like it."

EIGHTEEN

Nicole stood arrested in the doorway to the dressing room, staring at the huge pile of gorgeously wrapped packages. Each one was the equivalent of a colorful work of art; it almost seemed sinful to disturb their beauty. Although, bottom line, should she even look? It was outrageously too much. She wondered if this was a common practice for Rafe and if it was, she wasn't sure she wished to be viewed as one of his legion of women who expected gifts for services rendered.

In the midst of her discordant thoughts, her phone rang and, running back into the bedroom, she picked it up, glanced at the caller ID, and couldn't help but smile. So call her crazy, but damn he was easy to like.

"I'm about to walk into the computer room, so one last order, pussycat. Open the presents or I won't fuck you again."

"How did you know?"

"How did I not know? But look, I wanted to do it, and I want you to like the stuff, so don't give me any shit. And before you ask, I've never ordered gifts for a woman. Ever. So wear something new when you come over. I mean it: open the presents or else there will be dire consequences. Clear?"

"You've never ordered gifts?"

It was a question no woman other than Nicole would have asked; all the rest would have taken the presents without a qualm. "Not once in my life. Until now." Then his voice turned teasing. "That means open them or lose out on my dick."

"Fucking tyrant."

"Yeah, but you like the fucking part. Can't wait to see you in one of your new dresses. *Ciao.*"

Did he mean it about not fucking her? Yes. Probably.

Could she could talk him out of it? Uncertain.

Did she dare take a chance? She knew the answer to that one.

Funny how awesome, once-in-a-lifetime sex canceled out lesser priorities.

Wallowing in her what-the-fuck, thoroughly selfish happy place, Nicole decided to first smell the roses.

Slowly turning around in the bedroom, she surveyed the multitude of roses in every color of the spectrum before walking out into the hall. Whoa. She came to a sudden stop, glanced left and right, taking note of the considerable length of hallway massed with lush arrangements that stretched to the top of the stairway. Carefully navigating a narrow path leading to the stairs, she descended through a scented sea of roses spilling down to the ground floor, where she came to a wide-eyed stop. Drifts of colorful roses were spread out as far as the eye could see.

Her brain short-circuited, confounded by the incredible extravagance, trying to reconcile the gesture with Rafe's expectations. With hers. It wasn't as though she wasn't reasonably acquainted with wealth. Or that she hadn't been the object of male attention—even disconcerting levels of adulation on occasion. But this fulsome display was far beyond any previous tribute or interest accorded her. She wasn't entirely sure how to respond.

Fiona was always willing to listen to her angst or whining any time of the day or night and it *was* morning, however early. She'd give her a call. They'd always shared the good, bad, and middling in their lives, talked every problem to death, dealt with the doubts and drama of life, laughed a lot, cried a little, and generally saw the world through the same lens. Moving through the billowing roses, she walked back upstairs to where she'd left her phone.

Fiona answered with a wild giggle. "I'm having so, so, so much fun, Nicole! Tell me you're as happy as me! Tell me you're even half as happy as me, a quarter even, and you'll still be walking on air."

Nicole smiled. "You're seriously loaded. Where are you?"

"I-biz-ibit-fuck, where all the celebrities go in August."

"Ibiza?"

"Yeah, yeah, that's the place. Jack says hi. He's soooo sweet. You can't believe how sweet he is. He's takin' me shoppin' tomorrow, well today—we've been up all night. He says I can buy whatever I want! Crazy, hey? Nice crazy. Oops, sorry, me selfish. Whaz goin' on with you? Everythin' good?"

"Perfect. I just wanted to say hi." Apparently, Fiona wasn't going to be her voice of reason when it came to accepting gifts. But Nicole took one more stab at a sensible conversation about her doubts. "You don't mind taking presents from Jack? You're good with that? No problem?"

"Are you fucking kidding me?!" Nicole had to jerk the phone away from her ear at the screech. "What's to mind?" A second later, Fiona went quiet as though the gist of Nicole's question had suddenly registered and when she spoke, her voice was slurred, but no longer deafening. "Hey, somethin' wrong? Tell your BFF. I'm listenin'." She giggled. "You might have to say it twice, but I'm here for you, baby girl. Whaz up?"

"Rafe just bought me a ton of presents. I was trying to decide whether to open them or not, whether to accept them."

"Don' be stupit. He's richer than God. Assep, aksep—fuck, take'm. Take every damn present."

Nicole smiled. No equivocation there. Total vindication. Seriously drunken vindication, but an answer if she was looking to be persuaded.

"Jus' so you know, I gave him your sizes. Don' be mad. Be happy, okay? Hey, Jack wans talk to you. Lissen to him. He knows dudes."

A moment later, Jack was on the phone. "Hi. Fiona and I are having a great time. You okay?"

"You sound sober."

"Did a little blow. Keeps me going. Now, what's this about presents that has your knickers in a twist?"

Nicole sighed. "Rafe went a little crazy. The entire carriage house is filled with roses and now I have orders to open the huge pile of gifts in his dressing room."

"Orders?" Jack's voice was amused.

"Private matter."

"Got it."

"Rafe's at the main house. Ganz came in last night and they're dealing with some crisis."

"Ah. The recurring piracy. And you're left behind to open your gifts. I don't see the problem."

"It's just so much, too much. I'm not sure I like it for a bunch of weird, maybe silly reasons."

"In case it helps, Rafe doesn't buy gifts for women."

"He told me. I didn't know whether to believe him."

"It's true. So you're not just one in a long line, if that's what's bothering you."

She laughed. "Christ, are you a therapist?"

"Been to enough, but no. Since Rafe doesn't normally do this, I'd say you're pretty special. Why not just enjoy the gifts. He'd want you to." Jack chuckled. "Actually he ordered you to. So—did I talk you off the ledge?"

"Yeah, thanks. And thanks for being nice to Fiona. It sounds as though she's having a good time."

"Me too. It's my pleasure. Now go open the presents. Knowing Rafe, he's expecting to see you in whatever he bought ASAP. He's not a patient man."

"Understatement."

"I'll have Fiona call you later after she sleeps it off. Say hi to Rafe."

Nicole sat on the bed for a moment after the call, running the conversation through her mind. She liked knowing from a semi-reliable source—Jack was a cousin after all—that Rafe didn't buy gifts for women. She wanted to believe him, because call her stupid or Pollyanna, it felt superfine to know she wasn't one of a crowd. With a man like Rafe, that had been a given. Nice surprise.

Although everything about him was nice.

So seriously, she had to stop fretting about every little thing.

When she had the great good fortune to stumble into paradise, it was foolish to question the cosmic miracle.

Walking into the dressing room, she sat on the floor, trying to decide which exquisite package to open first. They were all tied with real ribbon, some embroidered, some metallic, others of silk so fine, she could practically see dollar signs printed on them. And each bow was adorned with silk flowers or small pieces of jewelry. My lord, it was just a little daunting to demolish such impeccable work.

She decided to start with a small package, like dipping her toe in the water. Flipping up the name tag, she read: To Nicole, love Rafe—and went still for a moment. Quickly reminding herself that she'd known him for less than twenty-four hours, that this was simple politesse—a conventional courtesy—she started breathing again. Jeez, it was easy to buy into the Cinderella myth with a man like Rafe, with this degree of largesse, with the impressive sexual satisfaction she'd recently experienced. But slow the fuck down. Rafe probably *was* richer than God and the cost of these presents was incidental to his bottom line. Chill.

But it still took another few seconds to dismiss that little word, *love,* on the name tag. Breathe in, breathe out. Okay, back to reality.

Setting the name tag aside, she untied the bow, placed the silk flower on the carpet, and unfolded the turquoise paper with care. When she lifted the cover on the box, she smiled. Maybe that's why the name tag said *love:* nestled inside silver tissue were four pairs of ribbon-embellished lace panties so sheer you could read the paper through them. Now that kind of loving she understood.

Less uptight now, she reached for a second package.

A half hour later, she'd opened them all. Rafe had found a replacement for her silver dress, in addition to two others like it in different colors. Along with several dresses, slacks, shirts, blouses, bikinis, bustiers, and shoes so cute it would have been impossible to resist even if she'd wanted to.

She was surrounded by a ministore of fabulous clothes.

A few of her favorites were stacked in a little pile: a pair of purple spectator heels that were meant to be worn with a purple sleeveless linen dress pleated in little tiny hand-sewn pleats that made the short skirt bell out perfectly. Victorian black-and-white lace boots that matched a black laser-cut skirt and top. Yellow suede high-tops that complimented multicolored fish-print slim trousers and a sweatshirt. Rhinestone, sparkly heels that resembled twining snakes that rose to her ankles. *Maybe those with the black lace bustier,* she thought with a smile. A brilliant blue cashmere hoodie and pants she could picture wearing at night on the beach. And a pale blue ankle length cashmere sweater dress with a deep V-neck, long sleeves, and a zipper that opened in front that was übersexy. She felt a little frisson just thinking about Rafe slowly unzipping the dress.

The jewelry was hand-crafted, modern in design, and modest. Obviously whoever had selected these items from the boutique in Rome saw them as no more than decorative packaging. For which she was grateful. It was enough to be overwhelmed by the roses and designer clothes. Expensive jewelry would have been impossible to accept.

Picking up a dress from the top of the pile, she walked into the bathroom. After a quick shower, she slipped on the simple black dress in sweatshirt material printed with flamboyant coral, yellow, and white tulips. It was comfortable and easy to wear, as were the black leather flip-flops with tulips painted on the straps that went with it.

After a last glance in the mirror, she set out to thank Rafe for his generosity. Although, considering the venue, her thanks would have to be well-mannered and polite. No wild hugs and kisses for his largesse. No showing off her pretty new panties.

NINETEEN

The computer room had two dozen computers running, and Ganz was overseeing the technicians, moving from person to person, issuing instructions in crisp, blunt commands, waiting each time for either a confirming nod or a question that required further clarification. Every man's facial expression was earnest and resolute. Everyone understood the stakes: Contini Pharma's R&D, clinical trial results, and potential blockbuster drugs about to come on the market were all targets for the state-sponsored hacking.

The system that Ganz had shut down for almost two days had come back online an hour ago with a vengeance, flooding the company's bandwidth with a brute-force wave of DDoS attacks. Under Ganz's direction, the technicians were defending with the full range of response tools, denying access, setting up additional buffers to any port that looked even remotely vulnerable, double-checking the security of their servers, bolstering their firewalls, ultimately funneling the massive amount of traffic through their own scrubbing center facility that separated bad from good. Everyone working at full capacity to stop the huge volume of challenges.

Security of another kind was evident on the entire back wall of the large room, where thirty security screens overlooked the property, inside and out. Three men sat at a long counter scanning the monitors, part of a shift that changed every six hours. The protection was simply a fact of life for Rafe. His father had generated a number of enemies in his destructive path through life and both as heir and now CEO, Rafe had value in terms of ransom. Personal security was routine.

Lounging on a wine leather chesterfield across the room from the technicians, Rafe was frowning, his phone to his ear. "How many?"

"Three," Carlos said. "We dumped them in the water two miles out. They won't be found."

"I expect they'll send more. Ganz is high target."

"Especially since he cleaned out the unit's bank account when he left."

Rafe grunted. "They owed him, he said. I'm sure they did. He had to have made them billions. Fuckers are greedy."

"Tell me something I don't know."

"Yeah. So. Here's the plan," Rafe said. "We have to be in Geneva no later than two. Ganz needs to check some of the corporate computers to make sure they're secure. I'm leaving you behind to take care of any missed tails on Ganz. We'll meet you in Geneva whenever you break free."

"Couple days, I'd say. Once they know they've lost Ganz and three of their men, if any of the team is left, they'll wait for new orders. These people aren't allowed to operate independently."

Rafe laughed. "Unlike Ganz. I'm surprised he lasted in Shanghai as long as he did."

"He was their star player, their prima donna. They were willing to bend a little for him, give him a little leash."

"But not enough."

"You don't have to tell me about the price of freedom," Carlos said drily. "I've seen a helluva lot of people die for it."

"Including Ganz's father." Rafe exhaled. "That was unnecessary; dumb as hell because Ganz is going to pay off that score in spades. As soon as he's done with us, he's going on the offensive. Speaking of settling scores, do you have enough men? We can send some down from Geneva."

"We're fine." Carlos chuckled. "Monaco is too rich an area for the squads after Ganz. They don't blend in. They need better clothes."

"Next assassin manual. Item one. You tell them."

Carlos laughed. "No way. I love those cheap windbreakers. They might as well have a sign on their foreheads. I gotta go. Malcolm just walked in. *Ciao.*"

Dropping his phone, Rafe noticed Nicole standing in the doorway. "Hey, baby. Have you been here long?"

"Not long. I didn't want to interrupt your call."

He tapped his phone. "Done." He smiled. "Don't you look fine. Perfect fit, perfect babe, come"—he patted his lap—"tell me what you liked best."

Rafe could have been a surfer, barefoot in shorts and a T-shirt, his hair pulled back in a messy ponytail, untidy bits of dark hair sticking out in disarray. But even dressed down, he was breathtakingly beautiful; not a single imperfection marred his flawless face and graceful, muscled body.

As Nicole approached, Rafe held out his arms and grinned. "Jump. I'll catch you."

Without hesitation, she did.

And he laughed out loud as he caught her. "You're my lovely wild thing, aren't you?"

She grinned from up close. "You make it supergratifying, Contini."

He dipped his head and brushed a kiss down her nose. "You are so awesome." Then he dragged in a breath and got his shit together before he went off the rails about how awesome she was and made everything more complicated. "We have to get out of here soon. That okay with you?" He smiled. "You understand only one answer is allowed."

"Where?"

"Geneva. Ganz has to lock down the software at corporate. Better safe than sorry, he says. Although he's been building barricades in triplicate this morning, closing even the most insignificant access points in our systems. He's headed them off at the pass." Rafe held up crossed fingers. "So far."

"Good." She smiled. "So take me and my new wardrobe anywhere. Thanks, by the way. The gifts were outrageously too much, but beautiful. You shouldn't have done it, of course. I kinda mean it. Even though I love everything."

"I'm glad." He ran a fingertip down the front of her dress, lingering briefly over one nipple. "You look nice. Umm... that feels nice." He grinned. "Do I have to get through panties or have you left me easy access?"

"You're not getting through anything with a room full of people watching."

"They're busy. They won't even notice if you don't scream."

She tensed. "Don't you dare."

He grinned. "You can't say that to me. Seriously, I take it personally."

She tried to swing her legs onto the floor.

His hand came out, clamped on her legs, and pulled her back. "Now, panties or not? Yes or no?"

"Yes. New ones. Expensive ones. Ones you better not tear."

"Then I'll slip in from the side."

"You'll do no such thing. I *will* scream if you so much as touch me—"

"Here?" he whispered, brushing her clit every so lightly.

She stifled a gasp.

"What about here?" He added a finger and slid both digits inside palm deep.

She began to tremble. "Please, Rafe." She swallowed hard. "Don't, oh God, don't do that," she breathed, flame-hot desire swelling through her senses.

"Just a little orgasm. I'll turn you so your back's to the men. Better?" he murmured, stroking gently, running his fingertips over the soft cushion of her G-spot, sliding up and down her aching flesh, easing in a third finger with a casual push.

Better was a relative word: sexually yes; scarily no, with potential exposure imminent. But she felt herself turn liquid inside, melt around his fingers, and like a coward, she shut her eyes. Like an addict, she gave in to the haze of lust beginning to engulf her. And when he whispered, "God, you're beautiful, tiger. Smoking hot, tight, slippery wet," she forgot where they were or didn't care where they were, and pressed into his hand with enough force to let him know she was eager, impatient as always when he touched her.

She started to quiver as his penetration deepened, softly moaned as he shifted into the exquisitely delicate, perfectly placed, lightly teasing strokes that had effectively turned her into a nymphomaniac in less than a day. Not that she was interested in any kind of therapy right now. Not that she was actually capable of logical thinking as her delirium mounted, and the aching pressure racheted up. "Are you okay?" he whispered just before he pressed his fingers in so deep she could only nod as carnal frenzy melted her brain.

But short moments later, she squirmed faintly against this hand, asking for more. "Good to go?" he murmured, smiling, knowing that artless eagerness, liking her uninhibited desire. Recognizing that he was on the clock too, with a roomful of techs in view. Quickly covering her mouth with his, he caressed her, testing the limits of her sleek, honeyed warmth until she was panting, barely breathing—his fingers and thumb flexing lightly, then harder, then with a subtle, tactile, targeted perfection guaranteed to make her scream.

Like that.

He swallowed her frantic sound as she convulsed around his fingers and glanced up under his lashes to see whether they had an audience. Just Ganz, who smiled, gave him a finger gun salute, and turned back to the tech huddled over his computer.

Rafe kissed her gently while she purred under his mouth and slowly returned to the world.

"I hate you," she murmured when she finally opened her eyes.

"Yeah, I could tell. Sadly, I'm going to have to wait for you to pay me back."

She stared at him for a moment before she winked. "Are you going to get off in public too?"

He gave her a lopsided grin. "Whatever turns you on, babe."

She rolled her eyes. "You're incorrigible. You know that, right?"

"Just trying to keep up with you, pussycat." He smiled and gently withdrew his fingers. "And you said you didn't want to come. Liar."

"Don't look so smug. You're good, okay? I turn into a wet mess of goo whenever you touch me."

"That is so hot, tiger. Better than anything, I kid you not." He glanced up when Ganz cleared his throat. "Looks like duty calls. Want something to eat? Henny can bring something up for you."

"Have you eaten?"

"Not yet." He pointed at a phone with about thirty buttons. "Call him. The one marked kitchen gets you there. Order anything. I don't care." He lifted her to her feet, gave her ass a little pat, then rose from the sofa. "I'll be over talking to Ganz. Feel free to interrupt."

They left for Geneva shortly after breakfast.

A helicopter landed on a wide expanse of lawn and Rafe escorted Nicole out to the plane, Ganz and Simon following behind.

"We're flying to Nice, where a jet's waiting for us," Rafe explained. "Have you ever been to Geneva?" He spoke with casual courtesy, as if they weren't in a race against a dangerous, unscrupulous enemy. As if collateral damage wasn't a possibility. As if his security wasn't on high alert with all hands on deck.

"No. You live there, right?"

"Part of the year. Depends on business. I travel a lot. Here we go. Watch your head getting in." He handed her up the small ramp into the 'copter. "Hi, Davey. Good weather for flying. Did you talk to Carlos?"

"Yeah. He's going to call when he's ready."

"Good. The usual precautions."

"We're on it, boss. Everyone buckle in. This won't take long."

TWENTY

Geneva was a thirty-minute flight from Nice in a private jet; no lines, no waiting to take off, only smiles and bows and "Welcome aboard, sir, whenever you're ready." Arriving in Geneva was equally convenient. Two cars were waiting for them on the tarmac.

"Ganz is going directly to our tech center," Rafe said, helping Nicole into the backseat of another armored black Mercedes. "I thought we'd stop by my flat first. You might prefer staying there rather than sitting around watching everyone punch keyboards."

"Where are you going to be?" Rafe hadn't changed from his shorts and T-shirt and hadn't bothered to put on shoes. "Just asking." She waggled her finger at his attire. "Dressed like that."

He grinned. "I'll fit right in with my tech crew. If their mothers or wives don't dress them, they're in trouble. I'll have to stay there until Ganz is satisfied everything's secure. Thanks, Simon." As the door was shut behind him, he turned to Nicole. "It might be hours, maybe days." He didn't say the longest DDoS attack Ganz had seen was twenty-eight days. "You'd be more comfortable at my flat. But your call." He smiled. "I wouldn't presume to tell you what to do."

She slid back in the corner of the seat and blew him a

kiss. "Smart fellow. I'll think about it. How far is your flat from the tech center?"

"It's close. A few blocks. They're both in Old Town."

"I could walk back then if I get tired of hanging around."

"I'll have Simon bring you back."

There was something guarded in his voice. "You don't want me to walk?"

He paused a fraction of a second, debating how to answer, how much or how little to tell her. He finally just said, "I'd rather you didn't."

"Is it dangerous? My uncle travels with security. I'm aware of the hazards of wealth."

"It's not just wealth. The country attacking our systems specializes in theft of technology, proprietary information, not to mention other less benign areas of attack." *Like assassinating Ganz's father.* "They're dangerous. If you want to walk, we'll find you somewhere else to walk."

"With security."

He nodded. "They'll stay out of sight if you prefer."

She took a deep breath; she didn't know the full extent of Dominic's security but apparently Rafe's was more than just Simon and the club bouncers. "How much security do you have?"

"A lot," he said, hoping she wouldn't ask for specifics, because he'd have to lie. "Especially now with Ganz here." Rafe's eyebrows arched upward briefly. "He has powerful enemies. I'm sorry this is all unfolding now. I should probably send you home"—he sighed—"but selfishly, I'd rather not. If you'd like to leave though, I'll see that you get back to Monaco, home, to Ibiza, wherever you like. I don't want you to stay if you're frightened." He had the resources, organization, and manpower to protect Nicole. She wouldn't come to harm, but he didn't want her living in fear while she was with him.

"You travel in armored cars for more than just these hackers, right?"

Rafe glanced out the window at the passing cityscape, a French-speaking, international city, the most expensive city in an expensive country, his home. "My father was the world's biggest asshole," he said mildly, as though speaking with a cool reasonableness could erase the abomination that was the man. With a shrug of dismissal, he turned back to Nicole. "I've inherited a number of his enemies. People who get fucked over hold grudges—no surprise. I ignore them as much as I can, but..." His voice trailed off. "Christ. I really should send you home."

"Relax. I'm not going anywhere. You have security. What can go wrong?"

He laughed. "About a thousand things. But I'll take care of you. I can do that. Thanks for staying. I would have found it hard to let you go."

"Speaking of hard..." She grinned.

Rafe shook his head, a small, almost infinitesimal, movement. "Can't. I need a one-track mind until Ganz has everything under control. And with you lounging in my backseat looking like my favorite wet dream it's not going to be easy, so don't give me any shit."

She put up her hands. "Got it. No more teasing. I'll stay out of your way. I'll be fine. I'll read or something. "

Rafe softly exhaled, surprised that it mattered so much

that she was content, satisfied, *staying*. "I have a pretty decent library at my flat. You should be able to find something you like there."

"Then I'll just grab a couple books, put on some slacks, and come with you. If you don't mind."

"Not at all. Have you thought about going to school in Europe? Or here? Geneva has several English-speaking universities." *What the fuck? Where did that even come from?* His adrenaline spiked into the stratosphere.

"I wish I could, but I can't." Nicole smiled because the pulse in his temple was beating wildly. "You're safe."

He outwardly winced. "That transparent?"

She chuckled. "Like glass, dude."

Leaning across the seat, he lifted her into his arms and tucked her close against his body. "Screw it. Go to school here if you want. Seriously. I'm good." Then he bent his head and just before he kissed her, he whispered, "Happy anniversary."

When she came up for air, he was smiling.

"You forgot." His brows descended in feigned chagrin. "I'm crushed. Twenty-four hours, tiger." He smiled. "It's a major record for me."

She wasn't sure that was good news or bad news, but being with him was right up there with surfing, chocolate, and being first in line for the world's best sex, so fuck the future. "We'll celebrate once your problems are over," she said, grinning like someone who'd been given the keys to the city, the world, the universe. "I just happen to have a new flowery silk bustier I'm thinking you might find attractive."

"You don't say," he said softly. "Looks like I'm going to have to offer Ganz some serious incentive to shut this down in a hurry."

"Did I mention the spike heels with sparkly straps twining up my ankles?"

He groaned. "Maybe prayer would work against computer attacks."

"You on your knees or me?"

Taking her chin in his fingers, he met the twinkle in her eyes with a hard stare. "You're going to get a goddamn spanking if you don't stop. I can take only so much."

Tension radiated off him in waves. "Lord, I'm being an idiot when your company is dealing with a cyberwar," she said with genuine remorse. "Not another word from me. I'll just sit in a corner and quietly read, okay?"

His fingers slid away and his hand dropped. "All I want to do is fuck you and I can't right now." He sighed, sexual repression a novelty in his life. "Later, we'll make up for lost time, okay?"

His flat turned out to be a four-story seventeenth-century building on the hill near the cathedral—smaller than the Monaco property but still impressive. They entered through security gates built into a high wall that shielded the lower levels of the house from the street. The gates closed automatically behind the car and after driving across a cobblestone courtyard, Simon brought the car to a stop before the main entrance.

"Nice flat slash palace," Nicole said drily, as they walked up to double doors that were being opened by two men in dark suits who looked as though they knew how to handle a weapon or two. Even a shoulder-fired missile wouldn't be a stretch; they were big.

"One of the dukes of Savoy built the house for his mistress," Rafe explained. "It's not massively grand, that's why I like it. Hey, guys, everyone fine?"

"Couldn't be better," the taller of the two men answered.

"I'd like you to meet Nicole Parrish. Nicole, Meyer, Rick, they help everything run smoothly here. We won't be long. Simon's driving us to the tech center as soon as Nicole changes and finds a book. Did the luggage get here yet?"

"An hour ago. It's in your suite."

Nicole shot Rafe a look and said under her breath, "My clothes got here before me? What if I'd said no to Geneva?"

"I would have sent them back."

"Liar."

He held her gaze. "You're wrong." Then he waved toward a monumental black marble staircase. "This way. Ganz is waiting."

She felt leveled by his calm, cool look. Chiding herself for pettiness in the midst of his challenges, she took his hand and whispered, "I'm sorry."

He turned to smile at her. "Once you get to know me better, you'll find that I generally mean what I say." His grin widened. "Not that omission hasn't been useful on occasion, but not so much with you, pussycat. I don't feel the need. So if you want to know something, just ask, I'll tell you. Same page now?"

She nodded, a dozen questions immediately racing into her brain as they ascended the grand staircase. But this was hardly the time to begin an inquisition, when his company was in peril. She could be a mature adult. She could stifle her curiosity. Well, maybe some of it. "Do you live here alone?"

He gave her a startled glance.

"I meant do your mother and stepdad live here too. It's a really big place for just one person."

"Ah. No, just me. My mother has a place on the lake a few miles outside the city. I prefer this old part of town." He didn't say that memories of his father haunted the house on the lake, or, more aptly, cursed it. "To the right here. My suite's at the end of the hall."

She didn't know if he was cutting off further inquiry or simply giving directions, but he'd sounded slightly distant, so she took the hint. Not that he didn't have a lot on his mind—important, grave concerns. This wasn't the time to be chatty.

His suite had stupendous views of the city and lake, the period furniture conforming to the date of the building with a few modern exceptions, like a long comfortable sofa and chairs in the sitting room and a wall of TV screens in the bedroom opposite the palace-size four-poster bed hung with cream silk bed curtains. The half dozen skateboards stacked in one corner were an anomaly in the splendor of the room.

She pointed. "Obviously, you skateboard."

"Occasionally. Basil and I used to compete when we were younger, thirteen, fourteen. Won a few trophies. Then I grew another seven inches." He shrugged. "My size became a disadvantage. Your things should be in my dressing room," he added.

She got the message, no matter the softness of his tone; he was in a hurry.

Leading her through the bedroom to his dressing room, he indicated a bank of mirrored doors to their left. "Over there, I'm guessing. I have a few calls to make, so I'll be in the sitting room. Take your time."

He clearly didn't mean it, with the muscle twitching in his cheekbone. "It won't take me long," she said. "If you'd like to save time, pick out some books for me."

He flexed his fingers, then smiled. "Sorry, nerves. They're pounding our systems hard. But whether you or I select the books isn't make or break. You don't have to rush." With a quick smile, he turned and left.

She knew better, so she found the brilliant blue cashmere pants and hoodie and her own flip-flops and changed in record time. Quickly returning to the sitting room, she found Rafe standing at the window, speaking rapidly in French on his phone. He must have heard her come in, because he turned and ended his call.

His brows lifted. "No bra?"

She opened the hoodie. "T-shirt underneath. I figured if I was going to sleep in these, I might as well be comfortable. You could be there for a while you said."

He stared at her, his expression unreadable. "I want to lock you away for my eyes only. I've never felt that way before." He slowly exhaled. "Not exactly possible in this day and age, so"—his smile was tight—"I'm just going to have to warn off everyone."

"Jeez, don't embarrass me. If you go all caveman on me, I'll have to put you in your place, and neither one of us wants that right now." She shrugged. "So in the interests of workplace harmony and not weirding you out, why don't I go put on a bra."

"Hang on." His teeth closed on his bottom lip for a second, then he said, "I'm a big boy. I'll deal with it. You weird me out in every other way—what's one more? Come on, we'll find you some books." But he paused briefly halfway to the door, kicked a pair of Vans out from under a chair, and slipped them on. "When the tech room's in panic mode"—his brows flickered—"everyone's overcaffeinated, distracted, jittery, spilling crap. Now what do you like to read?"

His library was huge, with floor-to-ceiling books, some, Rafe casually mentioned, from Gutenberg's time. Sliding ladders gave access to the higher shelves and an ancient globe that looked like it had been hand-painted by monks before the discovery of America sat on a stand just inside the doorway. Comfortable leather chairs were scattered about the room and the large, elaborately carved desk located center stage was clearly medieval.

Wide-eyed, Nicole turned to Rafe. "This isn't pretty decent, this is like illustrious. You better just point me to the books that don't cost a fortune."

He smiled. "All the books are meant to be read. Take whatever you like. Some of the new ones are on those shelves to your right. There's a first edition of *Fanny Hill* in the cabinet by the window though, if you'd like to get off before I have time to join you."

She snorted. "As if I'm going to do that with a room full of IT people."

"I have a nice, cozy office."

"Ummm..."

"Exactly. Let me get it for you while you check out the more recent fiction."

"You're way too nice." She looked up at him and licked her bottom lip. "I'm beginning to get all starry-eyed and impatient about our anniversary."

He laughed. "I'll have to see if I can get away for an hour or so tonight and celebrate with you."

"Really, you mean it?" She felt like some screaming teenybopper fan being offered her pick of rock stars.

"Really," he said, very softly. "Unless the fucking world blows up. Even then, I'm thinking somehow I'll get to you."

TWENTY-ONE

The tech center was housed in an ancient building on a narrow, winding street that was filled with crowds of tourists on a Sunday in summer. The computer room on the main floor was manic with activity, although strangely quiet, everyone intent on their keyboards and screens, only an occasional command from Ganz breaking the silence.

Rafe took a few minutes to show Nicole his office, the cafeteria, the exercise room, the small walled garden in back, then gave her a quick kiss on the cheek, said, "Make yourself at home," and walked over to Ganz, who was standing in front of a bank of computer screens that had code running so fast it was practically a blur.

Nicole found herself a comfortable sofa in a corner of the large room and after watching the intensely focused diligence for a short time, she opened a novel that had gotten critical acclaim and began reading about an officer in the KGB shortly after World War II who was beginning to question his conscience and duty. It was well written, well documented, and so suspenseful that she didn't notice the time until her stomach began growling.

Glancing up, she saw that the sun had set and the sky was gray with rain clouds. Putting her book down, she stretched and surveyed the operations still in full swing, the energy levels undiminished, Rafe seemingly moored to the spot he'd been in when she'd begun reading. Although a number of coffee cups were on a nearby table along with a footed mirror for Ganz's drug of choice.

Whatever it took, she reflected. They might be up for hours more.

As if Rafe felt her presence in the midst of the chaos, he glanced over and smiled when she rose from the sofa. She made a spooning motion to her mouth and with a wave, left the room and made her way to the cafeteria.

Even though it was the weekend, three chefs and a full service crew were on hand to accommodate anyone's food tastes. Selecting some items from the chalkboard, Nicole dined well on fresh corn chowder, lake trout with almonds, and a delicate genoise layered with ganache. Everything was so delicious, she ate every bite, the rich food acting like a sleeping pill.

Rafe's office had a small bedroom and bath: perfect.

Detouring back into the computer room, she picked up her books, waved at Rafe, who'd watched her since she'd walked in, then, leaving the high-tension atmosphere, she moved down the hall to Rafe's office.

"You follow her like a hawk its prey. I've never seen you so captivated," Ganz murmured, as Rafe's attention returned to the monitors. "What makes her so special?"

"I just like her. You're on the offensive now," Rafe remarked, not about to discuss his feelings, not sure what they were in any event; he'd never had any practice apportioning meaning to his emotions. "Does that mean we're out of danger? I'm assuming so."

Taking the rebuff with good grace, Ganz nodded. "They can't touch us anymore. It's over for you."

"While their whole network is disintegrating like it's been bombed." Rafe stared at the screens, then at Ganz. "How the hell are you doing that?"

"Two moles. I have all the passwords, routing info, identifying IP addresses, and firewall settings. Every fucking one. And now that Contini Pharma is out of the line of fire, I'm going to crash their systems." He shot Rafe a grin. "Armageddon, baby. Watch them self-destruct."

"Fucking impressive."

"Yeah, well, congratulate me once I get my two friends out. I need one of your planes in Macao."

"You got it. When?"

"Soon. I couldn't plan ahead because I didn't know when and if they'd hit you, although it was more when than if, which is why I got my ass down to Monaco. But fucking walls have ears, so I couldn't talk about it. With major shit like this, you can't tell who's dependable. After the dust settles, my friends will initiate their exit plan. They have to get from Shanghai to Macao, no small feat. So it should be a day or two before I need your plane in Macao."

"I'll make a call right now to get things rolling. It might be useful to have a backup team to get your boys to the airport. Macao's pretty wide open if you look like a high roller. I'll send some men along who can play at the big boys' table; they'll be ready to escort your friends to the plane."

Ganz nodded. "The fallout will be huge, so thanks."

"Fuck, you saved my ass. I owe you." Rafe looked up from punching in a number on his cell. "You can explain the details once they're in the air. I'll just get the plane off the ground."

"I'm going to need your help after this extraction too. The man who ordered the hit on my father is next on my list."

Rafe had wanted to kill his father so many times, he considered Ganz fortunate to have had a father he loved. Dragging in a steadying breath as Ganz's filial devotion brought up the old brew of repressed memories he'd locked away, Rafe forcibly brushed aside all the tiny barbs of recall and replied, "No problem. Who's the target? Hang on, Davey, or wait, I'll call you back."

"He runs the unit I worked for. Name's Zou Yao."

Rafe shook his head. "Don't know him, not that I should. Do you have a plan? If not, Carlos can help you. Even if you do, Carlos can help. He can get people in or out, dead or alive, your pick."

"Zou has a wife and family in Shanghai he sees occasionally. He has a young mistress and child in Hong Kong he adores. They're my bait."

"Just bait, I hope." Rafe lifted one brow. "Unless the mistress is some operative herself."

"Uh-uh. They're catch and release."

"Good enough. Whatever you need, it's yours. Money, manpower, me at your side if you like. You saved the company. Your war is my war. I'm all in."

"Until my friends are out, Zou's on hold."

Rafe punched his phone again. "Hey, Davey, file a flight

plan for Macao. Leave tomorrow. More details on their way, okay?" Hanging up, Rafe said, "I'll give you Davey's number and you can fill him in on your end. I'll see that he has all the men he needs to see this through—Mandarin-speaking just to be safe. It's a long flight, there's plenty of time to massage the plan." He flipped his hand toward the monitors. "This is winding down, right? How much longer?"

"Four, five hours to make sure everything's clean. I don't need you though. Take your sweetheart home."

"I can stay if you want. I told her it might be a while."

"Nah. Go. Although you can come and celebrate with me once the Macao venture is complete. I told Madeline I'd meet her in Paris as soon as I can get away. A couple nights at the Chandelier Club, and I'll be primed to go after Zou."

Rafe frowned. "I don't know. Nicole isn't really hard core. She might freak out at a sex club."

"Ask her."

"If she says no, I'm out."

"A grand says she won't."

Rafe shrugged. "I'm not betting. Either way, it's her call."

"As soon as I'm done here, I'll let Davey know what I need from your team in Macao. You're using the phone I gave you?"

"Why wouldn't I? Everything's encrypted. Call me."

A few minutes later, Rafe stood in the doorway of his office bedroom, a smile on his face. "So how's Fanny Hill getting along?"

"She's being rogered by a lovely young officer. I don't suppose you want to get a uniform from somewhere."

He smiled. "I know something even better to amuse you." He held out his hand. "Let's go home."

"Seriously? Home?"

"Yup. Simon's waiting downstairs."

She was already scrambling off the bed. "Wonderful, great, lovely, and every other word that signifies gratitude. I missed you."

"I missed you like crazy, but we're finally out of danger. Leave the books. Someone will bring them back later. Come on, it's our anniversary. I need to feel your body next to mine."

But Rafe was visibly wired when they got back to his house. While Nicole undressed, he restlessly paced, his gaze focused somewhere off in space; twice he started to speak, then changed his mind. Finally coming to a stop by the window, he stared out blankly at the lights of the city, plagued by long-suppressed memories of his father.

Normally, those nocuous memories were buried deep, but perhaps exhaustion was a factor, or too many hours of stress, maybe having to fend off the enemy Maso had initially provoked with his usual arrogant stupidity was reason enough. But all the disturbing ambiguities Rafe kept locked away were pouring out.

It wasn't just the heavy-handed and erratic discipline for offenses Rafe hadn't actually committed that flooded him. The memories of being pushed into sex too young, too hard, too fast, always made him cringe, as did the image of his leering father overtly or covertly in the background. He could feel it all washing over him again: the embarrassment, the discomfort, the awkwardness and baffling feelings.

He'd planned his retaliation for months.

A school assignment in Tokyo he'd told his father; Basil and Henny had the same class project. His father never asked what it was; education wasn't a significant concern for him. He saw boarding school as an opportunity to meet the right people—meaning other rich people—and make the necessary contacts that would be helpful later in life.

Rafe had researched tattoo artists and found a man renowned for traditional work. He'd made arrangements with the artist, then for lodging and possible medical care; he'd learned young to prepare for the unexpected. No surprise with a father like his. He'd discussed the design with the tattoo artist, the necessary time to complete it, whether the elderly man was willing to commit to the long hours. He couldn't be absent from school for more than a week.

The Hokusai tattoo had been deliberately provocative and ultimately successful in breaking him free of his father's noisome ideas of a youth's education. For purely personal reasons, his father detested all things Japanese. A business deal had gone bad, his opponent at the helm of the other company a woman who'd taken a huge sum of money from him and taunted him mercilessly in her victory. Maso had issues with women, huge issues. Deep-seated, Freudian issues.

As the proverbial icing on the cake of his liberation, one of the few signed Hokusai woodcuts of *The Great*

Wave figured largely in his father's botched deal; a bonus, as it were, to the victor. An empowering goad for Rafe.

With the first glimpse of his newly inked dick, paternal oversight disappeared from his sex life. Although, in a way, it was a Pyrrhic victory; Rafe had already been ruined, wounded, scarred, call it what you will, and his father knew it. For that smug conceit he'd wanted to kill Maso more times than he could remember.

At base though, beyond murderous urges, what screwed with his head even more was the fact that he'd learned what he'd learned and ultimately enjoyed knowing what he knew. For that schizoid mind fuck, he hated his father most.

Nicole glanced over her shoulder as she climbed into bed. "Hey, get your clothes off," she said. "You're holding up the show."

Rafe swung around, blinked, then dragged himself back into the world. "Give me a minute. I haven't come down from everything yet. I'm edgy and pissed, mostly for nearly being destroyed by the same assholes who've tried it a dozen times before. Can I tie you up? You'll like it."

"I beg your pardon?" The shift in subject was so abrupt she wondered if she'd misheard.

"I said, can I tie you up?"

She wrinkled her nose. "I was afraid that's what you said."

"You'll like it," he said again, matter-of-factly.

"Ummm—I don't think so."

"How do you know if you don't try it? I can almost guarantee you will," he said, like he'd say "Nice day if it doesn't rain."

"What if I don't?"

Rafe shrugged. "Trust me. I know you will." He didn't say that domination was one of his coping mechanisms, that he used it to normalize a discordant world, that he'd been encouraged in his taste. That there wasn't a woman who hadn't been sexually gratified when he'd untied her.

After a long indecisive pause, Nicole decided there was only one way to find out. "Okay," she said.

He didn't realize he'd been holding his breath, that it mattered she allowed this. "I'll be right back."

His gaze had been so vague, she felt a small frisson of uncertainty. When he walked back in from the dressing room, carrying the Japanese box of rope, she didn't feel any better when she saw that his mouth was drawn tight. "Hey, earth to Rafe. You're scaring me."

He looked up and shook his head. "Sorry, it's feels like I've been lost in a maze for most of the day with a deadly Minotaur breathing down my neck. Ganz is fucking good but it still wasn't a piece of cake. Annihilation was a real possibility." No way was he bringing up his psycho father.

"I understand." She smiled. "Just so you know who I am."

"Of course. You're my sweet pussycat." He set the box on the bed, leaned over, and gently kissed her. "I'm here. I'm glad you're here. I'm happy, okay?"

"Okay." She wiggled her fingers in the direction of the box. "But if I say stop you have to."

"Not a problem."

He spoke so casually, it was unnerving—like maybe he wouldn't stop, or he knew she'd enjoy it so much she wouldn't ask him to stop, or that he was so good at this every woman he'd ever tied up adored him for it. "Tell me you haven't done this before." Even knowing she was being completely irrational, she wanted the fiction. "Lie if necessary."

"Never. I told you before we went to the club that this was my first shipment of rope."

"Jeez, you're a good liar."

He smiled. "Thank you. We try. Now give me your hand," he said, unreeling a sweep of rope with a jerk of his wrist.

Helping her down from the bed, he took her by the shoulders, his slender fingers sliding over her warm skin, the slope of her upper arm, and for a second a rush of helplessness blew through Nicole's senses.

"You're safe," Rafe murmured, as if he knew. Pulling her back into his body with a one-armed hug, he gently stroked her throat. "Okay?"

She nodded.

He waited while she sighed; he didn't move.

"The thing is... you know the drill"—she took a small breath—"and I don't."

His fingers on her throat soothed her fluttering pulse. "No drill, pussycat. Just you and me feeling good."

She sighed again, then turned her head, her blue eyes laser bright. "Okay, I'm on board. Swear to God," she added because he was watching her from under his lashes.

He couldn't hide his grin. "Could we leave God out of this?"

"Fuck you." But she was grinning too.

"All in good time," he said with a wink, then dropped his arm, rested the center of the rope in his right hand, and smoothly folded it in two.

"The rope smells nice—like freshly mowed lawns." Looking over her shoulder again, her smile froze on her face, a prickle rose at the back of her neck. Lidded jungle-cat eyes were staring at her. "Rafe?"

Nothing, not a blink.

She half twisted around, her heart drumming. "Hey." A sharper tone. "Rafe!"

She got his attention. "Sorry." Smooth and easy, a lazy smile. "Still back in the tech room," he lied, sending all the wild shit back into the seething dark. A wry smile this time. "I didn't mean to scare you."

"Just checking that you're not in outer space."

"No way." Dipping his head, he brushed her cheek with a kiss. "I know where I am and there's nowhere else I'd rather be." He held up the rope, raised an eyebrow. "Ready?"

"As ever."

A wicked grin. "Good enough for me."

Taking her wrists, he swung her back around, swiftly bound her hands behind her, and with a quick, controlled movement raised her arms upward just enough so she could feel the tension in her muscles.

A gasp, then a small melting sigh as a completely new sensation coiled deep inside her and her sex began to throb and swell.

A familiar, recognizable sound of desire that struck a deep psychic chord. A physical one as well; his erection surged in response. Loosening the rope so her fingers were at the right level, he leaned into her, pressing his rigid dick against her hand. "You let me know when you want this." His voice was soft, mildly taunting.

Yet dominant male in the husky undertones, the blunt directive unequivocal, as though the decision was completely his. And a strange rush of longing swept through her at his assumption of power, the feverish sensation bone deep, delicious, hot, and impatient. She quivered, nodded.

"Talk," he said, a warning note in his voice.

"I want it, you, everything, please," she said, swiftly because the edge in his voice was raw, and if she wanted him, he had expectations. The rope around her wrists was only the beginning.

"I can smell your pussy," he murmured, ignoring her reply. "And your nipples are already stiff and hard." His voice dropped in volume, turned into a whisper. "You have no patience. We have to fix that."

His quiet assurance was both a lush invitation to play and annoyingly confident. But her body was purring and pulsing in a mindless, out-of-control, sex-addicted rhythm, so her voice shook a little when she said, "Speaking of patience, what's the deal with your rock-hard dick?"

"Not your problem," he said, without glancing up from adjusting the rope on her wrists. "I'm your problem."

She tried to turn and protest, but he held her firmly, jerking the ropes on her wrists higher, and her objection died in a sharp inhalation as a fiery flash of lust exploded in her sex, blazed through her senses, and laid out the welcome mat between her legs in hot, messy wetness.

His nostrils flared at the distinctive scent of arousal. "You're going to give every male within a mile a hard-on. I'll have to make sure you're locked up tight."

She barely heard him because every inch of her skin felt as though it was bathed in warm sunshine, her sex tingled and glowed, sweet desire enfolded her in bliss. "No," she murmured, but she was half smiling, in the grip of inexplicable passions so intense she was beyond rational thought, automatically raising her arms to his nudges as he quickly wrapped the silky, sweet-smelling hemp under and over her breasts, his hands moving smoothly in tandem. As the pressure on her breasts increased, she opened her mouth to complain, but Rafe gently massaged her nipples and she shut her eyes and purred instead.

And missed his satisfied smile.

While she was floating in her soft lustful haze, Rafe checked the underarm hitch with a finger between the rope and skin, cinched the line, then slid two perfectly placed half-hitches under her cleavage. Smoothly turning her, he wound the ropes in quick, sure movements, before standing back and cupping the underside of each tightly bound, jutting breast. Slowly raising his hands, he watched her arch her back to offset the pressure, then, deliberately continuing the upward motion, he forced her up on her toes.

"Feel that?" he whispered, his fingers sinking into her soft flesh, holding her balanced on the balls of her feet.

"God, yes," she said so softly, the sound scarcely moved the air.

Her cheeks were hotly flushed, her constricted breasts mounded high in their rope harness, her nipples swollen and taut, her desire so flagrant, pearly moisture was trickling down her thighs.

Down boy, he warned his dick.

This wasn't about a fast fuck.

This was about her submission.

And his power.

As he slowly lowered her back on her feet, she panted, "Please, I can't wait. I need you now."

"Not yet."

Her eyes flew open, stormy with frustration. "When?"

He smiled down at her. "When I'm ready."

Her eyes narrowed; she tilted her head back. "Fuck you, then." Her voice was clear and cool, all entitlement and attitude. "Untie me."

He grinned. "Does that usually work?"

"Always," she snapped, her resentment back full force. "Not that I'm usually"—she tried to wiggle her shoulders—"in this goddamn predicament."

"Glad to hear it." It surprised him, how much it pleased him. "And you'll like it when I finally let you come, pussycat, you really will."

"What I'd like is your dick inside me." Smooth as butter, a smile, trying another angle.

A flicker of amusement in his eyes. "I'm working on that."

"God, you piss me off," she said through gritted teeth, domination all well and good up to a point. But she wanted to come now. "You said you'd stop if I asked. Consider yourself asked."

"I didn't say I'd stop. I said, no problem. And it won't be."

"It is. Already. A huge. Problem." Enough outrage in each carefully pronounced word to shrivel most men's balls.

A relaxed half smile. "Jesus, you're so damned cute. Always in charge." He dipped his head, so his eyes were only inches from hers. "Now, I've got a little advice for you. Don't fucking move or you'll never come." His hooded gaze watched her for a moment—fixed and cool—and when she looked away, he said, smooth as silk, "There's a good girl," and reached for more rope.

She breathed in his unlimited power, the deep complications behind the cool gaze, the edge of trouble beneath the beauty, and rather than fear, she felt the white fire of arousal blaze higher, felt a flood of desire drench her sex, felt both a sweeping embarrassment and leaping pleasure.

She could call herself every kind of idiot for wanting him so desperately, but it didn't change the brightness of her need; she wanted his inked dick deep inside her.

Urgently.

Intent on his own rough desires rising like ghosts from his past, Rafe tied a double line rope in a knot at her cleavage, measured out three overhand knots, and slid one under Nicole's ribs, another on her silky pubic curls, the third on her clit hood, held it gently in place, then less gently, and watched Nicole shudder and drift off in a soft, pale daze.

"Look at me." His finger on the clit knot pressed a little harder, and, ignoring her tiny shriek, he said more sharply, "Look at me or I won't let you come."

She sucked in a fast breath that burned off the daze, her blue eyes so hot he didn't bother to hide his grin. "See. You're learning."

"I'm going to kill you." She was pissed to the bone.

He laughed. "Take a number. Now pay attention. It gets better." Leaning close, he slid the rope between her legs, spread her pussy open with the pressure, then ran the double rope up her back and fastened it to her wrists with a quick release tie.

He stood for a moment, gave his handiwork a swift up and down scan, then walked to the center of the bedroom and turned. "Come here," he said. Beckoned. A flutter of his fingers. Waited.

She didn't move.

He reached up, pulled his T-shirt over his head, shook his hair back in place, unzipped his shorts, stripped them off with his boxers, and kicked his clothes out of the way. Gave her a big friendly smile.

Under the pressure of the strategically placed knot, her clit was throbbing in a hard steady rhythm, her pussy, spread wide by the dual ropes, was drenching the soft hemp, turning it dark, and her breasts were cinched so tightly and wrenched so high she could feel every beat of her heart in the compressed flesh. She was certifiably horny and ready to fuck any dick except the bastard's smiling at her. She counted to ten, then twenty, trying to talk herself out of being a horn dog with relevant images of icy glaciers or slimy worms or smug pricks who didn't deserve to win this round or any round.

Rafe waited calmly, his huge painted dick stretched waist high, dictating the terms.

"I hate you," she hissed.

"How much?" He smiled. "Remember that? I do."

"And you're still here."

His hands spread out for a second before he slid his fingers down his dick. "As you see." A tiny nod. "We're waiting."

She took a shaky breath, a second one, then moved.

He watched her intently. Smiled when she finally reached him. Gently gripped her hard, taut nipples between his thumbs and index fingers and slowly tugged on them until she flinched. Then he took her face in his hands, raised her head until their eyes met, gave her cheeks a gentle pat, and said, "Down on your knees."

A quick in-breath through her nose. "No."

"I'm not going to hurt you. I'm going to make you feel good."

A small silence.

Then a faint shift of her shoulder, a louder, "No."

He flicked his finger at her. "Then you're going to need some help getting out of that."

"I'll manage. Scissors or a knife should do it."

"Where exactly would you be getting those?"

"In your dressing room—the scissors at least."

He lifted a brow. "Going through me, then?"

"You *wouldn't*!"

"Of course I would. Now, can we stop arguing? Get down on your knees."

"Never," she said flatly.

His eyes closed for a second, then opened again. "Fucking drama queen." Spinning her around, he grabbed a loop of rope in the middle of her back, gave her a gentle shove, and as she lost her balance, set her down softly on her knees. With a quick nudge of his feet, he spread her legs, held her with one hand, and with the other, bound her lower legs loosely to her thighs.

Leaving her helpless.

Another nudge and she'd be resting on her shoulders, her ass up, her sex spread wide.

He circled her, his gaze shuttered, weighing his options, the thousand skulking shadows flitting through his brain needing to be dealt with. Or he could save the hassle and deal with them later. Or not at all. Deciding on the latter, he came to a stop in front of her, squatted in a smooth flex of his quads so she was level with his face, and gave her a small, private smile. "How's it going so far?"

"You being a prick, you mean? It's working."

He stared at her. After a moment, he said, "I can keep you tied up."

"Fuck if you can." Her gaze threw off sparks like fireworks.

A split-second pause, then an easy smile. "I can do anything I want with you."

"No you can't." Scorn rang through her voice. "You know the word *obstinate* right?"

He went utterly still for a second, then surged to his feet, spun around, and walked out of the bedroom before he did something he'd regret. He didn't slam the door. He shut it softly. There was a quiet finality in the sound.

Shit. Her and her big mouth. What if he didn't come back? Where the hell had she left her phone? Better yet, how could she move? If Rafe Contini wasn't one of those masters of the universe who practically owned the world, she might not have been so worried. But he'd been pissed when he'd left.

Jesus, how did it feel to starve to death? Although she'd die of thirst first. What if he just left Geneva like he'd planned? No one would find her for God knows how long.

Although, realistically, she wouldn't die of hunger or thirst, because if her mother didn't hear from her every day, her mom would call Dominic. And he'd find her no matter where she was, even if she was at one of those remote Greek island monasteries where you needed to be hauled up the sheer cliff in a basket.

While Nicole was consoling herself that she wouldn't die alone or at all, Rafe was sprawled on the sofa in the room next door, thinking he should pour himself a drink, or better yet, empty a whole fucking bottle. He couldn't remember when he'd been so angry. Probably not since his old man died. Maso was about the only person who could send him into a rage; he was a fucking master at that. Rafe suddenly laughed. He wasn't so sure Nicole couldn't have given his old man a run for his money.

Little bitch. Sweet as candy bitch unfortunately—especially her lush pussy. *Christ Almighty,* he wanted his dick in her twenty-four/seven.

Scary as hell, that. Particularly for someone who'd always counted the minutes until he could send a woman home once the fucking was over.

Not that he'd turned into a saint since meeting Nicole, nor was he likely to reform any time soon. So the question remained: How was he going to negotiate the kind of fuck he wanted with his sweet-assed bitch?

She couldn't be bought off. A serious deterrent.

He could apologize, but that didn't mean she'd necessarily forgive him or, more to the point, play the game he wanted.

Did she have a favorite charity? He laughed out loud at that; a generous donation for a Japanese bondage fuck? That didn't happen every day.

With rapidly diminishing options, he decided to grovel—go into the trackless terrain beyond polite apology in an attempt to get his ass out of this sling. And what the hell, as long as he got what he wanted, who ever said sincerity was a requirement when it came to fucking? He knew the answer to that one and was still smiling when he entered the bedroom.

"It's about time," Nicole said, in a cooler tone of voice; she, too, had had time to reconsider her options. "I thought I was going to die in here."

"Jesus, tiger, it's only been six minutes. You barely had time to run out of swear words."

"I had time."

"Then you don't know very many." He sat down on the carpet, a few inches in front of her, crossing his legs in an easy yoga position.

"Where did you learn that?"

"What?"

"Yoga. My mother does yoga. I've tried. It hurts."

He didn't want the conversation to go off on a tangent, so he said, politely, "I forget. But I'd like to apologize. I was rude." At her lifted brows, he added, "Very rude, boorish and ill-bred, totally obnoxious. I'm sorry. And if there's anything I can do to atone for it, just let me know."

"Untie me."

"Besides that."

She laughed. "I knew that was coming."

Her laughter encouraged him. "You'll like it, pussycat. Guaranteed."

"You will too."

"Fucking A."

"Not because you've ever done it before."

"God, no." A teasing flash in his eyes, golden sunbeams. "I just have a good imagination."

"Okay, then, sure—why not?"

A hint of suspicion in his glance. "That's it?"

"I figured I was going to die of thirst. This can't be worse. And my knees are going to get sore eventually, so—"

"Is that my cue to hurry?" A real smile now, all shine and dazzle.

"I do like a clever man."

"Not because you've ever known one before," he said, paraphrasing her earlier comment.

"God, no," she mimicked. She winked. "Imagination. Not that you need any more flattery, but these ropes are beaucoup hot on all my hot spots. And a little satisfaction wouldn't go amiss."

A sardonic slant to his eyes. "Amiss?"

"You got a problem with that word?"

"Christ, no, I love that word, use it all the time. Especially when I'm golfing."

"Once my hands are free, Contini..."

"Not now, tiger. Just shut your eyes," he said, very softly, "and do what you're told."

She heard him move, felt him come up behind her, and sucked in a breath when he leaned over and his hands closed over her breasts.

"Whose tits are these?" he whispered, stretching her nipples.

She whimpered at the sharp sting, a second later felt the shimmering aftershock flare through her nipples, then slide downward like molten fire to her sex.

He squeezed harder. "Answer me."

"Yours, yours, they're yours." The words glossy, spinning, urgent.

"What's mine?" His fingers opened, spread wide over her breasts, closed like vises on her soft flesh. "Tell me."

"My boobs, nipples, everything," she said, breathless, shaking.

"No one else touches them. I'll need your promise."

"No one, I swear." She was struggling to find breath to speak, her spine rigid with the torment of her vaulting need. "Only you."

Fuck, his hard-on spiked six inches with that breathless promise. And if he'd been raised normally, he would have assuaged her impatient desires. But that pussy spread open for him, the helpless woman tightly bound, the flashbacks and hot libidinous urges flooding his body had never been house-trained. They were selfish, dangerous, intensely predatory; the kind that should be locked away.

Quickly releasing her bound calves, he raised her to her

feet. "Do you mind sitting?" he asked, deliberately polite, reminding himself that if any woman mattered, she did. *So don't go over the fucking line.*

Dr. Jekyll and Mr. Hyde, Nicole thought, but Rafe was smiling and she wasn't really afraid of him despite the rumors. "I'd like that," she said.

He laughed softly. "First date?"

"Not like any of mine." She grinned. "If you've noticed, I'm being very careful not to move."

"Because of these?" He touched the clit knot and pussy ropes, watched with pleasure as she drenched his fingers on cue.

"Please, Rafe." Her breath caught in her throat. "I'm asking nicely."

"It'll be better if you wait." He exerted a delicate pressure. "Understand?"

"No." Her voice was just a wisp of sound, the orgasmic momentum building.

He saw it too and, turning her around, quickly released the tie at her wrists, shifting the dynamic. Taking her hand, he drew her to one of two green, cut velvet upholstered chairs in a window enclosure. "Sit, relax. We'll talk about it."

After helping her into the deep, cushioned chair, he knelt in front of her, smiled. "Are you warm enough? I could turn the heat up if you like." Without waiting for an answer, he lifted her feet up on the chair seat, eased her legs open, and effectively redirected her attention. Seconds later, her wrists were loosely bound to the sides of her ankles, and a few quick loops of rope over her thighs held her legs open.

He looked up. “Comfortable?”

Her smile was half dreamy, the ropes over her sex tighter with her thighs spread wide. “This your idea of conversation?”

He shrugged, his motivations beyond the boundaries of polite conversation. “Does anything hurt? Look at me, tiger.” She was beginning to drift away with the pussy ropes doing their work. “Does anything hurt?”

She shook her head.

“Hey.” He cupped his ear.

“No,” she said, like she was listening to a faraway song, her gaze blank.

“Sure?” He touched her slippery pink flesh, open like a rose, heard her soft moan. “Answer me.”

There was something unsettling in his voice that gained her attention.

“I asked you if you’re sure nothing hurts?”

She didn’t notice the small wolf-curl to his lip, although it might have been too late even if she had noticed. “Yes, I’m sure. But I want to come. Please, Rafe.”

He almost relented when she uttered his name in such a soft, pleading tone. That he even considered it was testament to her unaccountable appeal. But old habits were, in his case, dearly bought and deeply entrenched. “Soon, pussycat. I promise.” He rose to his feet, took note of the sudden alarm in her eyes and slid a fingertip along one of her arched brows. “Relax. I’m not leaving you. I’m just going in the dressing room. I’ll be right back.”

When he walked back in, her smile lit up the room.

“You said you had one.” He held up her purple travel vibrator. “Should we give it a try?” He switched it on.

Her sex rippled violently at the familiar buzzing sound; she uttered a low moan of expectation that turned into a whispered purr. "You're such a sweetheart."

He slid the vibrator over her clit, teased her slick pussy with a lazy sweep of the tip, pressed it in fractionally and held it in place for a slow ten count before withdrawing it. Ignoring her groan of frustration, he moved it upward, slipping the sleek buzzing device over her stomach, higher still, to the knot over her ribs. Carefully easing the vibrator under the knot, he glanced up to fury in her eyes. Smiled. "I've never been called a sweetheart before."

"Now I know why," she muttered. Although in truth, with the ropes shimmying over her breasts and clit and sex as the vibrator steadily pulsed, all her feel-good nerves were humming a happy tune. But Disney wasn't enough. She wanted a graphic novel orgasm.

Rafe made a small adjustment to the rib knot. "Keep an open mind, pussycat," he calmly said as if they were debating climate change and he was the reasonable one. "Don't jump to conclusions." He turned the vibrator up to full power.

Her wild scream bounced off the ceiling and walls as all the ropes vibrated and every erogenous zone in her body was set ablaze. Pleasure washed over her in wild, seething waves, building higher and higher, lighting up her senses like a meteor shower, burning through her nerve endings. Trembling on the brink, she twitched and rubbed against the ropes, reaching for her elusive climax, the breathless rapture so *very* close—*almost, almost.*

The fierce, cresting thrill abruptly faded, spiraled away.

The vibrator had been turned off.

Her eyes snapped open, and, looking up, she saw Rafe standing by the chair. "You got a problem?" Her voice could have cut steel.

"More than one, but that's beside the point. You're going too fast, racing for the finish line as usual. You should slow down."

"Thanks for the advice." She lifted her chin, a small, imperious gesture. "Now, let's stop playing games. I want to come."

He'd stiffened at that small lift of her chin, and her unequivocal demand. Not that either altered his plans.

Reaching out, he took her chin firmly between his thumb and fingers and, ignoring her resistance, turned her face to him. "I need your help."

"And I need yours."

Leaning over, he flipped the vibrator switch back on. As her eyes began to shut at the immediate revival of the rich, gluttonous sensations in every pleasure center in her body, he spread his fingers over her cheeks, tightened his grip. "Nicole, open your eyes." His fingers were leaving marks, forcing her to respond. When she slowly opened her eyes and recognition lit her gaze, Rafe smiled. "Thank you," he said gently. "Now, look—here." He tipped her face slightly so she'd see what he was holding in his other hand. "Open your mouth."

Momentarily lost to a vibrator jolt of spiking pleasure slamming through her body, it took her a second to respond. Even half-stunned, and breathless, she instinctively said, "Me first."

"Jesus, you never quit. But under the circumstances"—he

indicated her trussed body with a lift of his fingers—"here's the deal. If I don't get off, you don't get off." He hit the Off switch on the vibrator.

"Jesus fucking *Christ,* you're a control freak."

"No argument there. So—you want to get off or not?"

In the end, he held her head firmly, waited for her to open her mouth, and eased in his dick cautiously because she was glaring at him. "Be nice now, and I might give your pussy a workout with that vibrator. It's up to you. But then everything always is, isn't it tiger?" he finished sardonically. "Don't bite. You do, you get punished."

With Nicole's insurgent temper, however, his warning might go unheeded. There was a certain sense of danger in having his dick in the mouth of a woman who was scowling at him. Then again, a little risk always made fucking that much better. Not to mention that his fiery, all-in-a-huff pussycat knew how to suck dick. If it didn't feel so good, he might take the time to be pissed.

He came in record time, thanks to her proficiency and his aching dick, which had been ready to explode since he'd walked into the bedroom.

Then, as predictable as clockwork, even before he'd wiped himself off, she tilted her head, rubbed the come off her mouth on her upper arm, and said, "Now me."

The synthesis of incivility and bland acceptance in her casual swipe of her mouth, along with her brusque demand, meant his nervy little princess was back in form. But when it came to insolence, he had the market cornered. "Not yet, tiger. By the way, you give good head," he said, tossing his T-shirt aside. "I needed that."

"Obviously you're not welcome." Each word chill as a mouthful of ice.

"Maybe you'll thank me later," he said pleasantly, kneeling between her legs, beginning to untie the ropes binding her wrists to her ankles.

"Nope, 'cause once you're done with your little games, I'll be on the next flight out."

His gaze snapped up. "You're leaving?"

"This was a day-by-day arrangement. You knew that," she said with a little sniff. "I have other plans."

"With anyone special?" His voice had dropped in volume, the query delicate as the air at twilight.

"I have lots of friends in Monaco," she drawled in a flawless fuck-you tone. "You met one of them at your club."

A veil dropped over Rafe's eyes, hiding the raw chill. "I remember." He untied the last knot holding her legs. "There you go." He lifted her from the chair. "Steady," he said, as she sucked in a breath, the jolt to her clit imploding through her body like a battering ram, the shocking pleasure immune to her censure. Her arms and legs were free, but her torso was still restricted by the ropes, captive to the sensual pressure points under the knots; she remained physically and sexually helpless, suspended between fury and a ravenous hysteria.

Aware of her hot-blooded passions and the erratic rhythm of her breathing, Rafe said, "Maybe you could accommodate me one more time before you go. If you don't mind," he added offhandedly. "One last fuck for old times' sake. What do you say?" He stopped her answer with a finger over her mouth. "That's not really a question." Picking her up easily, his hands spanning her waist, he pretended not to hear her hard gasp as the ropes went taut, nor her throaty groan.

Semigently—he still had nominal control over his temper after she'd baited him with de Barre—he lowered her to the floor on her hands and knees. "Ass up," he said, bringing the flat of his hand down in a quick slap on her butt.

She yelped in shock.

"Move it, babe." Two hard slaps. "I want easy access." His erection surged at the bright imprint of his fingers on her pale skin.

Momentarily stunned, it took her a second to respond. But her bottom was smarting from his stinging blows, her nipples had tightened as though heedless of restraint, and the incendiary heat pulsing between her legs was equally immune to his brute insolence. Hot and aroused, pissed, confused, driven by riveting need, she dropped down on her forearms.

"That's the way, baby—ass up nice and high." He gently stroked the rising red blush on her silken bottom. "Feel that glow, pussycat? My fingerprints are branding your ass."

As if on cue, the smoldering heat from his spanking spread flame-hot through her senses, coiled through to her throbbing core, shuddered through her body with terrorizing pleasure, made her frantic to feel him inside her. When it was indefensible to feel that way. When she should defy him.

When under different circumstances she might have.

But having been aroused repeatedly only to be denied each time just short of orgasm, bound with rope that repeatedly pushed and teased every sexual button and nerve ending, she was in a constant state of quivering desperation—beyond further resistance. Resting her cheek on the carpet, she obliged him, making her sex even more accessible.

They both wanted the same thing—at least now, this very moment. She almost told him that but didn't know if it would make things better or worse, whether he'd understand the inexplicable mystery of her longing—how she was almost faint for wanting him. She didn't understand it herself.

For Rafe, the only tangible reality beyond his blind rage at her threat to leave was Nicole's capitulation. She wouldn't be leaving him—of that he was sure. And de Barre wouldn't be screwing her; he could bet the fucking bank on that. Choking on resentment, taut as a crossbow, Rafe said harshly, "You're not allowed to come until I say so."

She bit back her protest, not daring to respond. Not now—this close to having what she so feverishly needed.

Kneeling behind her, he adjusted the ropes framing her pussy with a facile glide of his finger, making room; then, without warning, sullen and pissed, he drove into her slick warmth in one powerful thrust.

She gasped.

He quickly positioned his fingers over the clit knot, felt her immediately yield, turn pliant under his hands, and begin to pant softly. Fuck. As if he needed reminding of her ready acquiescence, not just for him but probably for her *friends* in Monaco, damn her. *They were just going to have to fucking wait their turn.* His grip tightening, he quickly withdrew, then plunged back in and settled into an unchecked, hard-driving rhythm. She readily met his fierce thrust and withdrawal, as frenzied as he, as overwrought, even more wildly impatient after her arousal had been curtailed and disrupted countless times.

It didn't take her long to begin peaking, but then it never did, Rafe reflected bitterly. *Not so fucking fast.* The second he felt her first tiny climactic ripples slide up his dick, he jerked out of her slick, overaccommodating pussy and ejaculated all over her, coating her with come while she screamed in frustration.

It took him longer than usual to return to the world after one of the most spectacular, world-class orgasms of his life. Seriously, his heart might have stopped for a second. Gasping for air, his focus still centered somewhere in the vicinity of his dick, he reached out for his semiclean T-shirt and was suddenly aware of Nicole sprawled on the floor. Crying. *Shit.*

Tears were seeping from under her lashes, trailing down her cheek to the carpet. He should have felt more than a brief pang of remorse; someone less perverse might. Someone more charitable. But he was still too resentful, images of de Barre's insolent smile spurring a hitherto unknown jealousy.

Lying down beside her, he gently cupped his hand around the back of her neck, pulled her closer, caught her jaw in his teeth, and closed his mouth softly with a low animal growl. Moving up her soft cheek, he left a faint trail of soft bites, coming to rest with her earlobe in his mouth.

She didn't move, as if she knew he was the predator and she the prey; that she was at his mercy. *Lie still, don't move; the law of the jungle.*

"You only fuck me," he growled, dominant male, staking his claim. "No one else touches you. Only me."

She nodded, incapable of resisting him, defenseless against her enigmatic feelings, vulnerable to an outrageous lust.

He'd moved back enough to see her eyes. "Sure?" He didn't know why he asked; it didn't matter. He was keeping her.

She nodded again, wordless in her complete abandonment of reason.

"I need a yes from you. You know that, right? No more arguments. Nothing but yeses."

"Yes, Rafe." Grave, quietly intent. A tiny nod to confirm.

"Thank you." An approving smile. "That's what I like to hear." He lifted his hand from the back of her neck and slid it down her back, over the twined ropes and cool stickiness of his come, slipping his damp fingers between her legs, stroking her parted pussy gently, a caress—a gesture of ownership. "Is this mine?"

She shouldn't immediately burn with desire. She should have more pride. Even the shame was decadently arousing. She whimpered, as though giving voice to her sordid disbelief, and when she tried to stifle the sound, he gently slid a finger inside.

"You want my dick inside you, don't you?"

She wouldn't look at him.

He nipped at the tender flesh of her shoulder. "Do you

think you deserve to come?" She didn't answer, but he saw the flush rising on her face. "Come on, tiger." He kissed the angle of her face. "Talk to me."

"Not if you're still just playing."

He suppressed his smile. His princess of the universe sounded like a child who'd missed out on a trip to the amusement park. "I'm not, I'm dead serious." He touched his tongue to her cheek where he'd marked her. "How many times do you want to come? Once?"

Her pale eyelids rose faintly.

"Twice?"

Holding his gaze, she nodded.

"Now?"

She shot him a fast glance.

He made sure his smile would pass judgment at the pearly gates.

"Okay," she said.

He unfastened the quick release knots, one after another, unwrapping her body tenderly between kisses. Taking special care when lifting away the clit knot, gently massaging her stomach and thighs until a little sigh escaped her lips.

Having been kept on the edge of ecstasy so long, once the pressure of the ropes was taken away, she was in limbo, sensually aware but drifting back from a state of constant arousal, content to simply absorb the calm.

He carried her into his bathroom, walked into his shower room, sat down on one of the benches with Nicole on his lap, hit the wall panel controls, and turned on all the shower heads to warm up the room.

"You okay?" She was almost too still, her eyes shut. He brushed her hair away from her face, kissed her cheek. "Look at me, pussycat." Had he pushed her too hard? "Hey, sweets," he said softly, "I'm beginning to worry."

Her smile appeared before she opened her eyes. "Good. You should."

He started breathing again. His darling bitch was back. "I am, truly. Just because I have no limits doesn't mean you don't. I should have known better. Sorry." He grinned. "Tie me up if you want."

She sat up a little straighter. "Really?"

His grin widened. "Maybe—although the phrase *when hell freezes over* is lighting up my brain. We could flip for it."

"That's all right," she said, grinning back. "It looks like way too much work anyway. You know me—keep it simple." She lifted her brows. "So anytime. I believe you said two."

"Only two?"

"Hey, Contini, the mood you've been in, I'll take the two and then we can talk about more. A bird in the hand, et cetera."

"Let me wash my come off you first."

She gave him a disgusted look. "About that," she said peevishly.

"Yeah, I know. Won't happen again."

"And?"

He saw one of those schoolteacher looks given to misbehaving students. "My sincere apologies, tiger. That probably wasn't the best idea in the world. Although, if we're comparing bad ideas, I'll take an apology for: *I'll be taking the next flight out.*"

"You pissed me off."

"Duh. That's why we're in the shower." As she scowled, he quickly put his hand over her mouth. "Let's not go another ten rounds okay? Sit back, enjoy your spa attendant, and once I have you all clean and sweet smelling, you'll get your happy endings."

"Okay."

He always liked how she could turn on a dime. Weigh the pros and cons, go with the good stuff—don't mess around. "Here, get comfortable." He lifted her so she was straddling his thighs.

She smiled. "Planning ahead?"

"You bet. Now shut your eyes. Shampoo first."

He was gentle, thorough, really thorough, so much so that she was seriously panting by the time he was rinsing off the last of the soap.

Setting the shower hose aside, he ran his fingers lightly over the waves of her hair. "Your hair was wet like this when I first saw you. I'll never forget it. You took my breath away."

"Even with your dick in Silvia Fermetti?" She couldn't resist; it was one of those gloating moments of female mojo.

"It wasn't quite in her yet," he said, like fractions of inches mattered. "And once I saw you—well, we know how that turned out."

She gave him a little wink. "I won Hokusai's *Great Wave.*"

"Along with the rest of me." He stared at her for a second,

then nodded as though coming to terms with the notion. "I've never said that before, never wanted to, never even thought about it."

She smiled. "I do like *all* of you—really a lot." Her voice went soft. "A whole lot."

"Ditto here. We're having a moment aren't we?"

"Sorta. Don't panic."

"I'm not. It feels good."

A small silence fell, only the dozen showerheads steaming up the room were backdrop to the quiet wonder of the moment.

Programmed to avoid emotion, Rafe spoke first. "Speaking of feeling good, I made a promise to you."

Understanding his sudden shift in mood, aware as well that neither of them were going to be setting a wedding date after knowing each other for a day, she politely said, "Yes, you did." She grinned. "Now deliver, Contini, or I'll make your life a living hell."

He laughed. "Too late. But it's the nicest hell I've ever been in." And with a wink, he took her by the waist, said, "See if he fits," and raised her enough so she could guide his erection into her warm body.

As she sank down his hard, rigid length, she wrapped her arms around his neck, shut her eyes, and sighed with such utter contentment, her smile mirrored only a very small fraction of her pleasure.

His low, throaty grunt as she came to rest, fully impaled, on his thighs was a sound of such intense satisfaction that he felt the echo resonate in his brain like a song loaded with bass.

Neither moved, breath held, filled with hope and fear and something beautiful.

Then his dick twitched, a reflex or a calculated transition, and they both took a breath.

"Amazing," she whispered, less afraid. "Like tasting a dream."

"Yeah," he said, learning to accept a world beyond lust, lowering his mouth to her lips. Tasting her.

And he made love to her then; made love to a woman for the first time in his life. She was more than a fleeting dream, something real and wonderful. And she deserved more than the heat and technique, the naked, dangerous lust—he smiled to himself as the word *romance* slid into the picture, but that's what she deserved. It was a little complicated at first; he had to slow down and think about what he was doing. No automatic moves, no do-it-by-the-numbers, but something better.

Although the first time wasn't precisely slow because she'd waited too long.

Rafe took Nicole to climax in a blazing rush, her orgasm so intense, whirling hot, and raw that she was sobbing at the end. "It's all right, tiger," he whispered, holding her close. "That first one after that long hits you hard. The next one's a piece of cake."

She slowly tipped her tear-stained face up and smiled, half shy, like she was still feeling the fizz. "It was good."

"I could tell."

She said, "You didn't come."

"You first." Not joking, not teasing, like he'd had time to think about it and was making a life change.

"Thank you." She smiled a little and wiggled on his primed, ready-to-rock erection. "You gonna be okay?"

He grinned. "I'm fine. Just waiting on you. It's your party."

He didn't mind acting the gentleman; he wanted to please her as if he were being graded. And he screwed the hell out of her in the nicest possible, five-star, straight-A, planning-every-move-for-her-pleasure way. Not just twice. But until she finally held up her hand, said, "Hang on a second. Let me think. Nope, I'm done. Don't wake me up when you come," and collapsed on his chest.

It probably wouldn't have traumatized her if he'd taken his turn, but she was played out. He'd live if he didn't climax.

Turning off the showers, he wiped them both dry and carried her to bed.

TWENTY-TWO

Resting against the headboard, Rafe cradled Nicole in his lap while she half dozed. She gave him such pleasure, he felt as though he were high. Crazy. He wondered if other people ever felt this good. It was extraordinary.

"Nice, hey?" A wisp of sound, warm with contentment.

"Nothing better, pussycat." He touched the top of her head with his lips. "Great anniversary."

"And we have another coming up tomorrow."

He chuckled. "You're going to keep me fucking busy."

She shifted in his arms so she could see his face. "I absolutely adore you. There, I said it again. Don't run. I won't let you."

"No way. I adore you too. Life's good right?"

"The best," she whispered.

"So now that I have you in a good mood," he said, lightly teasing.

"I'm always in a good mood."

"I don't want to fight. I repeat, now that I have you in a good mood," Rafe said, sensibly ignoring the little bunny twitch of her nose, "I have a question. Feel free to say no."

"Not more rope."

"As if you didn't get all sexed up, but no, it's something else."

"I *suppose* I'm going to learn a *whole* lot from you since you seem to know everything about—"

He put a finger over her mouth. "Listen." Having worked herself into a little snit, she tried to wiggle away, but he held her close. "Have you ever been to a sex club?"

Okay, that she wasn't expecting, but he was obviously waiting for an answer. "Like what kind of sex club?"

"The usual kind," he said.

"Define *usual*."

He laughed. "Or I could define *deviant*? Or you could just say no. I won't hold it against you if you're not a regular at sex clubs."

She sniffed. "I might hold it against you if you are a regular."

"Come on, I've known you for only twenty-four hours." He smiled. "How about I say I've never been to the one Ganz has invited us to in Paris? Better? So, want to check it out?"

"I can say no, right?"

"Absolutely." He didn't give a shit. He'd been to hundreds.

"What'll I wear if we go?"

"As little as you want, pussycat."

"Are people naked there?"

"That's what I've heard."

"You're such a liar."

"Survival, tiger. A crazy father, Darwinian boarding schools, a mother who loved me but didn't want to hear the bad stuff. Count your blessings if you had a normal childhood. So, do you want to go? Ganz needs an answer. He might be leaving for Paris tomorrow."

"Will I have fun if we go?"

"Oh, yeah," he said, soft as silk. "I'll make sure you do."

"You do have the knack." Her smile was rich with sated passion, her gaze warm with affection, a playful note in her voice when she said, "Don't panic now, and I have no idea why I'm asking except thanks to you I'm still feeling a crazy-ass glow—but have you ever thought about having children?"

He suppressed his shock, smiled back, and kept his voice mild as hell. "No, I've never thought about it. Too busy, I suppose." If any other woman had asked him that, he would have been far less polite.

"Me too. Busy."

"Someday," he said with disarming courtesy.

"Yeah."

He smiled and, ignoring the little voice in his head that was yelling, *Shut the fuck up,* he murmured, "Although, damn, right now, tiger, it doesn't sound like such a bad idea."

She laughed. "That's 'cause we're still floating in our warm, fuzzy bubble."

He didn't do warm and fuzzy; or, as a rule he didn't. He was a practical man. "I don't know—for me, watching you get fat with my baby inside you—I'm thinking that's seriously hot."

"Pervert."

"Hey, worshipful hot, okay? All tender and sweet shit."

"Okay, now you're just being crazy. My mom said that's

what happened to my uncle; he got baby crazy. She never thought it would happen to the great Dominic Knight, player extraordinaire."

Rafe's eyes widened for a second. "Your uncle's Dominic Knight?" If she'd mentioned it before he hadn't noticed.

"Yeah, you know him?"

"Not really," he said. "I've seen him here and there over the years. Not lately though."

"That's because he's turned into a saint—well...that's probably a stretch for Dominic. I used to hear my parents talk about his wildness and kink. Since he married, his life revolves around his family. Kate and the kids are darling though, so there's no question why he dotes on them."

Rafe's brows rose. "Kids?" Now there was a picture. The last time he'd seen Dominic Knight, he'd been covered in naked women.

"Yeah. Rosie's five and James is two and a half. They're cute and sweet and smart, as if Dominic and Kate put in an order for perfect kids."

"You don't say...

"I do say." But her voice in contrast was forceful, and quickly twisting away, she was straddling Rafe's hips in two seconds flat. "Now, Mr. Contini," she purred, "to change the subject from babies, which is way the hell out there, I was wondering if we could get back to talking about you being just a little bit nice to me again—in your *inimitable* fashion." She curled her fingers around his rising erection. "In *his* inimitable fashion." She looked up and smiled. "Have I mentioned he's my newest addiction?"

"I believe you have once or twice. And, speaking for him,

may I say the sexy sound of your voice alone is enough to make him hard." His golden gaze was warm with humor, and, sliding his long fingers around her waist, he lifted her slightly. "Put him in."

She smiled. "*Moi?* Again? Are you getting lazy?"

"Seeing as how I have my hands full, a little cooperation would be appreciated." A teasing lift of his brows. "Unless you don't want to come?"

A second later, his dick was fully ensconced in the woman of his dreams, her warm ass was resting on his thighs, and she was smiling at him like she was enjoying herself.

"We have to stop meeting like this," she said playfully.

"I don't see why."

She laughed. "Okay."

"That's the way, baby. Just yeses, always. Remember?"

"Yes, sir, absolutely, sir."

It was amazing how much his dick liked Nicole in submission mode.

She noticed too. "Jeez, for that much more dick in seconds flat, you can have all the yeses you want."

"Let me get that in writing. Seriously."

The quiet gravity in his amber gaze collided with her wild, irresponsible need. And suddenly she no longer cared who called the shots, who was in control, if control even mattered with an entire, blissful month before her in which she could be naively happy. Violently happy. "Just show me where to sign." She smiled. "Seriously."

"Done deal. August is turning out to be my favorite month ever."

"Because to love more and be happy is everything. That's a Hafiz poem I'm screwing up royally," she said with a grin.

"It sounds good to me. Perfect, in fact," he whispered and kissed her.

TWENTY-THREE

Two days later, after Ganz had successfully concluded what Rafe called some unfinished business, they flew to Paris.

Ganz was dropped off at his girlfriend's apartment and twenty minutes later, Rafe and Nicole arrived at the small fourteenth-century cloister house on the Seine that Rafe called home in the city. Rafe had purchased it when he left university and the building had been converted over the course of several years and considerable expense into a comfortable residence.

This time, rather than bodyguards, the door was opened by a small, plump, middle-aged woman in a gypsy skirt and a black T-shirt with henna-colored hair, enormous diamond studs in her ears, and a smile that was visible from space.

"You darling, sweet boy! How nice to see you again!"

She spoke French, but her enthusiasm was universal and when she opened her arms wide, Rafe moved forward to give her a hug.

Then he turned to Nicole, drew her forward, and made introductions.

"Natalie, I'd like you to meet Nicole," Rafe said in English. "Nicole, Natalie, who's kept me on the straight and narrow for many years."

"Tut, such a liar," Natalie said in heavily accented English, giving Rafe a little slap on the arm. "He does exactly as he pleases. You must change his bad behavior, *ma petite,*" she added with a smile for Nicole.

"I'll do my best," Nicole replied, shooting a teasing glance at Rafe. "But I may be too late."

"Nonsense, a man's better for a strong woman at his side." She smiled up at Rafe. "Isn't that so, *chéri*?"

"If you say so, Natalie," Rafe replied smoothly. "Who am I to question your magic?"

Her dark eyes hinted at arcane mysteries. "Indeed."

A small electric pause flickered in the ancient foyer.

Rafe broke the silence first. "Did my parcels arrive?"

"This morning. They're in your suite as ordered," Natalie said, staring at him, making it plain her deference was provisional.

"Thank you. If you'll excuse us," Rafe said, staring back, his voice conveying his own degree of provisional sanction: even a beloved employee would be wise not to go beyond a certain point.

As they moved toward a narrow curving flight of stairs, feeling as though she were refereeing an argument between her siblings, Nicole said, "She seems very nice."

"She is most of the time." A touch of complaint still in his voice. "Be careful," he cautioned more gently as they reached the stone staircase. "The treads are uneven."

"Has Natalie been with you long?" Nicole asked as they began their ascent.

"Yes."

"Then I'm assuming you somehow reconcile your struggles for supremacy."

He shot her a sharp look, then grinned. "Fuck no. It's a stalemate."

"But you like her."

"She tells fortunes."

"Jeez, I never would have guessed."

"Smart-ass." He sighed. "Natalie turned up here when I first bought the place. The cloister was an unholy mess after seven hundred years, the last two when the church was beginning to lose its political power, particularly austere for the order. Expenditures for maintenance had been deeply retrenched. Natalie walked up to me like she owned the place, took my hand, said, 'I know your fortune,' and proceeded to recount my life as if she'd read my nonexistent diary. When she finished, she looked at me with those snapping black eyes and said, 'You need me.' " He shrugged. "I figured someone who could see the past so clearly might be able to glimpse some of the future as well. Not that I'm particularly interested in the occult, but as you see, she's damned likable in her no-nonsense way. Although the deciding factor was her immediate command of the workmen; they were afraid of her. Ultimately, she oversaw the renovation with a keen eye, an iron fist, and the frugality of an accountant." He smiled and waved Nicole to the right at the top of the stairs. "Natalie considers this her home as much as mine."

"I sorta got that impression. Does she let you put your feet up on the furniture?"

A tic of a smile. "What she doesn't know won't hurt her."

Nicole laughed. "We have a housekeeper like that at home. She runs the place; the rest of us live there on her sufferance."

"Then you understand the dynamic." He stopped at a closed door, took a small breath, and spoke with a quiet formality. "I just want to say what a pleasure it is to have you here. I don't generally have guests."

She smiled. "I like being with you."

"Same here," he said, opening the door. "Come in."

His bedroom suite was a series of small rooms, one opening on the other, originally the mother superior's apartment with an anteroom, office, small dining room, and smaller bedroom. Rafe had restored the largest chamber into a sitting room, the office became the bedroom, the dining room a dressing room, and the nun's sleeping cell was now the bathroom. Colorful upholstered furniture, Turkish carpets, painted cabinets, and a number of modern paintings relieved the cool gray stone walls and floor.

He motioned to a scarlet silk-covered chair in the sitting room, the cushions invitingly soft and plump. "Sit down. I have something for you."

She didn't move. "You gave me enough already."

"Don't worry, you're not going to beggar me. Sit. Please sit," he added, since her mouth had firmed mutinously at his first brusque *sit.* He picked up a small box from Chaumet on a nearby table and after she sat, held it out to her. "Here, take a look."

She drew back as far as the chair cushion allowed. "What's this?"

"Take it." He shrugged. "It's not a bomb, I promise."

She took it from him, flipped open the top on the small jeweler's box, and went still. The ruby intaglio, surrounded by emeralds, was set on a simple yellow gold band.

"Wanna get fake engaged?" He grinned. "Just teasing. Call it a friendship ring, okay? I wanted to get you something myself. Don't ask me why. I was sober."

A quick breath, then a nod. "Sure, friendship, fake engaged, whatever." Taking the ruby ring out, she slipped it on the fourth finger of her left hand. "It fits. How'd you do that?"

His brows rose fractionally. "Sure? Just like that? You do this often?"

"No, don't freak. You said it's just for fun. You can have the ring back when I leave."

"Fiona said you like to take chances even if they're dicey," he said, clear and cool, watching her. "That it sometimes gets you in trouble."

"She said that?" Nicole held his gaze. "Did you want me to refuse the ring?"

He frowned. "No."

"What then? Am I supposed to be more impressed that the studly, every-woman's-dream Rafe Contini has done me this great honor?" Mocking. "Is that it?"

"Jeez, you're a bitch."

"And you don't know how to ask a woman to be fake engaged," she said flatly. "It's not a trip to the dentist, dude. A couple of smiles wouldn't be out of place."

He grunted.

An angel face, real as fuck. "That's not a smile."

"You drive me crazy."

"I know, but you like me anyway. And I adore you. I've already told you that."

His smile slowly unfurled, the corners of his gorgeous mouth tipping upward bit by bit until pleasure lit up his eyes, warmed her heart, and made them both glad they'd met. "I'm sorry. I'll try to be better," he said. "But even a fake engagement is pretty radical for me."

"Call it friendship then." She gave him a wink. "Although I like radical."

"Yeah," he said softly. "I know you do."

And his smile that time would have lured every nun who'd ever lived in this cloister into his arms and straight to hell.

"One more thing." He picked up the second package, wrapped in pale peach handmade paper and tied with green hemp string, from the table. "It wasn't easy to find on short notice. I hope you like it."

When she untied the string and unfolded the soft paper, she stopped breathing for a second. Two small books lay inside, the smallest, on top, the oldest from the looks of the worn cover. She glanced up, still breathless with delight. "Hafiz. You remembered."

"I checked him out. His poetry is incredible. The book on top is the first edition in English, 1771. But I also got you a later edition, 'cause the eighteenth-century fonts are hard to read."

"You're not getting these back. The ring, yes, but not Hafiz."

"Not a problem. I'm glad you like them."

"*Like* them?" She grinned. "Wrap my happiness in diamonds and pearls and pigeon egg rubies."

His happiness was somewhere in the same zip code, but he didn't want to think about any of this too much because he'd panic. To calm his historically uninvolved nerves, he told himself there was nothing wrong with a spontaneous, carpe diem, let-the-good-times-roll friendship with Nicole. Regardless of his occasional lapses into romantic sentiment, their time together wasn't forever. That's what made it manageable.

A month.

Perfectly acceptable.

Then back to normal.

"So did I do good? Did I do better on the smiles?"

"Better everything, Rafe. Thanks."

She hadn't called him by his given name before. It was stunning how good the small intimacy made him feel. As if she'd stepped over some prohibitive line and offered him more than her volatile sexuality. As if he'd ever wanted more than sex from a woman. That perhaps he did now stopped him cold for a moment.

But fuck it. It was what it was until it wasn't. Period. "You're welcome, pussycat. My pleasure. Now, what do you want to do? We have a few hours until we pick up Ganz and Madeline." He took one look at her expression and chuckled. "Silly question, right?"

"Well, we are engaged." Her smile was the image of innocence. "So you *are* allowed to kiss me now."

"I see," he said. "Had I known the rules, I would have given you a ring sooner. What do I have to do to fuck you?" An infinitesimal lift of one brow. "I'm assuming that involves a priest."

She met his eyes, blank-faced. "Being in a cloister house perhaps allows us some latitude with a sense of religiosity in the air. Surely a priest must have been here many times."

"From what I hear, some of these nuns might have *enjoyed* having him over."

"I'm shocked."

"I could shock you a little more if you like."

"You understand, I have to resist you at first or risk losing the moral high ground."

"Not a problem, tiger." He grinned. "I like it when you resist. Let me show you my bedroom." He took her hand and pulled her to her feet. "You can tell me if you like the decor."

His bedroom was cozy, even the bed was close to normal size—a simple pine bed without bed curtains, the coverlet plain quilted indigo cotton. A rush chair sat beside the bed like in Van Gogh's bedroom in Arles, a cherry wood table used as a desk, the only touch of luxury in the room—discounting the splendid late Kokoschka paintings—a sumptuous long sofa with down cushions upholstered in peach silk velvet.

Kicking off his sandals, Rafe dropped onto the sofa in a lazy sprawl and watched Nicole walk around the room surveying his paintings. "There's a very small Lautrec over the desk," he said.

After looking at it, she turned to him with a smile. "I see why you like it." The nude young lady was lying on her back, her legs spread wide, raising a glass of absinthe at the viewer in added invitation.

"She's a pretty young thing—not as beautiful as you, pussycat. Would you like your portrait done? I could have someone come over."

"Like that?" She flicked a finger at the painting.

He shrugged. "Not necessarily." After a decade of faceless women, he found himself wanting a memory of these days.

"Take a picture."

"Not the same."

"I'll think about it."

He looked at her. "No one else would say that."

"I'm not here for what you can give me"—she grinned—"other than the obvious. And I'll be greedy as hell about that."

"Not a problem." If nothing else, he'd take a picture; the mere thought made him flinch. So his voice was blunter than he'd intended when he said, "Speaking of greedy, what can you do for me?"

She shot him a sharp look. "Is that an invitation?"

"Yeah, greed to greed." At her quick eyebrow lift, he got himself together, telling himself to keep it casual, he wasn't going to feel this way forever. "Hey, sorry. Old habits. I don't want to fight. Okay?"

She scanned his face and made her own decision. "Me either. So while you have me in this forgiving mood," she said, suddenly grinning from ear to ear, "first as an apology and then as a thank-you for my fake engagement ring, would you like me to kneel at your feet and say—make myself useful?"

He grinned back. “Are you kidding? I'd pay to see that. Not you—just in general,” he quickly added to clear up any misunderstanding. “Hell, you don't even have to do anything. Just kneel there.”

She laughed. “Like this?” As she dropped to her knees in a pouf of her tangerine Missoni sundress, she watched his dick rise under his khaki slacks.

“Oh, yeah.” Narrow-eyed, he sucked in a breath. “That's way out of character, tiger. You take something I don't know about?”

“Come on—am I really that difficult?”

He looked startled for a moment, then broke out laughing.

“It's not that funny,” she grumbled, morphing into the pissy, difficult girl she was questioning.

Still chuckling, he said, “Okay, now there's my real pussycat.”

“I can be docile if I want,” she said with a flash of annoyance.

His laughter died away. “Show me.” Sitting up, he swung his feet to the floor and looked at her steadily. “Find that crystal bikini from Rome, change into it here”—he pointed at the floor near his feet—“then you can make yourself *useful*.”

She hesitated.

“See,” he said, shaking his head. “You can't do it.”

A small mocking smile. “And you can't control your dick.”

He flicked his glance downward, then up. “Come here. Take him out. We'll discuss it.” A small pause as he waited.

"You say you want to be useful"—his eyes met hers—"but you can't take orders. Only give them."

"I can too take orders... well, maybe I can." She sucked on her bottom lip, trying to come to terms with the complicated intangibles between desire and obedience, knowing full well that if he'd been anyone else, she'd have walked out.

"It was Empress Eugénie's ring," Rafe said, understanding her struggle because it was his—who gave what to whom, how much, how little, whether it mattered. Changing the subject to give her time. "The one you're wearing," he added, with a slight lift of his hand. "Did I mention that?"

She looked blank for a moment, until her brain caught up with her auditory senses. "No, who's she?"

He smiled. "Don't know your history?"

"Maybe your dick doesn't care if I do or not," she said with a glance at his blatant hard-on.

He laughed. "No shit. For future reference, tiger, Eugénie was Napoleon the Third's wife."

Nicole looked at her ring, then at him. "She had good taste. What was she like?"

She was a little bitch like you, but also beautiful like you. Instead of saying that, he said, "She was very pretty. I have a small portrait of her downstairs. Natalie supposedly found it at a flea market. I'm not so sure, but I like it, so I'll check its provenance someday and give it back. It's probably stolen. Natalie has interesting friends."

"Could I see it?"

"Sure. Put on the crystal bikini and I'll go get it."

"Jeez, is everything always about negotiation with you?"

He smiled. "Other way around, pussycat. Only with *you*. Everyone else does what they're told."

Not a blink, just a nod, then a graceful wave and Nicole was walking toward his dressing room. He felt as he had so many times since meeting her, that he was being given a gift; appreciative as ever, he smiled. "I'll be right back."

When he returned, Nicole was standing, slender and natural, in the center of his bedroom, unaware how stunning the image—all jeweled, pale beauty, the glittering bikini a whimsical illusion meant to catch the eye, invite interest, and cover very little.

"Oh," she said, her eyes lighting up as Rafe approached, holding the painting so she could see it. "She's lovely."

"She was. Every painter of note wanted her to sit for him." Rafe propped the portrait on his desk, leaning it against the wall. "Natalie has a good eye. Eugénie looks very young. Perhaps this was done before she left Spain." Bending, he kissed Nicole's cheek. "Take your time. I'm going to have a drink. Would you like one?"

"Uh-uh," she said without lifting her gaze from the portrait. "Why isn't this signed?"

"It could be under the frame. The lack of a signature may be the reason it was at a flea market—if that's even true." Pouring himself a whiskey, he sat on the sofa and enjoyed both his whiskey and his house guest. Either Alessandra had asked about Nicole's eye color or he'd mentioned it because the Swarovski crystals were sewn onto a blue silk fabric that matched Nicole's eyes.

She had the most remarkable eyes—like blue skies and

sunshine. Although when her temper was up, the brilliance turned explosive. What he liked best though was the warm, summertime blue as she floated in a postorgasmic daze. He smiled. She was sweetly vulnerable then.

"Something funny?"

He looked up to see her standing a foot away. "No, fond memories. Of you, pussycat," he added honestly, when, as a rule, honesty was rare in situations like this.

"Smooth." She smiled. "I almost believe you."

He shrugged. "It's the truth. Come here. I'll help you take that off. It's beautiful, but not very flexible, right? Then sit with me. You don't have to do anything. No orders. Promise."

"I might want more than just sitting." She said it kindly, examining him as she spoke, not sure what to make of this new, surprising individual.

"Sure. Just tell me what you want, and if it's something other than sex, I'll have someone find it for you. Anything at all." She was an island of happiness in his seriously fucked-up world. Carlos had taken out the advance team on Ganz's trail, but more were on their way. A helluva lot more. The danger was real, ominous, and unspeakably violent. Nicole would have to be sent away sooner than he'd anticipated. Sooner than he wished.

A small bewilderment drew her brows together; he seemed to be lost in thought. "You okay?"

He concentrated his gaze on her. "Yes. Fine. Sometimes life could be a little easier, that's all. Not your problem." For a moment it seemed he was going to say more, before he visibly regained command of himself. "But my dick's always interested in you," he said with a playful grin. "So what's on your agenda?"

He was trying to be accommodating; it was touching. "Nothing. I don't have an agenda. Sitting's fine, really. Here, help me with the hook in back." She turned and glanced over her shoulder as he sat up straighter and set his drink aside. "I think I fucked it up somehow."

A moment later, she was on his lap, sans bikini, his arms wrapped around her, his chin resting on the top of her head. "Tell me about your school schedule," he said, wanting the world to stop for just a few hours, wanting all the cold-blooded killers to disappear so he could enjoy this small private temptation properly.

"I don't have one." She shut her eyes, feeling his solid warmth melt through her body, wanting to never move. "Only Fiona knows. I haven't told my family. They think I'm on my way to Columbia next month."

"Why aren't you?" he asked with a mixture of flattery and real interest.

She sighed. "If I knew I'd tell you."

"Sounds like you need a break from academia." He almost said more—about staying, about a future, about impossible things with the various hit squads on the move requiring an aggressive defense and his full concentration. But he didn't; he rarely put a foot wrong. He'd learned that lesson very young.

She turned so she could see his face. "I don't know what I need." She made a little gesture of hopelessness with her hands. "Other than you." She smiled. "That part's simple. Twenty-four/seven, stay within touching distance."

"You've got my vote on that," he said easily, refusing to give in to destructive thoughts, thinking he'd remember the feel of her in his arms, the ridiculous little flash of warmth, for a million years.

She wiggled her bottom, wanting him to come back from wherever he was, wanting him to smile. "And him too?"

"Yeah, he doesn't know how to behave around you." He gave a wry chuckle "Gun to his head, he'd still keep going if you wanted him to."

"Thanks." She looked up at him with a discreet curiosity. "Feeling a little better now?"

God, she was appealing, all wide-eyed innocence, like she'd be stepping on his toes if she asked him to fuck her or what was wrong or if something was wrong. "I'm good. I'm always good with you." She was his treat in a world of endless chaos. "Come on, pussycat," he said, rising from the sofa with her in his arms. "Let's see if you can scream loud enough to make Natalie smile."

"Jesus, for sure I won't scream now," she said, as he pulled back the quilt and placed her in the middle of the bed.

And she didn't until the third time.

Several enjoyable hours later, Nicole was standing before the mirror in Rafe's bedroom in Paris, turning this way and that, glancing over her shoulder, finally facing him with a tiny frown.

"Will this outfit do? You know better than I what's proper in a sex club."

Rafe, having dressed with his usual speed, was lounging

in a chair, drinking a nineteen-year-old whiskey, admiring the view. Quickly censuring his first few comments about proper attire in a sex club, he said, "I'm not sure *proper*'s the right word, pussycat. But you look beautiful as usual, and that outfit is so damned sexy I'm going to have to spend all night fighting off the competition."

Her little frown deepened. "Sexy as in I look like I'm selling it on the corner?"

"I've never actually seen anyone selling it on the corner," he said, more or less honestly, "so I'll wing it and say no." Since Alessandra had sent him an e-mail of the invoice, he knew for a fact the only corner anyone would be selling *it* in this particular outfit was on the corner of six thousand euros.

"Good." She smiled. "Thanks. This is all a little new to me."

"Nothing to worry about. Just stay close so I don't have to punch anyone."

"I don't want anyone but you"—she blew him a kiss—"so no punching required."

He grinned. "Spoken with the peerless virtue I require in my faux fiancée."

"Pshaw—this little thing?" Smiling widely, she thrust her left hand in his direction, and the unpretentious ruby surrounded by emeralds on her left finger sparkled and gleamed.

"That little thing means I own you," Rafe said, smiling back. He was putting his mark on her for the world for reasons entirely unclear. But he wasn't looking for an escape route. At least not now.

"Only till the end of the month, when you get this back." Nicole smiled. "I've never been fake engaged before, but so far I like it."

"Good. I think it makes perfect sense. Like losing your brakes doing eighty."

"Or going for broke."

His grin had a reckless shine. "You and me on a runaway train, pussycat."

They were both fully committed to their exuberant, intoxicating, fiercely impassioned, provisional game that overlooked reality, contravened practicalities, and allowed them to please and gratify themselves for twenty-six more days in the euphoric world of their choosing. Realistically less, but only one of them was privy to that information.

"Seriously, though, tiger, you're not allowed to stray from my side. That outfit screams *fuck me*."

Nicole was barely dressed: all lush boobs, tiny waist, and legs that went on forever. Her flowery silk bustier was a colorful design of pale cream and yellow roses on a scarlet background, her waist compressed to hands-span width, the tiny cups barely covering her nipples, her breasts pushed up into high, plump mounds by the taut boning. A short, swingy skirt in the same fabric complemented the bustier and spike heels with sparkly straps that wound up Nicole's ankles pretty much signaled that *fuck me* wasn't out of the question.

She smiled as she tossed a tiny embroidered purse over her shoulder. "I'll cling to you like a lifeline in a storm."

"Damn right you will." This from a man who'd never asked a woman's name before he fucked her. "Maybe you should wear a jacket. It's cool at night."

She looked up from checking the contents of her purse: lipstick, phone, ID, credit card, cash, enough for cab fare home—her mother's mantra. "I'm not wearing a jacket inside."

"You will if I say you will."

Her gaze narrowed. "Hey."

He took a deep breath, exhaled. "Sorry." He drained the rest of his whiskey in a single swallow. She could say *Hey* all she wanted; no way, she was leaving his side. He'd amused himself in enough of these fuck clubs to understand the rules. There weren't any. "So," he said, setting his glass aside, coming to his feet, and holding out his hand. "Ready?"

She took his hand and even in heels, looked up a long way to his faint scowl. "I'm looking forward to seeing one of these clubs. And don't worry, I'll stick to you like glue. If you must know, I'm a little intimidated." She made a little face. "Naked people. Eeek."

"These high-end clubs only let in the beautiful people. So don't worry, you won't be seeing any fat German tourists." He smiled. "In fact, this club requires that entrants speak French, Russian, or Arabic—in addition to being young, good-looking, and rich. So the naked people are at least physically attractive. No guarantees on personality. Rich people can be massive douches."

She tapped his chest. "Even rich, young, handsome ones."

"Hey, babe, just do what you're told and everyone's happy."

"You better be smiling when you say that." Then she reached up and pulled his face down for a kiss. "Although during August," she said, the hum of her words warm on his lips, "I'm not entirely averse to a certain number of orders."

He chuckled. "True. You like orders with sex. Definitely a match made in heaven." And he kissed her back, lightly, in order not to ruin her lipstick. He knew about makeup and could be polite when required.

Dropping down on her heels, she made a little grumbly sound. "We don't have to stay long do we?"

"Or we could fuck there. That's kind of what these clubs are for. Don't panic," he quickly said as her eyes opened wide, "I'll get us a private room."

"Whew. You had me worried there for a minute."

He felt a sudden warm, protective zeal, a feeling so alien he mentally scrutinized it for a moment before fully embracing it. "No one sees you but me. You're my girl."

Maybe that warm protective wave was operating on a duplicate plane because Nicole felt it envelope her in tender, lambent affection. "I like being your girl."

"Good," he said gruffly.

When Nicole and Rafe exited the cloister house, Simon slid off the front fender and moved to open the back door of the car.

"Picking up Ganz?"

"That's the plan. Then do you mind sticking around in case we want to leave early?"

"No problem. Probably not a bad idea anyway," he said, holding Rafe's gaze for a moment as Nicole slid into the backseat.

"Right." Rafe smiled. "How soon we forget."

"Best not do that," Simon said cryptically. "Carlos wouldn't approve."

"Agreed." Rafe arched one brow. "We have company I hear."

"She won't notice."

"Excellent."

Rafe stepped into the car and Simon shut the door.

Simon took a roundabout route to Madeline's apartment, making certain they didn't have a tail. It was still early days since the two men had been spirited out of Macao, but no one was taking any chances.

They picked up Ganz and Madeline and once everyone was seated, the two women were introduced.

"Nice to meet you," Nicole said, smiling across Ganz at the lovely blond woman who almost matched him in height. "I hear you're as good as Ganz on the computer."

"Sometimes. We met online a few years ago. Are you enjoying Paris?"

"Rafe has been making it enjoyable." Nicole smiled up at Rafe, who had his arm around her.

"She's easy to please." Dipping his head, he kissed Nicole's cheek. "We might not stay all night. Can you get home on your own or do you want Simon to send for another car?"

"Some friends of mine are going to be there," Madeline said. "We can ride with them or catch a cab."

Rafe leaned forward enough to see Ganz. "Why don't we have a car there for you?"

"Sure." Ganz had been careful to keep his relationship with Madeline hidden, but after the recent upheaval in Shanghai, pursuit was bound to be ratcheted up.

"If I don't see you later, I'll talk to you tomorrow," Rafe said as they pulled up to a nondescript facade in a commercial neighborhood.

A doorman guarded the entrance, but he knew Ganz, so their party was waved in without delay. The club had a dress code requiring a suit or sport coat for men and no trousers for women, so Rafe was wearing a sport coat and slacks. He'd always found that money took care of any dress code requirements, but Ganz had told him what to wear and they were going in as his guests. No point in acting like a fuckwad.

The Chandelier Club was an upscale club, a favorite of celebrities and politicians, a place to see and be seen. Rafe didn't go to sex clubs to be seen. He went to engage in hard-core kink, so he preferred privacy and perversion rather than the spotlight. But for Nicole's initial foray into clubs like this, the Chandelier was relatively tame.

After a round of drinks at a neon-lit, glitzy bar all sleek glass and white marble, red leather chairs at the tables, scoops of shiny aluminum for bar stools, Ganz handed Rafe a key to a private room, held up another key, said, "We're next door to your room if you need us," and he and Madeline left. A DJ was spinning records and a few dancers were on the minuscule dance floor, although the majority of the patrons were watching a couple at a nearby marble-topped table who were beginning to undress. Nicole couldn't tell if it was a performance or spontaneous, their disrobing was so languid. But when the man suddenly pushed the woman facedown on the table and began fucking her from behind, a small gasp drifted across the room.

Nicole glanced up at Rafe, who appeared unmoved. “Are they for real or actors?”

He shrugged. “Hard to tell. Want me to ask them?”

“Jeez, no. I was just curious.”

He slid off his bar stool. “Let’s see what else they have here. Someone’s screaming in the next room. Could be interesting.” He lifted her down and took her hand. “Stay close,” he murmured and moved toward a large archway.

As they entered a more luxurious bar, darker, mirrored walls, plush carpet, black leather sofas and chairs, lit with several large crystal chandeliers, Rafe pointed to a small stage set in a corner where a performance was under way. A standing woman was tied to a black velvet-covered wall, her wrists and ankles shackled to metal hoops. She was nude except for heels, her back was to the room, and a large man, also nude, his erection impressive, was forcing a huge dildo up her ass.

The bound woman was whimpering now, her screams having quieted, and she could hear the man’s voice over a sound system, telling her if she screamed, he’d ram it in harder.

“Understand?”

“Yes, yes.”

“You can take it all. I know you can. And if you’re good, I’ll let you have my dick after the dildo. Understand?” He paused. “You must answer me.” He nudged the dildo in a fraction more as though to encourage a reply.

She gasped, tensed, whimpered, “Yes, yes.”

“You want to come don’t you?” A low, husky whisper.

She nodded frantically.

"I can't hear you."

"I do, I do."

"That's what I want to hear. Now, relax, I'm going to push this deeper."

Her wild scream boomeranged around the room, Nicole sucked in a breath, and Rafe said, "That's enough of that," and quickly guided her out of the room. Leading her to a quiet corner of the grand salon next door, he dipped his head and said, "Sorry about that. Would you like to go home?"

Nicole shook her head. "Not yet, but wow, that was rough."

"Some people like it that way."

"Really?"

He stifled a smile; that was blushing innocence. "So I hear. Would you like to sit down, have a glass of champagne? Pretend you're in the palace at Chambord? They brought this room wholesale from there."

Nicole surveyed the large, high-ceilinged room, an eighteenth-century masterpiece of walls painted with pastoral scenes of beautiful young men and women amusing themselves in the country. Some clothed, others not, the ambiance one of languid arousal. The furniture was antique, upholstered in pastel damask, the carpet a plush reproduction of an Anatolian design, the chandeliers dimmed to a soft luminescence. "Me in a palace with champagne?" She smiled. "Why not?" But as Rafe turned to guide her to a chair, Nicole's eyes widened. "Ohmygod, Rafe!" she said in a shocked whisper. "Look! That couple on the bar! Don't they care if people watch? And those two against the wall. She's giving him head and the crowd around them is—"

"Fucking noisy," Rafe grumbled as the advice being offered rose in volume. "Unless you're seriously interested, why don't we go to that room Ganz got for us, order some drinks, food if you like, and forget about these people. Or if you'd like a private performance, I could order up that too. We wouldn't have to deal with the goddamn noise."

"I don't know…really, a private performance? Is it embarrassing?"

"If it is, we'll ask them to leave. You decide though. I don't care." This was pretty tame stuff, for which he was grateful. He'd grown virtuous, for Christ's sake, when it came to Nicole.

"Okay, let's. We can always come back, right?"

"Sure, whatever you want. Let's go find our room."

They'd made their way halfway through the crowded salon, Rafe protecting Nicole with one arm around her shoulder, the other in front of her, when a dark-haired man with slicked-back hair, dressed in a showy pearl gray double-breasted suit, stepped in front of them.

His smile was more of a leer. "Nice piece of ass, Contini. Can I have seconds?"

Rafe's arm tightened on Nicole's shoulder. "No. She's my fiancée."

"Really?" His glittering gaze looked Nicole up, then looked her down, before flicking to Rafe.

"Really," Rafe growled. "So unless your papa wants to visit his little prince in the hospital tomorrow, I suggest you back the fuck off."

The interloper flashed a cocky grin. "My papa wouldn't like that."

"You've met Carlos, right?" Rafe paused, waiting for the name to register. "In case you or your papa are inclined to be stupid."

Even in the dim light you could see the man turn white.

"So either I punch your fucking lights out right now and we can start a small war or you can back the fuck off. Your call."

As the man spun around and shouldered his way through the crowd, Nicole looked up. "Have I met Carlos?"

"You might have. He was on the yacht. Brown hair, my height, but built like a bull."

She shook her head.

"You'll see him tomorrow. He's here in Paris. You'll like him. He plays Chopin like a professional. Good hands." *Especially with a knife.*

"You must play too." She'd seen the Bösendorfer grand piano in his Geneva home.

"Not much anymore. Occasionally for my mother." Rafe glanced over her head and nodded at one of his men who'd closed in as Yuri blocked their path, then watched him turn and follow the Russian. "Sorry about that. Yuri likes to think he's as tough as his father. He isn't." He smiled. "Should we see if we can make it to the hallway this time?"

When Rafe opened the door to the private room, Nicole stood on the threshold and breathed, "Jeez..."

When she didn't move, Rafe said, "Want another room?"

She looked up and smiled. "This little love nest will do just fine."

He laughed, easing her forward with a hand on her back. "I thought it might have been too much." He shut the door.

"Seriously, I'm going to be a princess tonight. Gold bed, white satin coverlet, murals on the walls, those big chairs made for poufy skirts, and, if I'm not mistaken, I see a mirror on the ceiling over the bed." She glanced up at Rafe. "Tell me, do palaces come with those? You'd know."

"Just for the record," he teased, not answering the question about ceiling mirrors, "I'm not playing a prince."

"You can be my stable boy then. That would be, like, forbidden and sexy, right?"

He laughed. "Jesus, tiger, where the hell do you get your ideas?"

"What? It's not common knowledge? Stable boys are always studly."

He grinned. "Maybe you're thinking about their horses."

She put up her hand. "Okay, that's too kinky."

"And this place is too refined, pussycat. So I'm thinking, drinks first," he said, changing the subject. "What do you want?"

"You said there was a menu."

Walking over to a gilded desk, he pulled open the drawer and lifted out a leather-bound folio.

"How did you know that was there? I thought you hadn't come here before."

"I figured." He flicked open the pale blue cover and glanced at the table of contents.

"Do all sex clubs have menus?"

Not exactly, unless the question What do you want?

counts as a menu. "I'm not sure. I haven't seen one like this before. Here, see if there's some drink you like." He handed her the blue leather folio.

Dropping onto the soft pink sofa, Nicole flipped through the pages of liquors. "What do you want?"

"I don't care. You decide." Sitting beside her, he leaned back and surveyed the dramatic stage set of a room that reminded him a little of a Bollywood version of Versailles.

"Have you ever had absinthe?"

"That's pretty strong, tiger. Pick something else."

"How strong?"

"One hundred thirty-six proof. Seriously, it'll put you on your ass."

"I'll just have a little."

He gave her a look from under his lashes. "Can I talk you out of it? You won't remember a thing."

"How do you know?"

"Someone told me, I guess."

"Liar. So you were with a woman who passed out on you?"

He uttered a small, low growl. "Don't pick a fight."

"I want absinthe."

"You got it." Coming to his feet, he walked to the phone and on his return, said, "You heard me. You can try it the old-fashioned way and then with champagne. Death in the Afternoon tastes better."

"I'm not allowed to ask you how you know that, I suppose."

"Not a problem. I like it better." He flicked his finger at the booklet. "See if you want a personal performance of some kind in here. Ganz tells me his girlfriend likes the two men and one woman sex act."

"Right here?" She waved her arm. "Like up close?"

"So I hear."

"Do you want to see it?"

"Not really. You're the only one I want to see. But it's up to you. New experience and all that shit."

"I'm trying not to be pissed, really, but—"

"Hey, hey," he whispered, pulling her into his arms. "All that's a million years ago, okay? You're my sunshine. You make me happy. I'm not fighting about one fucking thing tonight. Your call on everything."

She glanced up and grinned. "Everything?"

"Well, I might have one request." Lifting her onto his lap, he kissed her lightly. "And that never changes."

"Good. It better not."

"Not while there's still breath in my body, pussycat."

Twenty minutes later, after two drinks of absinthe, one with sugar and water, one with champagne, they were undressed, lounging on the bed, and at least one of them was well on her way to feeling good. "Okay, I feel adventuresome. Give me two men and one woman."

Rafe leaned over and touched her cheek gently. "This isn't audience participation, pussycat. You understand that, right?" Which wasn't necessarily true, but no one touched Nicole but him.

She giggled. "Let me reword that. Give me the performance. And while we're waiting for them, give me another Death in the Afternoon. I like that Hemingway named it. It makes it more celebrated and, like, historic."

"You still should pace yourself, tiger. Just saying."

"Pshaw." She giggled. "I love that word. Pshaw, shpaw, oh hell, you know what I mean. Don't frown at me, just a little drinky, okay? But call for the people first."

He didn't roll his eyes, but he thought about it. Like he thought about taking her home before she passed out. On the other hand, he could carry her out whenever and she was having fun. So he was having fun.

He made the call, made the drink—very weak—and listened to her tell him how much fun she was having in a real sex club for the first time in her life. And enjoyed her kisses and smiles and chattiness more than he ever thought possible. He heard about her and Fiona's friendship, which was just the very best; he heard about her sisters and brothers, one of whom was named Rafe. He almost asked her why she hadn't mentioned it before, but then she started talking about how much she liked surfing, how he had to come out to California and surf with her someday.

Until the knock on the door stopped her.

"Oh, God, oh, God—are they here? Where do I look? Can I look right at them, I mean directly at, well—"

"You can look anywhere you like," he said, climbing from the bed, nude and unconcerned. "Tell them what you want if you wish."

"Like what?" She pointed. "Are you going like that?"

"I think they've seen naked people before."

"Jesus." She pulled the sheet up to her chin.

He laughed. "Would you like an introduction? Would that help?"

"God no! Quick, give me another drink before you open the door."

He had his hand on the latch and turned. "I think you've had enough. This liquor is potent."

"Just a little one. Please?"

He eased the door open a slit, said, "Give me a minute," and shut it again. "I wish you wouldn't. How about just some champagne?"

"And a teeny, tiny bit of absinthe."

Her smile was dazzling, her voice soft and breathy, and a more punctilious man than he would have had to be standing there to refuse so sweet a request. "Just a little bit now."

"Yes, yes, whatever you say."

Good God, it was hard to resist such honeyed wheedling. He didn't. But he did say, "This is the last, even tiny, drink, tiger. I'm cutting you off."

"Of course," she said as if she actually meant it, then proceeded to drain the glass in one swallow.

As he walked to the door, he glanced at the clock, because no way was Nicole going to last much longer. As he let the nude performers in, he said, "This might be over in a hurry, so watch for my signal to leave. The lady is feeling no pain."

The pretty woman of the trio smiled at Rafe. "We could stay for you."

"Thank you, but no. My fiancée was the one interested in your performance."

Returning to the bed, Rafe settled Nicole in his arms and murmured in her ear, "Now you can give instructions if you think of something. Or tell me and I'll specify what you want."

She shook her head in a frantic little motion on his shoulder. "No way."

"We're ready," Rafe said.

The men were large and muscled, the woman small in relation to them, so one of the men set down a small wooden platform he'd carried in and helped the woman up onto it. In the meantime, the other man hit a switch on the wall and a bar suspended between two chains slowly descended from the ceiling above the woman. When it reached a suitable position where she could reach up comfortably and grip it, the switch was turned off. The woman stood between the two men, one in front of her, the other behind, her pussy and bottom at a level with the men's erections.

The men began kissing and caressing her, stroking her softly with their hands, fingering her gently, testing her readiness, their dicks engorged and fully prepared for action. Her eyes shut as one man slid two fingers up her pussy at the same time the other man tested her rear entrance with the tip of his dick.

"Non, non," she whispered, writhing slightly at the pressure. Whether acting or real, was uncertain. Her hips were stilled in a hard grip by the man behind her and she shuddered.

Nicole gasped, held on tightly to Rafe's arm, and shifted slightly on the bed.

The next few moments, the man in front gently sucked on the woman's nipples, added a third finger to her pussy, and soon she was softly panting. He gave a nod to his partner, who eased his dick in her ass a fraction more.

Nicole jerked at her soft cry, sucked in a breath, and groaned.

Rafe slipped his hand between her legs, ran his fingertips up her slick, pulsing cleft, felt her hard, steady throbbing beneath his fingers. "Can you wait until they finish?" he whispered.

Eyes shut, she shook her head.

"You sure? There's more."

Her fingers closed hard over his dick, squeezed harder. He glanced up, said, "Thank you. You may leave." And before the performers were out the door, he was deep inside Nicole and trying to keep her from coming in under five seconds.

"Hey, hey, wait." He withdrew slightly.

She dragged him back, pulled him deep inside her, whispered, "Don't want to," and promptly began to come.

What the hell, he thought, *it wasn't as though she ever waited.* And kicking ass, he caught up to her and came that first time right on cue.

She was all warm and cuddly in her half-wasted state and in the mood to kiss him all over repeatedly. This was a side of the feisty woman he'd come to adore that he hadn't seen before.

And as if she was a mind reader, she looked up from sucking on his dick, giggled, and asked, "Do you mind if I'm overzealous kissing-wise tonight?"

He laughed. "Anytime pussycat. I'll never say no."

"Oh, good." And she got back to business.

TWENTY-FOUR

Christ, two twenty-five a.m. Don't they know the time here in Paris?" Dominic grumbled, understanding his calls came in from all over the world. Rolling over, he grabbed his phone on the bedside table and hit the Answer icon.

"You're not going to like to hear this, but I just saw your niece Nicole."

Dominic recognized Julian Wilson's LA drawl; they'd run into each other yesterday at a business dinner. "So?"

"At the Chandelier Club."

"What?" Dominic sat up and swung his legs over the side of the bed.

"She was with some young dude a while ago. Then I got sidetracked. She looked like a newbie though."

Dominic was striding toward his dressing room. "No shit. Look, have Raoul stall them or lock them in if they're already in a room. Discreetly. No scene. I'll be there in fifteen minutes."

Kate, his wife, had followed him and was standing in the doorway. "Be where in fifteen minutes?"

He quickly explained in an edited version while he pulled on boxers and jeans. He called it a nightclub.

"Nicole's twenty-two, Dominic. Maybe she's okay."

He pulled a navy sweater over his head. "Nicole has a

history of making bad choices." He'd quietly bailed her out of a few over the years.

"Shouldn't that be her parents' problem? I'm just saying. She might not like you barging into some nightclub," Kate cautioned him with a yawn.

"I'm not asking her, and her parents don't know what she does. How much did you tell your grandparents about your sex life?"

"There wasn't a whole lot to tell."

"But you didn't tell them anyway. Right?" His voice was muffled as he reached into a closet and pulled out some shoes.

"Gramps would have scared them off."

"From what I've heard about Roy, I'm guessing he'd vetted them already and just let it go." He stepped into burgundy suede desert boots and swiftly tied them. "I'll be back in less than an hour. Shut the children's doors, will you? In case Nicole's screaming at me when we come back."

"Be nice, Dominic. She's not going to like you monitoring her activities."

"I'm not. Fuck—although I should have. Thank God Julian called." He grabbed some car keys from the top of the dresser. He didn't want to take the time for Henri to bring up the car. He stopped for a moment to give Kate a kiss, then patted her bare ass. "Close the kids' doors, then get back into bed, baby. No sense in ruining your sleep."

When he arrived at the club, he braked hard, cranked the Mercedes coupe nose in, straight up to the door, got out, pocketed his keys, and snarled, "Fuck you," in French to the valet who started shouting at him to move his car. "I'm here to see Raoul."

The man backed off like he'd been burned. Raoul owned this high-end sex club and ten others in Europe. He was connected and not to the aristocracy. Dominic had known him a long time, had done a lot of business with him in the past. They were friends, acquaintances, and, formerly, partners in vice.

Raoul was waiting for him in the foyer.

Dominic smiled tightly. "She still here?" He spoke quietly in French.

Raoul nodded. "I didn't know she was your niece. They wouldn't have let her in if we'd known."

"I fucking didn't know, so don't sweat it. I don't suppose you have a robe—just in case. I'm going to walk her out of here in about ten seconds."

Raoul snapped his fingers and a bouncer rushed over. "I need a robe. Meet us in room fourteen. I want you there before us." He was speaking to the man's back at the last.

The club owner and Dominic walked through the luxurious bar—all glass, onyx, crystal chandeliers, and plush carpets—then through the even more richly appointed main salon with murals on the walls, antique furniture, and dim lights. Both rooms were packed with clothed and unclothed bodies, everyone high or drunk, sexual exhibitionism graphically on display.

"You're happily married now, I hear," Raoul said as if people weren't fornicating all around them.

"I am," Dominic replied blandly. Having frequented places like this for years, he didn't react to the spectacle.

"And damned lucky to be. You've got kids, right?" Raoul was pushing fifty, personal-trainer trim, well-dressed, good-looking. He'd been married forever, Dominic recalled.

"They're in Barcelona with their mother. They're great kids. Both at university now. Yours are young?"

"Yes." Dominic smiled. "And precious." He sighed softly. "My niece was sugarsweet too not so long ago. Last I heard from my sister, Nicole was at my apartment in Monaco taking a break after college. There's a fucking snow job for you," he muttered. "Goddamn little liar."

"Give her a lecture from me too. This is no place for a young girl."

"Who brought her?"

"I didn't see. We'll find out. Want me to bar him from the club?"

"Nah. I don't care what he does so long as he's not with Nicole."

A bouncer was standing at the door to the room when they arrived, a black silk robe over his arm. "Door's open," he murmured.

Dominic nodded, took the robe. "Thanks." Then he turned to Raoul. "I'll go in alone. God knows what she's doing. Appreciate your understanding."

"Anytime, *mon ami.*"

Dominic turned the knob, pushed open the door, walked in, slammed the door behind him, took one look at the naked couple swiftly disengaging at his intrusion, and tossed the robe at the bed. "Put this on," he growled.

Nicole let out a shriek, scrambled up into a sitting position, and pulled the sheet up in front of her. "Uncle Dominic, what are you doing here!" she screamed, all wild huff and indignation.

And zoned out or drunk. "Shut the fuck up. I'm taking you home."

She didn't move, her eyes narrowed, her mouth set.

"Put the goddamn robe on," Dominic snapped, then glared at the bastard lounging naked beside her on the bed. "Who the fuck are you?"

"Who's asking?" A languid drawl, a small shrug that rippled the long black hair on his shoulder. Rafe wasn't going to argue with Dominic Knight, but he wasn't going to kiss his ass either. Righteous indignation was a little out of line for a man who'd spent years in places like this.

"Just answer me, asshole." But recognition was slowly dawning as Dominic surveyed the man's tattooed erection. He'd seen that inked dick in Tokyo in the days before Katherine. Even in a group orgy, even concentrating on getting off, you couldn't help but notice something like that. The young heir to the Swiss pharmaceutical fortune had been a wet-behind-the-ears kid at the time. So he'd be twenty-five, twenty-six, now and he was either on some pharmaceuticals that kept his dick hard or he was turned on by people looking. "Actually, I know who you are. So keep your painted dick away from my niece. Got it, douche bag?"

Okay, so maybe he didn't feel like taking Knight's shit. "You should fucking talk," Rafe said. "Aren't you the king of kink?"

"You're pushing your luck, kid."

"Jesus, I'm really scared."

"Good," Dominic said, ignoring the sarcasm. "You fucking should be." He shot a look at his niece, taking note of the absinthe bottle on the bedside table. "Christ, Nicole, how the hell drunk are you?" She'd fallen back on the bed, her dark hair a tangle of curls splayed out on the pillows, her eyes half-lidded.

"She wanted absinthe. I'm guessing you know she's hard to talk out of things." Rafe reached for his slacks. "I'm taking care of her. We don't need you."

"I know how you take care of women, Contini. So fuck off." Softly swearing, Dominic moved to the bed and manhandled Nicole's arms into the robe, feeling a major sense of déjà vu, remembering all the times he'd struggled to get her into her clothes when she was a baby. "Jesus, asshole," he muttered, glowering at the rich punk who was zipping up his slacks. "You like them unconscious?"

"I don't. How about you? It was a close one in that Bangkok club I hear. Those kinds of rumors are hard to suppress, right?"

The muscle over Dominic's cheekbone twitched like crazy, but he kept his mouth shut and, wrapping the robe around his inebriated niece, he tied the belt and picked her up in his arms. Then he abruptly stopped and scanned the room for Nicole's purse—credit cards, phone, ID—all the things you didn't want to leave in a place like this. Ah—there. Walking over to the brilliant pink sofa, he leaned over, grabbed her purse strap with one finger, then strode to the door.

Not inclined to start a public brawl in a place like this for any number of reasons, but mostly because it would cause problems for Nicole, Rafe said, "Tell Nicole I'll see her tomorrow. Early."

"Good luck with that, motherfucker," Dominic growled. Bending slightly, he flipped the door handle, swung the door back hard with his foot, and walked out to the echo of wood smashing plaster.

There were two bouncers in the hall waiting to escort him, and, following his muscle through the crowd, Dominic reached the front door in record time. The men accompanied him outside and down the steps, and after handing Nicole to one of them, Dominic took out his keys, opened the car doors, threw Nicole's purse on the console, and started the car to warm it up. Walking back to the man with Nicole, he took her in his arms, carried her to the car, carefully placed her in the seat, buckled her in, and quietly shut her door. With a word of thanks to the bouncers, he moved around the car to the driver's seat and slid behind the wheel.

As he swung the car back out into the street, he had a quick twinge of alarm.

What if he had to collect Rosie from a place like this someday?

Jesus fuck.

He shot a glance at Nicole sleeping peacefully and softly sighed. *Who would have thought?*

Not that he'd given a flying fuck about the time he'd spent in clubs like Raoul's. Of course, he hadn't given a flying fuck about much of anything in those days. Conversely, he had to admit to a rare sense of prudery when it came to Nicole. Maybe it was just that he knew his sister wouldn't approve, not to mention her husband would probably kill the little rat bastard in bed with her. Bottom line though, Nicole hadn't lived the life he had; she'd had a normal childhood. Raoul's club was way the hell too hard core for her.

She wasn't ready for a place like that.

He drove slowly, so Nicole's head wouldn't slide off the headrest. He took the steep ramp into the underground garage beneath the apartment building even more slowly, to keep her from slipping down the seat. But the low roar of the powerful engine in the confined space echoed off the walls in a loud, pulsating rumble.

Nicole woke up. "Where are we?" she asked in a wispy voice, like she was a thousand miles away.

"Almost at the apartment. And don't you dare raise your voice when we get there because the children are sleeping." He pulled into his parking space.

"He's like you, Nicky." Her voice was husky, half asleep.

"Jeez, don't say that." Dominic turned off the ignition. "That's the last thing I want to hear."

She turned her head to look at him, her eyes the same blue as his, clearer now as though returning to the world was a possibility. "I don't mean the sex club." She raised her hand in a small dismissive gesture. "I mean Rafe is smart and funny and he's good to me."

Dominic took a deep breath. "Nicole, honey, you're so damned young. You'll find all kinds of guys who'll be good to you. Pick someone else." He reached over and unsnapped her seat belt. "Now, come on. I'm taking you upstairs." Dominic owned the building on the Île Saint-

Louis, his apartment the entire top floor, the view of Notre Dame stunning. "Katherine will find some pajamas for you. And no one has to know about this. I told Katherine it was a nightclub. You ripped your dress and one of the dancers found you a robe. Unless you can think of something better."

She shook her head. "That's fine. Kate won't say anything to Mom, will she?"

"There's nothing to say. That particular nightclub was too rough. I brought you home. End of story."

"Thanks, Nicky. I mean for not telling anyone."

"You better thank me for getting you out of that fucking bed. Your boyfriend is bad news. Take my word for it, Nicole. You don't know. I do. Okay?"

"Okay, Nicky." But she'd noticed the faint vibration of the ringer on her cell phone in her small embroidered purse that had slid off the console and lay next to her hip. She looked away and smiled.

It was Rafe calling.

She knew.

Rafe slipped his phone in his pants pocket and looked up.

Simon was standing in the doorway, flanked by two bouncers who, in turn, were flanked by two of Rafe's men. Carlos wasn't taking any chances.

"You saw?" Rafe asked.

"Yeah, I was parked across the street. You staying or going?"

Rafe grinned. "What do you think?"

"A week ago I would have said staying. Now?" Simon shrugged and smiled. "Even the bookies won't give you odds."

Rafe reached for his shoes. "We'll see."

Simon snorted. "Fucking dreamer."

"Speaking of dreams, we have to wake up some people," Rafe muttered, sliding his shoes on. "I need a slew of presents by morning."

TWENTY-FIVE

Once Nicole was in bed, Dominic kissed Kate and said, "I have a few calls to make. Go back to sleep. I'll be in shortly."

"You're not calling Melanie are you?"

"No. There's no reason for her to know about this. It was a stupid mistake"—Dominic rolled his eyes—"one of many for Nicole. I don't want my sister upset. She thinks her children are sweet, innocent, and can do no wrong."

"Like you with our children."

"Yeah, well, ours are." He smiled. "You made them for me, why wouldn't they be perfect?"

"Sure, butter me up, but someday," Kate said with a sliver of a nod, "you're going to have to stop giving them everything they want."

"No I don't."

The corner of her mouth lifted in a small smile. "You're going to ruin them for the real world."

"That's what I'm here for, baby," Dominic said softly. "To keep the real world at bay. Now go to bed. I'm going to give Max a call. See what he knows about this nightclub. I don't want this incident to turn into a scandal."

"Don't stay up too late. The children wake early." Dominic had never missed a breakfast with his children.

"I know. I'll keep an eye on the clock." He blew her a kiss. "Sleep tight."

A short time later, Rafe walked into his house and wasn't surprised to find Carlos seated on the stairs in his usual uniform: black jeans, black lace-up boots, and a T-shirt from some obscure Basque or African band.

Carlos lifted his chin just a fraction. "Now what?" he said mildly.

Rafe kept moving. "I apologize to Knight, then get Nicole back." He gestured to him to follow. "I have some calls to make. After that you can bitch at me."

Simon had come in and followed Carlos into Rafe's office. "Get comfortable, guys," Rafe said. "Have a drink. This'll take a few minutes." Grabbing a mineral water from the drinks caddy, Rafe moved to his desk, dropped into his chair, and reached for the phone.

It rang at length, then kicked to voice mail.

Rafe redialed. Twice.

"You're persistent," Alessandra mumbled when she finally answered. "Are you sober?"

"More or less. And this time I *really* apologize for waking you," Rafe said in Italian. "Charge me for the inconvenience, but I need some gifts delivered to me before breakfast. Children's gifts. I'm in Paris. A girl five, a boy two and a half. Don't have the gifts wrapped. It's just a gesture."

"How big a gesture?" Alessandra had come alert, her voice crisp.

"Four or five presents each. Whatever you think children that age would like. Their mother is some incredible computer brain, so maybe something electronic for each of them. This is in the way of an apology to Dominic Knight. They're his kids. We had a little run-in tonight. He took Nicole back to his place."

She snorted. "He's not going to let you get near them. I don't mind taking your money, but he has security on top of security."

"I'm working on that. By the way, Nicole says thank you for the clothes."

"No, she doesn't. I talked to Basil. She didn't want to take them."

"She likes them now. I can be persuasive," he said, a smile in his voice.

"I've heard that," she murmured, amused. "Didn't you know she was Dominic's niece?"

"No. If she mentioned it, I didn't hear it."

"So tonight he came to save his niece from the notorious Rafe Contini. Where were you?"

"The Chandelier Club."

"Could have been worse."

"That's what I thought, but apparently he's become a fucking saint. Or hypocrite."

"Or just protective of his niece. Men make those kinds of distinctions."

"Whatever. His female classification system's not my problem. Nicole doesn't want to be at his place. She's been texting me. So find me something his kids will like. Diplomats always bring gifts, right? No later than nine thirty. Now, I still have some calls to make, so I gotta go. Thanks, Alessandra, you're my savior. *Ciao.*"

Leaning back in his chair, Rafe opened his arms wide and smiled at Carlos, who was sitting across the desk from him in a high-backed tapestry chair, his fingers lightly stroking the lion heads carved on the chair arms. "Hit me. Once you're finished telling me to cut her loose, I have to call Gina." A small lift of his brows. "So how did I step outside the lines?"

"Irrelevant," Carlos said, not prickly or urgent, just moving on. "We're on damage control now. First, you should let her go. Seriously. No joke. Send the lady a nice gift and a thank-you—even write it yourself if she matters more than the others. But she's in the way. You have too much going on right now with Ganz's war on the horizon. You don't have time for fucking."

"I'll make time. And it's not just that. It's"—a slow headshake—"different and strange and I don't know...a revelation."

"Whatever it is, you'll be putting her in danger. Knight's not going to like that."

"He won't know."

"He'll know. He's on the phone right now checking out every detail of your life down to your dick size. He protects his own—without mercy. A few years ago, when the Balkan Mafia tried to mess with him, they lost so many men they gave up; when he and his boys got caught in a firefight in Angola they all came out alive—which is more than you could say for the other side. The two big-time bankers in Singapore he personally threatened are still shitting their pants. He's not someone you want to fuck with."

A flash of impatience in amber eyes. "You think I give

a damn about his power? You think I can't push back just as hard? Jesus Christ, Carlos, how the hell do you think I stayed alive until you showed up? I took care of myself, my mother too, okay? So don't give me any shit about how Dominic Knight can take me down. He can't."

"Just be sensible. That's all I'm saying. This lady won't be around long."

"We're engaged."

"Jesus. Are you high?"

Rafe grimaced. "I wish I had that excuse." He blew out a breath. "Let's just say I'm not ready to let her go." He slid down on his spine, sighed, looked up from under his lashes, held a finger up. "I'm going to try to explain something, so just listen." He kept his voice even, as though the undercurrent of emotion was so strong he had to fight against it. "You know those video game images or fantasy stories where a band of men, hunters, warriors, are traveling across a barren landscape—some gray, endless dystopia? Anyway, I have this picture in my head where I come up on a single flower blooming in this vast wasteland of dark skies and gathering clouds. The flower is blue, delicate, and fragile, and I just want to stand there for a few minutes and take in the rare beauty. So I'm going to just stop and look, drink in the goddamn perfection for a few minutes. Okay? I'll start walking again when I have to, when staying longer will risk having the flower trampled by my enemies. But till then we have enough men to protect Nicole." He looked up. "I know what we're up against. She'll have to leave soon."

Carlos nodded. "A week, ten days at the most—maybe two weeks if Zou has to protect his flank before he attacks.

After Ganz's defection, he's got other enemies besides us. So this time he's not going to stop until someone above his pay grade decides it's not worth losing another man or we manage to cut off the head and the monster dies."

"Or we do."

"Yeah."

Having survived years of punitive emotional and physical trials, Rafe viewed the world with a certain fatalism. You did all you could until that option was gone. "Mother and Anton are competent," he said, shrugging off extermination. "The business will be fine. And Anton can protect Mother." Both men knew Anton's background; neither were naïve about his capabilities. Rafe shoved himself upright in his chair. "So first things first—total security for Nicole. No half measures." He smiled faintly. "You taught me well."

"You were in charge of your life long before I showed up. I'd never seen such an accomplished and aware twelve-year-old."

"Survival."

"Yeah, I know."

Rafe glanced at his watch. "So everything clear then?"

"One last thing. Shanghai's going to be the mother of all mothers. You know that, right?"

"They have been for a while. We could have lost a fortune in R and D a dozen times in the last few years. Except for Ganz. It's time to pay him back."

"You've been paying him."

"This is different. They killed Ganz's father. Ganz loved him." Rafe's head came up a fraction and he held Carlos's gaze full on. "I envy the feeling."

A couple seconds stare back, then a nod. "Okay. But if you get Nicole back from Knight, you can't stay here. It's too hard to defend."

"We'll go to Split."

"ASAP."

"Yes." Rafe reached for the phone. "If Gina can get me in, I'll explain to Knight that he's still the lead wolf, I mean him no disrespect, and when he's smiling again, Nicole and I will leave. See that a plane's ready."

Both eyebrows up, a lighter tone. "You're a spoiled shit," Carlos said. "He's going to see right through that."

"Yeah, I know." Rafe grinned. "That's when I tell him he's right and we start talking. And admit it—without me to manage you'd be bored out of your mind. Chasing women and gambling gets old and you know it."

"Did I ever say I was tired of either?"

"You're an adrenaline junkie. Too much tail and cards gets monotonous. You fucking need me to feed your high."

Carlos came to his feet and cracked a smile. "Sometimes—maybe. Keep in touch. I'm going to send enough troops to Split to secure the place."

After Carlos left, Rafe shot a glance at Simon, who was lounging on the sofa, a drink resting on his chest. "No friendly advice?"

"Fuck no. If we're going to Split, my life is golden."

"Do you mind sticking around? I'll need a ride in a few hours. Take a nap, I'll wake you."

"Will do." Simon kicked off his shoes, set his drink aside, shut his eyes, and was sleeping two seconds later. Fighting in the hellholes of the world, he'd learned to ignore artillery that wasn't close, find some out-of-the-way burrow, and sleep when he could.

Familiar with Simon's second sense about danger, knowing he was dead-to-the-world on his sofa, Rafe made his next call unconcerned he'd wake Simon.

"First, it's not an emergency, Gina," Rafe said quickly in French. "Relax."

"Then why the fuck are you calling me at four in the morning?" She slid her handgun back under her pillow; an automatic reaction when she was startled. She took a breath.

"I need your help."

"And I'm going to help you because?"

"Don't be a bitch. This is important. Don't forget, I'm nice to you when you want me to be." He could hear her breathing, trying to decide whether she wanted to be nice back, whether he'd still answer her booty call if she said no.

She sighed, sat up in bed, and ran her fingers over her face. "All right. What do you want?"

"Can you get me up to Dominic Knight's apartment? My girlfriend, his niece, is there under duress."

"He has a private elevator, keeps to himself, real family man, never travels without his wife and children."

"I've heard. You wouldn't happen to know his elevator code."

"I might. But I'm living in this building for a reason and I don't want to piss him off."

"Got it," Rafe said. "I understand he has good security?"

"The best. No offense."

"None taken. He probably has more enemies."

"Not anymore," she drawled.

Rafe exhaled. "Christ, is it on the fucking world news?"

"Only in a very specific circle. Why the hell did you poke that beast?"

"They started it. They've been trying to steal my R and D for years. I'm just defending myself. Or rather Ganz is. They recently killed his father. I'm sure you heard that too."

"An attaché at the Mongolian embassy in Paris. In broad daylight. That's sending a message."

"The guy in charge was too pissed at Ganz for finesse."

"I heard Carlos's in town. That should help. Rumor has it he finished up the last of Ganz's trouble in Monte Carlo and the fish are eating well."

"You hear a whole fucking lot." A slice of a laugh. "Care to tell me how many more are on their way?"

"A wave of locusts, *mon cher,*" she said softly. "But you already know that."

"Yeah. We're working on the incoming."

"Good idea. So when do you need the code?"

"Ten this morning."

"Okay. So you're going up to kiss his ring."

"I'm hoping to avoid that. I just want to apologize."

She laughed. "Good luck. He's not the forgiving type. He hasn't talked to his parents in years, although maybe I'm telling the wrong person that."

Rafe laughed. "Christ, maybe we have something in common after all."

"You're both badasses, I'll give you that. Ring me when you get here. I'll come down and see if I can help you get your girlfriend back."

"Thanks." *He was halfway to his goal.* "You're a sweetheart."

"Fucking A—hearts and flowers all the way."

She actually was a sweetheart at times, Rafe reflected, hanging up. Sexy sweet. At other times—ex-Mossad—she was a freelance lethal threat.

Rafe glanced at the time. It probably wouldn't hurt to sleep for a couple hours. He had to be alert if he wanted to convince Knight to let him leave with Nicole.

Dominic had been on the phone with his ADC, Max, off and on for hours, gathering the information he needed—none of it encouraging. The news from Macao was fucking catastrophic.

"If Contini's mixed up in that defection," Max said, "he's got a world of trouble on his hands. A friend of mine who runs security for a Singapore financier happened to be in Macao when the shit hit the fan. Rumor has it the plane was Contini's, the team that walked the defectors to the plane was Contini's, and the Shanghai gang is frothing at the mouth. Their entire cybernetwork was bombed to dust."

"Jesus, Nicole sure knows how to pick 'em."

"And Gora married Contini's mother a couple years ago. Right after Maso died, right after Gora's wife was found dead of an overdose in Istanbul."

"Fucking convenient."

"Yeah. You're looking at a real salt-of-the-earth family unit."

"Fuck, Melanie would wet herself if she knew where her baby girl was playing house."

"Nicole is a lot like you, Nick. Just saying. Don't get righteous."

Dominic laughed. "The day I get righteous, you have permission to put a bullet in my head. But she needs protecting from herself, from him, from this shit storm that seems to coming his way. So call up the troops. In case we need them."

"I've already sent out the message. Everyone's coming in from holiday."

"Okay, thanks." Dominic had been watching the clock. "I have to go. Kate expects me in bed when she wakes up. As for Nicole, I'll know more after I talk to her. There's no question she's going to balk at going home."

"She'd be safest there."

"We both know that. Getting her to agree is the fucking elephant in the room."

Max laughed. "Déjà vu. You never did what was prudent either."

"That's not fucking helpful," Dominic grumbled. "We'll talk later."

Dominic had just pushed away from his desk, calculating that he had twenty minutes to shower before Kate woke up, when his phone rang. He pounced on it, not wanting the ring to rouse the household. His private number was private. It had to be someone he knew.

"I hear we might be relatives," Gora said gruffly in Italian, their common language.

Dominic recognized the rough accent. "Did you set this up, motherfucker?" he growled at the mafioso, Anton Georgescu, who had almost ruined his life a few years ago.

"No. I just found out. The boy doesn't confide. He's also too young to know what he wants." There was a flash of anger in Gora's voice.

"That works out then, because my niece isn't his type."

"And Rafail's not hers," Gora said just as grimly. He'd done some checking too.

"What the fuck does that mean?"

"She's fickle, impulsive, men always buzzing around her. Rafail's getting involved. It worries me. I don't want him hurt."

"Him hurt? Are you fucking kidding me? Your stepson and a friend of his have some serious enemies from Shanghai mobilizing against them. A goddamn armada coming in for the kill. What the fuck's wrong with you? Aren't you watching your kid?"

"It all just happened in the last few days."

"Fuck if I care when it happened. It happened. I'm warning you now, if there's any blowback to my family, I'm coming after you with everything I've got. Full-scale war, Gora."

"Calm the fuck down. I'll deal with it."

Dominic crushed back a snarl and spoke very slowly. "You. Do. Not. Understand. This isn't your brain-dead, no-neck enforcers. This is a state-sponsored, fucking no-holds-barred bunch of thugs who'd kill their own mother if they were given the order."

"Don't you think I fucking know that?"

"It sure as hell doesn't seem like it when you tell me to calm the fuck down. I haven't been calm since I found out who my niece was shacking up with."

"I agree. The arrangement isn't wise. I'll talk to him."

Dominic hissed a breath between his teeth, pissed that Gora had the fucking gall to disapprove of Nicole when his goddamn stepson was the byword for lecherous vice. "You do that," he said with a bite to his voice. "In the meantime, I'm sending Nicole home. So when you talk to him you can give him the message."

"I might need some names from you. My contacts are more limited since I retired. But I'll send out a hit team, ten times ten teams, if necessary. I still can do that. He's my boy and no one's going to hurt him."

"Your boy?" Dominic's voice was barely a whisper.

"Stepson."

"Don't fucking lie. I heard your voice." For a second, clear as a bell, Gora's heartbeat rang in the word *boy,* and the truth slipped out into the world like a wisp of smoke.

"I don't care what you heard. It's none of your business. It's no one's business but mine. As far as Rafail knows he's my stepson, so shut the fuck up."

"If I wasn't so pissed, I'd find it amusing that you cuckolded that head case Maso."

"I didn't know about Rafail until after Maso died. Long story. It doesn't matter now. But he doesn't know he's my son and I want it to stay that way. If you tell him, I'll see you in hell."

There was the hard, cold vehemence Dominic had heard before in Rome years ago. "Take it easy. He won't hear it from me. But if I needed added reason to keep my niece away from him I have it now. Keep your boy away from her," Dominic said, his voice as deadly as Gora's. "Now and forever." He set the phone in the cradle softly, as if he needed to compensate for the rage boiling inside him. Then he sat utterly still, telling himself it couldn't be possible. In all the world, this was who Nicole had picked? He sucked in a breath, said, "No," under his breath, then "No way," in a louder tone, then "No way in hell," with such fury, he could barely breathe.

TWENTY-SIX

Rafe, wearing only boxers, was standing in front of an open wardrobe door flicking through hangers. Three discarded shirts and two pairs of trousers were in a pile on the floor. He was softly swearing.

"Wear your gray linen slacks and one of your short-sleeve shirts."

Rafe swung around to see Natalie standing in the doorway. A flash of impatience lit his eyes. "Do you mind?"

Her shrug set her dangly jet earrings quivering. "You're not naked. And it's not as though I haven't seen you naked."

"Great. That's what I want to hear."

"I'm an old lady. You're not the first man I've seen without clothes."

"Hey. This isn't a conversation I want to have." He lifted his chin. "Do you want something?"

She held up Nicole's backpack. "Here's the change of clothes you wanted. And a word of advice. Relax. You're nervous as a bridegroom."

"Jesus, Natalie, if you want me to relax, don't say words like *bridegroom*."

"Everything's going to be fine."

Suddenly his gaze was nailed on her. "You saw?"

She shrugged. "It wasn't all sunny skies, but you can do it."

"You try to keep things casual, then it changes. Gets real." He did a quick shoulder roll, winced, every muscle tense. "It throws me."

"She's a lovely woman. Special in ways that touch you, that make you stop and think you might be missing something." A bare nod in his direction. "Why wouldn't she matter?"

Rafe examined her, did some quick calculating behind his eyes, finally flashed a wry smile. "You're right, take a bow. Damned if the world just seems better when Nicole's around, colors brighter, sun more dazzling. Nicer."

"Explain that to her uncle."

Rafe groaned.

"I have a feeling he might understand. He wasn't always happily married."

Rafe's eyebrows flickered. "Christ, how do you know that?"

She look amused. "As you recall, I have a gift." *And a thousand street contacts in the gypsy community.* "Now get dressed. I woke Simon. He's showering. Come downstairs and I'll make you a good breakfast before you go into the lion's den."

"Jesus, he's just a fucking man."

"I didn't say he wasn't. Although, if you're sensible, you'll mind your manners."

Rafe laughed. "That's the plan, Natalie."

At the same time Rafe was talking to his housekeeper, Nicole was on her way into the kitchen. She'd have coffee, then find something to wear. She wanted to be ready when Rafe came for her.

Dominic heard Nicole in the hallway. Quietly sliding out of bed, he threw on sweats and a T-shirt and left the bedroom without waking Kate. He preferred privacy for what was sure to be a difficult conversation.

When he walked into the kitchen, Nicole was standing in front of the espresso machine in a pair of Kate's pajamas, looking uncertain.

"Let me," he said. "Every machine is different. What's your pleasure?"

As she spun around, her brows dipped into a scowl. "Double espresso, and I'm still pissed at you so you can stop smiling."

"I understand. Sit." He pointed at the scrubbed pine table surrounded by colorful painted chairs in the center of the large, sunny kitchen.

She bristled. "Don't tell me what to do."

"Sorry, please sit," he said gently. "The coffee will take a few minutes."

The only sound for the next small interval was the hiss of the espresso machine and the ticking of a tall case clock in the corner.

Pissed as hell that Dominic had interfered in her life last night, Nicole came out guns blazing. "I met someone you know in Monte Carlo," she said, her gaze trained on her uncle. "Her name was Bianca—a tall, dark-haired bitch."

Dominic froze. A heartbeat later, he turned and looked at Nicole's smug face. "I'm sorry you had to meet her. Forget it."

She lifted one eyebrow. "It's a little hard to forget when she said you two had a child. Does Kate know?"

He wanted to slap that smug look off her face. He knew what she was doing. A good offense is the best defense. "Yes, Kate knows. And the child wasn't mine. The situation was taken care of a long time ago. End of story."

Nicole made a face. "Funny. *She* says the child is yours."

One of his eyebrows flicked; that was all. "Since you met her, you have to be aware that she's a gilt-edged, lying bitch. Now, we're done with this conversation and if you mention it to Kate, I'll have you on a plane home so fast your head will spin. Do we understand each other?"

"I'm not going home, so fuck you and your threats," Nicole snapped.

"You're going home if I say you're going home," Dominic snapped back.

"Jesus, Dominic, who made you God?" she shouted. "I'm twenty-two years old, I'm not your child, you have no say over what I do."

"Keep your goddamn voice down or you'll wake the kids," he growled. "And little missy, right now, I'm the only one who *does* have a say. Or would you like me to tell your mother who you're mixed up with? No? It looks like you don't think that's a great idea. I won't even mention your dad because he'd lock you in your room for the next decade if he knew what the hell Rafe Contini does in his free time. And I'm not talking about the Chandelier Club. He took you there because it was tame. Yeah, look all wide-eyed. That place is like nursery school for hard-core players. Okay?"

"And you would know," she hissed.

"I did. Not anymore. But that's the difference between him and me. The serious, anything-goes, twisted, fuck scene is still his playground." His gaze narrowed. "You wouldn't like it. There's nothing pretty about it."

"You can't scare me. If other places are worse, he didn't take me to those, okay? There's nothing about him that frightens me." Unblinking, she stared at him. "So stop with the bullshit. And I'm only here for the summer anyway—a few weeks more. Then I have to go back to school. You don't have to make a federal case about this. We're both just enjoying the holiday."

"He's got other problems," Dominic said flatly. "Business shit that could be dangerous."

"If you're talking about the attack on his company computers, that's over."

Dominic slid two small cups of espresso out from under the machine spouts, and walked over to the table, wondering what lie would best serve. "There might be more attacks," he said simply, setting the cups down and taking a seat at the table.

"Rafe has plenty of security. Like you. He protects me the same way you protect your family."

She didn't have a clue in hell. "I'm not sure that's true."

"See, you're equivocating." She jabbed her finger at him. "You don't know."

"Maybe if you just went home for a week or so," Dominic suggested, perjuring himself without a qualm, intent on getting Nicole to the States, where she'd be safe. "Once things calm down you—"

Two young children suddenly burst into the kitchen screaming, high-pitched and repetitively, "Auntie Nicole! Tanti Mic! Auntie Nicole! Tanti Mic!"

And a moment later two little pajama-clad bodies hurled themselves at Nicole. She leaned down, scooped them up on her lap, and the adult conversation was over.

Kate arrived a few minutes later, tying the belt on her robe. "Morning, everyone. Isn't it nice Auntie Nicole is visiting?" She smiled at her children crowded together on Nicole's lap. "Tell Auntie what you've been doing this summer."

Both children began talking at once, giving Nicole a breathless rendition of their activities: how they'd been learning to swim, *underwater,* they both explained in an excited rush of words. How they were going to go to the seashore too before they had to go back to school. How they'd had classes in computer games, James explained with such swelling pleasure, his words tumbled out in an unintelligible flurry that required interpretation from his older sister. "Isn't that so, Jimmy," Rosie said, after making everything clear. He nodded furiously, his dark hair flopping back and forth and went off on another tangent, requiring further explanation.

Their indulgent parents watched and smiled.

Nicole was smiling too. She and the children were close.

Suddenly, the back door to the kitchen opened and a tall, gray-haired woman walked in, carrying a market basket with fresh produce and two baguettes tucked under her arm. She greeted everyone with a smile and a cheerful, *"Bonjour."*

Preferring their privacy, Dominic and Kate didn't have live-in help, but the cook came in each day and saw to their meals. The children immediately jumped off Nicole's lap and clamored for the morning pastry Emilie always brought from the market. After handing them each a small caramel bun, the cook asked, "Now, what would everyone like for breakfast?"

Relieved that she was free from any further arguments, at least until after breakfast, Nicole smiled at the cook and put in her order for a veggie omelet. Rafe would find a way to liberate her; he'd texted that he'd come for her in the morning. She wasn't going home. Dominic might not like it, but that wasn't her problem.

Breakfast was almost over, the last of the children's pancakes sizzling on the griddle, when the doorbell rang.

"Me get, me get!" James shouted, sliding out of his chair in a flash. "Me, me, me!" he screamed, running from the kitchen.

Dominic was right behind him, followed by the rest of the family. Visitors were rare. No surprise, when it practically took special permission signed in triplicate from the pope to reach the front door. When the concierge always called for confirmation before anyone was allowed up.

Dominic opened the door and froze.

Rafe smiled. "Morning." Wearing perfectly pressed gray slacks, his white linen shirt buttoned up to the neck, his shoes shined to a high polish, his hair pulled back in a ponytail smooth as a matador's, save for a pocket protector, Rafe looked like an accountant—albeit an uncommonly handsome one.

"Papa! Papa! Up! Up! Hold me!" James screamed in French; he had his father's gift for languages. He already spoke four, including toddler Malay and Cantonese.

When Dominic picked up his son—a smaller version of himself, with identical hair, eyes, and cute rather than handsome looks—James pointed his finger at Rafe. "Who he?" he asked in English, having heard Rafe's greeting. "Who you?" he added when his father didn't immediately answer.

"My friend Rafe," Nicole interjected, stepping forward, her heart pumping wildly, feeling happiness bubble inside her; Rafe was trying so hard in those ridiculous clothes.

"You tan be *my* friend too," James said with a wide smile, then repeated the sentence in French in case the man didn't understand because he hadn't responded.

"Thank you," Rafe finally said in English. "I'd like that. I have a little brother like you."

"You do?" James grabbed a handful of Dominic's hair and swung his father's head sideways so he could see into his eyes. "He got bruver yike me, Papa."

Dominic nodded. "Yes, I heard."

"Bruver got name?" His gaze back on Rafe, James jabbed at his chest. "Me Jimmy."

"Hi, Jimmy. My brother's name is Titus."

Rosie tugged on her father's pant leg, sensing something was wrong. Her attachment to her father was strong, almost mystical; they were a team. "Daddy?"

Dominic looked down and smiled. "It's fine, sweetie." He winked at her. "Everything's fine."

Rafe saw that spark, that magic between parent and

child, and knew that Dominic Knight wouldn't make a scene in front of his children. Lifting up the shopping bags he was carrying an inch or two, Rafe said, "I brought the children some gifts, if that's okay?"

"Me, me, gif!" James screamed and wiggled frantically in his father's arms, trying to get down.

Rosie lightly brushed her father's leg, more composed than her brother, remembering her manners, but excitement shone in her eyes. "May we, Daddy?"

Goddamn fucker, Dominic silently swore, then turned his full attention on his daughter, giving her a little smile. "Of course you can, sweetie." His gaze shifted to Rafe, turned into a glare. "Come in." With a quick glance over his shoulder, he lifted an eyebrow to Kate. "Why don't you show the children what Rafe brought while he and I talk for a minute in my office." Another sharp look for Rafe. "That okay with you?"

"Absolutely. No problem." Rafe handed the two bags to Kate, then slid Nicole's backpack off his shoulder and held it out to her.

"I'll come with you," Nicole said.

"No you won't," Dominic snapped.

Dominic's tone made the children jump. They'd never heard a harsh word from their father.

"Katherine, take Nicole with you to help with the presents." Dominic smiled at his children. "Go with Mummy. I'll come see all your presents in a few minutes."

Rosie didn't move until Dominic bent down, brushed a fall of red hair from her forehead, and kissed her. "Go on, sweetheart. I'll be right there." As the family walked away,

Dominic said under his breath, "You're a real pain in the ass, you know. Let's get this over with." And he turned and moved down the hallway.

A few moments later, Dominic's office door was closed and the two, dark-haired men, both tall, powerful, indisposed to failure, exercising authority in all facets of their lives, eyed each other like fighters in the opening round of a cage match.

Dominic's eyes were blue flame, his voice gentle—no threat, just stating a fact. "You fuck with any of my family, you fuck with me. It's as simple as that. Now what the bloody hell are you doing here?"

"I'm here for Nicole."

"I must be a genius. I already figured that out. You can't see her. Now leave."

"I'll just come back."

The air sharpened, turned cold. "That would fall into the category of fucking with my family. Are you stupid?"

"She doesn't want to be here," Rafe said simply. "You know her better than I but even I know she won't stay if she doesn't want to."

"You don't know me very well either." Dominic gave Rafe a warning stare. "If I say she stays, she stays."

A small curl to Rafe's mouth, a faint grin. "Really? You're sure?"

"How the fuck *did* you get in?" Dominic growled. "Did Nicole give you the code?"

"No. She wouldn't do that." The last thing Rafe wanted was for any blame to fall on Nicole. "I haven't talked to her since last night." A half truth, but she hadn't texted the code. "You saw her then. She was out of it."

"Yeah, that pissed me off. You should have taken better care of her."

"You have to know once she decides to do something no one can stop her." Rafe shrugged. "She was in a mood. She wanted to drink."

Dominic grunted—not an answer, but a form of acknowledgment. "You still haven't told me how you got in."

"I know someone in the building."

"That doesn't get you to the top floor."

"Gina lent a hand."

"You know Gina?"

"We're friends."

Dominic's brows rose at the word *friends* spoken in that tone. "How do you get along with her boyfriend, the Saudi prince?"

"I've never discussed it with him. Gina's an independent woman."

"I've heard."

There was a curious nuance in Dominic's voice. "How well do *you* know her?" Maybe he wasn't a total family man after all.

"Not well. She's a tenant, the kind I prefer. Capable."

"Ex-Mossad."

"Yes, as I said, capable. Keeps to herself."

"You had her up to your apartment not long ago, a contact you needed. She paid attention. You should probably change your code."

"Okay, so we know how you got here. Now, *why* are you really here? So far, I'm not buying your story."

"It's not a story. I texted Nicole and told her I'd pick her up this morning."

"From someone like you, I'll need a more definitive explanation, something with a little more feeling than your usual *pickup* tale. No bullshit or I'll chuck you out the window."

"You could try to chuck me out the window."

"Cocky."

"She's worth staying for." Rafe's chin went up just a fraction. "Worth taking shit from you. Worth whatever hassle you feel like handing out."

Dominic's eyebrows rose faintly. "Tell me more. And I'll think about it—not very hard, because you're nothing but trouble for her, but let's just say I'm curious what a guy like you thinks is worthwhile in a woman." Dominic smiled tightly. "Other than the obvious."

Rafe let the dig pass; it was counterproductive to rise to the challenge. He wanted to walk out of here with what he came for and if he had to ignore a few asshole remarks to do it, he would. "I just met Nicole a week ago, or hell—four days ago. I don't know if a woman has ever had you considering words like *miracle* and *crazy, tender,* and *mystical* even, but—ah . . . your wife."

A small flinch, like something had hit home. "Okay, so that's not what I thought you'd say, but the problem is—I know you from places I'd rather not know you from."

"You were there too, and you're not there anymore," Rafe said.

"After four days?" Dominic's brows spiked upward. "Come *on,* you can do better than that."

"Did you go back to those places once you met your wife?"

"That's different." Dominic blew out a breath. "In hindsight, it's all a massive waste of time. But you don't know till you know."

"Maybe I do now."

Dominic gave him a steely-eyed look. "At your age? Gimme a break. You're still racking up your score. So, look, we're both"—he sighed—"experienced. With your track record you have to know this isn't permanent. I don't want Nicole hurt. You be nice to her too long and she's going to suffer when you decide to move on."

"She's the one who's moving on. She's going back to school at the end of the month."

"Which brings up another point. I'm not sure you *have* a month of leisure with Shanghai on your ass. That's major fire power coming your way."

"I'm taking care of it."

"You might not be able to. You don't have the troops."

"I do. You know who my father was. I was dealing with his enemies before most kids had their braces out. So my security is strong, more than capable, and currently expanding. Carlos has the word out. And Ganz can hack into their communications. They give an order, we know it." Rafe blew out a breath. "I'd rather stay out of it. I would if I could. But it's not likely."

"Not a chance," Dominic said.

"Right." Rafe sighed.

"Except for your friend you'd try?"

"Yeah—I would. But Ganz and two other guys are my family, or as much family as I have, aside from my mother. And everyone needs someone at their back. I can count on them, they count on me. You fuck with my family, you fuck with me," he said, smiling faintly. "It's that simple."

"Smart-ass." But Dominic's mouth twitched slightly and he thought of his sister, who'd been all he had growing up. Suddenly, he was looking at Rafe Contini through a slightly different lens.

"I really will take care of Nicole," Rafe said, recognizing a small breakthrough in their disagreement. "Hand on my heart." He made the gesture. "And I wish I could walk away from these pricks who've been trying to steal from my company for years. Piracy is a fucked-up business model if you ask me. I have a company that contributes to society both in product and charities. My grandfather planned it that way. He was a good man."

"Maso?" A test question.

Rafe shrugged. "A place holder. He wasn't interested in anything but—"

"I know. You don't have to say it."

"Personally, I like R and D—have since I was very young. We help make the world better, safer, healthier. In fact, we have a new nonspecific flu vaccine coming online soon that's revolutionary. And we just discovered an on/off switch in a genome sequence that shuts down tumor development in certain tumors." Rafe smiled. "Sorry, off topic. Anyway, if you'd allow it," Rafe added, with exquisite deference, with a conciliatory, respectful tone he'd never before employed, "I'd like to take Nicole to my property in Split. It's completely secure and the moment it isn't, I'll see that Nicole goes home."

Rafe took a small breath before he added, "I've never been with a woman for more than a few hours, so—this feels like the happiest day of my life. Ask Nicole. She says the same thing. Neither of us ever thought we'd experience the sappy, once-in-a-lifetime stuff. It's like free-falling into a brave new world. It's that good. Ask her, she'll tell you."

Dominic's lips were pursed, but there was something different in the brilliant blue of his eyes, like maybe some test had been passed, like there might be an alternative to *fuck off* and *no way in hell.* "Sit." Dominic pointed at a chair. "Give me a minute to make some calls."

While the children were busy tearing boxes apart, Kate and Nicole confided in each other, as they had for years. Nicole had been instrumental in bringing Kate out of the sadness engulfing her after her miscarriage; they'd been close ever since.

"Rafe seems nice," Kate said. "He thought of the children."

"He *is* nice. That's why I like him. Dominic thinks he's too disreputable, but I told him he should talk. I heard what Dominic was like before he met you. And look at him now."

"Your uncle worries about you, that's all. He's protective."

Nicole rolled her eyes. "Controlling, you mean."

Kate smiled. "Dominic likes to think he can manage the world. Not that he doesn't do a pretty good job of it, but there are times. I understand. Oh my goodness, a doll with red hair just like yours," Kate said, responding to Rosie's squeal of delight. "Isn't that lovely."

And the next few minutes, they were kept busy oohing and aahing over the gifts that both children pronounced as just *perfect*.

"Could I talk to you for a minute, Nicole? In my office. You and Rafe."

The women looked up.

Dominic was standing in the doorway to the conservatory, smiling, like everything was nice and friendly. Like the sun wasn't shining through floor-to-ceiling bulletproof glass, like he and Rafe were buds, like he was inviting Nicole into his office for milk and cookies.

Nicole hesitated.

"If there's a problem, let me know," Kate said, patting Nicole's arm. "I'll talk to Dominic for you. Now go."

As soon as Nicole walked into the office, Rafe came to his feet, went to her, and took her hand. "You okay?" he whispered.

"What's going on?"

"I think we're good."

Despite a truckload of misgivings, there was something about Nicole in unicorn pajamas and Rafe buttoned up tight that almost made Dominic smile. They looked so young and dreamy-eyed when they smiled at each other, even Contini, who had so many miles under his belt he should be jaded as hell. Something almost naïve burning there. Something beautiful.

Understanding the heart of it, the light and glow of

it, Dominic said quietly, "Come, sit down," and motioned to a sofa. "I think Rafe and I have arrived at a workable compromise."

"I don't have to compromise," Nicole protested, but Rafe squeezed her hand and stopped her.

"Dominic and I agreed on this," he said, drawing her to the sofa. "There's more trouble on the way and I want you safe. So listen."

"Here's what Rafe and I were thinking we'd do," Dominic said a moment later, sitting on the corner of his desk, swinging one bare foot. "I'll tell your mother I saw you in Paris and you were enjoying your holiday. You okay with that so far?"

"Thanks, Nicky," Nicole breathed, shooting a quick glance at Rafe, who was smiling before looking at her uncle again. "Thanks a lot."

"Hey, what's a summer break for, right?" Dominic gave her a little sideways smile. "And Rafe's going to take good care of you till you go back to school."

Nicole turned and grinned at Rafe.

"Make sure you call your mother and be nice, make her feel good," Dominic said. "Tell her you're going to Split for a few days with some friends, to see the sights, swim, sail, all that holiday shit. I'll be sending Leo along with you. Your personal bodyguard." He stopped her protest with a raised hand. "No negotiation. Rafe and I have agreed on this. He knows the situation better than either of us."

She looked at Rafe, who nodded.

"Okay," she said.

Dominic smiled. "Good. That's settled. Now give me a hug and we'll go see the children."

A moment later, Dominic took Nicole in his arms and, holding Rafe's gaze over her head for a second, said to her, "Now, listen to Rafe when it comes to security. Don't give him any trouble, okay?"

"Yup." She smiled up at her uncle. "Thanks for understanding."

"Your boyfriend's a good talker. Thank him."

After joining Kate and the children, Nicole and Rafe got down on the floor and began helping Rosie and James with their video games. "My brother, Titus, is six now and getting pretty good at these games," Rafe said. "Here, try this...see how it works?"

"Me dood too!" Jimmy exclaimed, grabbing the game device from Rafe.

"You are. Look, you hit that bouncing squirrel in the corner. Perfect. You got ten points. Push the squirrel icon again."

Nicole reached up and opened the top button of Rafe's shirt.

He smiled and shifted his shoulders. "Thanks. I was being strangled."

"I noticed."

Then Rafe turned back to the kids. "Shall we see if we can climb all the way to the top of this mountain? That's the way, Rosie. Perfect. Here, Jimmy, put your finger right there. There you go."

"You've done this a few times before," Kate said, smiling at Rafe.

He grinned. "A few thousand times, Mrs. Knight."

"Call me Kate, please."

He dipped his head. "Then Rafe, okay? Nicole just started using my given name." He winked at Nicole. "I think that means she's getting serious."

"You better believe it," Nicole said with a grin.

A half hour later, after Nicole had changed and she and Rafe had said their good-byes and left, while Rosie and James were still engrossed in their new toys, Kate turned to Dominic lounging beside her on the sofa. "All is well now?"

"More or less. Leo's going with Nicole as my eyes and ears."

Kate's brows lifted. "Really. That's necessary?"

"Just a precaution," Dominic said mildly. "I feel responsible for Nicole when she's so far from home."

That Rafe Contini had pathological, professional killers on his ass was also a cogent reason for having eyes and ears on her. The second Rafe even smelled a hint of danger on the breeze, he'd promised that Nicole would be spirited out of Split. Carlos and Max were coordinating additional troop movements to the site to augment security. Leo was there to help.

TWENTY-SEVEN

What did you say to Dominic?" Nicole asked, as Simon drove them away from the apartment on the Île Saint-Louis. "I was surprised he didn't put up more of a fuss."

"I told him we're both feeling the magic," Rafe said, holding her in his arms, thinking it was the right word for what he was feeling, that the world was breath held and gold and dazzling. "I said it to him a dozen different ways and he finally got it. I hope you don't mind about Leo, but it wasn't a bad compromise," Rafe said blandly, in lieu of the extensive massing of troops at Split. "He's on his way to the plane. We're taking off soon."

"Leo's fine. I like him." Then she twisted in his arms so she could see his face. "I'm so happy it's bewildering. But perfect too, like the universe is doing us a favor. And I don't want to miss a thing, I want to pay attention to every second of every day."

"Don't worry, pussycat," Rafe whispered, kissing her gently. "We have lots more than seconds." But even as he spoke, he felt the slash of grief slide up his spine. They had more than seconds, but not many days. Leo was there to take Nicole home when Rafe could no longer protect her. That was the bargain he'd made with Dominic Knight.

Please turn the page for a special,
brand new extended scene from

POWER AND POSSESSION!

Dear Readers,

I've added a few pages to the scene with Rafe and Nicole in the Paris sex club. Whether it was a whim, a rash impulse, a voice in my ear—who knows? My characters talk to me. I have no control. And after all, Rafe had been on his best behavior all evening.

This particular sex club was tame as hell by his standards, but that was the whole point, he told himself. Be good. Don't get out of hand. Nicole will enjoy herself. So the brakes were on his libido; no problem.

Then out of the blue—well not exactly out of the blue—since she'd just made him very happy as in—best ever happy—he told her he owed her big-time. "Anything," he said.

A little blink, a tentative smile. "Anything?" Then she shut her eyes as though that made her invisible and blushing bright pink said in a rush, "I've never tried, oh God, oh Jeez, I don't know how to ask for, you know."

Rafe understood. But Nicole had had several absinthe drinks, so he gave her a whole lot of opportunities to change her mind about *you know.*

She didn't want to.

So really—what man could refuse?

And who wants a man that would?

I hope you all enjoy this extended scene!

C. C. Gibbs

(Continues scene in sex club in Paris)

And as if she was a mind reader, she looked up from sucking on his dick, giggled and asked, “Do you mind if I’m overzealous kissing-wise tonight?”

He laughed. “Anytime, pussycat. I’ll never say no.”

“Oh, good.” And she got back to business.

A few minutes later, sprawled on his back, still breathing hard, Rafe reached down, pulled Nicole up on his chest and rubbed his fingers over her lips. “Such a—sweet— mouth.” His voice was ragged. “Best. Ever.” Raising his head in an impressive display of rippling abs, he kissed her lips, then flopped back down and grinned. “I’m still fucking levitating somewhere on the edge of wrecked and dazzled. I owe you big-time. Seriously, anything.”

Her heart started beating overtime. Whether it was the absinthe, the way Rafe said, “Anything,” his deep voice low and sexy as all hell or whether the tantalizing image of the threesome, particularly the part where the man’s hips met the woman’s ass and his cock disappeared from sight. It all made her tense, hot, hungry, the possibilities sending a rush of little shocks and shivers and aching need spiking through her body.

“Anything?”

Rafe hauled his ass back from his happy place at the startling tentativeness in Nicole’s query. She didn’t ask much. At least not like that. Like some virgin teenager thinking about her first kiss. A quick blink, a quicker smile. “Absolutely. Whatever you want. Hey.” He smoothed away her little frown. "No limits, pussycat. You want something. You got it."

"I've never tried"—she shut her eyes—"I don't know how to ask," she mumbled, the blur of words at the end not entirely due to alcohol—dangerous temptation sending a surge of adrenaline to her brain.

She didn't have to ask. Her cherry-red blush was signal enough. "Wanna try it?" His voice was ultra soft, his golden gaze extraordinarily gentle. "We'll take it slow. You can tell me to stop anytime. You're in charge. Now you have to open your eyes," he said, the familiar teasing surfacing once again, "or I'm going to figure you didn't mean it."

A brief, little peek from one eye.

His brows canted upward. "If you're shy, we can just forget about it. Go home. Watch TV."

Both eyes opened wide. "I'm not shy."

He smiled. "You could have fooled me." He wanted to say he'd make sure it was good for her, but that would suggest a history of other times and places, so he said instead, "Should I get the girl and guys back? Check out how it's done? Like lesson two?"

She took a small breath. "Maybe. Wait. I need another drink first."

"You have another drink," he said with a little head shake and an easy smile, "you're going to miss out on the fun."

A shiver of lust, a hint of the unknown teased her senses. "So it's fun?"

"I can't speak from experience but I've watched a lot of porn," he said, only half-lying. He didn't personally use his ass for a playground.

"Oh, God, I can't decide." Bewildered and awed at the same time, she couldn't think straight. "Maybe we shouldn't—you know... call them."

He tugged her a little closer until her lips met his. Warm, gentle, his face so close his amber eyes so beautiful, every buzzing nerve in her body started twitching up a storm. "Hey, either way, okay?" Soft, comforting, his hands slid down her spine. "You're in charge."

"Promise?"

"Every second."

She smiled, a tiny smile, dipped her lashes just a fraction. "Okay."

Fuck. Nicole shy as hell was like ordering up every male's number one fantasy. "Same people?"

She gave him a flicker of a nod.

Reaching for the bedside phone, he held her gaze. "Last chance." None of this was worth making her upset or uncomfortable.

A breathless, small laugh. "Fucking call already."

He grinned, gave her a quick pat on her ass, said, "Brilliant," and picked up the receiver. He spoke rapidly in French, his voice soft and low. A small scowl creased his brow while he listened briefly, then his tone sharpened, and speaking fast, he delivered what even to a casual bystander were brusque orders—although the only word Nicole recognized in the rush of French was euros.

Moments later, Rafe set down the receiver with deliberate restraint and turned to Nicole with a smile. "I told them we didn't want to wait. They were happy to oblige."

"Jeez, Louise, remind me not to get on your bad side," she said with a grin.

"Impossible. You're the sunshine of my life. Now, let's see about finding some useful"—he purposely used a non-clinical word—"amenities for this brand-new playtime. Don't move. I like you right where you are."

Holding Nicole against his body, he rolled a quarter turn, pulled out the drawer on the bedside table, rifled through the supply of packaged items, selected two and swiveling back, dropped the lube and butt plug on the bed.

Her eyes widened.

"You can change your mind. I'll send the people away. We can go home or stay here and do missionary position—whatever. It's up to you."

She shook her head, took a breath. "I trust you."

Whoa—that was a new phrase; a novel obligation as well for someone like him in places like this. But then everything about Nicole was a first-time feeling. "Just remember—you don't like something, tell me stop. Anytime, okay?"

Before she could answer someone knocked on the door.

"One more quick drink. Come on," she said, wrinkling her nose. "What's the worst that happens? I forget all the fun and games?"

"When you put it that way," he said with a warm, crinkly smile. "How can I say no?"

"There you go. Pure logic. Go let them in and bring me back a drink."

Seriously, it was a keys to the kingdom moment.

Casually lifting her up in a showy flexing of upper body muscle, he settled her half reclining against the pillows, covered her up to her chin with the coverlet like an over-protective, non-sharing, super jealous boyfriend. Gently brushing a curl off her forehead, he gave her a little tucking-in kiss, rose from the bed and indifferent to his nudity, walked to the door.

Opening it, he nodded at the trio who'd been dragged out of someone else's room. "Appreciate the quick response," he said, ignoring the woman's obvious interest in his inked dick, and standing aside, he waved them in. "My fiancée was in the mood for an additional performance." *He'd already defined the specifics on the phone.* Shutting the door, he moved to the liquor cabinet and made Nicole the weakest drink on the planet.

Like inebriated people were wont to do, she watched him pour and said, "More."

"Just a little then," he said, blowing her a kiss. Although he considered kissing the performers too because the woman suddenly squealed, the two men laughed and he was able to set down the bottle of absinthe without adding any more to Nicole's drink.

"Did you see," Nicole whispered as he returned to the bed and handed her the glass. "They brought a whip this time."

Glancing over his shoulder, he saw the woman bent over a small leather padded hurtle that had been unfolded and set up. Her wrists were being tied to the frame by one man, the second was behind her, casually swinging a braided quirt while he waited. "Do you want me to tell them no whipping?"

"Can you do that? I mean . . . tell them how to"—

"You can have them do anything you want right here on the bed if you like. You give the orders, they do it. It's a business."

"Wow, like wow—okay . . . no, no, don't," she said as Rafe took a step toward the trio. "I didn't mean I wanted that. They're fine where they are." Upending her watered-down drink, she swallowed it like a man dying of thirst in the desert, then handed the glass to Rafe.

Setting it down on the bedside table, he smiled faintly. "How much whipping do you want? A lot, some, none? I think they're waiting for your instructions."

Her blush was so fucking hot, he almost cleared the room.

"God . . . don't ask." She sucked in a breath. "I couldn't possibly—I mean . . . I don't know."

"When you do, if you do, tell me—otherwise, I'll get them going. How's that?"

Wide-eyed and sweet as fuck, she nodded.

Lifting the covers, he slid into bed beside her, leaned back against the headboard, pulled her into his arms, and said, "Anytime. We're ready. Nothing too excessive."

The quirt came down on the lady's pale ass, lightly, then less lightly until her skin was bright pink, streaked with faint red lines. Until she was squirming and panting.

Until Nicole was squirming and panting.

"You like that?" Rafe whispered, sliding his hand between her legs. "Ummm, fucking yes, you do." He slid his fingers down her wetness, tapped her swollen little clit. "Can't come until it's over though. Understand?"

"No." Her gaze swiveled up to Rafe and she gave him a smug smile. "Or yes. Because I can tell them when it's over—right?"

He chuckled. "If your French is good enough." What he didn't say was that he was paying them extremely well, they knew it and that meant they took orders from him. Like now. He uttered a few short directives in French.

The man holding the quirt acknowledged Rafe with a nod, then began lubing up the quirt handle. When Rafe added another brief instruction, he gave another nod to his partner who moved in front of the woman, lightly holding his stiff cock in the curve of his fingers.

A low murmured command and she looked up, opened her mouth.

Without further comment, he slowly fed his rigid dick into her mouth until she audibly gagged.

Nicole stopped breathing for a second, then softly exhaled as the woman shifted her head slightly and swallowed another few inches of his huge cock.

"I don't think she can take it all. What do you think?" Rafe's voice was soft, his arm around Nicole's shoulders proprietary, his fingers stroking her throbbing pussy. "You give world-class head, pussycat. Want to give her some tips?"

She frantically shook her head, her silky hair sliding back and forth on his shoulder.

"Sure?" His voice was teasing. "You do it better."

"Hey, I'm barely holding it together, okay?" she said in a feverish whisper.

"Sorry. No more teasing. We'll just watch."

The man with the quirt apparently was the leader and mindful of Rafe's directions no matter how subtle. When Rafe dipped his head, indicating they move on, the man slowly slid the lubed quirt handle into the woman's ass until she moaned around the cock in her mouth.

He stopped pushing.

Nicole shuddered, exhaled a low, breathy groan.

"Can you feel that, pussycat? All your virgin nerve endings getting into the game?" Rafe's voice was whisper soft. "Ready to give it a try?"

A little whimper, a squirmy wiggle, a half suffocated breathy, "I think so."

Lifting her onto his lap, he draped her in the sheet, covering her up as if she were an inviolate nun. Or more aptly, for his eyes only. He'd become an incredibly possessive man, a thought that didn't bear close scrutiny considering his former views on independence. "I'm moving you just a little." His slid her bottom back a few inches on his thighs. "There. Comfortable?"

"Horny," she said, turning to nip his shoulder. "Super horny." She bit harder.

"Hey," he grumbled. "Watch it or I'll bite back."

"Later, okay?"

Her huge blue-eyed gaze met his, the smoldering heat damn near combustible. "Got it," he said, husky and low, and gave the man with the quirt another glance.

The man left the quirt handle buried in the woman's ass and started lubing his erection, his fingers sliding up and down, around and around, slowly, lingeringly, taking his time like a stripper in the spotlight. Even across the room, he could hear Contini's lady's heavy breathing, and he wished the sex club legend pleasure of his new innocent piece. Gossip would be rife about her role in his life; men like Contini didn't reform. But he was paying them six months wages for showing up in under five minutes. His motives were irrelevant.

Another quick glance toward his paymaster.

An infinitesimal nod from the billionaire playboy.

Removing the quirt, the large man lined up the head of his cock on target, pushed into Minette's primed ass, slipped a hand between her legs and continued his role as stud.

"You want that?" Rafe asked, watching Nicole's mesmerized gaze, not sure what he'd do if she said yes.

She glanced up, shocked. "No." Her eyes narrowed in that half-second time lapse occasioned by excessive alcohol. "You want her?"

"Fuck no," he growled.

She blew out a breath. "Sorry. That was the bitch in me. But I'm really having fun in case you were wondering," she added in a velvety purr.

"Good for you." It made the all-too-familiar staged bullshit worthwhile. He smiled "Ready for more?"

She giggled, nodded, said, "Anytime, dude," like she was feeling no pain, on board and rocking.

Rafe gave a lift of his chin to the man with the shiny lubed dick. "Let's see the lady come."

Both men took it up a notch, the thrust and withdrawal of two huge cocks moving in a hard driving rhythm, the woman's sex expertly worked by hand. With her ass filled brim full, the man with his dick in her mouth forcefully milking her tits, her pussy being lavished with attention, the woman's frenzied cries rose higher and higher.

Nicole was hot and wet, squirming as she watched the sex act, panting feverishly, sweet as hell, Rafe thought, flat-out perfect in every way.

Lubing the fingers of his left hand, Rafe lightly massaged her virgin ass as she sat back on his thighs, circling the tight little rosebud, gently thrusting a finger in a fraction, withdrawing and penetrating again in a careful, slow, deepening invasion. Stroking her pussy with his other hand, finger fucking her with finesse, making her sweet spots quiver and tremble, making her wetter.

Sliding his long fingers in deeper, he caressed her sleek, throbbing tissue until she was lit up from inside, squirming against his fingers, front and rear, whimpering, "Please, please, please," like she did at the last when she was frantic. Like he needed her to do if he didn't want to hurt her.

"Out," he said, the sound barely audible and seconds later, the door closed softly on the performers.

He kissed her tenderly, his fingers gentle on her nerve-rich clit and pussy, even more gentle on her sweet, chaste ass.

"Hurry. Please." Frenzied and pleading, her body racked with shudders, dizzy with want, she sobbed, "Rafe! I need you!"

He had her up on her hands and knees a second later,

the head of his erection nuzzling her ass, two fingers buried in her throbbing pussy, his thumb on her clit.

His heart was beating like a drum.

"Still time to say stop." His mouth was near her ear, his dick so hard it hurt.

"No, no, I mean yes, do it—hurry, hurry..."

He shut his eyes briefly, reined in his wildness and cautiously pressed forward.

She tensed.

He froze. "You okay?" He told himself he could stop; he hoped he could stop. Although he wasn't so sure with his dick in full out ramming speed. "Maybe you should come first," he said, quickly. Making it easier for her, or making a bargain with the devil for himself.

Then he sucked it up and did what he did so well, what he knew she liked, what her hard-core sexual cravings had been panting for from the very beginning of the staged performance. He made her G-spot bundle of nerves flutter and dance with joy, made her tempestuous little clit take jolt after jolt of provocative thumb pressure until she was screaming so loudly his ears were ringing. And at the very last when she flipped out and went ape shit in a gasping, seething, cunt clenching climax, he pushed his way into her virgin ass as far as he could go without hurting her and came so hard he saw stars.

When the fury abated, when their breathing stilled and their new radical position was acknowledged, Rafe spoke first. "Did I hurt you?"

She was completely motionless. "No, but move will you?"

"Sorry, of course." He very carefully withdrew, then

gently turned her and lowered her on her back. Her eyes were closed and he felt a rush of sheer panic. *What the fuck was wrong with him? She was a goddamn innocent.* "Oh Christ, I've hurt you haven't I? I'll take you to a doctor, have Aleix come here. Jesus, I'm so fucking sorry."

Her eyes slowly opened and her smile was like a thousand perfect sunrises. "I'm fine. Just"—

"Hurt. Dammit, I should have known better. You're not used to any of this. Christ, you're pale as hell."

"Hey." Reaching up she touched his mouth. "Nothing hurts. Well, maybe I'm just a tiny bit sore, but it's not major. Relax."

"We're never doing that again," he said, brusquely. "No way."

She lifted one brow. "I believe I'm allowed a vote, Contini."

"Fuck if you are," he growled.

"Why don't we talk about it later? When you're done beating yourself up. I'm an adult. I know what hurts and doesn't hurt. I screamed so loud when I came I must have scared the shit out of anyone in the vicinity. You did good, okay? That was a very, very, very fine orgasm."

One eyebrow flicked up, there was a grin at the corner of his mouth. "You're crazy."

"Yeah, I know. That's why we get along. Now I'm hungry. Could we have something to eat?"

"Sure," he said, a note of dubiousness still in his voice. "But no more sex tonight."

She smiled. "Let's see how it goes. Do they have steak frites? I hope so."

Fine. He wasn't going to argue. If she wanted sex, she'd have to go solo. He wasn't touching her anymore tonight. But one look at the challenging glint in her eye and the feel of her fingers rubbing his bare skin and he could already feel his resolve weakening a little. "I'm sure they do," he said, polite as hell. "Something chocolate for dessert?"

As Nicole and Rafe cross the dangerous line between love and lust, pleasure and pain, power and possession, the only thing that remains is…

SEDUCTION AND SURRENDER

See the next page for a preview of this scorching new novel.

ONE

A private island off the coast of Croatia

The shoreline was a spectacular run of high limestone cliffs, punctuated with small, secluded beaches, the windswept native pines and colonized palms an exotic melding of history and cultures typical of the region. A partially restored medieval castle dominated the heights, while a well-appointed Venetian villa surrounded by lush gardens served as Rafe's residence.

After a late morning swim and a luncheon al fresco, poolside, Nicole and Rafe lay together on a sun-faded chaise, the too-tender-to-touch happiness they were feeling underscored by small stirrings of melancholy. After eight days in their own special paradise, they both knew time was running out.

The shadow of fear sent a shiver down Nicole's spine.

Rafe felt it, looked down. "You okay?"

No. She hated feeling this way: restless, stifled, powerless against the future. Not knowing what was real and what was skidding mist. But the blue of her eyes suddenly flashed spotlight bright and a familiar echo of defiance rang through her voice. "Tell me we can stay here forever. Just you and me. Say it." A ferocious stare. "Officially."

He heard the small twitch of fear beneath the hard ding

of her words, knew what she was asking, and he cared enough to lie through his teeth. "Why do you think I brought you to my hidden lair, tiger? So you can't get away." Lightly tracing the delicate arch of her brow, he wondered if he'd ever be this happy again. "Just you and me forever." His smile was a blaze of beauty. "That's the plan."

It was too late for anything but lies.

There was no forever.

The statute of limitations had run out.

Even knowing their world was being shaken to the core, a rush of gladness shone in Nicole's eyes. "That works for me."

Rafe's face closed over for a moment, before he smiled. "We're a good pair, pussycat. Right from the beginning. A triumph of serendipity over reason."

"And me not taking no for an answer without a hissy fit," she said, all playful sass; sure again.

"Yeah, that too." A wolfish glint darkened his amber eyes; he wasn't so sure he would have let her walk away. He suddenly stifled a yawn. "Sorry." His voice was thick with fatigue.

"Poor baby," Nicole murmured. "You're not getting much sleep." Rafe was often gone when she woke in the middle of the night, his schedule brutal. "Don't feel you have to entertain me. Go take a nap."

He rolled his eyes. "Thanks, Mom. We're just dealing with some fallout from the Geneva attack. Nothing for you to worry about. I'll sleep when it's over."

"You're bringing in an awful lot of men." Security was visibly ramping up, Leo was frowning more or less full-time, and while she understood she was being *protected* from the war plans, something beyond ordinary defense was in the works.

Rafe smiled. "Okay, it's major fallout. But we weathered their twelfth attack, so I've been to this dance before. It's pretty routine. More wine?"

"Sure. A little." She gave herself points for responding like a mature adult; Rafe didn't wish to discuss the subject. She understood. "Lunch was fabulous as usual." She waved at the debris of luncheon on a nearby table.

"Teresa's a gem. I was lucky to find her," Rafe replied, blandly, levering upward in a supple flex of abs to reach for a bottle of local rose.

Nicole picked up her wineglass from a small mosaic table beside the chaise, then quickly set it down as tears suddenly welled in her eyes and all her stiff-upper-lip intentions melted away. "Oh hell," she whispered, incapable of Rafe's cool control with farewell and loss twisting her gut. "How much longer before—"

Dropping the wine bottle, Rafe swung back, put his finger over her mouth. "Come on," he said, softly. "Don't rain on my parade. I like feeling happy."

Sucking in a deep breath, then another, she finally managed to conjure up a wobbly smile. "Gotcha."

"There you go." He gave her a sweetly wicked wink. "Compliance. That's what I like."

Cautioning herself not to ask for more than Rafe could give when he was only looking for a degree of normalcy in the eye of the coming storm, she grabbed handfuls of his sleek, black hair and pulled him close. "Then you better make it worth my while, Contini. Got it?"

"So you give the orders now?" A slow lazy smile, an eyebrow lift.

"Was I somehow not clear?" she purred.

His grin was bad boy perfect. "Just checkin'." Although, he'd been on his best behavior the last few days, wanting to offer Nicole unalloyed pleasure, wanting what they had to matter somehow, wanting it to be better and brighter and sharper so even when the lights went out and the signals were lost, the memories would still be vivid. He had two, maybe three days of sweet, urgent happiness left. "Okay, now don't give me any shit, but my orders first. Shut your eyes."

Her gaze narrowed. "Seriously?"

"Seriously the orders or seriously shutting your eyes?" Not that it mattered; he knew how to make her obey.

"What if I say both?"

He smiled. "It'll just delay your orgasm."

"Hmmm."

He knew that sound and look. "Ready to move on? If so, I apologize for the cliché, but it's something I want to do."

"Do what?" she asked warily.

"I said cliché, pussycat, not depraved. Trust me." He waited calmly.

She finally shut one eye.

He flashed her a wide grin. "You have trust issues, tiger?"

"Maybe."

"Do what you're told," he drawled, "you get the prize."

"I'd better," she said in her bossy little bitch voice that always made him smile.

He leaned forward a little, gave her a small intimate smile. "Have I ever let you down?"

A second later, her eyes closed and he gave himself a moment to relish the lush image of her lying on his chaise, eyes shut, her skin warm and golden, her lush form on almost full display in a tiny red polka dot bikini, her beauty so precious she took your breath away.

And she was his, at least for now.

Stretching out his arm, he plucked a plump, red cherry from the bowl on the table. "Open your mouth," he said, quietly, raising his hand with the cherry. "Uh, uh, you can't look yet. Trust, okay?" He waited until her eyelids drifted downward again, then waited a fraction of a second more—committing to memory the sweetly erotic picture of her waiting open-mouthed and expectant—before he lowered his hand.

The instant the cherry touched her tongue, her eyes flew open and her giggle warmed his heart.

"See, perfectly innocuous," he said with a lopsided grin. "Am I a good boy or what? Now bite."

"You're a romantic too," she teased, giving him a poke in the ribs. "How hard should I bite?"

He laughed. "Goddamn sex fiend. No wonder we get along."

"Did you ever doubt it?"

"Jesus, and I thought you liked me because I made you laugh and we both enjoyed walks on the beach."

"Fuck you."

"All in due time. You gonna eat this cherry or what? Or would you like it somewhere else?"

She grinned. "Same old pervert." But she pulled the cherry off the stem and began to chew.

"Yeah, well men are fucking predictable," he said, holding out his palm for the pit. "Feel like another one in a different location?"

She took in his playful leer. "So I have choices?" she said with a tantalizing glint in the blue of her eyes.

He chuckled. "You always have choices, tiger. The menu's large and my dick and I are always on board for whatever you want."

"The tower room."

He chuckled. "Walls, twelve feet thick—your kind of perfect. No one can hear you scream."

She grinned. "Do I detect a note of censure?"

"Hell no. Your enthusiasm is music to my ears, tiger." He held out his hand. "Want me to carry you? Don't answer. I'm carrying you." His need for her burned hotter with each passing moment, the thought that he might never hold her again so sharp it hurt.

Nicole pressed her hand to her chest as though he'd spoken aloud, as though his thoughts had scalded her skin, as though mental telepathy was real and not just coincidence. "I don't want to leave," she blurted out, her eyes huge, pleading. "Tell me I don't have to. Oh God, I'm sorry—I shouldn't have said that—no I'm not!" Her voice pitched high, she stared at him with heated challenge in her eyes. "I'm not one bit sorry! And I'm *not* going!"

He couldn't think of anything on earth he'd rather hear, nor anything more impossible. "Hey, hey, it's okay," he whispered. Leaning in, he slid a finger under her chin, dipped his head, and kissed her gently. "You don't have to leave," he lied. "No way."

He felt her smile on his lips, heard her soft, "Thanks," and sitting back, met her warm, sunlit gaze.

"Fairy tales really can come true, right?"

"I'll make sure they do." *Three days tops,* he thought, giving her a reassuring smile because she was watching. Although there was a small chance in hell he might win this crapshoot. "Since you walked into my life, I've become a believer in miracles. So why not a few more." His smile was heartbreakingly beautiful this time. "Are we all good now?"

Swallowing her tears, she nodded.

He kissed her cheek. "That's my girl. Now let's check out the view from the tower room. We'll slam the door on the world, you give orders this time, I'll take them," he said, sexy and low as he lifted her into his arms, "and we'll—"

He recognized the ringtone.

"Give me a second," he said. Picking up his cell phone from the table, he answered cautiously with Nicole in earshot. "Yes?"

"I'm in Split," Dominic said, crisply. "I've come for Nicole. It has nothing to do with you. Nicole's sister was in a bad car accident. She survived, others didn't, but they don't know whether she'll live. I need you to alert your men that my chopper's coming in. Fifteen minutes."

"I'll take care of it," Rafe said.

"Is Nicole's phone on? I'll call her next."

"Yes."

"Help her out."

"Of course."

A second after Rafe ended his call, Nicole's cell rang. Even before she answered it, she knew something was wrong because Rafe picked up her iPhone from the table and without looking at the caller ID, handed it to her.

Don't miss more books from C. C. Gibbs!

Dominic Knight is a man who is always in control. A self-made billionaire by the age of twenty-three, a genius of innovation, and CEO of a global tech empire, Knight always gets what he wants. And he wants Kate Hart...

A rising star of cyber forensics, Kate is well aware of Knight's reputation as a master manipulator, uncompromising leader, and demanding lover. But she's determined to stay cool and professional—no matter how hot and bothered her new boss makes her feel.

First he appears in her dreams. Then he comes to her in the night. And so begins a journey of erotic awakening and discovery as rich and powerful as Knight himself. In locales from the sultry red-light district of Amsterdam to the private sexual playgrounds of Hong Kong, Kate will shed every inhibition and surrender every part of herself—body, mind, and soul—to give her lover all he craves, all he needs, and all he demands...

Brilliant. Wealthy. Powerful. Dominic Knight is one of the hottest tech developers in the world—and the most demanding lover Kate Hart has ever known. Whether in the boardroom or the bedroom, he is always in charge. But there is one thing he cannot control: Kate's fiery heart...

As a master in her field, talented Kate surpassed Dominic's wildest expectations. As a woman of uncommon intelligence and beauty, she unlocked something deep within him. Yet since their professional relationship—and erotically charged affair—came to an end, the fire in him has only grown stronger.

Now, the man who has everything will do whatever it takes to reclaim the woman he lost. From Boston and Paris to Singapore and San Francisco, he will lure Kate back into his elite world of privilege and passion. Together, they will test the limits of desire and the boundaries of discipline. For both, this is uncharted territory—naked, reckless, and uninhibited. But when Dominic's deadliest enemies target Kate, he must face his darkest fears...and admit to himself that she is all he needs.

Self-made billionaire Dominic Knight has always been the master of his destiny. From the boardroom to the bedroom, he takes charge of every situation, every impulse, every lover. But now he is ready to tie himself down—to one impossibly alluring woman...

Kate Hart thinks of herself as strong and independent. With a brain any tech genius would envy and a body built for pleasure, she has always been in full control of her life. Then she met Dominic Knight...

From the moment she first succumbed to temptation, Dominic and Kate have explored every fantasy, every need, and every desire. Bound together in an intoxicating game of passion and possession, seduction and surrender, they have nothing left to conquer—except the possibility of forever. Now from the bright lights of London to the sultry lairs of Paris, Dominic must convince Kate he's ready to make the ultimate commitment. But how long can two lovers teeter on the brink of ecstasy...before they fall off?